PRETERNATURAL SAGACITY

A novel concerning life and its mysteries

by

Davies Lynch

Published by

Llyfrau Cambria Books, Wales, United Kingdom.

Cambria Books is a division of

Cambria Publishing.

Discover our other books at: www.cambriabooks.co.uk

"He slept in a stable – generally on horseback – and so terrified a Newfoundland dog by his preternatural sagacity, that he had been known, by the mere superiority of his genius, to walk off unmolested with the dog's dinner, from before his face."

From the preface to Barnaby Rudge by Charles Dickens, 1841, referring to his pet Raven, Grip.

This novel has been particularly inspired by two human qualities; *Courage to Journey* to the frontiers of knowledge and *Freedom to Imagine* what lies Beyond.

CHAPTERS

Introduction

I imagine that anyone engaged in researching their family history harbours an excitement that they might stumble on hidden secrets that reveal more clearly the personalities of those long-gone, often stone-faced relatives in faded photographs. The further back we go, the foggier becomes the information trail until it goes completely dark, when even the names run out. Our ancestors lived within gradually evolving societies, each generation facing the challenges of their times, in their local communities and amidst their family dynamics; some coping with these, even shaping the evolution, some unable to cope and suffering varying degrees of pain and suffering, trying to make sense of their lot. How our own lives might be shaped by our ancestors' experiences is a topic for speculation but generally seems a mystery, unique to individuals; but the question can be a stimulus to research, even if expectations of discovering any kind of causal relationships might be low.

In my ancestry research, ongoing in various fits and starts for more than a decade, I found that the line stretching back to my grandfather's parents had a particular fascination for me. My digging had turned up only a handful of facts about my great-grandparents; birthdates, dwelling places, date and place of marriage, birth of children and deaths. But Henry and Sarah, first cousins, had left Somerset in their late teens, to build a new home together in the Welsh mining valleys. While this was not unusual, after all there was widespread labour mobility in the 19th century, facilitating the industrial revolution, the possible circumstances of what I suspect was an elopement, intrigued me. Apart from a few smudged dots, the canvas was blank but I found myself imagining things that joined the dots, filled the picture in, and I decided that I would create a fiction, one possible version of what might have happened; shine a magical torch on a month in my great-grandparents lives during the period of their elopement; let them 'live again' through their great-grandson's imagination.

But, I also wanted to make the connection with modern-times and so I created their fictional great-grandson, Bran, an aeronautical engineer who researches his ancestry in his spare time, gradually building the picture, informed by his research, and by a series of dreams that lead him through the fog, bringing him more and more in touch with his own mortality. I wanted to create a multi-dimensional character, more real if you like. He is a professional and passionate about improving aviation safety. So, to reinforce this, the modern-times story is sprinkled with technical stuff; not so detailed to put the layperson off but just enough to, hopefully, give you a flavour of the intensity, the reality, of high-tech engineering; trust me, I am a high-tech engineer.

You'll also find the influence of Bob Dylan's lyrics threading their way through the story in several ways. Metaphors and symbolism used to bring new perspectives on life. With the lyrics and musical creativity of Bran and his band Orion, practising every Friday night for the upcoming Love-Sick concert, I am attempting to illustrate the existential pleasures available to modern man, contrasting with the just-emerging awareness and presence of Henry and Sarah in their working-class world of the 1870s.

And then there are the ravens, and their Preternatural Sagacity, like Dicken's Grip, that lace the tale with a slightly mystical content. They feature as a kind of go-between,

2

guiding both generations to value, trust and follow their instinct, and carve out their paths to increased self-awareness.

*

One reviewer suggested that the tech stuff, the ravens and Dylan's lyrics were distractions from the main plot and could put the reader off. I replied that this was a risk I was prepared to take, but that I hoped readers would appreciate that I was trying to create a multi-faceted story, each facet bringing out different sides of the whole. Weaving the connecting threads between the facets felt very important to me, and to my characters as well.

So, this is a tale of life in two communities, conditioned by two social systems, separated by 128 years of time; of the aeronautical engineer in the year 2000, and his great-grandparents in 1872. Historical fiction woven with a modern adventure, weaving values and emotions, love and friendships, hopes and dreams.

As many authors will recognise, at various points in the telling of a story, their characters take over and lead the way. That happened for me on many occasions, and I was compelled to follow them as they 're-lived' their lives, often surprising me with their initiatives and their discoveries. As the story unfolds, Bran comes to realise that he is carrying a kind of generational torch for safety and it sits well with him, as it does with me.

I hope you, the reader, enjoy my efforts; they may put you in touch with the torch that you are carrying.

*

Finally, I draw attention to three short pieces at the end of the book; a list of my characters, in case the reader loses touch with who's who; a list of acronyms, so familiar in technical

3

papers, to aid the reader, in case they appear out of nowhere. Finally, I include an acknowledgment section to highlight from where I drew support and inspiration.

Davies Lynch

1. Let the Creative Juices Flow as the Raven Lifts off

The sound was like distant thunder rumbling and ending in a single roar as the cage hit the pit bottom nearly 1000 feet below the surface. The silence, at first deafening, was broken by a growing number of voices shouting out in anguish. Men and women were running across the fields, down the lanes, along the canal towpath and gathering together at the pithead. The scene was changing fast, the viewer hardly able to keep up. A young boy holding a younger girl's hand, had a terribly confused expression on his face. She looked across and caught his eye. Wives and mothers wept, their pain expressed in moans that filled the air around the place of death where four broken bodies of the miners were laid out. The moment when safe became unsafe, with the break of the rope, and normal became abnormal. A pit pony stood motionless and two young ravens stood on its back, making low gurgling croaks as if talking to each other. An old man smartly dressed and looking out of place, gazed at the birds with wonder and muttered to himself. "Just like Dickens' Grip, surely these creatures have preternatural sagacity."

Bran sat up in bed, shaking his head as if to clear the invading thoughts, the weird dream. "What was that all about, and what on earth does preternatural sagacity mean? I've never invented words in my dream before."

"What are you talking about Bran?' Bran had woken his wife Mary. "Preternatural is like, beyond the natural but not supernatural, if that makes sense. And, you normally have sagacity, the quality of being wise, but I'm having my doubts this morning; have you just had a dream?"

"Yes love, a weird one. I think there was a coal mine, children holding hands, women crying. I think there had been an accident. Then this old chap is looking at two big black crows sitting on the back of a horse, muttering something about preternatural sagacity and Dickens. I'd swear the young girl looked at me."

"Write it down Bran, it might make sense one day. But for now, time to get moving, you have a big day ahead with your aviation safety conference, and John will be arriving in an hour. Oh, and Dylan wanted to ask you a question about gravity but he'd gone to bed before you got back last night; seems his teacher doesn't understand it and he didn't believe my explanation. I told him that gravity has many ways of pulling people down, but he didn't find that funny, or helpful. So, it's over to the expert."

"Gravity, now there's a real puzzle. Most people first ask that question when they are very young, when their wonder is fresh, but then go through their lives with gravity as a mystery. I'm a Newtonian, down-to-Earth kind of guy, but I'll see what Dylan thinks of Einstein's curved space-time when he's eating his boiled egg."

That was 1990, ten years before this part of our story begins. Bran had written about the dream in his notebook, now archived in his library; the dream had never made sense to him and he had all but forgotten about it, as we all do with our foggy dreams. Dylan was even more confused about gravity after his father had attempted to explain it at breakfast, but it had stimulated his imagination and he was now studying physics at University, equipping himself with the abstract mathematical tools needed to make sense of gravity and the other forces that shape things in the natural world.

3   2   1   0

Once again, it was early in the morning, 5.28 to be precise, and Bran woke, alone in his bed. Mary was on sabbatical in Berkeley, so he couldn't share the thought, the question, on his mind. Why was he so fascinated by his ancestry? He wasn't sure but felt it was something to do with his mortality; maybe an attempt to connect with past lives in the hope that future life could connect with him and he would somehow endure, become immortal. But the cynic might say that the past and the future are just memories and false hopes, so could they be trusted? Whatever, Bran was not a cynic, and there was something ethereal about his interest, but also slightly annoying. He felt it was taking up valuable time that could be better spent on the living and live issues; "and surely the future is more important than the past?", he said to himself. For now, he would follow the gossamer threads of curiosity wherever they led him.

The remnant of a dream was fading into the mist of his mind; a woman's face, lips moving but no words coming out. Bran didn't recognise her, and yet it was unsettling because she seemed vaguely familiar, but she had gone. It was Wednesday and Bran was taking a few days off from his work. His secretary Joselyn had written in his diary 'on travel', which meant he should only be contacted in emergencies. He would be visiting a museum where documents and stories were kept, describing life in the Somerset coalfields during the 19th century. Bran's great-grandfather Henry had been a coal miner in the Camerton area from an early age, until he left with Sarah in the early 1870's to dig coal and become a mines inspector in Ebbw Vale. Bran's research had also turned up Henry and Sarah's marriage certificate. The date was June 1872 and they were married in the Old Blaina Baptist Chapel.

Henry and Sarah's sons and grandsons, including Bran's grandfather George and father Alwyn, would follow in his coal dusty footsteps, but Bran had been freed from this dark, shadowy underworld of coughing, pain, constant danger and emotional blackout by education; or so it seemed. The more he learned about the life of his coal-mining ancestors, the more he valued his education and the more he was driven to achieve. It was as if the coal pits had a gravity to them, hauling him down, that he had to struggle against, reaching from his ancestry through into his future. These images would weave their way through Bran's thoughts and they were intriguing. Maybe his valuing education should be enough to explain his fascination and intrigue, but he felt there was more. The story had a root in Somerset and he wanted to explore where this root led.

Visiting the museum was not the only thing taking Bran away from his work and home this week. He had received a call from Suisan Morgan, daughter of Professor John Morgan, Bran's PhD supervisor and mentor in his early career, with the news that John had passed away after a short illness; *"would Bran be willing to read a eulogy of John's professional achievements at the funeral?"* Bran knew John had been ill and was deeply saddened when he heard the news of his death. John had been very influential to Bran's career, a strong role model and good friend, inspiring him to regard quality and ethics as professional cornerstones. Bran felt proud being asked to speak at the funeral and preparing the eulogy had brought back many good memories; yes, memories could indeed be good, and reassuring.

Bran was an aeronautical engineer and a pilot, and his speciality was making sense of the behaviour of aircraft through mathematical analysis and flight testing. John had opened Bran's eyes to the power of critical analysis, searching for physical understandings through the lens of mathematics. Before this had happened, Bran had been very sceptical, even fearful, of maths. It seemed to be a language people used to divorce themselves from reality, communicate with others who preferred an unreal world. He was wrong, or at least partly wrong; he had several colleagues who had escaped reality this way and academia gave them a safe home. Bran had learned that through using maths, scientists and engineers could explain why things happened the way they did in the complexity of the physical world. In aviation, predict how aircraft might behave when they fly out of their safe envelope and, importantly, when things fail to function as designed, or pilots do the wrong things. Explaining and predicting had become purposeful pursuits that defined Bran's approach to his work. He had put them to good use in problem-solving throughout his career. Explain and predict, watchwords for living, interpreting the past and imagining the future.

$$\alpha \Leftrightarrow \omega$$

Bran turned into the crematorium driveway that wound its way up to the chapel-esque building. The alternating green and copper coloured leaves of beech trees, flickering in the sunlight, providing a tranquilising contrast for those passing below. But not enough to prevent Bran from feeling a shudder as he imagined what happened behind the curtain inside the innocuous looking structure. He had arrived early and inadvertently joined a group of mourners waiting to be called for another funeral service. At first, he hadn't realised this and looked around for familiar faces; there were none, and he saw his mistake. Feeling embarrassed, he sat down as the group moved out of the waiting room into the chapel. A man approached Bran.

"Good morning, are you joining us?"

"I really do apologise", said Bran, "I arrived early and thought this was John Morgan's service. If you don't mind I'll just wait here until the family arrive."

"Yes of course" said the man, "it's my brother-in-law, killed in a helicopter crash; tragedy is he was the pilot and people are blaming him for what happened." Just then, a woman came out of the chapel and walked purposefully towards the two men, her eyes staring at Bran, as if trying to read his thoughts. It unsettled him even more than his embarrassment.

"Frank, I'm not sure I can cope with this, I need you with me," still staring at Bran, as if addressing him.

"I'm sorry Sandra, of course I'm with you, I just wanted to greet this gentleman, I thought he was one of Peter's friends." Bran repeated his excuse.

"I arrived early for my friend's funeral and joined your group by mistake, please forgive me."

"Don't worry", said Sandra, "an easy mistake in these beastly places; I'm sorry about your loss."

"And I'm sorry about yours; I'm Bran Sage" holding out his hand. Still staring at him, the woman introduced herself as Sandra Peel and held Bran's out-stretched hand for a little longer than felt comfortable. Then she released him and Frank and Sandra walked into the Chapel leaving Bran to sit on his own and reflect on his relationship with John Morgan and the eulogy he would be reading; but Sandra's stare and the feel of her hand were still in his thoughts, causing discomfort. Her face wore an expression that drew out Bran's male saviour, but he'd felt it before, was familiar with it and most of the time managed to control that hapless part of his character.

As John's family and friends started to arrive, Bran felt

more comfortable and the warmth of the greetings and shared sadness reminded him of how funerals were a time of coming together; pain is less severe when it is shared. Bran had known Suisan for almost as long as he'd known John. She had initially tried to protect him from what she described as John's obsession with his work. But this was futile since both John and Bran were equally committed to advancing aeronautical science and making aviation safer. Suisan, along with Bran's wife Mary, grew to understand this, as their husbands' work came into the public eye on several occasions following aircraft accidents. Suisan had wanted a quiet ceremony with only John's closest friends and family and the small group sat in a semi-circle around the coffin. A small vase of wild flowers had been placed on a stand in front of the coffin, just behind the lectern where a man stood, dressed in a black suit and sporting a neatly trimmed grey-gold beard. Listening to the eulogy of John's life from his brother Kenneth, Bran wondered if his family really understood John or at least the side of John Morgan that Bran thought he knew. Kenneth painted a picture of a good and clever man, but who was perhaps a little too engrossed in his work to be in touch with the here and now, to be in touch with his emotions. Bran knew that Kenneth had a chip on his shoulder connected with his brother's successes. But did Suisan agree, Bran wondered as he made his way to the lectern, and would they recognise the John Morgan that he was about to talk about.

Bran began his eulogy. *'The maths is quite advanced but the right student should be able to master it and the aeronautical science behind it is really quite wonderful.'* "I recall with amazing clarity Dr Morgan, as I addressed him then, saying this about the project he was offering final year students. We all sat in the lecture theatre listening to the academics describe the projects on offer. One was about supersonic wing design, another about the flow over and under racing cars, yet another about how wings bend and twist in turbulence, and was there one about flying a helicopter on Mars? I remember being excited and thinking, '*now, this is the reason I am studying aeronautical engineering, to solve these really tricky problems, to be the first to discover something; and my project would take me there*.' John had described how a pilot could make an aircraft go unstable, when they might be struggling to control the flight path and keep the aircraft stable. This seemed illogical, counter-intuitive, a real puzzle and it was about flight control and stability, my favourite subject. But it involved advanced maths, John had said. 'How advanced?' I asked, wondering if I was the 'right student' that he had referred to. 'In what way, wonderful?' I don't remember how John answered my questions. I think I had already decided that I wanted to do his project, and so began a professional relationship which would turn into a long and lasting friendship."

"Trust is a precious thing in relationships. Often hard earned and can take time to grow, but I knew at once that I could trust John Morgan professionally. A layperson might wonder what that means and for me, in my profession as an engineer, it's about being 100% confident that what a person says is correct, or that they would share their doubts if they had any. Now, John would offer strong opinions on things political and social; he wouldn't hold back from castigating politicians for their ineptness, or suggesting how we might make a better world, but when it came to technical stuff he was something of a hardliner. Unsubstantiated claims, waffle and bull were not part of John's vocabulary and he took great pride in getting things right. I remember him telling me that he had learned that from his father who would remind him that self-worth can only be gained by being true to yourself. So, I was lucky; my project supervisor was trustworthy and he was only satisfied when getting things right. I had to shape up to become the 'right student' who could master the 'advanced maths' and learn to get things right. John showed me these footholds for becoming a good engineer and I am grateful; thank you John for you also showed me that aeronautical science could, indeed, be wonderful."

"I'd like to give an example of the importance of being right. I remember a time when John and I worked on a joint project which involved reviewing the causal factors in aircraft accidents, particularly related to pilot errors. We were both amazed at the number of what seemed simple mistakes that were made by pilots. They were highly trained and highly skilled and, most of the time, they did their job well, flying people around the world, from town to town, to work and back, on vacation to far-off places. I remember John saying that he was not sure if he would ever feel safe in an aeroplane again, but we kept reminding ourselves that, statistically, flying was the safest way to travel, and it was getting safer every year." Suisan interrupted Bran; "I remember that and he talked about his anxiety of flying with me; and, you know, I don't think he ever flew again." Suisan was crying and Bran paused in respect for Suisan's grief. He continued, "John used maths to show how the automatic pilot, designed to aid the human pilot, could be programmed to protect against the pilot applying the wrong commands. There was quite a bit of resistance from the pilot community but John showed that his technique could have prevented some fatal accidents and the authorities were persuaded. This led to changes in the airworthiness regulations, developments in technology and improvements in safety. Another aspect of John's legacy of getting it right."

"An irony is that most of John's work was actually about approximations, about things being 'almost right'. Everything we do in engineering is approximate, but the key is to understand the limits of your approximations and John

Morgan was truly a master at this. His books on the subject are standard references used the world over, in academia, research laboratories and in industry. They form core material for most modern degree courses on engineering analysis. I know that he was particularly pleased receiving the gold medal from the National Academy for his contribution to engineering education; it is so good to know that his influence lives on and is in effect, immortal."

"It always helps in a relationship if you share humour and the value of metaphor, and this was certainly true for John and myself, especially when metaphor is tinged with irony. And John was particularly good at using humorous metaphors to stimulate new insights. In this I'd say that he was gifted. I'd like to give you an example, not because I want to lighten the tone, far from it; please forgive me if you think I have overstepped the mark here. We were out hiking with a group of colleagues who were meeting in a country house for a workshop on engineering ethics. John was undertaking a study for the Engineering Council on the ways that ethics, as a subject, was taught in University courses. He had assembled  a group of engineers from academia and industry to brainstorm the subject and explore whether new approaches could work better at preparing engineering students for their professional life. On the walk, we became distracted by a pair of ravens cavorting in the skies above us. Suddenly one of the ravens appeared to stall, and dropped down to the same level as the other raven, quickly re-gaining control and flying in formation with its partner. John explained to the gathering that this was an example of a pilot, the raven in this case, being able to recover from an upset by using the other raven as a visual cue to help stabilise their flight path. Later, after dinner, John gave a talk

14

to the group on ethics in engineering and recalled the raven experience. He described how, as engineers, we sometimes find ourselves in upset situations; maybe we discover a mistake in the design calculation, or we're under pressure to take a short cut in testing. We can feel out of control, fall out of touch and lose track of the ethical standards that we signed up to. To correct this, it may be necessary to turn to someone who can guide us back onto the ethical track; like the raven was able to stabilise by lining up with his, or her, mate. The raven's cues were visual, John said, and our cues for recovery are the ethical principles. John was a visionary and could stimulate new insights with his, often spontaneous, metaphors."

"Coming back to the ethics project, some of you will be aware that John's efforts led to a formal revision of the ethics content in engineering degree courses and his recommendation that all engineering academics be required to register as professional engineers, and therefore comply with the Council's ethical principles, is getting increased support from our profession's leaders."

"We would laugh together at the weirdest things that others would not understand because they were personal to our experience together. And this was not about other's misfortunes. It was more about seeing ordinary situations before our eyes and turn them into little theatricals – like the old man and his dog who were pulling in opposite directions, with John claiming this to be a demonstration, proof even, of Newton's third law – every force has an equal and opposite reaction. Or the car reversing down the hill suggesting to John that we were moving back in time and maybe he would be able to fix something that went wrong yesterday. John was good at imagining these little cameos of life. It was part of his creativity and it encouraged the same from others, if they were up for it, if they were the 'right student', if they could see the 'wonder'. I am going to miss John Morgan."

"To finish, I'd like to thank Suisan and John's family for asking me to prepare this eulogy; its brought back some very precious memories and helped me to climb out of my busyness to share this celebration of John's life with you, his friends and family. Right now, I would not want to be anywhere else than here with you; I just added that line. John was both open-hearted and open-minded, quite a rare combination in academia in my experience. He became a good friend of mine, someone I could trust, and in a competitive world that's unfortunately also quite rare. His professional legacy is there for future generations to benefit from. Even though John Morgan has left us, through this legacy he will continue to be an excellent role model. Thank you." Bran paused before leaving the lectern, felt a surge of emotion and reached out and touched John's coffin. One by one the other members of the group came up and laid their hands on the coffin until about 30 hands, criss-crossed and overlapped, covered the coffin; many were crying and they would all miss John Morgan.

During the service, periods of meditation were accompanied by pieces of classical music, giving Bran time to reflect. When he wrote the eulogy, he'd had a strong emotional response and reading it, these feelings came flowing back. He was in the moment but also, at the same time, looking back over a rich history and forward to the impact of a powerful legacy. Bran thought that this related to his own search for meaning in his ancestry; it seemed to pervade much that he did these days. And what a strange coincidence that the funeral before John's was for a pilot who people were blaming for the accident in which he was killed. Then he remembered reading about a recent helicopter crash, probably the one that Peter Peel was piloting. Bran connected with some words from his favourite poet, merging them with new thoughts; ravens and pilots, can they ever be free from the chains of the skyway?

$$\tau_x = k\tau_g$$

Bran checked into his hotel that evening after saying farewell to Suisan and John's family. Suisan had thanked Bran for his speech and wanted him to visit her sometime soon to help go through John's things. She thought that Bran would be the best person to sort out the many documents that John had collected over his long professional career. He had started the sorting before he'd died, Suisan had said, so maybe it would not be too daunting. Bran was grateful for this invitation. He wasn't sure what to expect but knew that John was very organised so the task should be straightforward. Bran telephoned Mary but there was no answer, she was probably in a meeting. He left a message saying that the service had been an emotional experience; Suisan had sent her love and was looking forward to seeing Mary again soon.

Bran always found hotel breakfast a strange experience. Normally content with a bowl of cereals at home, on travel he was always drawn to the cooked breakfast, the 'full English, full Welsh, full Irish' or 'full wherever he was'. It looked like a piece of artwork, bright reds and yellows, browns, black and white and, of course, the orange beans; such a shame to spoil the image by eating it. Around the hotel breakfast room, people were talking quietly, reading newspapers, clinking cutlery, drinking coffee, making toast; all very measured, very controlled; humans preparing themselves for the day ahead. A new day for everyone, and for some it would bring surprises, good news or bad news, a change in the weather, new acquaintances, successes and failures, old memories re-kindled; all things in a day in the life of a human being. Breakfast was the launch pad for the new day. Would you be

17

able to control the flight path of your life with sufficient attention that you didn't crash or upset those in your way? Would the breakfast help? Bran was conjuring with these abstract thoughts when he noticed a familiar face across the breakfast room. To begin with he couldn't recall where he'd seen the woman, or her name, but he knew he had. Then it came to him; it was Sandra, and that was Frank sitting with her. When he had seen her at the funeral parlour, he had been struck by her penetrating gaze and sad eyes. Her direct way of speaking and formal black dress contrasted with the vulnerability expressed in her eyes. Bran was thinking these things while sipping his coffee, and he looked over the room to notice that Sandra was gazing at him with a smile and raised open hand; a slight smile and a gentle greeting. Bran returned the gesture but felt that it was enough communication. Breakfast might be a launch pad for the day but he wasn't ready to climb on board, just yet.

The day ahead would involve meeting the curator at the Somerset Coalfield Museum, and going through archives from the 19th century, searching for ancestral traces. Bran wasn't expecting to find any direct evidence of the Sage's but by exploring the lives of the people from the place that Henry and Sarah were born and lived through to their late teens, he hoped to form a picture of them, albeit sketchy, in his mind. For sure, life must have been hard; did they have the time or the inclination to talk about their ambitions, about life and love? Why did they move to Ebbw Vale? They were cousins so maybe they eloped without parents' approval. Were they happy? Bran could think much quicker than he could speak or write, so these thoughts passed through his mind in a moment as he was checking out of the hotel. He turned around to see her standing there; she was rotating a gold bracelet on her wrist.

"Good morning Dr Sage; it is Dr Sage, right? I asked at the crematorium chapel after I discovered who Professor Morgan was; it seems that people are quoting your esteemed mentor in the case against my husband." Sandra spoke very purposefully and Bran was caught off guard.

"Good morning Mrs Peel. I'm sorry I'm not sure what you are saying; as I understand it, the accident investigation is still ongoing, so the cause of your husband's crash has not been established." Bran said this as sensitively as he could while being as direct as he needed to be.

"I do realise that, but it seems that they always blame the pilot," Sandra replied, "isn't that right Dr Sage."

"I am sorry about your husband's death Mrs Peel but you shouldn't believe the speculations that the media thinks helpful, but usually aren't. The accident investigation will gather the evidence and experts will weigh it up before concluding on the cause; but they never, ever, attribute blame." Bran could see that Sandra wanted to say something more, so he suggested that they sit at one of the tables in the hotel foyer.

"Peter was a very careful pilot, Dr Sage," still rotating her bracelet, "and he had a near perfect safety record; near-perfect because he did have one accident about 12 years ago. You might remember it; the rear rotor stopped working and the aircraft crashed into a lake. Peter managed to escape but two passengers were killed." Indeed, Bran did remember it and he remembered helping John Morgan make sense of the accident data; the details came flooding back. The case was presented at an aviation safety conference in 1990.

"Yes, I do remember that accident Mrs Peel, very tragic, but as I recall, your husband was exonerated by the fatal accident inquiry; in fact, wasn't he praised for steering the helicopter into the lake rather than crash on a populated area?"

"That's correct Dr Sage, but the press hounded him for weeks during the investigation since he was the only person to survive. I fear that the memory of that accident will act against him this time; and it seems so unfair. Could you help me?" Bran wondered what she wanted but was careful with his reply.

"I don't think that my involvement would be helpful to you at this stage Mrs Peel. If I am called on to advise the investigation, I need to be free from a conflict of interest; just like if a friend or relation of mine was involved, I could not provide unbiased support. I hope you can understand this Sandra." Why had Bran called her Sandra? Maybe to comfort her, to reassure her, but it seemed inappropriate as soon as he'd said it. She got up to walk away.

"Well, thank you anyway Dr Sage, I'm glad to have met you." Once again, her gaze remained fixed on Bran's eyes as she held his hand; it was not a handshake at all and Bran had to free himself from the physical contact before he re-gained composure.

"Goodbye Mrs Peel." She gave him that slight smile again as she turned away and walked gracefully out of the lobby. Whew, 'careful' thought Bran, 'careful my friend, and don't get caught in a net that you will find difficult to disentangle yourself from.'

Sandra had been committed to supporting Peter's career as a pilot, initially in the military, then as a test pilot and latterly as a commercial pilot working for a helicopter operator. About nine months ago they had separated, acknowledging that their interests and needs had diverged. Peter was based away from their home and only returned every few weeks. Absence was not making either of their hearts grow fonder, but rather leading them to forge their futures in different directions. Sandra felt that she had lost a lot of her own identity in the drive to support her husband's career. She now wanted to develop her own career as a musical instructor and musician. With her degree in music, she had taught their three children to play piano, violin and guitar, would help them compose pieces to play in school concerts. She had also recently joined a small jazz band, and she derived a great deal of solace and emotional strength from this new venture. This made her feel young again, with moments of joy and excitement that she hadn't felt for many years. She had fallen out of love, but she didn't know if she would be able to love again. She knew that she had a reserve but it needed the right person to tap into it, and she would not easily be drawn in this direction. Peter's death had shocked her and she was deeply sad that they had not had a reconciliation. Their separation had seemed natural and painless but now it pierced her heart as she remembered all the good times and felt a deep remorse. She quietly thanked Peter for those good times and cried for a long time after she arrived home.

$$\delta \approx g/\eta^2$$

Driving through the Somerset countryside, Bran wanted to think about the task ahead; his ancestry, and particularly his great grandfather Henry and great grandmother Sarah. He wanted to know them, and even though he knew he could never know them, he had questions that he hoped the museum could help answer, help fill the blank spaces. But he couldn't focus on this and his mind kept wandering back to Sandra, her sad eyes, her gold bracelet rotating with easy hand movements, her soft voice coming out of those small lips and her graceful movements. 'Stop it you idiot', he said to himself, and he turned the music on in his car. A Bob Dylan song was playing and it helped him out of his tangled-up thoughts. "Bob gets it right, says it right, in so many ways," Bran said to himself. He was a big Dylan fan, and played and sang Dylan songs in pubs

21

and clubs and enjoyed the theatre of performance. This coming Friday, Bran would be meeting with his band to practice for their upcoming concert featuring Dylan's love songs and his use of symbolism. He was looking forward to it and always came away from these get-togethers inspired by the new insights gained from the music and through discussion of the bard's creativity.

As he drove along, Bran took in the panorama of the passing countryside. Hills collapsing into valleys with rivers flowing through and birds flying on their missions across the sky. It was a sunny day and Bran thought about his wife Mary. She loved the natural world and her interest in life was intoxicating for Bran; from Mary came Bran's love of nature. Mary had obtained her doctorate in environmental sciences 25 years ago when it was a fledgling discipline. Her colleagues had warned her that it was a narrow road, but she had a passion and she needed to follow it; she would learn to broaden and extend the road. Passion drew them together; not just the passionate love they felt for each other, although that was powerful enough, but being passionate about their chosen careers. Mary could make anything interesting and she had a natural and intuitive understanding of the sciences. She knew that biology, physics and chemistry were all connected; all part of the one big picture of life that only made sense when perceived as the one big picture, and she wanted to be at the new frontier of interdisciplinary science where new discoveries were being made. Something was waiting there beyond the horizon for her to discover; that missing piece.

Well, this is what she thought when she was very young. Her biology teacher had asked the class what the difference between life and non-life was, from a scientific perspective? The class discussed this, including its philosophical overtones, and one of Mary's classmates said that she thought the difference was in the atoms; live atoms were somehow different to non-live atoms. "No" the teacher had said, "although that's a good answer. The atoms in life forms, like animals and plants, are the same as the atoms in non-life forms, like rocks and water; in fact, most of both are made up of atoms from only a handful of elements, like hydrogen, oxygen and carbon." She continued. "But what is different about life is that the atoms are grouped together to form what we call organic molecules and these, in turn, group to form cells; cells group together to form organisms, like human beings, daffodils and worms. But there is much more; life can take in energy from its environment and use it to grow and reproduce. Life forms have senses that interpret the environment and respond to changes. But perhaps most wonderful of all, living cells contain very special molecules that are passed from one generation to another and contain an individual life's program; and everyone, every living thing, has a different program. And, of course, life forms have memories, holding imprints of past experiences. The people who undertake scientific research in this field of genetics are finding out new things every day, at the frontier of knowledge, for everyone to understand."

Mary listened in wonder and the ideas connected with what she already knew; she learned quickly and questions would bubble up in Mary's mind that took her on quests to find out more, to learn more. She had read about Darwin and evolution and realised that this was another key property; life survives because it evolves. Every now and then a mutation of a life form, with a slightly different program, would come along that was better suited to the changing environment, able to find a better food source, make and use tools, communicate better, and so on and so forth; there seemed no limit to evolution. There seemed no limit to life's diversification; another characteristic of life Mary discovered. There might be as many as a trillion different life forms, different species, but we really don't know. But how did life begin? No-one seemed to have the answer to this. As a young teenager, Mary was bowled over by science and how it revealed the way things are. There would be no looking back; she would become a scientist and search for jigsaw pieces that made up the big picture of life. Everything else seemed ordinary, and ordinary did not appeal to Mary.

Bran had met Mary when they were both studying for their doctorates at the University of London. Bran attended a debate on the theme 'Technology – in control or under control?' The chairman gave an introductory talk on the history of technology, with a 'rise and fall' theme; the rise through the 19th century to the middle of the 20th century, spurred by the scientific revolution. Since then, technology had been getting an increasingly bad name, de-humanising people, the cause of so much environmental damage and an enabler for weapons of mass destruction, terrifying armed conflicts and terrorism. The chair was deliberately provocative. Bran had felt mixed emotions hearing this and spoke out about the positive benefits of technology, acknowledging the need for constraint to minimise unintended negative consequences. Several members of the audience were on the chairman's side and aimed their criticism at Bran; 'am I the only one who sees the positive side to technology?' he thought as he took more and more flak from an increasingly aggressive group of anti-technologists and neo-luddites, mostly from the arts and humanities disciplines. The chairman managed to calm the audience down and pointed to a woman who held her hand up, wanting to say something. She stood up and the light from one of the stain glass windows shone on her face. Bran was mesmerised and flooded with feelings that were new to him. He couldn't put his finger on what was happening and just gazed at the woman bathed in light. When she spoke, her voice drew everyone's attention, not because of its assertiveness or commanding tone, but because her words flowed out as if in song and she moved her body gracefully in stressing her rhetoric; she was a joy to watch. This woman's arguments were also powerful. Science was exposing the ignorance of dogma. Technology was freeing people from burdensome work, alleviating suffering and ill-health and dismantling the shackles of control imposed on the ordinary people by the elite. Science was lighting up the road to achieving environmental balance in the biosphere and engineers were tackling the renewable energy challenges to ensure a carbon-neutral future for our planet. It was as if this beautiful woman, this beautiful voice, was painting a picture, revealing a vision for people, of how things could be, and her audience was being led towards this willingly. How did she do that, Bran was thinking?

He had to meet her, that was his only thought. After the debate, he saw her across the crowded room, in a group of animated characters, all vying for her attention he thought. He didn't even know the girl so how could he feel jealous? He wanted to share ideas with this woman, to talk about science and technology, but most of all he just wanted to be with her. How could Bran explain that? She would think he was a weirdo; she would not be wrong Bran thought, he felt weird, but not in any threatening way. He needed to understand what was going on within before he would take this any further. He walked out of the conference foyer onto a balcony with his glass of wine and looked out over the city. Focus on what is real, he said to himself. The neo-luddites don't understand; they don't try to frame and solve problems like engineers do. They simply can't; their education has taken them away from science, and scientific understandings, since they were in their mid-teens. What a terribly shackled education system we have. Reflecting on this problem always got Bran hot under the collar and he knew he had to cool down to stay rational.

"Bran", he heard the chairman's voice behind him; "Bran, I'd like to introduce you to Mary Norris, seems she liked what you said there in the debate." That moment was frozen in Bran's memory, marking the beginning of a new life. They talked for hours, sharing thoughts and ideas, laughing at each other's humour, discovering the other and themselves. At the end of the evening, they agreed to meet again the next day, Bran's head was spinning as his imagination worked overtime. This woman was genuinely interested in his aeronautical research and he had listened to her ideas on global warming with fascination. The joy of the union of two minds was fuelled by another feeling; Bran believed he had fallen in love. He walked home with wings on his heels, in a mix of the precocious Hermes and the melancholy Rodgers and Hammerstein lyrics. A new life had begun. He was no longer alone and his new friend, his soulmate, would shape this life in powerful ways.

As Bran drove into the car park at the coal mining museum, he sighed and reflected on the value of driving through country lanes for stimulating the free play of thoughts. His memories didn't surprise him but sometimes they reminded him of important things, and of how important some things were. Waiting for the museum to open, Bran let his thoughts settle; yes, letting thoughts settle is a task in itself. Each thought had to find its own resting place in the canyons of his mind, until called on again or popping out of its own volition. Bran reflected on this process with wonder and chuckled to himself as he thought that this must be the height of introversion. His mind carried 50 years of memories, interwoven with thoughts and ideas, and dreams of what might be. Some had borne fruit while others lay dormant; the life you lead and the lives you wonder about, which is the more real? He seemed to be wanting to bring his great grandfather back to life; maybe he should write a novel about him? But connecting with the lives of others is challenging even when you think you know someone. When they are lost in the mists of time Bran would have to build the picture, the story, beyond his senses. He reminded himself that this was why he was visiting the museum. Mary would say that our senses can only take in so much and the mind is where we interpret and make sense of our relationship with the environment and other people. Bran's recall of his first meeting with Mary had enlivened him, helped him to feel grounded and he thought of the paradox of his love of flight and the need to feel grounded, just as the door to the museum opened and broke into his reverie like a stone in a rock pool. A man dressed as a coal miner welcomed Bran at the door.

"I bet you'll be Dr Sage? I'm Ron Flintworth, Jenny passed your email to me. Excuse the clothing but we are doing a little theatre for a local school group, that you would be most welcome to sit in on by the way. Come on in, would you like some tea or coffee?" The museum was filled with artefacts, hanging on the walls, resting on shelves and protected within glass cases; the past preserved with a mixture of modern smells filling the air.

"Thanks, coffee, black and no sugar," replied Bran. Ron was a small, elderly man, in his early 80's Bran guessed, and he spoke with a mild West Country accent.

"We've arranged for you to go through the archives this afternoon and Jenny has pulled out a few things that you might be particularly interested in. Was it the 1872 disputes you were curious about?"

"Yes", said Bran, "any details on those might be helpful because I think my great grandfather Henry may have been involved. My father told me that he thought Henry Sage had left the Somerset coalfields after some altercation but that's it, the rest is a mystery."

"You're fortunate to have that straw to clutch; my dad died when his aircraft crashed on takeoff. He had only just joined the RFC and it was his first solo flight in the Camel. Pilots were warned of the control difficulties but they weren't properly prepared for them. I was less than 1 year old when he died in 1917." Bran recalled reading about the Camel's problems; unstable in pitch which made it highly manoeuvrable, and the importance of close pilot attention on takeoff to counteract the torque from the heavy rotary engines and propeller. Pilots could easily be caught out if they did not anticipate the aircraft yawing to the right as they raised the nose on take-off. An aeronautical engineer's classic gyroscopic-effect case study, but a novice pilot's nightmare. Ron continued.

"Later, I decided that I would work in aviation and try to make aircraft safer; my Dad should not have died that way. I joined the Holtan Aircraft Company as an apprentice, then worked as a flight test engineer, then later in the design office until I retired. But you aren't here to listen to my family history, let's go up to the archives." Bran was interested in any and everything 'aviation', but he did want to be purposeful during this visit.

"Jenny, this is Dr Sage; Dr Sage, Jenny Partridge, Jenny looks after our archives and is our research officer."

"Oh, that's too grand a title Ron, we're all obsessed volunteers here Dr Sage and I'm the one obsessed with keeping the documents organised." Jenny's round face seemed to feature a permanent smile that glowed brighter with the enthusiasm in her voice.

"It's a pleasure to meet you Jenny, please call me Bran, and thanks Ron for sharing a little of your history; it helps to know you better and, I agree, your dad should not have died because his aircraft was unsafe." Ron nodded in appreciation of Bran's words. Jenny continued,

"I have found some documents on the disputes of the 1870's. We have some of the Somerset Miners' Union and Association records which you might like to browse through, but I have not yet found any mention of your great grandfather. Did you say he was involved in the disputes?"

"Well, my father thought he was," replied Bran, "but he had no details."

"I am just going to check through another cabinet so I'll leave you here to read through what you want and come through to the library when you are ready." Jenny left Bran with a folder of papers as she closed the door quietly and walked down the stairs talking with Ron. Jenny Partridge was dedicated to her tasks at the museum. She had been a primary school teacher before retiring a few years earlier and brought her skills as an educator to her work at the museum. She organised most of the educational activities as well as writing the scripts for the theatrical events, including todays.

Bran felt a kinship with Ron and Jenny; they were preserving a piece of history so that folk like him could explore and make sense of it, for whatever reasons. Reading the papers, Bran found that the 'disputes' were mostly concerned with pay and safety. The unions wanted a fairer system of wages and colliers met in large numbers to protest the exploitation of the workers by the managers and owners who were primarily interested in profit and their own personal gain.

The introduction of a sliding scale for wages, that related to the price paid for the coal, came in the late 1870's and would improve relationships for a while, but the tension was always there as the method was open to abuse; and it was a national tension, across the Midlands, Yorkshire, South Wales and Somerset. The raw material driving the expansion of the British Empire and the Industrial Revolution was hewn from the ground at a huge cost to miners and their families. They wanted more recompense, a fairer deal. Miners also wanted safer working conditions, free from the daily threats of explosions, tunnel collapses and suffocation and longer-term health problems due to poor ventilation. Bran's father, grandfather and great grandfather had endured lives as colliers. As Bran read through documents describing the terrible conditions underground in the Somerset coalfields, he wondered at the poverty, the literal starvation, that induced people to work in the mines. But there was no mention of Henry Sage. Jenny appeared at the door to the archive room.

"I've found something that you might be interested in Dr Sage." Jenny hoisted a cardboard box onto the table and opened the top to reveal an assortment of documents. "This box of material was donated to the museum by the couple who bought the old pub in Camerton, The Colliers' Rest. The label on the box says that it was found when the new owners were clearing out the basement in 1990, but I don't think anyone has been through this yet and it looks like personal material from the family who ran the pub, Tony and Sonia Johnson. It was built in the early 1800's and run by the Johnson's for the last 20 years before it shut down. They tried to persuade their son Ollie to take it on but he went to college and started a business in Bath, but he still lives locally; can't blame him really, publicans have a hard time these days. I imagine that your great grandad had a few pints in the 'Rest' as they used to call it."

"Yes, I imagine he did", said Bran as he gazed at the dust rising out of the box. How old is that dust he wondered? Bran carefully removed and examined each item in the box; receipts and bills, newspaper cuttings with articles about the pub, business letters to Tony Johnson, letters to Sonia Johnson from friends and relatives; all dated in the mid-late 20th century. At the bottom of the box were three small watercolours in delicately carved wooden frames. Bran laid all three alongside each other on the table. One showed a painting of a coal mine, the headstock winding gears standing stark against a slippery grey sky with a figure of a man leaning on a post in front of the timber yard. Another showed a kingfisher perched on a branch above a stream; the colours were faded but it was a beautiful sight. The third showed a couple walking along a path beside what might be a canal. All three were signed SJ. So, Sonia Johnson had been an artist thought Bran, and a good one. Jenny looked at the pictures.

"I think they were hanging in the pub lounge; we should give them to Ollie, I'm sure he would like to have some of his mum's paintings."

Although Bran had not found anything relating to Henry in the museum's archives, he felt a little closer to his great grandfather and imagined him standing up for the workers in the disputes, maybe even resorting to fisticuffs to take a stand. Bran was re-creating the man from tiny pieces of information, giving him a heroic character. When Henry was buried he had the largest coffin in Ebbw Vale. He wasn't described as the tallest man in Ebbw Vale, but rather that he was buried in the largest coffin. Bran had never asked his dad why Henry's passing was remembered in this way and it was too late now. "Damn, I wish I had asked more questions," thought Bran; "the past disappears like smoke unless it is talked about, or written about." Maybe Bran would get around to writing an autobiography one day; one day maybe but not yet, too many other things to do.

Before his journey home, Bran had planned to take a walk in the local area as part of the connecting with his ancestors. Although there were none left in the area, records showed that the Sage family had lived here for more than two centuries and probably before that. Bran wanted to soak up the atmosphere of the place, smell the aromas, feel the wind on his face, breathe the Somerset air, and take it home with him. As he was leaving the museum he thanked Ron and Jenny for their help and hospitality.

"You have both been very helpful, I can't thank you enough."

"You are most welcome" said Jenny, visitors like you make our job more interesting, adds an extra purpose, and we are purposeful, aren't we Ron?"

"Indeed, we are Jenny," said Ron, "all this stuff only begins to mean something when people look at it. Will you stay to watch our little theatre at 3.30 Bran, just 30 minutes' worth."

"Yes, I will Ron but I wanted to take a walk into the countryside before that, I'd like to get some exercise."

"There is a footpath along the old coal canal towpath, the canal was filled in years ago but we've been clearing the route to make it a nature reserve using some of the heritage funds we secured a few years ago."

"That's a great idea, thanks Ron; I'd read about the coal canal and the restoration work, and I will be back for the theatre; bye for now."

Bran walked along the old canal towpath. The canal itself had not been used for over a hundred years, and was filled in and overgrown with grass, nettles and wild flowers, but some of the side walls were still  intact and Bran closed his eyes to imagine what it might have looked like 130 years ago. Did Henry walk along this path, maybe on his way to work in the early hours, or returning home 14 hours later weary from a day digging coal. What were his thoughts? Was he thinking about his future, making a better life somewhere else? Was he at all reflective or just too exhausted to do anything but walk home? Bran had discovered that Henry had married Sarah after they had moved to South Wales, so had they eloped? What did their parents think and say? Bran had also discovered from ancestry records that Henry and Sarah were first cousins. Sarah's mother and Henry's mother were sisters. What did the mothers, the sisters, think? Did they disapprove terribly and ostracise their children? Whatever, the feelings in the Sage family must have been strong around this union. From the records, Bran also knew that Sarah had her first child in Ebbw Vale in 1873, but when exactly had they moved to Wales?

The blossom of late spring filled the air with scent and a blackbird was singing his heart out. Did the blackbird's ancestor sing when Henry trod this path? Bran's thoughts were exploring these unanswerable questions when he caught sight of a humped-back stone bridge over the canal, coming into view around the bend. He imagined a coal barge being towed by a horse along the canal and under the bridge. He then noticed that the towpath did not pass under the bridge and he wondered how the barges got through; a question for Ron when I get back, he thought. The sight of the bridge was strangely familiar to him and he had a déjà vu feeling that took him by surprise. Einstein's space-time theory posits that the concept of 'now' as a unique moment, that's here and gone, only exists in human minds, while really all events in space and time exist as a continuum. Did this mean that the past is never gone and the future is already here? Bran found these very difficult concepts to grasp, beyond any kind of common sense. Yet, just as in Plato's cave allegory, Bran was all too aware that there were likely to be many things beyond the, so-called, common sense. Perhaps déjà vu moments are when we catch a glimpse of another event in the continuum. Bran always felt thrilled playing with these thought experiments, but brought himself back to the here and now, remembering that he wanted to watch Ron's theatre. With one last look at the old canal ditch going under the bridge, he turned around and headed back to the museum.

Bran arrived just as the school children in the audience were making their last shuffles and coughs; the main lights were dimmed and the curtain raised. Ron stood on the stage as a younger man slowly pushed a cart loaded with coal along a track, while another man lay under a rock hewing at a simulated coal seam beyond. Yet another was fitting wooden props in the two-feet space between roof and floor. Water dripping was heard, and the noise from various machines was accompanied by clunking, rapping, grinding and scrunching sounds oozing from the dark industry. As the drama unfolded, Ron described how it was for the colliers working underground.

"The confined, poorly ventilated spaces, constant threat of roof collapses unless the pit props were secure, long periods in contorted positions trying to dig the coal from the narrow seams. Yet men and boys were willing to do this day after day, week after week, month after month and year after year to earn enough to feed their families. Large families meant more income into the home as the children were old enough to work. It was not unusual for boys as young as 5 to be found underground, helping their elder brothers with the carting. It wasn't until 1842 that the coal mines regulation act made it illegal for women, or children under the age of 10, to work underground. However, families became dependent on the income from the women and boys working underground so the practice continued illegally into the late 19th century. When the inspectors came to review practices at a colliery, the women and children would stay at home. Before the culture changed, the ruling was easily abused as owners and workers colluded to both their short-term benefits. The culture would only change when the men got a living wage for their day's work, and with large families, what was a living wage? So, we sometimes wonder why so many men flocked to work underground in the middle of the 19th century. One reason was that they could earn double the wage of an agricultural worker. That might be enough of a reason but colliers were also drawn to, dare I say enticed by, work in close confines with other men, sharing a solidarity, a camaraderie, that could only be experienced in one other scenario, wartime; isn't that amazing?"

Ron left the rhetorical question hang in the air and asked the audience of scholars and teachers if they had any questions. And, so began a dialogue between age and experience and youth and innocence. Bran found it fascinating to listen to and

35

afterwards he congratulated Ron on an excellent talk and his skills as an educator.

"Thank you, Dr Sage, Jenny writes the script but when I get to do this I really feel the part, even though I never worked underground myself. I had several school friends who worked in the mines and, like me, were engaged in essential industries during the war so did not have to join the forces. I've got most of my understanding of what it was like for colliers from them. They are all dead now, mostly from mining-related diseases." Ron spoke these words with finality, his eyes looking beyond Bran but focussed within.

Bran felt a deep respect for Ron. He carried more than 80 years of memories, seemingly without cynicism or burden; he was still youthful and gracious but then his face turned grave as he looked at Bran and continued speaking.

"You know Dr Sage, I went up to Bath yesterday for my grandson's funeral. Can you believe that Dr Sage, going to your grandson's funeral? It really seems wrong, doesn't it? Peter was a helicopter pilot and he died when his aircraft crashed, along with his three passengers, so all very tragic." Realising that this was the same funeral service that he had inadvertently stumbled on, Bran shared this.

"Ron, I also went to a funeral ceremony for an old friend of mine in Bath yesterday and I think it was just after your grandson's. I met his widow Sandra and brother-in-law Frank. Sandra shared a little of the circumstances with me; I am so sorry Ron."

"Well dear me, what an amazing coincidence Dr Sage. I didn't see you there but then I was sitting in the chapel with my daughter, Peter's mother Sophie, and his father Philip. Sophie is terribly distraught by Peter's death and worried that he might be blamed for the crash; it's mostly pilot error these days isn't it Dr Sage? I'm afraid that Peter and Sandra separated a year or so ago. It seemed an amicable affair, if I can call it that. But Peter was so young, only 45, and he was a good pilot." Bran thought carefully what to say but then decided to share the conversation he'd had with Sandra. "Ah, so she asked for your help Dr Sage? And this is your line of work, investigating the causes of flying accidents?"

"Yes, I run an aerospace consultancy Ron, and we do sometimes support accident investigations. I advised Sandra to wait until the Air Accident Investigation Branch publishes its report. They should soon have access to the flight data recorder, if there was one on-board, and will then begin making sense of this. Their initial findings should be published within a few months. I can understand how you and your family might feel in limbo but, please be assured Ron, the investigators do a good job and, if anyone can get to the bottom of this, understand the causal factors, it's them."

"Causal factors, is that what they call them, so my grandson might be remembered as a causal factor? My father was killed because he did not have sufficient training to overcome the Camel's nasty flying characteristics, and my grandson because, well we don't know do we? But, you know something Dr Sage, I worked for years in the helicopter industry and I was always, every step of the way, aware that flying machines not only had to be made well, but also needed to fly well. When I worked in the design office at Holtan, I dedicated myself to safety and became the lead engineer for the analysis of failure modes and effects; I'm sure you know what I mean Dr Sage. I felt that every action I took, every detail I examined, made things better, safer, for the pilot. When automatic pilots came in during the 1960s, there were a host of new types of failure that we had to consider. The autopilots were supposed to make things easier and safer but they brought with them some unintended consequences."

"Yes, I'm very aware of that," said Bran, "failures of the automatic control systems have led to many accidents. The regulations state that if there is a failure, the aircraft's handling should not be worse than if the automation had not been there. That's all very well but I've seen cases where a failure puts the pilot in a really difficult situation."

Bran and Ron continued talking about this subject, precious to them both. Ron reminded Bran a little of John Morgan, who also had a keen interest in the positives and negatives of automatic flight control. Bran decided to make a commitment.

"Ron, if I can I will let you know of the progress in the investigation when anything is published; would you like me to do that?"

"Yes please, Dr Sage, that would be marvellous, and I will let you know if we find out anything more that might help in your ancestry research. Your visit has motivated Jenny and me to get a better understanding of the disputes you referred to. It is such an important part of the human story within the coal mining history here." They walked towards the exit of the museum and Bran noticed that the three paintings he had looked at earlier were displayed in the foyer.

"It's good to see those lovely paintings in the light of day again, and for others to enjoy them, said Bran."

"Ah yes," Ron replied, "Jenny was so taken with them that she decided to display them for all to see as they come through the door; but it may not be for long as Sonia's son will probably want to show off his mother's talents in his own home."

"Looking at that view of the towpath and the bridge

reminds me of a déjà vu moment I had on my walk earlier. I think I passed that very spot and had the impression that I had seen that view before, although it looks very different with the water and the barge in view," Bran replied.

"Yes, Sonia must have had a good imagination because the canal has been disused for more than 100 years, and that image of the headstock must have been painted from a photograph" said Ron. Bran remembered his question.

"How did they get the boats under the bridge, I noticed that the towpath doesn't go under the bridge."

"That's right, the horse would have to be taken up over the top and down to the towpath on the other side. Meanwhile, a man or maybe a man and a boy, the leggers as they were called, would lie in the barge, on what were called wing boards, but sometimes on top of the coal, and push with their legs on the tunnel wall. Another risky, unsafe practice, which resulted in accidents; we can't escape accidents in all manmade endeavours, can we Dr Sage." Bran nodded in agreement.

"Thanks Ron, that clears up that point and could you please thank Jenny for me." Bran left the coal mining museum with no details of Henry Sage, yet he was beginning to glean an impression of what life might have been like for his great grandfather. He wanted to establish why and when Henry and Sarah left Somerset. For some reason this intrigued him and maybe some answers would be found in the place of their elopement, Ebbw Vale. Bran had no evidence that they had eloped, more of a suspicion, and he knew that he may never find the truth.

On his journey home Bran was taking stock of his experiences over the last two days; meeting Sandra and the curious effect she had on him, the eulogy he gave and the bitter sweet experience of John Morgan's funeral service, the warmth of John's family, the insights gained at the coal mining museum, finding new friendships in Jenny and Ron, the déjà vu experience of walking along the tow path. His recall of first meeting Mary had been exhilarating and he felt grateful for his fortune. How life can be shaped by the unexpected experience he thought, and how he embraced that; he hoped he would never, ever, lose sight of the importance of chance encounters. He would soon be getting back to the discipline of his consultancy work, where clearly defined, analytic processes can also reveal the unexpected, but only if one's senses are open to new things. Bran had developed a strong sense of humanity and practised this within the ethos of his consultancy. Staff were encouraged to think and work with open minds, to be on the alert for pieces of evidence that might

help to create the bigger picture. In one of his regular staff meetings, Bran had made the point that, at the frontier of what we know and understand lies the unexpected and, as explorers, we do well to remember that and expect to be surprised. He liked to think of his team of consultants as explorers.

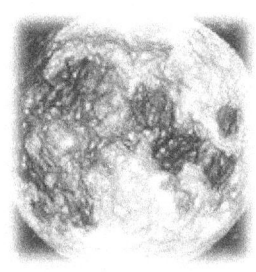

That night, Bran sat out on the decking in his garden and reflected on the week gone by as he gazed up at the moon which was full, shining bright; Tycho glaring like a star within

the moon's surface, and the Seas of Serenity and Tranquillity merging together like a pair of sunglasses. The man in the moon with shades on and he smiled at the thought. He wondered what the Earth looked like from up there and imagined the amazement experienced by those who had first walked on the lunar surface and looked back at their home planet from Mare Tranquillitatis; seems more mysterious in Latin he thought. Looking back was something that captivated Bran but he still did not fully understand why. It had troubled him yesterday and he'd penned a poem to capture thoughts about juggling his two worlds; he read it to himself.

Working on the theory, learning to sing the song

Sometimes feeling weary, sometimes very strong

Patterns form within my mind, I lay them down with care

So that I can bring them back one day, without a single tear

Laughter 'round the corner, courage on its knees

Sometime after I cried out loud, I learned to hide the tears

Frankincense means nought to me, that myrrh is just a gloss

But gold it makes me stop to think and wonder about my loss

Juggling seems new to me now but I'm giving it a go

Try to find the patterns, learn how to catch and throw, let
the creative juices flow

Yes, let those juices flow; mustn't fear what they might bring. He felt that he would sleep well tonight; making new friends puts to rest some inner torments. He whispered goodnight Mary, wondering how she was, thousands of miles away. Before he went to sleep, Bran picked up his guitar and strummed a tune on the major sevenths, and quietly sang Dylan's *Most of the Time*. Why he associated so with the lyrics of such a sad song he wasn't sure, but sometimes he had feelings that chimed with being less than fully content, maybe hiding from feelings buried deep. Bran only knew that Dylan had the right words for this kind of mood. As he fell asleep he was back on the canal path and he could see a woman's face, she was staring at him. Was it Mary, Sandra or someone else; he'd think about it in the morning, when he could clear his focus all around and be able to deal with situations down to the bone; Bran fell asleep with Dylan's lyrics and the woman's face going around inside his head.

2. The Knots People Tie as the Raven Croaks with Rage

They walked along the old canal path, talking together and she was looking up at his face, while he gazed into the sky as if for inspiration. Henry held Sarah's hand but he let go as he began to conduct with his hands and arms to accompany his words. It was  as if he was struggling with his inner self, conducting an orchestra in the sky. Sarah knew what was happening, she had been close to her cousin all their lives, and she folded her arms to protect herself against Henry's strength of conviction. She was with him, her heart felt for him, but she needed to shield herself from any unintended shrapnel coming from Henry's angst.

"Oh, dear cousin, if only I could make changes, make things safer down there, make them understand how important safety is. Ever since Ritchie started carting, I'm at all sorts with the way things are, or rather the way things aren't. I'd have the whole mine checked out every day  before we begin work; the cables, tracks, tunnels, shafts and headstocks. Everything, and we'd do it ourselves so those artful managers can't take their short cuts." Ritchie was

 Henry's younger brother, only 12 years old and bright and sharp as a new pin, but underground most of the day, hauling the coal in sledge-like putts from the coal face to the track, then loading the coal into wheeled tubs. Ritchie wore the guss and crook, with a rope around his waist attached to a chain that went through his legs to be hooked onto the putt. They took some getting used to, crawling on all fours and dragging the putt hundreds of feet to the main tunnel and track. Henry had made sure that Ritchie worked with him so he could help him learn the job and show him how the hewing was done. Ritchie was keen, and seemed to have endless stamina, wanting to show his older brother what he was made of; the same hard stuff.

Henry was a tall man and could not work in the thinnest seams, but was often still cramped into a narrow coal seam for long periods. Henry was also very strong and the most productive miner at the New Pit, sometimes hewing more than 12 tons in a single day. He was proud of his work but also keenly aware that working conditions could and should be improved. With hands wringing and exasperation in his voice, Henry continued; "if only they could see that everyone would benefit from things being safer down there, and we'd be more productive." Sarah took his hand again.

"Henry my love, you are right and you are doing the right thing but you should be more patient and you will get what you want."

"It's not just what I want Sarah, it's for all of us who slave away underground nine or ten hours a day; but I do sometimes wonder if most of them care. You know, up on the hill the other evening some men were talking about forming an association so we could pressure the owners to give us what we want, not just one or two of us but hundreds of us, in union. My heart jumped at that idea Sarah my love. When it seems that you are a lone voice, and then you hear others saying the same thing and calling for action, Lord it does inspire me. But we're up against it love on both sides. The managers want to keep control and keep us in shackles, fill their own pockets with more profit and some of the men don't want to kick up a fuss; afraid of losing their jobs, they are." Sarah reached out and gripped his hand firmly.

"You know Henry, Martha said to me the other day that Fred was worried that you would make things worse for the men. She said that some were thinking that the owners were looking for the chance to let some of the miners go."

"No, that won't happen," said Henry. "There is a shortage of coal across the country and we need to be digging more, need more miners, not less. The artful managers just use that as a threat to frighten people into doing what they're told for a low wage. Pay is another thing the union wants to get hold of. You know yourself Sarah that some of the families hereabouts have six or eight mouths to feed and even with men like Fred, and four of his youngsters working, it's hardly enough to live on. The men are meeting again on the hill Saturday night and I said I would join them." Sarah looked at Henry and squeezed his hand.

"You will do what you must Henry and you know I am with you whatever that is, but promise me you will be careful." Henry smiled and nodded to Sarah in response. She loved that smile; it was an outward sign of his inner happiness. They walked on quietly into the evening, bathed in early summer aromas of Pineapple Mayweed growing on the sides of the towpath and the new mown hay drifting off the field below, the nightingale whistling a fairy tale drew them closer.

Henry had worked in the mine since he was 12 but only full time since he was 18. Before then he had another part-time job gardening for the Fernhill family who lived in the Manor. He loved working in the garden but it was not well paid and he was ready to go underground full-time as soon as a hewer position came up. In the Manor garden, Henry would have long chats with 'Grampa John', as he was known, a gentle, wise old man and the grandfather of the lady of the Manor, Anna Fernhill, who also owned the lands in the surrounding area. John had helped fund the local school and wanted to educate Henry, help to give him better chances in life and open his mind to the many things going on in the big wide world outside Camerton. Henry became particularly interested in what was described as the industrial revolution and the increasing use of machinery powered by steam engines. The New Pit had a new engine installed that drove the winding gear and the tandem headstocks, those giant wheels in the sky. Henry was fascinated as a child to watch this at work. No longer were any horses needed to walk round and round the gear pulling the cages up, just a steam machine with the pulling power of 10 horses. Grampa John described the reciprocating-piston steam engine; how the water boiled and the steam expanded, applied pressure to the piston, pushing it down and pulling it up, and, through a crank, driving a wheel around, connecting to the winding gear and the cage. This allowed the mines to go down to the thicker seams deep below the surface at the New Pit.

Grampa John had friends in the city of Bath and would still visit on occasions. He would come back and share with the young Henry what he had found out about the big wide world. It seems that John was as enthusiastic to share as Henry was to listen. A new theory of evolution had been proposed but was causing a lot of trouble because some people refused to belief that humans were related to monkeys. In America, a civil war had ended but the President had been assassinated; while in Britain, the reform act of parliament allowed many more working people to vote in elections. A new canal had been opened between the Mediterranean and the Red Sea, so boats no longer needed to travel around the Horn of Africa to get to and from the Far East. A Russian friend of Grampa John's had described how a new piece of music, based on Shakespeare's Romeo and Juliet, and a stunning new book, titled War and Peace, would both confuse the literary critics before drawing praise. War and Peace, like his mum Maria and her sister Elizabeth, thought Henry; Romeo and Juliet, like Sarah and himself. All this news from afar made Henry's head spin with wonder, building a tree of knowledge in his mind. Another friend, who was a teacher at Somerset College, had shown Grampa John an electrical wire device for sending messages between rooms at the college. John had met the inventor on one of his visits, a man named Bell. Henry wondered why he would want to talk through a wire and how did that work anyway.

The 60's had felt like a special time to be alive and Henry had been captivated by discovery and learning about things going on in the world from an early age. He had a big appetite for knowledge but he also knew that he had to bring an income into the home. His father James had been killed in a mining accident ten years before and Henry and his brothers James Jnr and Ritchie were the bread-winners now; their mother Maria depended on them. His younger brother Tom had moved to mine coal in the South Wales Valleys and older brother George was married with his own family to support. Henry's keen interest in all things made him different from other colliers, many of whom were illiterate and drew on camaraderie to endure the hard work. To some of them, Henry felt like a

47

threat to this blissful ignorance. They thought him too zealous regarding safety and laughed when he talked about the importance of skill training. Colliers should be grateful to the owners for the work, and not kick up a fuss when things go wrong, when someone is injured or when their pay did not increase; these were the inevitable consequences of hard, manly occupation and if you didn't like it, you should shuv off. And anyway, a collier's pay was double that of a farm labourer, so who could complain? Henry Sage was a very mature 21-year-old in 1872, and possessed a strength of character that showed little weakness, except what was revealed to his best friend, Sarah.

Sarah Jane Wallace, daughter of Elizabeth and Albert Wallace, had been born a few years after Henry and they had grown up as the closest of friends, confidants to each other in all that was important. Sarah possessed a mysterious beauty, glowing auburn hair surrounding a face with expressions for all moments, and bright eyes that could capture and hold the attention of anybody. Sarah's smile was endearing, and many a man would collapse in love with her or become bewitched by her attention. She would use these gifts carefully in her life, wary of their power. From an early age, Henry was Sarah's protector, and Sarah had become Henry's conscience, her thoughts connecting with his in a natural way. She was also his restorer; when he was unsure, she helped him to gain confidence; when he was confused, she would help him see clearly; when he was angry she soothed him and when he was sad, she knew how to bring him out of his malaise. It was as if she knew what he was thinking and knew exactly what was needed to ease his pain, steady his nerves and make him feel good. Henry knew that he was very fortunate and his friendship with Sarah was the most important thing in his life. It both did and didn't make sense to him, but while it held him he would always submit, in the light and the dark. They were in love, and as they had advanced into adolescence, they were careful to try to keep their special relationship to themselves. But their mothers knew and could see what was developing. Henry's mother Maria was supportive of the relationship, although it was rarely discussed. On the other hand, her sister Elizabeth was very possessive about Sarah, needing her attention, and discouraged her daughter from seeing too much of Henry. Elizabeth was very frosty to both her sister and nephew and this caused a divide; she was something of a heartbreaker, ignorant of the light that shone from their union. Well, looking back it seems that way.

Sarah's family ran the Collier's Rest public house in Camerton and Sarah had worked doing domestic duties there from a young age. At the age of 17, she was industrious but was also careful how she spent her time. Time and life were precious to her. The pub was busy most nights, and Sarah made the miners feel welcome. They would thank her for her good spirits, her cheerfulness and some would confide that, when they got home, they were often met by a cross and ill-disposed wife who rebuked them for their drinking weaknesses, made them feel bad. Many miners were caught in this cycle of hard work underground, the need to extend the camaraderie into the evening at the Rest, and then being told off at home. Working hard the next day, with their fellow miners, relieved their guilt but most miners were hardly aware of the cycle they were trapped in. To some, the lovely Sarah was part of this cycle, as she made them feel good about themselves. If Sarah liked you, why not like yourself? If Sarah gave you a warm smile, why not give yourself a warm smile? One group of miners would start singing before they left the pub; humorous songs about working underground, written by Henry's older brother George. George could make up lyrics as he sang and soon the group had learned the new song and were singing in harmony. *"we are the Camerton colliers and we work for the love of coal, we spend all day deep underground, and sing to save our soul."* The Rest gained a reputation as a good place for miners to gather and relax. Sarah's father Albert was a good landlord and was pleased to see his daughter make the miners feel good. But he was also protective towards her and would be quick to challenge any unhealthy attention from miners. One, a sullen man, who often drank with a couple of other shady characters, had made advances to Sarah; would she like to come for a walk with Billie, who would like to show her the wonders of nature? Sarah would politely refuse but Albert would make it clear that he did not like the advances and it had to stop. Billie would just grin at Albert and declare that he was only being friendly; but the sickly grin disguised a deep lust that seemed to have just one aim.

Henry didn't often visit the Rest in the evenings. He did not like to see Sarah so friendly with other men. He felt jealous, but he knew that Sarah was his special friend and he could trust her. But what if another man wanted to marry her, provide for her, love her? Henry could easily torment himself with these thoughts and he knew that he and Sarah needed to talk about their relationship and the future. They were first cousins but it was not unknown for first cousins to marry thereabouts, although Elizabeth would say that idiots come from these unions. Elizabeth's parents had been first cousins but she seemed in denial of this. She was bitter for all kinds of reasons, some well-hidden to most, but Maria would later reveal that one reason for this was that their cousin, Jack, who Elizabeth was very fond of, had eloped with another woman, and would never be seen again. How our ethics get twisted, but Elizabeth could see none of this and was fearful of what her imagination brought her.

So, Henry would read in the evenings and walk and talk with Ritchie, who looked up to Henry, as if a father. Ritchie had only vague memories of their father James, but Henry filled in the blanks as he told stories of how their father had worked on the land before he became a coal miner. How he had worked on the canal locks heading east to Midford. James Sage was famous for his work on the canal but even more famous for his heroic rescue of five miners trapped underground after a tunnel collapsed when the props were crushed. James laboured for hours to clear the rubble from the narrow shaft and get to the trapped miners. When he eventually reached them, they were deep in water as the pump system had broken in the collapse and they were able to escape to the pit-bottom with minutes to spare. This accident had occurred at a time when the cage was being repaired so it was not possible to send more miners down to help James. By the time the exhausted miners reached the pit bottom the cage had been lowered and they were able to reach the surface. From that time on James was the local hero. But Henry was all too aware that his father was the victim of carelessness in the pits. The props had broken because there were too few of them and they were poorly maintained, and the hoist repairs should not have been happening when miners were still underground. James was killed when the hemp winding rope attached to the cage he was in broke; he and three of his fellow miners fell to their death at the bottom of the shaft. Henry had nightmares about his father falling, and often wondered what his last thoughts might have been. He resolved to do all he could to make the mines safer, and this became one of his missions in life. Another was to marry Sarah.

Henry and Sarah walked quietly along the towpath until they came to the bridge where they sat on the wall and looked out together across the fields. A coal barge was approaching from the west and they watched as the leggers climbed onto the boards and took the barge under the bridge. They waved to Henry and Sarah as they passed below. A woman in her late teens led the horse over the path to the other side of the bridge.

"Good evening to you Sarah," said the woman, "taking the air then, how be you?"

"Hullo Rita", said Sarah, "I'm well thanks, that's a pretty bunch of flowers in your hair."

"A present from Billie Oats," replied Rita, "I know he's a bit of a rogue but I do think he fancies me."

"Be careful of the rogue Rita dear" said Sarah, but Rita just chuckled as she tied the horse back on the barge and she and her two brothers went on their way. Henry got up from sitting on the bridge and turned to face Sarah.

"Sarah, I've something I want to say and ask of you." Sarah smiled and took Henry's hands in hers. "I know we are close kin, the closest of friends you could ever find and you make my life Sarah, my love, make it real. Will you marry me and make me the happiest man alive?" Sarah reached up and tenderly moved her hands through Henry's long curly dark brown hair. Drawing his head down she kissed him fully on the lips. They had not kissed quite like this before and for both it was a most erotic experience. Neither of them wanted that kiss to end as Henry drew Sarah's body close to his and felt her breasts pressing against him. His hands moved through her auburn hair and over her shoulders, down her back as he enveloped her in his arms. When the kiss ended, they both gasped for breath and Sarah began to laugh and cry at the same time.

"Yes, I will marry you, my lovely sweet Henry; I knew you would ask me when you was ready and I've been waiting for some time, didn't you know?" She looked deeply into his eyes as she held the lapels of his jacket. Henry could hardly speak, he felt so happy and he too began to cry.

"Oh, my Sarah, I'm sorry I have kept you waiting. I don't know why but I thought you might say no. We are like brother and sister and I know you love me but somehow I thought you might, might not…" Henry paused, "… well I'm not sure what I thought my love, but maybe that I didn't deserve you; that you wouldn't want me as a husband." They held each other for a long time that evening and watched the sun going down and the reflection in the dark water of the canal shone as brightly as the sinking sun. Blackbirds were competing for territory by singing their songs boldly. Henry thought they were singing just for Sarah and him; everything seemed connected with the union of man and woman on this special night. Sarah whispered in Henry's ear.

"I love you Henry and I will travel with you throughout your life, through the ups and downs, and I want lots of children with you, so be prepared for lots of loving Mr Sage." She kissed him again, and a warmth crept through Henry's body and soul; he couldn't imagine a more perfect feeling. The purple dusk of twilight rose in the sky saying goodnight to the sun.

Henry and Sarah decided to keep their engagement a secret until they could tell both families at the same time. They anticipated problems from Elizabeth but Henry felt sure that his mother Maria would be very happy for them. When Sarah arrived back at the Rest, her mother complained that she was out late and there was a full house so she should get to work behind the bar. One of Rita's brothers had told Elizabeth that he had seen Henry and Sarah on the canal bridge near

Timsbury, when they brought a barge through earlier on, so Sarah's mother was already angry. She had a little plan for Sarah that would put a stop to the developing relationship with her cousin. Elizabeth's uncle had moved to the Midlands a few years before and was a publican at a very busy coaching house in the coal mining area. He had written to Elizabeth asking if Sarah might like to come up and live with them, do domestic work for her uncle; he would pay her well. Now Elizabeth thought that she would arrange for this to happen. Before Sarah went to bed that night her mother told her what she had planned; there was no point arguing, it had all been arranged and she would leave in a couple of weeks when Arthur came to visit. When Sarah was alone with her father, she asked him if he had agreed to this.

"I'm sorry Sarah, I will miss thee but your mother has a determination about this that would shock a ghost, she has. She be worried that you and cousin Henry are too close, and some time away for you would help you see things different. What do you say to that Sarah, my dear daughter?" Sarah looked at her father and spoke quietly with emotional conviction.

"Father, I know my own mind, I know what I want and what I don't want, and my friendship with Henry is precious; he is precious to me. Sending me away will not change that, it is very cruel." Albert's expression was one of deep sadness.

"I be caught here my dearest as your mother is so strong on it. Could you just give it a try, maybe you would see it her way in time?" Sarah went to bed that night in a very confused state. She had experienced the most wonderful moments with Henry and committed herself to him, but the happy feelings flowing from these thoughts were tangled up in the blue mire of her family's wish to send her away. "I can't let this happen", she said to herself, and she slept very poorly that night, if at all; she would need all her strength to overcome her mother's destructiveness.

Henry awoke, got dressed and went down for breakfast with his mother and brothers. It seems that the bailiff had called around the night before wanting to talk with Henry; could Henry see him during his break today. He and Ritchie made their way down the hill to the colliery, throwing and kicking a football along as they went their way, talking and joking about the day ahead. It took about ten minutes for the cage to descend to the bottom of the mine shaft, and then the small group of miners had to walk and crawl about half a mile before arriving at the coal face. They each wore a helmet with a burning candle to light the way. Camerton was not a gassy pit so burning candles were considered safe even though Davy lamps were now available but were expensive and miners had to buy their own candles or lamps from the company store. The tunnels and tracks should have been cleared of rubble overnight and the pit props checked for stability but Henry could see that this had not happened, yet again, and he made a mental note to bring this up with the bailiff when he saw him later. Henry lay down and arranged himself so that he could hew at the coal seam with sufficient force to break the coal. He was skilled at this, knew how to apply a force without wasting energy, and how to ensure that the coal broke off in large lumps. The larger the lumps, the less waste and more valuable the coal. Henry kept his tools sharp, giving him the best possible cutting edge. When sufficient coal had been cut to fill a putt, he would help Ritchie haul it to a level where Ritchie could drag it to the track to load into a tub. From there it was easier to push the tub to the bottom of the shaft but this needed two other men to help. The carters spent their whole day pulling and pushing, hunched over in the low tunnels, gradually causing more and more damage to their bodies. When Ritchie returned to where Henry was working, there would be more coal to load into the putt, and so the day went on. When the accessible coal had been cut from the seam, Henry would have to hew the rocks above, and other men would arrive with the wooden props to secure the safe space for Henry to go further into the seam. The men depended on each other here in the darkness, but the hewer was the main man in all of this. The productivity of the hewers ultimately determined how much coal was brought up and this was weighed to establish everyone's wages. Henry was known as the most productive hewer and was respected by his fellow colliers for his hard work and tirelessness. Some would grumble that he made them work harder than they needed. They were often the same men who complained about Henry's concern for safety, but the grumblers were few and didn't get much attention.

During his lunch break, Henry went up to the surface to meet the bailiff, Colin Amble.

"Henry, you're my best worker and, don't take this wrong, but the owners are concerned about the gatherings that are taking place; they feel threatened by this union of colliers and where it will lead. There has been talk of strikes and violent protestations and we want to avoid these, don't we Henry?" Colin looked at Henry and nodded, hoping for a return nod in agreement, but none came; Henry was thinking carefully. Colin continued. "I know that you have influence with the men and they listen to you. We want you to persuade them to stop making it difficult for the owners. It will only end up in more hardship for the miners. I know it's only a few troublemakers but they spread their bad ideas like a disease. You explain to them that the owners have expenses that the miners can't see and make them realise that they are getting a fair enough wage as it is. When the owners can sell more coal, or get a better price, then the wages will rise. Anyway, a lot of miners spend most of their earnings down the Rest, and if they would give more to their wives, we'd all be better off, if you see what I mean. The other thing Henry is that the Somerset mines are not as productive as the mines in South Wales and the Welsh can get their coal over to the cities in England nowadays. So, we have competition and, where there is competition, we need more efficiency, and more productivity Henry; you can see that can't you?" Colin looked at Henry, nodding his head again. "You'll do this for us Henry, right?"

Henry took a deep breath; he knew this was a very important moment and he had to get his words just right.

"Mr Amble, the other evening I spent some time with my brother George and his family; his wife and four young children and his mother. He is the breadwinner, the only one who brings home a wage from his hard work in the mine. He has a drink in the Rest two or three times a week but does not get drunk and he entertains all there with his singing and song lyrics. The men gather at the Rest to share stories from their day underground and that's important to them; it's good for their morale. George's family are hungry most of the time. He is one of many poor people I know like this, careful with their limited resources, but living on the edge of starvation all the time. Most of these men value their positions as hewers, breakers, putters, loaders or leggers. They know there are others waiting to take their place if they don't pull their weight, and most work without misgivings or resentments for the owners. I know this because I work with them every day Mr Amble. But they see the colliery owners and the landowners living a life of luxury, their children receiving education in boarding schools and they wonder Mr Amble, they wonder, why such inequality? And they ask themselves, is this fair?"

Colin Amble was a good man, a Christian, but he did not have the will, or the courage, to fight for a cause that was unlikely to be won.

"Henry, I understand all of that, but these same people would be far worse off working on the land and if they showed more prudence, they could do better for their families. The Chapel door is always open to them and our messages are of salvation, hope and courage to endure and not to be overtaken by misery, envy and self-doubt. I have found that Christians can endure more because of their faith." Henry wondered what it was that Colin had found, and where he had found it, that gave him this conviction. He thought of what the miners endured underground and how the camaraderie helped them to endure the extreme hardship. Maybe Christians were comrades digging for another kind of coal. But now was not the time or place to get into an argument about religion.

"Mr Amble, I am not the miner's leader and others are determined to see changes. They argue that a change for the better sometimes needs extreme measures, so that people, especially the owners, see the determination. Changes to working practices and pay structures have already happened in other parts of the country without the owners suffering too much. But I am, generally, a peaceful man and I won't participate in any violence against the owners. I will tell the miners that you want to have a proper discussion and that you are willing to listen to their claims and grievances and maybe things will turn out right if agreements can be made. That's what I can do if you want, but they may not listen to me; what do you say to that Mr Amble?"

"Do your very best for us Henry and the improvements will come, but the owners won't give way to threats from a few ill-disposed men, mark my words." Colin Amble thanked Henry and walked away. Henry sat down on a bench by the canal and thought about the conversation he'd just had with the bailiff. Yes, he would talk to the miners at the next meeting but he expected resistance because he knew the strength of feeling amongst the men and their families.

Back underground, Henry was glad to be with Ritchie again. He was good company and seemed not to have a complaint or bad thought in him. Ritchie also shared Henry's pleasure in working hard, they spurred each other on, contributing to Henry's high productivity. Ritchie was always asking questions, mining for what Henry knew, and helping Henry understand better the things that Grampa John had told him. Henry often thought that when a person really wants to learn, or needs to know something, the mind opens and makes space for new things; there seemed no limit to this as he thought about Grampa John's tales of things going on in far off places. Ritchie, like his uncle George, would make up little poems out of what he saw and felt around him at any moment. *'One more load, haul it up the road, send it on its journey to the light. Back for another, working with my brother, together with all our might, the end in sight.'* Henry thought that one day Ritchie should make something of his skill with words; yes, one day he should do that and Henry would help him.

Henry and Sarah met that evening before she started her work in the Rest. Henry could see that Sarah was distressed. She explained that her mother had arranged for her to live with her uncle Arthur in the Midlands, work at his inn there; Arthur would be coming down in a couple of weeks and that was that.

"I ain't doing that Henry my love, never." Sarah spoke

with a determined tone and Henry held her close.

"This is because of me, isn't it Sarah my love."

"Not you Henry, but us; my mother has a dreadful hate for us. She knows that I love you and that you love me. We have made our everlasting bond and that is everything to me."

"And to me, dearest Sarah." Henry moved his hands through Sarah's hair and kissed her.

"I must go to work Henry but let's take a long walk again on Sunday morning and we can work out a plan of what we must do." Sarah kissed Henry, pressed his hands and walked back down the lane towards the Colliers Rest. As Sarah approached the pub, Henry noticed a man crossing the lane and walking beside Sarah. He put his arm around her waist and she quickly pulled away, only to be pursued again by the persistent and unwelcome man. Henry ran down the lane towards them and shouted,

"Hey, stop that, can't you see its not welcome?" Billie turned and saw Henry coming towards him.

"Only having a bit of fun Sage, but what's it to you, Sarah's my friend, don't you know."

"I'm not your friend," Sarah spoke with anger in her voice. "And I don't want you putting your hands on me."

"You heard her Oats, now move on your way before I help you on your way." Billie looked fiercely at Henry, and wore a sickly smile as he walked on to the Rest. "Sarah, I know you don't encourage him but be careful my love and have nothing to do with him tonight."

Things were quiet that night in the Rest and Billie Oats made no more advances to Sarah but he was a bitter man who carried a lot of grudges from his past – a poor family without

60

much love and care, losing out on colliery work, and saddled with a laziness and an attitude that made him only suitable for menial farm labouring. He was one of those who wanted things to fall on his plate and felt aggrieved that others were more fortunate. He couldn't see that most of the working people around him strived to make their own fortune, or they too would be left to stew in their own misery.

The next day, Saturday, Henry received a letter from his brother Tom who had moved to work in the South Wales coalfield a year before. Henry put the letter in his pocket and read it during his break in the middle of the day. He and Ritchie sat on a pile of logs that were to be cut into pit props. They made a great bench but you had to be careful that they didn't roll away from under you, when you could get some unfortunate bruising. Tom had worked on the land and had been waiting for a position in the New Pit to come up when he heard of opportunities in the South Wales Valleys. Henry read the letter out loud so that Ritchie could hear what their brother was up to. It seemed that Tom was doing very well, had received good training and was already hewing at the coal face and earning more than Henry; but he was missing home and his mum's cooking. Tom had met a girl who he had become very fond of; and she seemed very fond of him too.

"That helps," said Henry and Ritchie chuckled. "Tom says that she speaks funny and it took a while to understand her, but that's true of all the Welsh; apparently, they have a great sense of humour, Tom says. Oh, and he's coming home next weekend with his girl Megan and he's sure we'll all love her."

"That's great" said Ritchie, "I love Megan already."

"Tom says that Welsh coal is blacker than Somerset coal, shines bright, gleaming with gold flecks. Seems like the valleys are a thousand feet deep Ritchie, and then the pits go another thousand feet underground and one of their mines produces as much coal as ten of ours." When he had finished reading, Henry's mind was buzzing with thoughts, with one big one coming back again and again; maybe he and Sarah could move to South Wales. But how would his mother cope? Henry didn't share these thoughts with Ritchie, who was jumping amongst the logs and reciting a poem he had just made up.

"Tom's coming home, Megan's coming too, is she blonde or a dark brunette, are her eyes bright blue." Ritchie liked to ask questions in his poems and he liked to imagine women; he was at an age when they were beginning to get his attention. He wondered what it might be like to have a girl as a friend; what would you say to each other? He could see how Sarah made Henry strong and confident and they were easy with each other. Ritchie thought that must be perfect.

"Come on Ritchie, back to work, me to hew and you to haul, the only way that you'll grow tall."

"Hey, Henry, you're a poet, and you know it when you show it." They both laughed and Henry put his arm around Ritchie's shoulder as they walked to the pit head and climbed into the cage to descend into darkness.

That evening Henry made his way up to Clandown Hill, a good mile from Camerton, to hear what the men from the miner's union were saying. Henry was mulling over what Colin Amble had asked him and he felt that this was an important time for him to decide where he stood. He was being asked to

act as a go-between but he could only do that if he felt he could trust the owners. The miners were his friends, he lived and breathed with them and to lose their trust would be very painful, and he wouldn't let

that happen. When he arrived at the top of the hill, he was surprised to find that there were already what looked like several hundred miners gathered and talking together.

"Henry, good to see you, this is Ivan Evans from the South Wales miner's association and Charlie Smith from the Midlands, they've come down to tell us how they do things in the other coalfields." Henry's brother George introduced him to the men with strange faces and strange accents. Miners were still gathering from the villages around and it was about 8pm before Ivan Evans climbed onto a mound and addressed the crowd.

"Good evening fellow colliers, fellow miners of the black fuel. I dig for coal deep underground in a town called Ebbw Vale in South Wales. On Wednesday I was underground for 12 hours and I hewed nearly eight tons of coal. After my shift, I walked a mile to my home and family to find my loving wife waiting with a cheery welcome and a plate of good food. My three youngest children were asleep in their bed; my three eldest sons, who also worked underground, sat around the table waiting for their father. I said a prayer of thanks and we ate our food. My brother's seat at the table was empty. Last year he was killed, along with eighteen of his friends, when there was an explosion underground. Four died from the powerful blast when the fire-damp gas ignited, but my brother and the others died when they breathed the deadly after-damp gas. You can't smell it or see it but one breath and you are gone. One of the casualties was from your area, young John Cooke, I knew him well; dark clouds pass down from our valleys over the waters to your farmlands. This accident happened because the ventilation system was inadequate to keep the air clean and protect the men against disaster. The ironmasters and coal mine owners knew this but had ignored the recommendations of the Government's inspector of mines. And there are problems across the country; yes, across the country nearly a thousand miners die every year because of mine accidents? So, it is up to us to make sure that it is safe underground, don't you agree?"

A loud roar came from the miners gathered around, followed by clapping of hands and stamping of feet. Ivan Evans was in good company, he had captured their attention, he was one of them. He continued.

"I can see that you are miners of the black fuel because you wear the blue scars on your dark faces and I see the broken bones in your tightly gripped fists. But I also see bright eyes, strong shoulders and I feel your independent spirit; oh yes, I can see you are colliers. We need to feel safe, and to be safe working underground, and the owners must take responsibility for safety. Now I'm told that your mines are not gassy like ours but you still have safety concerns. You need to be sure that everyone working underground is properly trained in their job; be confident that daily inspections are carried out by people who are certified and, by the way, we should be deciding who these are, not the owners; we need to know that the managers are certified to manage and run mines, and have the colliers' interests at heart. I've seen cases where managers have blamed the men for not propping up the roofs of tunnels in time; causing falls by overcrowding into the hudges in which they were lifted to the surface; letting boys aged 10 do a man's work and pay them a pittance. Things are getting better, safer, and a large part due to the tireless efforts of miner's association like you are building here in Somerset." Another roar and vigorous clapping from the listening miners.

"And then there is our pay." An even bigger roar could be heard across the countryside. Ivan began to talk about how miners had been treated like slaves, downtrodden for more than a century, paid as little as possible to allow the owners to use the profits to improve their own lot. How we had allowed the privileged magnates and their financiers to decide the course of our industry, without any consultation with the workers.

"Yes, we have allowed them to do this, but the abuse must stop; things must change if tomorrow is to be better than today and yesterday. We want our voices heard, our rights respected, improving standards of living, better chances of education for our children when they reach coal-mining age. These things are ours to claim, and if necessary, to fight for. I don't mean going to war, but rather using the main weapon at our disposal, the ability to remove our labour and stand our ground for change." Ivan continued his powerful rhetoric, winning more and more hearts and minds as the cheers burst through the warm evening air. The miners were enlivened, their imaginations fuelled by thoughts of a new future, with things getting better every day. They didn't mind the hard work, indeed they thrived on it, sharing experiences with common dangers and mutual dependence within a common independence, special skills that they passed on within their underground world at the seams, through the tunnels and up and down the shafts. They were colliers and Ivan Evans reminded them of their nobility.

They shouted out loud so the world could hear '*for union and for right.*'

How could Henry challenge any of Ivan's words, spoken with such a lyrical tongue, when he believed them and was cheering with his friends; but he did speak up.

"Friends, my heart has been pumping to Ivan's words, my mind bubbling with ideas of what might be possible. I'd like to suggest that we need a plan for how we approach the owners with our proposals." A voice shouted out,

"Our demands Henry, not our proposals." Henry nodded, but continued,

"Ok, but I believe that the best way to negotiate is to be clear about what we want, to argue our case and to listen to how the owners and the managers react and take it from there. I know there are some of the managers and bailiffs that don't seem to care a damn for us but there are others who will listen and if we can persuade them to give us what we want, we should try and then we all win, surely?" The air was full of miners murmuring as if a giant swarm of bees was passing overhead. A voice shouted out,

"Those bastards do treat us like slaves, like they own our every muscle, and we should make 'em pay us a fair wage. And they bloody cheat us when they weigh what we bring up and claim half of it is slag. I seen you talking to Amble yesterday Sage, you're one of them so why should we trust you, eh?" There didn't seem to be much support for this outburst, most of the miners knew that Henry could be trusted,

66

but Henry still felt hurt and annoyed by what the man had said. Henry recognised him as Martin Ferris, a fellow collier in Camerton. Ivan spoke again,

"I know your anger boys, we've got it in the Valleys as well, but Henry is right, you must decide what you want your association to ask for and you can't expect the managers to agree unless they see the benefit. You need the right person to do the negotiating; that's something we have found in South Wales. A belligerent, blustering radical who curses all the time is more likely to put the other side off than win their hearts and minds. But you need to be prepared to use the withdrawal of labour weapon." Henry hadn't thought of the owners and the managers being 'the other side', or using 'weapons' before, but he could see that he needed to stand by the miners, to stand by their side, if he was to be part of this.

Just then one of Henry's friends, Robert Barnes, came out of the crowd and stood next to him. Robert was a self-educated, thoughtful miner, and someone who Henry had a great respect for, and enjoyed his company.

"Listen men, I propose that we form a small group who can gather opinions, discuss ideas and take proposals to the owners. I'm sure that Henry will join me, but we should have two or three more, if you agree." Henry nodded his head and looked at Ivan with a 'is that a good idea?' look on his face. Ivan stepped up again.

"This is the way we started our association in Ebbw Vale and there were several volunteers who joined the task force; our initial focus was safety but we were aware that there was, and still is, a national movement to improve the lot of the working man and his family. You may be aware of the reform acts of Parliament that give more democracy, give the workers more say in the choice of their politicians."

Most of the miners in Somerset were not aware of the bigger political picture in mid-late 19th century England, but big strides were being made to improve the lives of poor people. The 2nd reform act of 1868 had given three times as many men the vote, including rate payers in rural areas and other *'respectable working men'*, but excluding the *'feckless and criminal poor'*. However, the reform did not include most of the miners and they would have to wait until 1884 for the 3rd Reform Act before they could vote. The passing of the 2nd Reform Act backfired on the Conservative government of Benjamin Disraeli, who lost the election of 1868; clearly the new voters were not impressed and they exercised their influence by voting in the radical Liberals under William Gladstone. Henry was aware of these things, and the bubbling unrest in the country, from discussions with Robert and Grampa John who he still met up with frequently.

The crowd of miners were talking amongst themselves and Ivan shouted out.

"All those in favour of setting up a task force, to work out what we want to do, say aye." The miners were hesitant but gradually the ayes could be heard until there resounding aye soared up to the heavens, echoing around the hills. "All those against shout nay." There was silence but much murmuring continued. Ivan continued. "Then I suggest that all of those who want to join the task force, come up and speak with Robert and Henry before you go home tonight." George called the meeting to a close and the men began to disperse, heading home in different directions and Henry was relieved when a smaller group of miners gathered around Robert and himself.

"Count me in for the task force," one said, "I've got some ideas," said another; "I'm in, let's get this right" said a third. The task force was taking shape and talked for about half an hour before agreeing to meet in a few days to draw up a plan;

all must bring their ideas. Ivan had stayed with them and shared ideas from his experience in the valleys. There was an excitement in the group. Where one man alone may lose enthusiasm, a task force of six men could support each other so no-one felt alone. They could bounce ideas off each other and sharpen up their arguments. They agreed to meet the next evening in Robert's house. Ivan, Robert and Henry stayed talking for a while longer. Ivan would be going home to Wales the next day and thanked Henry and Robert for their support.

"Peaceful negotiations and agreements are always possible when the two sides want to find a way and what they carve out will last longer. I don't know your managers but if they are reasonable men they will listen. But I have known some very unreasonable managers, who have a deep distain for the working man, regard him a slave."

Robert and Ivan headed off to the west and Henry sat down on the hill for a while thinking about what had happened. Up the hill, on the horizon, a pair of deer were prancing on the skyline; probably been frightened by the sight and sound of Ivan and Robert passing by, Henry thought. They looked free but he  wondered if the deer really were free if they had to be constantly on the alert for dangers. He thought of Sarah and their meeting the next day; he longed for her company to calm his thoughts.

Walking down the hill Henry heard the croak of the raven as it crossed the darkening sky, as if speaking to him; "hale raven, did you like what you saw?" The raven was Henry's favourite bird and he often wondered if they thought like humans. There is so much we don't know, he thought as he approached the wood, about the natural world around us and

the man-made world around the globe. Man's place within the fury and serenity of the natural world. These lofty thoughts were running through his mind when he noticed a group of four men standing by the stile at the wall. Henry felt a sensation pulsing through his body, alerting him to danger. He noticed that one of the men was Billie Oats but he didn't recognise the others. Billie spoke as Henry approached.

"Evening Sage, out for a stroll and causing trouble again. Martin told me what you've been saying to the miners, bringing unrest, making some lose their jobs." Henry had no intention of discussing anything with Billie.

"Stand aside Oats, you're blocking my way."

"Oh, we're blocking his way boys, whad'ya think he's gonna do 'bout it?"

Henry's father James had taught him to fight when he was very young and made it very clear that to win a fight you must be focussed and determined and be prepared to hit hard; you needed to be in the now. Henry did not think that Billie would have much of a fight in him but the big man on his right looked hard, and the two men on Billie's left looked mean and had clubs in their hands, that they had concealed behind their backs, so their intentions were clear. 'Thud,' Henry hit the big man very hard in the stomach and he let out a groan as he doubled up. He would be out of it for a short while, and Henry's second blow hit Billie in his face, breaking his nose, with blood splattering across his cheeks as he cried out like a baby. Henry's fists were hard as iron from years of hewing, and toughened by the constant battle with stone. The two club men had jumped forward, one dived at Henry's legs and the other lashed out at Henry hitting him on the right ear and down onto his shoulder. Henry stumbled back and freed himself from the man trying to tackle him, bringing his knee up to crunch on the man's jaw. Whatever happens, stay on your feet in a fight, his father had said. Henry dragged the man and holding his arm, swung him around throwing him against the stile. He felt another blow on his back and turned to catch the club bearing down on him for the third time; he wrenched it free and brought it hard down on the man's head.

The big man had recovered and was diving at Henry from the other side, with Billie shouting, "get him John, break his head, the bastard smashed my face." Henry quickly stepped aside and tripped John up, catching and twisting his arm as he went down. There was a clunk as his arm dislocated from his shoulder as big John hit the ground with a cry of pain and was out of the fight. John's cry had brought the rooks out of their nests above in the trees and they created an uproar, a  noisy commotion. How dare those humans disturb our peace, and the rooks had no thought for how they themselves disturbed the peace of the humans in the village, but who knows what rooks think. The raven swooped low to see what was going on.

On that same night, somewhere in South Wales, a Lady gave birth to a boy in a house called Ravenscroft, called him Bertrand and he would grow up to try to bridge the sciences and humanities. He would write how philosophy teaches us to live with, and not be afraid of, uncertainty, and to free us from the paralysis of hesitation. Romeo and Juliet played war and peace together around every corner, beyond every horizon, and somewhere in St Petersburg an orchestra played Tchaikovsky's Overture, the Capulets and Montagues clashing swords to crashing symbols. Around the globe humankind fought and killed, made love, creating a new generation and  Henry sent Billie reeling with a blow that broke his front teeth as the raven gave one last croak before heading over the valley to his home. One of the club men managed to hit Henry in the face and he would surely have a black eye. Henry's anger and fury were strong and he wanted to hurt these useless men. He was hitting one of the club men repeatedly with his fists, as the man fell to his knees, when Henry heard someone shouting his name.

"Henry stop or you'll kill him." Robert ran down the slope, "we heard the shouting and came over to check if all was ok."

Henry's rage began to subside. All four of the villains were badly hurt and were making their way over the stile and through the wood to lick their wounds, and to who knows where they might find solace for their nastiness. Henry's ear was dripping blood and the bruising around his eye was swelling up; his clenched fists and knuckles were covered in blood and the pain arrived, while his eyes stared into the wood as the villains retreated out of sight.

Robert came closer, "Wow Henry, looks like you gave them quite a battle and you have some wounds to show for it; sit down on the log here and rest and let me check your head where it's bleeding."

Ivan spoke. "Jesus Henry, pity the man who'd pick a fight with you, what was that about; were they miners who don't like what you are trying to do?" Henry lowered and shook his head from side to side.

"The wasteful hate in some men's hearts, thugs who think they can bring a man down, I will fight against it all my life and I might die for it." Henry paused to catch his breath. "My guess is that Billie Oats was behind it, I've had to tell him off a few times for bothering my cousin Sarah. But who the other men were, I don't know. Maybe from another pit out Radstock way or from one of the farms, but I've never seen them before?"

"Me neither," said Robert, "come on Henry, we have to get you home to bathe those cuts and bruises." Henry rose from the log and his legs were shaky; he leaned on the wall and took deep breaths trying to calm his rage which was still being fuelled by the adrenaline pumping the blood around his body.

"Thanks for being with me Robert, and Ivan too, I am so glad you stopped me then or Lord knows what would have happened with this fire of rage burning inside; I'm ready to head home now."

On the way down the hill, through the wood, there was no sign of Henry's assailants and Ivan took the opportunity to describe what it was like in South Wales; trying to help Henry recover, help him take his mind off the fight and cool his anger. It sounded a dynamic place with lots of work opportunities as the coalfields were developing. Most mines also had seams of iron ore and there were huge iron-making furnaces being erected. Ivan also described the new plant, making a new iron alloy called steel, much stronger and more malleable than wrought iron and this would be the metal of the future. In the Ebbw Vale valley, more than 9000 men worked in the mines and the iron and steel plants. It was an industrial city, the skies lit up at night by the flames from the furnaces. Ivan spoke poetically about how the workers felt at the heart of an industrial revolution. Steel made and coal dug in Ebbw Vale were sent all around the world to make railways and fuel steam engines. Henry felt excited by scenes in his imagination and wanted to be part of this new world. He imagined that he could grow and learn more in such a place and he also began to think of how he might be better able to fulfil his ambition to make coal mining safer; the grass seemed greener in Ebbw Vale and the pain in his wounds began to subside.

He didn't want Sarah to see his injuries, although she was on his mind, and so he went home, after saying farewell to Ivan and Robert. Ivan shook his hand carefully, even though it was covered in blood, and looking up at Henry said,

"I'm looking forward to meeting you again Henry" and walked off down the road with Robert.

Henry's mother Maria was distraught when she saw Henry's bruised face. She made him sit down and cleaned his wounds while Henry explained what had happened.

"You must go to the police Henry, tell them all about it; these thugs need to know that they just can't go around picking a fight with people because they think different to them."

"I don't think they'll be picking a fight with me again Mum, I hurt them more than they hurt me, and I don't believe it was because of what I think. That Billie Oats has a deep dislike for me." Just then George arrived home.

"Henry, what have you done to Billie Oats? I passed him down by the Rest and his faced looked smashed to pieces. Someone said that you had picked a fight with him." Henry told the story of the fight again.

"He got what was coming George, and he is a weak coward, bringing others to do his fighting." Henry didn't tell them about the rage he felt and how he might have kept beating the clubman to death; he didn't tell them that he really wanted to kill him, to destroy the evil.

Henry had difficulty sleeping that night. He was filled with thoughts racing around inside his head about the fight, about coal mining, about Sarah and about his life and what the future held; tomorrow, next week, next year and beyond. He knew that what he did today shaped tomorrow and he was both thrilled and scared about what the future would bring and how much he could shape his own destiny. All around him he could see the consequences of men's endeavours to change things, to shape their futures; the coal mines and the transporting of coal to cities of people and cities of iron and steel. His chats with Grampa John had opened his mind to the panorama of life, to mankind's struggle, not just for survival like other animals, but also to conquer the environment, control nature and build communities where people could live and work together and share; yes, sharing and building was what he wanted from life. He wondered if people like Billie Oats and his thug friends ever thought like this; he doubted that they did and maybe something was missed out in their early development. Henry's thoughts were not particularly coherent until they came to rest on Sarah. Whatever the future held, whatever shape it took, he wanted to build his life around Sarah. When he thought of her, nothing else seemed to matter and he knew that the road he would travel would be safer, more loving and exciting with Sarah by his side.

They met on the old canal towpath on Sunday morning. Sarah stared at Henry's face as he told her all about what had happened the night before.

"You hit first Henry, is that right?" Sarah spoke gently as she ran her fingers over Henry's bruised face.

"Yes Sarah, I hit first. I knew my chances would be better if I knocked the big guy down quickly and from then on I was on the attack with every move." Henry was always calmed by Sarah and he spoke about his experience as if referring to another person, a friend of his.

"Something changes in me Sarah when I fight, a burning rage fires up and takes over, my heart pumps like its gonna burst, all other thoughts disappear and my movements just happen, like sudden instinct; it's the way I am made Sarah. I don't feel any pain from the hits I get, only afterwards when the wounds and the regrets open up." They walked into a field and sat on a log together, Sarah kissing the wounds on Henry's face.

"Then your instincts are good Henry and it seems to me that you are learning more about them, about yourself, with every new experience. I do like that about you Henry, you are alive to the good and the new and you fight against the bad and old, worn out ways. These things will take us through life together Henry and I will help guide you when you are uncertain." They looked into each other's eyes and no words were said. Words could not compete with the intensity of their gaze, could not add to the powerful feelings that grew as they saw deep inside and their bodies began to respond, to rise to the occasion. They kissed with such intimacy that their lips seemed to merge, soft and moist, a perfect fit. Sarah and Henry lay down in the grass in the hidden corner of the field and made love. The feel of Henry's rough and broken hands on her body was intensely erotic for Sarah and she welcomed him into her body as they experienced amazing ecstasy, becoming lost in the moment together. They lay locked together for a long time before Sarah spoke.

"We are one, Henry Sage and, yes, I will guide you if you are uncertain, I will feed you when you are hungry, give you drink when you are thirsty and soothe you if you are troubled and loving when you want it. However long we have together, every day will be a gift and our love will make it a precious gift." She spoke with a lovely melodic tone in her voice that captivated Henry in more ways than one.

They walked hand in hand, arm in arm, further along the canal path and Henry told Sarah about his idea of them moving to South Wales, about the things that Ivan had shared and how he and Sarah could build a new life together, free from the bitter taste of loneliness that they felt when they thought of the future without each other. They shared excitement but also sadness about this idea. Henry and Sarah were both fearless adventurers, their courage forged out of their union. But Henry was worried about how his mother Maria might cope with one wage less coming into the home every week. But if he stayed that would still be the case when he and Sarah were married so he told himself that things would work out, things had to work out. For Sarah, there would be no going to live in the Midlands with her uncle and she would be free from her mother's petty jealousies and spite. She would miss her loving father Albert terribly, but she would write to him every week telling him all the news from their life in the valleys.

The wind blew gentle in the trees growing alongside the canal path and they stopped at the bridge to sit and just be together. They were two people with separate minds and bodies and yet they were also one, connected in ways unknown to them but very real. They felt each other's feelings, could read each other's thoughts and these things made their union much stronger than they were, and could be, as two separate people. That is why Henry knew something was bothering Sarah.

"Tell me what's wrong my love." But Sarah was staring at the path ahead and seemed not to hear Henry. "Sarah, come back to me dearest." Henry put his arm around Sarah's shoulder and gently pulled her towards him. Sarah came back as if waking with a start.

"Oh Henry, I was gone there for a moment; how strange that feels, like I've been asleep, but I'm not even tired."

"You were staring down the canal path Sarah; were you looking at something?" They both looked along the path but the only movements were the trees swaying back and fore and the raven crossing the valley, flying along the skyline.

"I don't know, Henry, maybe our lovemaking has sent me into dreamland. Let's walk back now, I've made some lunch we can stop in our field and enjoy it."

3. A Day in the Life as the Raven Climbs to Safety

Her eyes were penetrating and engaging, pulling Bran deeper into his dream. He stood still on the canal path, breathing deeply, the trees swaying above him. He'd seen this canal bridge before but now a couple sat there and the man was speaking to the woman; he had his arm around her and Bran knew they were lovers. But she was staring at Bran and Bran was trying to free himself from the dream. Yes, he knew he was dreaming, but he was frozen, unable to move a muscle and he was trying to send a greeting to the woman but couldn't. Most of the time he could solve any riddle but this one had him caught. Then the raven dived down in front of Bran and let out a fierce cronk before passing across the canal to the other side of the valley; that brought Bran back to reality.

Bran woke with a jolt as his muscles suddenly came back to life. "Wow, that was real." It was 5.28am on Friday 19th May and Bran came crashing back into his normal routine. "I must write this down, before it all  fades away," he said to himself as he stumbled to his desk. He had seen the woman's face before but had no memory of who she was. He wrote a few lines down; "woman staring at me; I've seen her face before in my dreams but I don't recognise her; beautiful in a mysterious way, auburn hair, piercing eyes; on a canal tow path; felt the cool breeze in my face; saw and heard a raven, very real; seems like the same canal path that I walked along yesterday but the canal was full of water; wanted to wave to the woman but my body was frozen and I could not move a muscle; felt a desperate frustration." Bran settled back in his chair; that's all he could remember. He made a note to discuss with Chloe when convenient. Chloe played the piano and keyboard in the band, was a psychotherapist, and knew things about dreams and dreaming; she might be able to shed some insight into recurring dreams. This was the first time he had dreamt of being on the canal path, but the woman, or at least her face, he was sure he had seen before in his dreams.

After Bran finished his breakfast he telephoned Mary. It would be about 10pm in San Francisco and it was often a good time for them to talk; Mary ending her day and Bran starting his, keeping their fire burning 24 hours a day.

"Bran, it's so good to hear your voice; how was it on your trip, did you find out anything about Henry?"

"Good morning, evening, Mary love, good to hear you too; no new information about Henry but met some interesting people at the museum and they are following things up for me. John's funeral was a very cathartic experience and I was happy with my eulogy. Suisan seemed to like it and wants me to go through John's things, maybe see if there is some unfinished business. I doubt there will be since John was very well organised in his work. How are the global warming meetings going, are you heating 'em up?" Bran liked to joke with Mary about the strong impact she had on others, but he was well aware of the seriousness of the work she was doing.

"Oh Bran, if we only lived in a more perfect world where political and industrial leaders were as motivated by a sense of duty to humankind as they are to money and power, things would be a lot, lot better, and easier to change. But we don't, so being a realist with ideals helps me get through the messy stuff, manage my expectations; you know what I mean. I've said before Bran that I much prefer to do the science but we also need to build the bridge across the cultural divides. It's so important that we frame and present the data in a non-ambiguous way that politicians can understand, then guide the industry and rule makers towards a cleaner future; towards a future, whatever its condition."

Bran felt Mary's passion coming through and he knew that if anything could be done, Mary's best efforts would ensure that it would be done; she never got tired of trying. They talked for about ten minutes, sharing news, talking about their children, who were both studying at University. Mary asked Bran if he could check her mail box at the University if he had time; her secretary normally let Mary know about anything urgent, but she was away on vacation for a week. After he put the phone down, Bran reflected that he had held back from sharing his dream with Mary. He wanted to think it through first and didn't want Mary to pick up any anxiety he was still feeling about the strange experience of the dream. When he could make more sense of it he would share it; maybe send Mary an email; yes, an email would be best, not worry her over the phone.

Bran Raymond Sage and Mary Anne Norris were married soon after they had both completed their PhDs in 1975. Bran secured a job in the aerospace industry, developing flight control systems for a new aircraft venture. He was in at the deep end, learning fast, and able to apply his knowledge and research skills with minimal supervision. He advanced to group leader within two years. Mary was offered a post-doctoral fellowship at the University and they set up home in a nearby town. Mary had conducted her PhD research on greenhouse gases in collaboration with the Meteorological Office. Their Director, John Sawyer, had published a major report on 'man-made carbon dioxide', predicting dangerous rises in temperature over the next few decades. Her PhD research had also featured an analysis of the impact of chlorofluorocarbon molecules in the atmosphere. She was inspired by the work of James Lovelock on this theme, who showed that these molecules were massive absorbers of infrared radiation, heating up the atmosphere. Earlier, Mary had been advised that there were more exciting fields of study than environmental sciences, but she had trusted her instincts and now found herself engaged in cutting-edge science with huge implications for humans and planet Earth.

Like many hard working and ambitious young scientists and engineers, Mary and Bran did not have a lot of time for the fractious, adversarial world of UK politics. For sure, things were happening that would impact their lives. The Labour Party had won the 1974 general election, promising to re-negotiate the UK's membership of the European Economic Community and hold a referendum on continued membership. Prime Minister Harold Wilson and his ministers were relatively successful with their re-negotiation and, in the referendum, held on 5th June 1975, 67% voted for staying in the EEC. Among other things, this enabled sustained collaboration within Europe for all kinds of science, increasing the impact of the UK's research on the well-being of its citizens and beyond. This was particularly true in environmental sciences, where the gearing achieved through the working together of the best minds across the continent had a powerful effect on progress. Mary became a key player in this story and soon secured a tenured academic position, later being appointed Chair of Environmental Sciences. She was now working with the Inter-Governmental Panel on Climate Change, re-assessing green-house gas emissions and their impact on global warming and climate change. Three years before, Mary had been involved in developing the Kyoto rule book, that would legally bind Nations to defined emission cuts over the next decade. The binding was proving difficult, as players with vested interests in maintaining the use of high carbon fuels got involved. A meeting was planned for November in The Hague to finalise the Kyoto rule book. In anticipation of this Mary was taking a 3-month sabbatical at The University of California, Berkeley, where some critical work was going on. Climate change impact-science was a developing discipline and Mary was helping it to grow; but that's another story.

In the early days, Bran would sometimes sneak into the lecture theatre to listen to Mary giving a talk to students. He always found her subject fascinating but he was also very aware of how much Mary's style of lecturing mesmerized him and reminded him of the occasion of their first meeting. He had grown to know Mary very well but still felt she was a mystery; "that's good, that's healthy" he would say to himself, "and long may we both yearn to discover more about each other." But while he regularly persuaded himself that he was good enough for her love, he would also torment himself within with self-doubt, and he knew not where this feeling, and the baggage of doubts, came from. Mary was aware of Bran's difficulty and did her best to re-assure him of her love, whenever she could.

In their 25 years of marriage, Mary had given birth to their son Dylan, named after Bran's uncle, and their daughter Julia, named after Mary's mother. The Sages moved to a larger house in the village of Bladyn and engaged in various community activities as their children grew up. Bran was offered a Visiting Professorship at the University and from there established his technical consultancy. Both Dylan and Julia were studying at University and as the new millennium began, Bran and Mary were on their own again. For both their careers, the next decade looked likely to be the most productive in their lives. They shared a keen sense of duty to humanity and practised this in their work; shared ethics binding their friendship.

Bran cycled to his company's offices located within the University's Science Park. After showering and changing into his work clothes, he walked through the general office where most of the staff worked, to his own office at the end. He had named his consultancy, Flight Science for Safety, or FS2 for short, and grown it to 15 staff and more than £5M annual turnover. Bran understood the importance of having peace and quiet to enable engineers concentrate on their work, to be able to do the hard engineering science with focus, and he had designed the interior space of the office to contain cubicle-style pods for individual staff, all with a window to the outside world. In addition, there were three meeting rooms, one large enough for staff meetings. All technical staff were qualified to PhD level, and three held supervisory responsibilities for the sub-disciplines of Flight Science, Modelling and Simulation, and Training and Products. FS2 earned about 20% of its turnover from short courses, licensing its modelling and simulation software, and from supporting uses. At any one time, FS2 might have up to eight active projects, some coming to an end, some starting up and some in mid-stream. All staff were trained in the Company's project management and ethics framework, ensuring they could manage the projects they were leading, focus on understanding customer requirements, undertake quality engineering science, improve their knowledge and skills, abide by the professional engineer's ethical principles and deliver to cost and time goals. Problem-posing and problem-solving were core to the business.

"This is what we do," Bran would say to new staff and he laid it out in the FS2 practice manual, emphasising the importance of these cultural aspects when science becomes engineering. The skillset and knowledge contained within the consultancy was integrated by the supervisors such that the total was much greater than the sum of the parts. Staff were also trained to develop interpersonal and communication skills, things that were often completely left out of formal higher education. Staff were usually involved in several projects at any one time, so a mutual dependence was also part of the company culture. "You all need each other," Bran would say, "so work hard, overcome the demons that inhibit your focus, and you'll discover the wonders of engineering." He still believed John Morgan's words, that felt as fresh as when he first heard them 30 years before.

FS2 also owned a share in a flight simulator, based in the University, that was accredited for conducting flight research and development. This facility could simulate any kind of flying vehicle, by re-programming the flight model and the cockpit interface. Test pilots were hired to support projects and this flight-testing capability had reinforced the standing of Bran's company in government and industry circles. FS2 was an integrated team and Bran had followed his instincts in putting it together and grown it to a size where he could stay in touch with all activities. This oversight was important to him and business volume was limited accordingly. FS2 had gained an international reputation for excellence and one of Bran's problems was controlling the company's growth. "Not a bad problem to have" he would say to himself, but job satisfaction was critical to Bran and being able to be hands-on wherever, and whenever, needed was key to this.

Bran met his secretary, Joselyn Amble, for a briefing on things that had come up while he was away, plans for the day and the following week. After an exchange of greetings, Joselyn was brief and efficient, as always.

"No emergencies, Holtan Aircraft called for discussion

about a potential project; Roger has discussed with them and will brief at the Technical Leads meeting at 0800. The Air Accident Investigation Branch also want your input to a new investigation, I've forwarded the email to you; the University want to discuss some continuing professional development for their academics; I've arranged for Felicity to pick this up and you don't need to be involved unless you want." Felicity Freeman was the Tech Lead for continuing professional development, or CPD, in FS2. "Frances Rogers from the Royal Aeronautical Society will call at 1100 this morning to interview you on ethics for professional engineers; that's been in the diary for a while and I've put the summary sheet you asked for in your notebook. This afternoon Roger will host a visit by a team from Claston on the Skycruiser3 project; Roger will present on our progress and he said that he thinks Claston want us to do more; and that's about it."

"Thanks Jos, that all sounds good and I wonder could you pop over to the University and pick up any mail for Mary sometime; let me have it by the end of the day please?" The 0800 Tech Leads meetings, or TLeMs as they were known, were a regular daily event and provided an opportunity for the staff to discuss the status of projects and whether capabilities were adequate for future business prospects. Although there was deep knowledge and expertise in the team, they still needed to conduct a thorough capability analysis for any new prospect to ensure that FS2 could take the work on.

The TLeM's were usually contained within one hour, but Roger wanted to discuss the Holtan project and an issue he was having with a staff member, Jim Waterhill, "so today's might last a little longer, if that's ok". Roger led the Modelling and Simulation capability and Colin the Flight Science capability within FS2. Felicity also joined the meeting. All three had about ten years' experience since completing their PhD's, and

86

they were fully wired into the FS2 working practises. It seems that Jim was having difficulty finalising his work, achieving closure on analysis; he always wanted to do a little more and wasn't happy stopping while he still had ideas of how to improve things. Roger explained.

"Jim appears to be so concerned about his progress, and continually wants to improve things, that he loses sight of the goal; where and when he needs to draw the line. The project lead, Ralph, has had to get involved to extract the fruit from Jim's work, and it is good tasty fruit, for sure. But it's not the best use of Ralph's time and managing Jim's enthusiasm for perfection is a draw on resources and starting to create tensions."

"Is there any hostility emerging Rog," Bran asked.

"Not yet; Ralph is a very patient guy as you know, but I think we might be close. No need for your direct involvement yet Bran, just keeping you in the loop." Bran wanted to know a little more.

"So, what's the solution, the remedy." Roger leaned forward and rested his arms on the table.

"I've had a chat with Jim and he has reluctantly agreed that he will meet Dr Rosie Lynch, a Social Psychologist at the University, who understands about the different traits people have in the workplace. She says it will be useful for her research, so won't charge us; hope you agree with that route Bran?" Bran smiled at Roger and Colin, they all recognised the problem.

"Ok, let's try Dr Lynch," but he wanted to say more. "The trade-off, the balance, here is between achieving our cost and time goals on the one hand and the level of excellence and quality of our outputs on the other." Bran was looking carefully at Ralph and Colin as he said these things, holding out and moving the palms of his hands up and down, mimicking the balance. "You both know that we sometimes need to do more than expected, because we meet the unexpected. So, from a business perspective, it's a question of risk. From a technical perspective, I'm very aware that we all sometimes put in more hours than we've costed because we enjoy the rewards of discovery and want to resolve any outstanding questions fully. But, the customer comes first, so we must exercise our risk management procedure to make judgements in specific cases. Is there a specific case of issue now? I'm free up until about 9.30 so let's see if we can clear this up."

Roger nodded, "Ok, so Ralph will present our results and conclusions on the Claston project this afternoon and he has selected only the mature results from Jim's work; Jim is unhappy that Ralph won't show his latest results that cast some doubt on the conclusions."

Bran chipped in, "can you be specific, how big are the doubts."

Roger continued, "as you know, we are working with the Safety Agency, reviewing the certification of the Claston Skycruiser3, their new business jet. FS2 were contracted to review 36 safety cases. For several of these, we have used our flight simulator, with an independent test pilot, to explore what might happen following a failure of some of the control functions. Claston provided us with their flight simulation model software and the hardware for the automatic flight control system, both of which have already been approved by the Safety Agency. We've integrated these into our Flight Sim and confirmed that they give the same results for the safety cases that Claston have already examined. On a different project, Jim has been developing a new math model for the wing-tip vortex, to examine the aerodynamic loads on the tail-fin in extreme sideslip flight cases, when the tip vortex might reach the fin. He thought he would check this out on the Skycruiser3, in a worst-case scenario; engine failure just after take-off. The vortex is then at its strongest and the sideslip transient at its largest value, with the engines being on close to full power. Jim predicts that the vortex hits the tail causing loads very close to the structural limits. The problem is that we haven't validated Jim's new model with any test data yet and even he doesn't fully understand what is happening. He only discovered this yesterday, and is asking for more time to complete the work. Recall the last time this kind of thing happened, we gave him another 3 months and his results were still inconclusive."

"What's Ralph's take on this?" Bran asked Roger.

"Ralph is sceptical of Jim's new results, partly because Jim's model is still very much in development, but also because it shows a strange vortex expansion between the wing and tail that we can't explain. If this expansion didn't happen, the vortex would have only a minor effect on the tail, but it could be a red herring within the maths that Jim is using, if you get my point?"

"Yes, I do, but another way of looking at it is, if Jim is on to something, and he may be right, it really could be the worst-case scenario. Will they be checking this in flight-test?" Colin responded to this as it was his area.

"Flight testing for controllability following engine failure is part of the certification, yes. But many of the safety cases will not be tested in flight, either because Claston and the Safety Agency are sufficiently confident in the simulation or because they would be unsafe to test in the real world. I know that sounds ironic; a safety case too unsafe to test, but there are some scenarios where the probability of the failure is so remote, extremely remote to be specific, and the consequences so severe, that the Agency only needs to see the evidence for the probability. My understanding is that, following the completion of our work, they will decide on the extent of flight testing necessary to fulfil the certification requirements, partly based on our conclusions." Bran thought for a moment then responded.

"Let me summarise; if we stay with our initial conclusions from using the Claston model, we report that the critical case of single engine failure on take-off does not result in a tail loading problem and presumably that might reduce the extent of flight testing. Or, if we report the new findings, and Claston decide to test the critical condition in flight, they would risk experiencing the high loads and possibly loss of control. Sounds like a Catch-22 situation. Also, correct me if I am wrong, but the single engine failure on take-off case does not have an extremely remote probability?"

"That's correct," said Colin, "and they must test for controllability, no question about it. The risk is reduced by conducting the testing at altitude, effectively simulating the take-off scenario up and away. This is primarily to determine the minimum airspeed for controllability following an engine failure on the take-off run of course, not connected with tail loading. What Jim has identified is a potential problem that could occur within the flight envelope that is certified for controllability; an unintended consequence of Claston's advanced design concept."

Bran made his next point firmly.

"Ok, we have to report this to Claston, there is no question of that. But we do it in a way that helps them plan and conduct their pre-certification testing safely." Colin and Roger both nodded their heads.

"I'll work with Ralph to include something in the

presentation," said Roger.

"And they'll need to use their test aircraft with the loads instrumentation, gradually working up to the critical condition," added Colin; he continued. "Claston won't like hearing this and will ask us to quantify the risk of relying on the results from using their model. Based on our discussion, I suggest that we say that we consider the risk is sufficiently high to recommend additional pre-certification testing." Bran agreed and concluded the discussion of this issue.

"So, we've agreed on the way forward and, Roger, could you brief Ralph and then explain to Jim what we are doing, with Ralph present. He needs to know and he will need guidance on how much further to take the work; I'll leave that to you, but I've made it clear where I stand; this is at the heart of our code of ethics guys. Oh, but he still needs to see Dr Lynch, right? What's next?" Roger nodded and continued.

"Geoff Scrag, Chief Engineer at Holtan, called yesterday, he wants to discuss a serious issue they are having with the HoneyB, one of their new civil helicopter designs. They want a teleconference on Monday afternoon to discuss; your diary was clear so I agreed."

"That's fine," said Bran, "but serious sounds like it could be urgent, so could you review what spare capacity we have in the short-term Rog?"

"Will do." Roger nodded.

The TLeM continued until 0930, when Bran summarised his understanding of decisions and actions and then Felicity, Roger and Colin left, Roger taking the recording of the meeting out for Joselyn to transcribe. All TLeMs and full staff meetings were recorded, transcribed and kept on file; another practice Bran had instigated, and it had proved important for going back to establish when and how things were decided.

91

The details from meetings and staff interactions can often get forgotten in an engineer's busy day. Bran reflected on the discussion on the Skycruiser3 and Jim's apparent obsession with getting things right. Bran knew that he also had this trait and recalled a time when his manager rebuked him for trying to perfect his work. Bran would argue that it was only by taking things into the unknown that you really discover, find the wonder. "It's not about icing on the cake," he would say, "staying with the tried and tested might be low risk but hardly ever sheds new light on a problem"; and, in the engineering of complex systems, new light was often needed to reveal a flaw or to gain insight into unusual behaviour. *But its more than the customer wants, and is paying us for, Bran; come on, get real here.* On one occasion, Bran's extra analysis had revealed something that had not been considered, not been expected, which had saved the company a lot of money and embarrassment, and enhanced its reputation. This led to Bran's advancement to group leader and his manager was moved to another Department, carrying a bitterness with him. So, Bran had empathy for Jim and he did not want to discourage his desire to explore, but rather help him manage his time better.

Bran also reflected on the certification support that FS2 were providing Claston. Certifying an aircraft for civil operations was about safety and it underpinned the confidence the travelling public had in the safety of air transportation. He sometimes formed the impression that the Industry and the Agency colluded to find the shortest route to certification. With so many safety cases to study and assess, they needed a methodical approach for sure, but it had to be much more than box ticking, and it didn't help that the documents were full of boxes. So, the FS2 contribution had to be thorough and any concerns needed reporting. I don't want that woman staring and scaring me again, he thought, but would she approve? But

Bran wasn't sure what he meant, just an untethered thought floating around in his brain. What had the face in his dream got to do with aircraft certification? The question floated away with the thought, like a whiff of smoke, but it found a resting place in his mind.

Bran read the email from Stuart Carter from the Air Accident Investigation Branch, the AAIB, and asked Jos to phone Stuart, see if he was free.

"And a good day to you as well Bran, thanks for calling and always nice to hear your voice. You might have guessed that it's about the Odona crash a couple of weeks ago and I wanted your advice on the curious flight path the aircraft took. Can I send you our initial analysis? If you think you can help we'll make it an item on the tasking agreement we have with FS2, would that work?" Bran had worked with the AAIB before, often small tasks to review their assessments before publication, but occasionally more detailed analysis was required by FS2, often using their flight simulator, with AAIB test pilots getting involved.

"Please send what you have Stuart, and why not refrain from pointing out what you think is curious; see if I can pick it up."

"That makes sense Bran, will do; I'm putting it together in a short note, and I plan to get it to you by the end of the day, ok?"

"Thanks Stuart, what's the timeline on this?"

"Well Bran, as you know it could take two or even three years before we have the whole story for the full report, but we need to get a special bulletin out within about a month. If we can establish whether there was any technical failure from the wreckage and flight recorder, we usually include this and try to establish the fundamental causal factors."

"Anything obvious from the wreckage Stuart?"

"There was a fire Bran but it looks like main and tail rotors were intact when it hit the ground; I'll put these details in the note I send through. When you've digested it, please get back to me and we can chat."

"Ok Stuart, it will probably be the middle of next week; I'm still catching up on things after a few days off."

"Really, I didn't think Bran Sage took time off." Stuart laughed saying this and Bran joined in but was conscious of a twist of dark humour. The kind of work Bran did could absorb every breathing moment, and more if you weren't careful, and Bran had a huge appetite for trying to solve difficult problems, still trying to prove he was the 'right student, able to master it, caught by the wonder of it all.' Some things seem to stay with you forever once they are locked in, found a place to settle within your psyche. Bran was all too aware that Stuart was talking about the accident to the aircraft that Peter Peel piloted, husband of Sandra Peel, grandson of Ron Flintworth; what a small world we inhabit.

The phone rang and Jos said she had Frances Rogers from the Society on the line; Bran took the call. He had arranged to give a telephone interview on ethics for professional engineers based on the FS2 practice and Bran's interpretations of the Engineering Council's Codes of Conduct. The late 20th and early 21st century were a time of turmoil for the UK's Engineering Council, as its staff attempted to coordinate and regulate the activities of over 100 institutions and associations, including the Royal Aeronautical Society, the Institution of Electrical Engineers (IEE) and the Institute of Materials,

Minerals and Mining Engineers. The latter developed out of a Society formed in the mid-19th century to discuss the ventilation of coalmines, prevention of accidents and safety in the general working of coalmines. The IEE had developed from the Society of Telegraph Engineers, formed in 1871, around the same time that Alexander Graham Bell was testing out his experimental telephone in Somerset College. The telephone would replace the telegraph as a means of electric-communication but Bell would have to go to America to find business opportunities receptive to his invention. The inability, unwillingness even, of the British establishment, the so-called ruling class, to turn science into technology highlighted again their ineptitude and short-sightedness.

Bran was all too aware of the history of how champions of codes of ethics for engineers had fought their way through the tangled webs tensioned between profit and public welfare, but he wanted to focus on the current issues in the interview. He described his company's code of ethics and agreed to send Frances a copy. They discussed the importance of professional engineers holding paramount the safety, health, and welfare of the public, independent of their employer's business economics; the role of whistleblowing and legal protection of engineers who are forced down this route; how conflicts of interest might develop and be resolved and how ethics can be built into higher education programmes. Bran was enthusiastic about drawing on the historical perspective of ethics, building on Aristotle's extensive thesis, and having some of this material taught by academics from the Humanities, rather than Science and Engineering, Faculties. But Bran emphasised that,

"Engineering case studies are essential for getting the importance of ethical practice across to student engineers, and these case studies need to be presented by practising engineers, drawing again on Aristotle, and his 'art of rhetoric'. To persuade a student that they need to take something on board, the teacher needs to show that he or she has the experience and knowledge to tell the story, that they are authentic (the ethos), then tell a good story, full of rich content and strong arguments (the logos) and finally the appeal to the student's humanity that the consequences of being unethical are dire (the pathos). These three parts are equal in importance, and together are necessary and sufficient for persuasion." Bran went on to describe how they built in ethics case studies in the FS2 CPD courses. He finished up by saying; "being ethical is about being noble. The rush and gush for profit and adulation obscures and diminishes nobility; alas, promoting nobility is a poorly resourced endeavour."

Frances thanked Bran for his time and said she would let him see the draft of her article before it was published. Bran then needed a few minutes to let his thoughts settle before turning to the next thing; ethics was serious stuff and fired up his engines. He stood looking out of the window of his office, drinking a coffee. There were a multitude of events unfolding across the campus, people coming and going, and Bran gazed through them, seeing none of them. Letting thoughts settle involved reflecting on what he had said, what he hadn't said. He decided that he had covered all the major issues that related to the way that FS2 embodied ethics into their working practises. Bran had described how, when giving a seminar on this topic, he used the case of the Boeing 737 rudder actuator reversals causing United Flight 585 and USAir Flight 427 to crash, killing all passengers. The accidents had occurred in 1991 and 1994 respectively, but the US National Transportation Safety Board had only fully understood and reported the design flaw in 1999, eight years after the first accident. The actuator reversals were very difficult to replicate in test and reluctance from industry to admit to design failings held things back. This was one of many case studies that were full of lessons-learned that could be passed on to a new generation of student engineers to reinforce their appreciation of the importance of ethics to safety. Yes, Bran was not only obsessed with quality but also safety, both picked up from John Morgan; but they also seemed to be defining characteristics of himself, in his very makeup, his genes, whatever that meant.

After lunch, Bran decided not to sit in on the Claston briefing, but to let the FS2 project team do their work. He was confident that they would not need his intervention. So, he continued catching up with the status of various projects, by way of short briefing notes produced by the project leads; what they called the Friday Briefs. The FriBri's were another of Bran's initiatives and provided him and the teams an opportunity to take a weekly stock of progress. At 3.30, the Claston briefing ended and Jos came in to ask Bran if he would see Tobias Hamel, the Chief Designer for the SkyCruiser3.

"Yes, of course, come in Tobias, please sit down, can Jos get you something to drink?"

"No thanks Bran, your guys went through their work and its very impressive, shall I say. Would you mind if one of my engineers came with our pilot next week, when you investigate Waterhill's wake impact on the tail in your simulator? It looks like it could be a defining moment in the certification and we'll want to fully prepare for our own flight trials."

"Did you mention this at the briefing Tobias? I'm sure it will be ok but I'd like to check with Roger that things will be sufficiently mature by then; I'll just ask him to join us if you don't mind." Roger came in and sat down next to Bran. They discussed the possibility of a Claston engineer joining them during the following week and Roger considered that the new vortex wake would be ready to investigate tail impingements following an engine failure on take-off. They agreed that Juergen Gmelin would join the FS2 team from Wednesday to Friday. Bran could see that Tobias wanted to discuss something else so, after Roger had left, he asked, "what's on your mind Tobias?"

"Yes Bran, to get to the point, we're getting feedback from some airlines, one in particular that their pilots are complaining about our new autopilot on the Skycruiser2. It seems that they think the mode selection process is too complicated for flight management during the terminal phase of the approach to landing, and could lead to confusion. There have been a few go-around incidents and the pilots claim the system isn't helping them maintain a stable approach. It was certified last year and is now operational with seven different airlines; that's about 120,000 landings and three reported incidents."

"One in 40,000 Tobias, in aviation that's a fairly high probability," said Bran.

"I know Bran, but it's just one airline and we are wondering if they are maybe not training their pilots properly in the new system. Claston have provided an update to the training simulators and manuals, so they should be clear how to manage the new system."

"How can we help, Tobias," Bran asked. Tobias looked at Bran with a concerned expression.

"The Safety Agency has asked for an independent review and I'd like to recommend FS2 to them; how would that be Bran, do you have the capacity to take it on, do you have the interest?" Bran thought for a moment then answered.

"Tobias, we certainly have the interest but we will need to scope this out, look at the timeframe, and it would be best if this is done in close collaboration with the Agency and yourselves; you know how important understanding customer requirements is to FS2. If this is urgent then we ought to arrange a meeting next week, do you agree?"

"Yes, that's what I was going to suggest Bran; maybe during the period when you are running the Skycruiser3 trial and the Agency guys can get some insight into that as well? I will speak with them and see if they agree with our approach, if you don't mind?" Bran agreed, they finished their discussion, shook hands and Tobias left the office.

Bran had a high regard for Tobias Hamel and he sometimes wondered how a Chief Designer managed to keep it all in his head, keep all the balls in the air, managing the multitude of events and activities involved in the design of a system as complex as an aeroplane. It was a job that required special skills and very few people would be up to it, thought Bran.  You'd need a good team, good lieutenants; yes, the lieutenants would be critical, a deputy for each of the main systems. The airframe, engines and transmissions, avionics and control systems, etc.

Bran thought of Wilbur Wright, the first aeroplane designer and pilot, and how he had taken a systems approach to design. Every facet of the design, every element of the

99

system, needed to be shaped by requirements. Facet was a good word here thought Bran; the various faces of the design. Form, fit and function, the three main facets would evolve together as the design matured and the form part included the aesthetic; to fly good it must look good. What a huge responsibility Chief Designers have, he thought. To Bran, they represented the epitome of human creators of machines;

 the human instinct to create draws people in a powerful way. Most people, even some engineers, didn't understand design. Bran would ask a student group what they thought a designer did, and while they mostly got it wrong, the ensuing discussion brought out some of the key ingredients of creativity, like keen observational ability and imagination. What happens in the mind is crucial to the practice of design. A good understanding of the fundamental science at play, and the technologies involved, blends with artistic beauty and existential pleasure in the minds of the great designers. The ability to think visually, as a designer once said to Bran, is essential; to be able to close your eyes and imagine a complex mechanism working, how inputs affect outputs, how causes lead to effects, these things are what visual thinkers can do. You would have a hard time designing if you weren't a good visual thinker and didn't have a good imagination. Then there is the designer's ability to compromise and optimise; to try to get as close to the best for every facet, knowing that you will have to compromise, trading off one for another. So, a chief designer uses life skills every day in their job. They were indeed special people. Bran wondered, if he had stayed with Claston, would he, could he, have become a Chief Designer?

Well, it would have been a different journey for him, that's for sure. The question lingered, but with Bran so engaged with FS2, he had no regrets about his choice of journey, and maybe he wasn't such a great visual thinker, so he would have struggled. Friday night was band practice and Bran couldn't wait. Jos had already left to get home to her family, so Bran packed his rucksack. He noticed the pile of mail for Mary on his desk and he put that into the sack, changed into his cycling gear and was ready to go.

"Have a good weekend guys," he said to the group in the conference room still working, and he was on his way home.

The band called themselves Orion, after the constellation of stars that was visible throughout the whole world, sitting as it does on the celestial equator. The six band members jokingly associated themselves with different stars of Orion. Sam played bass, was a journalist with strong socialist views on the world, and associated with Rigel, the foot of Orion. Chloe played keys, was a therapist in her other life, as she described it, and was Meissa; Bran had suggested this as she really was the shining star in the band. Jacob provided the percussion, was a self-employed creative artist, and shining on one side of Orion's belt as Alnitak. That brings us to Oliver, playing jazz guitar, a post-doc researcher in Political Science at the other end of Orion's belt as Mintaka. Georgia played the violin, described herself as a hippy and ran an organic health shop with her partner. Georgia was the warrior

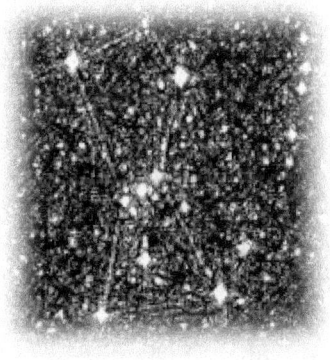

101

Bellatrix and loved the part as she bewitched the audiences with her fiddling. And, so to Bran, who played guitar and the role of Saif, the sword of Orion. If the band ever recruited a seventh member, the job description would include their stage name as Betelgeuse, Orion's armpit. They weren't expecting to recruit a seventh member, "unless they brought some burning attack ships with them", Sam would say, although secretly Sam would prefer to be Betelgeuse. Most of the band also sang, and they often sang in three-part harmony, very Beatlesque, Sam and Bran liked to think.

Orion met every Friday night to jam and practice at the local arts centre, a converted church hall now owned by a local artisan Toni Bow who used it to hold creative-arts workshops. We've already met Toni's son Jacob, as the drummer in Orion, and he keeps all his percussion kit at the Centre. Bran arrived to find most of the band already there and tuning up. They would play for three hours before heading out to the local pub for food and drinks, so they kept the chit-chat about their lives until then. Those three hours were precious music time. They were mainly practising for a concert they would be playing for charity at the Arts Centre in the middle of June. The concert was titled *Love Sick'* and featured love songs of Bob Dylan, with the band members own interpretations of the symbolism used by the writer. Each band member could choose four Dylan songs, would work out a rough arrangement and then request contributions from the other stars. Tonight, they would be working on six of the songs, one each from the band members. They would spend about half an hour on each, with Oliver keeping an eye on the clock and moving things along as required. During their vocal warm-ups, they would hold hands and stand in the shape of Orion; that was a powerful way to strengthen their bond.

First up was Jacob; he had selected the title tune, *Love*

Sick, and wanted the band to help him create a mysterious, moody sound with his percussion pounding the slow pace to the song. Chloe kept the keys simple and flowed along with the drums and bass. Jacob sang the lyrics with his rustic voice. Bran was taken by the words. Was Dylan referring to a dream he'd had, when a woman smiled at him, and why did it destroy him? Is this what Bran was feeling when his dream woman looked at him? Jacob put a lot of his emotion into the song, singing with a soulful, crying tone, one moment wishing he'd never met the girl and the next willing to give anything to be with her. The man understands the paradox of human love, thought Bran. Bran strummed his Lowden, muting the strings to create a percussive effect in counterpoint to Jacob's bass drum. Oliver called time on Jacob after 30 minutes but the band had progressed very well and had almost completed the arrangement.

Sam described how he heard *Wedding Song* with the bass featuring as a main part, quite unlike the original acoustic guitar version on the *Planet Waves* album; but he did want a finger picking acoustic and Bran had volunteered for that part. The harp piece was to be replaced with Georgia on the violin; maybe Chloe could try a brooding organ in the background and Jacob might add some light snares. They were ready and Sam and Bran got the song going with a couple of bars of the verse, with Sam coming in with the song on the third. They started in Am, climbing up to C and then up again to D, but Georgia emulated the cross-harp on the record by playing her part in the key of Fmaj; she did a great job and her mannerisms were a sight to see. Georgia wanted to draw attention to herself and made wonderful theatre of her instrumental parts. The lyrics were strong, and Sam sang them in a purposeful way, like Dylan, as if in a hurry to get the whole story told before she left; about time and love, about the way she made his circle complete, taught him how to give, taught his eyes to

103

see; oh, and he'd love her in eternity, if there was eternity. Bran thought of Mary and how she made his life complete, and a richer one to live. He wondered how people could live without love; he was afraid of being without love, and he surprised himself with that very scary thought.

Chloe began to sing *Make You Feel My Love*, initially just playing the piano and it sounded beautiful, but after finishing she asked Oliver if he could play a lead guitar solo in the middle and again at the end, with backing from the whole band, who would then quieten down for Chloe to sing the verses with her own accompanying piano. Oliver had not worked out a solo for this so time was spent trying to get this right. He eventually settled on a Something-styled solo that worked for Chloe and the band played it through several times. Chloe sang the song with a wonderfully lyrical voice, gently caressing the notes. She sang free of any schmutz and sentimentality; she saw the song as a love song, but of unrequited love, a plea from the singer who wanted his or her lover to feel his or her love. The way that Chloe sang, the listener was left with the impression of her sadness; whether the love was felt or not, it would not be reciprocated.

Georgia had been working on her violin solo at the beginning and end of *You're a Big Girl Now* for some time so it already sounded very good and she just needed a strong bass part from Sam, finger style classical guitar from Oliver or Bran (they tossed and Oliver won) and she wanted to hear if Chloe could add a soft organ sound during the plaintiff pieces when she was singing through her tears. Georgia brought tears to all eyes when she sang this song; sounded like it was really coming from a heart pierced by broken love. Bran reflected how friendships had grown over the few years the band had been together; grown from their music but also the sharing of personal issues which trust allows, encourages even. The sharing improved their singing, particularly the harmonies, and Georgia had asked Bran if he would find a harmony part in her song so they explored Bran singing the notes D, C and B to accompany Chloe's B, A and G during the fall. It worked, Georgia loved it and they locked it in.

Oliver had worked out a great solo guitar part for *Born in Time* and called on the whole band to contribute; "so much to do here," he said, "and so many ideas, so let's get going." The bass and drum kept up a persistent beat, the heartbeat, during the verses, piano keys echoing the singer's lines and creating an ethereal sound that was just what Oliver wanted. He had a soft voice, but kept the notes perfectly as he hung onto them at the end of the lines. Bran played slide guitar, adding a muted country flavour to the mystical words. When it came to the guitar solo, Oliver let rip, and the contrast with his gentle rendering of the song was amazing, quite perfect. At one point Georgia joined in with her viola bringing a darker flavour to the song. It fitted very well and suggested a second instrumental solo or maybe the lead guitar and viola could duel it out. They would try that next time; Oliver's 30 minutes were up and he called time on himself. Bran thought that he and Mary were born in time and he felt they were made of dreams; he was reminded of his dream that he had woke with, ages ago that very day.

Bran had chosen *Most of the Time*, another song that spoke of time. He'd been playing this as a solo piece since he first heard it on the *Oh Mercy* album eleven years before, so turning it into a piece with many parts was a challenge. Sometimes he sang it in Cmaj at a jaunty pace like Dylan's almost nonchalant version from *Tell Tale Signs* and other times he would slow it right down, switch to major sevenths, and using facial expressions to help tell the story of lost love. Whatever the lyrics were saying, you knew that the singer was hiding from his feelings, the ones he'd buried. Sometimes Bran would cry singing this song, but how could he get the band to help him. They played the *Oh Mercy* version with the Lanois-style production. Bran wasn't keen on the shimmering background sounds on this version so they decided to start the song with Bran and his acoustic guitar and harp, accompanied by light snares, with a new instrument coming in for each of the second and third verses before everyone was on board for the bridge and final verse; as the song closed, the instruments dropped out one by one until it's just Bran fingerpicking and playing harmonica, having tried to persuade himself he didn't care if he ever saw her again. He wasn't singing about Mary, but could it be the woman in his dreams?

"Thanks guys, I really appreciate that and I'm very happy with how its evolving." Bran looked at the clock as he spoke and noticed that his time, and Orion's three hours, were up.

"Where did that time go," said Jacob.

"Flies when we're having fun, like a jet plane," said Georgia, as she played the chorus from *The Times They are A'Changin'* on her violin and they all joined in with the singing.

"And flying time makes me very thirsty," added Sam, "shall we pack up and go get a pint and a pie?" As usual, they had booked a table in one of the side rooms at The Red Lion, the privacy helped them to talk more openly with each other about the music and their lives. They spent about half an hour reviewing what they had accomplished at the Arts Centre; they were pleased with themselves.

"I think we've nailed most of those songs," ventured Jacob, "and with last week's work, I'd say we're probably about half way there; what do folk think?" The band did not have a leader as such but each member had their own strengths which others acknowledged and generally accepted. Jacob was often the first to voice his opinion on matters, but he was a sensitive man and his intonation showed that he was seeking approval rather than being dogmatic.

"Yeh, I agree Jacob, we've done well," Chloe responded first and Sam raised his glass, with a "let's drink to that and may it continue all the way to the concert."

"To the concert," said Oliver and Georgia together and they clinked glasses and supped their beer and wine.

Chloe was very knowledgeable musically, could quickly identify notes and keys, and this was particularly helpful to those who could not read music, like Bran. The band looked to Chloe for musical guidance. They looked to Bran for organisation and structure; his work as an engineer helped, although he was conscious that a light touch was important, not to squeeze the innovation out, frighten it away, with too much structure. Bran was also good at finding harmonies; he had a good ear and had worked on Beatle harmonies with his brother when they were younger. Bran also played guitar of course but that's for someone else to comment on. Sam and Georgia could be relied on to keep the humour flowing; their banter was pure creativity. Oliver was the quietest of the band when it came to conversation, but his guitar work was delicate and captivating and he'd say that his Gibson did the talking. But Oliver was also clever with interpreting the symbolism in Dylan's music and he would be sending band members his ideas on that before the next practice. Oliver opined that,

"Dylan might speak to us in riddles but it's how we interpret them to be meaningful in our own lives that really matters; don't struggle with what he might or might not have meant, it'll get you nowhere fast."

It had become their practice to each talk for about five

minutes on some aspect of their lives, then open for discussion. This sharing had helped to bond friendships and trust, so important for creating good music together. It also allowed them to let off steam in a safe environment.

Sam began with what turned into a rant about the New Labour government cheating socialism. He described an article he was writing for the local newspaper, exciting a wave of opinions from the band members.

Sam; "At 100 years old, my party doesn't look much different from the Tories, serving the elite more than the workers. I'd like to see a dramatic change in the inequalities that pervade our society; inequalities in opportunity but also inequalities in the routes to opportunity, so people who are stuck at the bottom are given lifelines to improve their lot. You can read my ideas in my article when it comes out next week." Earlier in the month the Tories had won decisively in the local elections, despite Chancellor Brown's £2b boost to the health service and £1b for education.

Georgia; "British people are fickle, and always will be. Only 30% of them turned out for the local elections so they don't deserve good government."

Jacob; "Unless they make things better for us self-employed they won't get my vote next year."

Oliver; "Talking about voting, did you know that before the Reform Acts in the late 19th century, only landowners and householders could vote in general elections? The industrial revolution was creating a middle class of reasonably well off people who wanted a say in how they were governed. More and more people were leaving the land and working in factories and the coal mines, forming working communities, small societies of like-minded people who spoke as a group and with conviction about what they wanted. And power to the people in the form of local councils only came with the Local Government Act of 1888; just in case you wanted to know," he said with a wry smile on his face, adding that "democracy was on the rising curve as the 19th century came to a close," with a nod to his choice of Dylan songs. Oliver's research was taking him back to the 19th century and he was writing a thesis titled *The Fragility of Democracy.*

Sam; "I'm looking forward to reading your thesis Oli, and I hope you write something about how voting must change to be fairer, more representative, iron out inequalities."

Oliver; "oh yes I will Sam, especially for you."

Georgia shared that she was extending her health food store to be able to promote healthier diets.

"We are installing a small theatre where we can show videos of the benefits of good food, healthy diets; and what a healthy diet actually means. Did you guys know that we carry trillions of bacteria in our guts, most of which are critical to our survival? These alien creatures can be good or bad for us and the idea is to find the diet which gets the right balance; maximises the survival of the good bacteria for an individual. We have a local herbalist and a doctor of alternative medicines coming in to give talks and sign people up for courses. You are all welcome to come along, check it out when we are done; should be ready by August."

"I'll be at the door as your first customer, ok. I'm all for trying to remake the world at large?" Jacob quickly responded with a chuckle.

Chloe wanted to talk about something not a million miles from Georgia's topic;

"I'm reading a book titled 'Molecules of Emotion' and I know it's going to be very helpful in my therapy. Its written by a scientist, Candace Pert, whose research has shown that we have molecules attached to our neurons that are receptors for different chemical messages sent by the body. So, our mind and our body are coupled and our emotional state can have a big impact on our physical state. Pert suggests that we may even be able to control our health with our minds; gives a new meaning to psychosomatic. And there's more, a lot more actually," Chloe took a sip of her wine and leaned forward with a profound expression. Bran really liked that expression and felt a great warmth for Chloe. "The part I'm really getting involved with is the idea that dreams are one of the ways that the body communicates with the mind. The mystery is learning the language of this communication, and what's fascinating is this is all coming out of scientific research. The Eastern approach to well-being may be validated by western science which I think is both restorative and ironic. So, stay tuned folks and you'll hear more."

Jacob was the first to chip in. "Just like Dylan in *Series of Dreams*, although he does say it's not too scientific." Jacob had sung that song in a previous concert and was still trying to figure it out.

Georgia; "maybe you could come and give a talk at our health store when we've got the little theatre up and running."

Jacob; "or maybe a talk at the Centre, open it up to a wider audience, Chloe."

Chloe liked both these ideas and said she would let them know when she had finished preparing a talk she was going to be giving at a psychotherapy conference in the autumn.

Jacob described the exhibition he was working on. "It's going to be about expressions, people's facial expressions; about a dozen local artists will display their work and talk about how we communicate with expressions, intentionally or unintentionally. Listening to you Chloe, I suspect that its always intentionally if the body and mind are integrated in the way you say. There's a woman who focuses on how expressions change as we hear different things; how the whole face can light up or dim down; she'll talk about how expressions are very primitive, must have been archetypal in human evolution. Then there's fake expressions, giving false impressions, something I'm working on; you know the line about smiling at your face while hissing behind your back?"

Sam; "not more Dylan, Jacob, gets into everything that guy. But yes, I do know what you mean, I call it the politician's grin."

Chloe; "I'm reminded of the faces that go from desperation to realisation in five steps; you know the advert for chocolate? Your turn Bran, what are you bringing to the party tonight?"

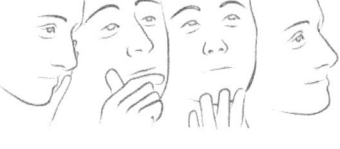

Bran; "I'm sure you don't want to hear about vortex wakes hitting aircraft tails or pilot-vehicle interfaces."

"Oh please, please, bring it on Bran," shouted Georgia to a round of chuckling.

"Maybe next time, but tonight I thought I'd share a bit about my ancestry research. I'm digging into the past to explore the lives of my great grandparents, Henry and Sarah. Before them it gets really dark, but I have a few pieces of the jigsaw around these two. I visited a mining museum in Somerset this week and got a taste of what life was like for a coal miner and his family in the middle to late 19th century. I'm finding it all very therapeutic, not sure why I'm doing it but it somehow feels like it's adding more meaning to my life."

Sam; "you short of meaning Bran? Get involved in

111

politics and our social problems, that'll give you meaning mate." Sam often challenged Bran and it made Bran feel both challenged and irritated. Sam was a good friend and maybe that's why he felt he could speak with the sharp edge in his tone.

Bran; "no, not short of meaning at all Sam, far from it but there's something missing." He looked across to Chloe who smiled gently at him. Bran continued; "I know my life began 50 years ago and will be over sometime in the next 50 years, who knows when, but maybe birth is not the beginning and death is not the end." Bran got a cheer from Oli as he referenced another Dylan song. "Look friends, my days are full of applying science and engineering to problems with man-made flying machines; incredibly satisfying work and socially responsible because it makes aviation safer. I'd challenge anyone who says there is no existential pleasure in engineering; it brings out the whole man, or the whole woman. Maybe it's because the search for meaning in my profession is so rewarding that I want to find it in just being human as well; there is so much I don't understand." Bran could share these things, share his vulnerability, because he was with friends. He missed Mary when she was on travel and he knew that she missed him. He missed talking to her about his vulnerabilities, many of which he wouldn't share with his musical friends. He looked around and realised that he loved them all in different ways, and it was time for all to go home.

He gave Chloe a lift home, it had become a regular practise and it gave them a chance to talk a little more intimately. Chloe was married with two wonderful children; he was uncle Bran to them and they didn't have any real uncles.

"Ok," Bran once said to Chloe, "I'll be their pseudo-uncle." But now he wanted to talk about his dream. "I had a weird dream last night, or rather this morning, Chloe." Bran described the dream and felt a huge relief talking about it.

"And you didn't recognise this woman Bran; that's not unusual, but there are lots of theories and interpretation methods for dreams. It would take a little longer than we have right now but why not meet for coffee one day and I can take you through them, pro bono," Chloe said with a smile.

"I'd like that Chloe, yes please, maybe we could meet for lunch, on me, any space next week?"

"I'll email you and let you know, ok?" They drew up alongside Chloe's house, Chloe leaned over and kissed Bran on the cheek and with a goodnight closed the car door and walked up her drive. She hasn't done that before, thought Bran; maybe sharing my need for meaning touched her. The impression of the kiss stayed on Bran's cheek and he didn't want to wipe it away; he wanted to remember what her lips felt like.

At home, Bran emptied his rucksack onto his desk and poured himself a glass of wine; not drinking in the pub helped him keep his head clear, but he was ready for the soothing effect of a Burgundy when he arrived home. He went through Mary's mail; mostly from this or that Society or Organisation but there was one letter, handwritten address on the envelope. He thought he would share that with Mary in the morning. Ah, Saturday morning, he could lie in, but he knew he wouldn't. His internal clock would shake him up at 5.28 and, anyway, he wanted to talk with Mary before her Friday ended.

So now we know a little more about a day in the working life of Bran Sage. Some of it may be a bit confusing for the non-technical mind, but it's the kind of thing that goes on in thousands of offices and factories all around the world; engineers being creative and grappling to solve problem after problem. You, the reader, will benefit from many of these solutions. Hopefully a glimpse hasn't done any harm. But, it wasn't typical, because it was Friday, and anyway every day was different, full of stuff to make decisions about and Bran was a very deliberate man, he liked to make decisions. It helped him to feel in charge of his life, but inside he knew this feeling was quite fragile.

Before he went to bed he picked up his Lowden and sang one of his own compositions that reinforced his sense of fragility; hardly guaranteed to help him sleep.

In a quiet moment, I had the fright of my life

I thought I heard the whistle blow, it cut me like a knife

There's no such thing as peace and quiet unless I'm by your side

Free from all that solitude, not cut off at high tide

Wandering around these scattered thoughts, piecing them together

Tryin' to make sense of a confused world at the end of its tether

Tryin' to make sense of the knots people tie instead of listening to their hearts

But would you trust your instinct, if it caused you to sink

As you climbed up to the brink of your own ramparts

Perhaps you would hold back, showing that you've got the knack

Of demonstrating what you lack, the courage to look back
But stay focussed on the cause, weave around the laws
You'll never know the moment, until the end's in sight
It doesn't really matter, when you're heading for the light

"Feels like I'm heading for the dark and, anyway, I am looking back," he thought as he was falling asleep.

"Not far enough," he heard a woman's voice calmly reply.

4. Trust your Instinct as the Raven Wonders

 Sarah and Henry sat in their loving field and ate their sandwiches quietly. They were together but deep in their own thoughts. Sarah was disturbed by what she had experienced on the bridge. It was as if her mind had left her body and she was looking back at herself; *not far enough* she thought but didn't understand what that meant. She described it to Henry, sharing her disturbance.

"Oh, my dear Sarah, don't be afraid, our lovemaking took me to another place as well, but we both came back, didn't we, back to each other." Henry put his arm around Sarah and kissed her softly on her forehead, her cheek and found her warm lips.

"I wasn't afraid my love, I'm never afraid when I am with you, but I wish I knew what happened to me; it was a new thing Henry, a very new thing for me and I'd like to understand it." Sarah was very in tune with her body and her emotions. She felt they were connected in some way, and this feeling seemed to give her a special grace; a unique insight into her natural self. Where Sarah had grace, Henry had nobility and an urge to do useful things, for the benefit of others; it made him feel good, more complete and self-assured.

"Sarah, can I tell you the things the miners talked about last night, on the hill?"

"Yes, my love, it will help pull me out of my mystery, bring me back."

"We talked about forming an association, a union of colliery workers, who would draw up a plan for the improvements that need to be made to our working conditions and pay. Seems like they've already done this in other parts of the country, in South Wales and The Midlands, and made things happen."

"Tell me what you want to happen Henry love?"

"A few of us are meeting up this week to make a plan for just that Sarah; I want the pits to be safer places to work; I want the colliers to be involved in the daily inspections and to be able to propose what should change. We are the best people to make these proposals, because we know what it's like down there. And it seems that whenever the owners aren't making enough profit they reduce the pay of the colliers; now that isn't fair Sarah. We should be paid a decent wage for a day's work. And the owners should share the pain when business dips."

"And will the owners agree with your ideas Henry?"

"Well, we will see Sarah; but listening to Ivan Evans from the Valleys, I was inspired, and excited by what they have done and, if they can do it, we can do it, with a bit of luck."

"I think you'll need more than luck Henry my love but if changes can be made, I know that you're the one to make 'em."

They started to walk home and Sarah asked Henry, "how will your mining plans affect our dream to move away together my love?"

Henry squeezed Sarah's hand. "We should go as soon as we are able Sarah; with Robert, George and a few others all fired up, they won't need me, but I want to help them get it going. I want to go back to Colin Amble and explain what we are doing; help him understand that we only want what's good for the miners and their families, without causing problems for the owners. If I can help build this bridge between us and them, between the owners and the workers, where sensible talk can happen between reasonable people, then I will feel I have done my job. Tom will be down on Saturday and I'm going to talk with him about us moving to the Valleys, maybe even travel back with him next week."

Henry stopped on the pathway and looked at Sarah. "Our future is together Sarah, it's all I can see clearly, free of the pains of the past and open to the adventures of the future; create a new world for our children, our grandchildren and great grandchildren. I see them all through the eyes in my mind and your great granddaughter is beautiful like you." Henry laughed as he said this.

"You must have big eyes in your mind Henry Sage and I'm glad you have; your urge for adventure excites me. I think our great grandson will be tall and handsome like you and he will…" Sarah paused for a moment before going on, "…and he will be noble like you Henry, I am sure of it. Yes, noble and Welsh, I'm sure that's how he will be." Sarah put her arm in Henry's and they walked on under the trees, listening to the sounds that nature offered for free on a Sunday afternoon.

When they got close to Camerton, they embraced and Sarah walked on along the path to the Collier's Rest. It was closed on Sunday so she was planning to take her easel out and paint nature later that day. The lady of the Manor, Anna Fernhill, had given Sarah a present of the painting materials many years before and Sarah had a natural skill, able to project the images in her mind onto parchment with easy strokes of her paint brush. Henry went on up the hill and across the fields towards his home in Tunley. As he approached the house, he noticed a tall policeman standing outside, talking with his brother George and mother Maria. Henry greeted the man.

"Good day to you Sgt Pepper, we don't see you

118

hereabouts much, any trouble?"

"Good day to you Henry; yes, I'm afraid so, Billie Oats said that you assaulted him and his friend last night when they were on their way to the Rest, is that true?" Henry described what had happened. George had already told Sgt Pepper that he had seen Oats and his friend walking past the Rest.

"You say there was three other fellas and they ran off when Robert Barnes and the Welshman came down the hill." Sgt Pepper was writing in his notebook. "Did you recognise the other men Henry?"

"No, I didn't Sgt, but I would if I saw them again. Billie called the big man John, that's all I know; oh, I think you'll find he has a dislocated shoulder. What does Oats say happened?"

"Says that you attacked him on the lane above the Rest and he didn't do anything to upset you; says you just laid into him for no reason. He looks pretty bashed up Henry. His friend Charlie Grange was with him and says you hit him with a club."

"Oats is lying Sgt and I know that Robert will be my witness in this. One of his thug friends, probably this Grange fella, hit me with his club, as you can see." Henry gestured to his bruised face. "Their intention was to beat me up, that's for sure, so I acted in self-defence. I got the club off Grange and, yes, I did hit him."

"You say you was at a meeting Henry, with other miners; can I ask what that was about?"

"We were discussing the safety in our mines Sgt and how we might improve it, so there wouldn't be so many accidents." Sgt Pepper continued to write his notes.

"Billie Oats says that you are planning to disturb the peace by calling the miners to strike against the owners, to withdraw their labour, is that right Henry?" Sgt Pepper asked this while writing and moved his eyes up to look at Henry when he stopped.

"No, it isn't Sgt, we want to have a reasonable discussion with the bailiffs and the owners and work to reach an agreement." Henry wondered why Sgt Pepper was still writing in his notebook.

"All right Henry, that'll do for now. I'll need to speak with Robert to get his evidence and if Billie Oats wants to press charges for assault, I'll be back. Meanwhile stay in the area till this is cleared up."

"Why would I leave the area Sgt, it's my home and a man has a right to defend himself so my conscience is as clear as day." As he said this, Henry realised that he had an answer to his own question, 'why would he leave the area,' but it had nothing to do with the fight and he had no intention of sharing his plans with Sgt Pepper.

It was late Sunday afternoon and Sarah had placed her easel on a flat patch of ground to the side of the footpath. In front of her the path wound its way beside the canal, over the side of the bridge, disappearing out of sight, only to reappear on the other side with the canal sweeping around to the west under the trees. On the right, a rail track came down over the field, from where the gugg wheel wound the cable, lowering the full coal tubs down the hill to the canal and hauling them empty back up to the roadway at the colliery. Mankind leaves another dirty black scar on the soft green landscape. But it was Sunday and all was still, the way that Sarah liked it. Stillness allowed her to be at one with herself, in the moment with her art, the images outside reforming as shapes and colours within her mind. These images were the raw material for her artwork. Sometimes they looked just like the real-world images but mostly they took on a character, colour, size and shape, of their own. Sarah sometimes wondered where this ability to see these impressions of reality, and the skill to paint them, came from. No-one else in her family were artists, but she was gifted and she felt that this natural ability must come from somewhere. Maybe she could pass it on; yes, she would teach her children to paint the Wallace way; she liked that idea and smiled at the thought. Sarah imagined Henry and her walking along the path, sitting on the bridge, talking about their love and their future and the images appeared in her art; two people so close it was as if they were one. After Sarah had finished the painting she walked up to the bridge and sat where she and Henry had sat earlier that day. She recalled the strange feeling of being outside her body, looking at herself and Henry from a distance. She'd told Henry that she wasn't afraid, when she was with him and it was true, but now she did feel afraid. She was afraid of what she didn't understand and she felt unsettled. Then she noticed a tall man with his arm in a sling walking along the canal path towards her and she decided that she didn't want to meet anyone here, in Henry's and her special place, when she felt the way she did. She picked up her easel and headed back to the Rest, comforted by the early evening bird song.

Henry and George arrived at Robert's house to find four other men already there; Farnham Nash from Timsbury, William Hodge and his brother James from Paulton and Archie Flintworth from the Radstock area. Henry was very pleased to see them; 'now we have a working group' he thought. Robert had told them about the fight and they joked together about the state of Henry's face and the likely condition of Billie and his thug mates. Robert welcomed Henry and spoke first.

"Sgt Pepper came to see me earlier Henry, so I told him what I'd seen; seems that Billie Oats has made an assault complaint."

"Thanks Robert, I hope that will be the end of it but Oats may well pour in more lies before this is done with. Can we talk about our plan, I need to get my mind onto new and better things?" They talked together for more than two hours and William said he would write down what they agreed; it would be the beginning of their plan. Three main issues dominated the discussion. First, and most urgent, a review of all safety issues relating to the working practices at the mines must be undertaken in collaboration with representatives from the owners, and this review would include recommendations for improvements. Second, the method of determining workers' wages would be reviewed, including how coal was priced and how this could be connected to the wages. Third, the ongoing discussions around the development of the Somerset mines should include miners' representatives to ensure that their views were considered. The developments were intended to increase performance and efficiency, and Robert noted that these could lead to changes in working conditions so miners needed to be consulted. They agreed that Henry and Robert would try to meet with Colin Amble the next day and explain what they were doing, set up an exploratory meeting with the mine owners and the land owners. Robert ended the meeting with a few words of thanks and inspiration.

"We have a stake in our health and safety at work, in our wages and in our future working practices and we can drive this stake deep, so it stands strong for all to see. It is time that our voice was heard, our views taken account of, in the planning and decision making in our coal industry." Robert stressed the 'our' as he looked at his friends. "But, having a stake also means taking responsibility for any changes we propose or we support; sharing ownership of decisions with the owners. Ivan told us how this is happening all around the country but not without difficulties and confrontations. We must be prepared for conflict, and build a strong association of coal miners, to challenge any ill-disposed managers and their bailiffs; you know who I mean, the ones who treat us as if we are the slaves of the owners. We are bigger and more noble than them so let's show them." Robert paused and, looking at his friends, nodded his head to indicate he had finished. Archie started to clap and was soon joined by the others, raising the men's elation and their confidence that, yes, they would show them and, yes, they could do this.

Henry felt good as he made his way up the hill to his home. He wasn't sure what his part in all this would be, but he remembered that he had agreed with Colin Amble that he would talk with the men and try to build the bridge, so that was his main role for now, and it would start tomorrow. He was also thinking that he might not be here much longer so did not want to take on a leadership role. So, Robert had agreed to be the working group leader, William and James wanted to take the lead on safety matters, Farnham on pay and Archie on mining developments. They had all the topics covered. As he approached the gate leading to the road up to Tunley, Henry saw a man with his arm in a sling waiting there; he recognised him as Billie Oats's friend John, from the previous night. The bruises on Henry's face started to throb and he prepared himself for another fight. But surely John couldn't fight with his shoulder dislocated?

"Evening Henry, don't be alarmed, I don't want no more trouble. You beat us fair and square last night and I am here to say I regret my part in Billie Oats's quarrel with you; he is a mean man and I should never have joined him in his vengeful action. He said that you was planning to call the miners to strike against the owners and he just wanted to warn you off, frighten you but I see now he wanted to do you harm. You whacked me good and hard and I will be reminded of that until my shoulder heals. But I'm here to say sorry." John held out his hand to Henry.

"Well John, you are a surprise and a good one at that. Today has been full of them for me and I've been glad to receive them all so I will shake your hand." Henry and John were both tall, strong men with good physiques and vice-like grips. Their handshake was firm and long, a sign of a new friendship starting but Henry had to let go when the bruises from the previous night started to hurt. "Come John, have a cup of tea with my brothers and me and tell us your story."

John Riddle was a coal miner from the Midsomer Norton area; a similar age to Henry and living at home with mother, brothers and sisters. His father had also been killed in a mining accident. He had been hit by a runaway coal tub, and John had carried him home where he died of his injuries a few days later. John had been distraught by his father's death, became withdrawn and out of sorts for a long time, hardly talking to anyone. He started drinking and would often cry himself to sleep, wondering if he could have done more for his father; could he have saved him? The burdens of guilt and shame we carry with us shape our lives for sure. He didn't have any real friends but got talking in the local Inn with Charlie Grange, who persuaded him to join them last night, saying that they wanted to stop Henry Sage from disturbing the peace, from stirring up trouble for the miners. It was only afterwards that he met one of the miners who had been at the Clandown meeting and he'd told him about the good things that would come from forming an association. John had seen the doctor on the Sunday morning who had popped his shoulder back in place and had advised John to wear a sling for a few days. John felt an urgent need to speak with Henry, to apologise. So, he was grateful that Henry had asked to hear his story; the fight had woken John up and it was time his story came out.

"I've never been a particularly clever man Henry but I do seem to be valued for my strength and willingness to work hard. So that's how I value myself as well, if you see what I mean." Henry nodded and suggested they sit on a log by the roadside; he could see that John wanted to get something off his chest. Maybe the invite to "tell us your story" had sparked something. John told Henry how he had lost his father.

"I carried his broken body up the hill to the mine after he had been hit by the coal wagon, but he died two days later from the damage inside; well, that's what the doctor said. He was talking to me all the way up the hill Henry but I couldn't make out what he was saying. The doctor gave him morphine and he did not speak again. I torment myself Henry, asking could I have done something different to save him? Maybe if I'd waited until the doctor could come to where he lay, but that may have been hours, and I couldn't just leave him there; I wanted to rescue my father Henry, can you understand that?"

"Yes, of course I can understand that John. You see, my father was killed when the cage he was in fell to the bottom of the mine shaft. I wasn't there to help him, but I was too young anyway; what could I have done?" John's story had taken Henry back to when his father had died, his body broken at the bottom of the shaft; what were his last thoughts as he fell to his death? Henry tormented himself with that thought, that question. He remembered standing at the pithead, holding Sarah's hand, and staring at his father's body laid out on the cold ground. The wailing of heartbroken wives and mothers accompanied by the chattering of two ravens who stood on the back of a pit pony; memories, fresh as the day they were created.

"Dear God Henry, well I'll be damned, so you and me, we have something else in common. Strong men without fathers." The two strong men talked more about their lives and Henry suggested they go have that cup of tea. He told John about the meeting he had been to, about the working group planning for how to improve the miners' lot. John said that he would like to be involved; yes of course he could. He introduced John to his mother Maria, and brothers George and Ritchie. Maria invited John to stay for dinner but he said he needed to get back to his own mother who would be cooking their supper.

"Well, hopefully another time" said Maria. Henry walked out with John and bid him farewell as John began his trek home.

"Thank you, Henry, you've helped me turn a corner and now I need to find my way along a new road. I know that I am more than just a strong, hard-working man and I want to find out what that more is?" John walked off on the road and Henry wondered about the roads people travel along in their lives. He sat pondering for some time and thought about the journey he would be taking with Sarah, started feeling excited by this thought. He also thought about friendship and how important it was; how his friendship with Sarah gave him purpose. He looked across the valley to see John walking along the canal path on his way home and thought that a new friendship had been born. Friendship between men based on common understandings, mutual trust and caring for the things they do together. Physical things like digging coal, ploughing fields or building houses and bridges, where safety and productivity require cooperation between men. And mental things, like what the working group was doing, planning and negotiating, trying to influence how other people thought and acted. These were different from the physical things but no less reliant on trust for the friendships to endure and for the outcomes to be successful.

Sunday was ending, the sun sitting just above the horizon, the rooks returning home and chattering to each other about their day's exploits, or so Henry thought. Those rooks haven't had a day of rest and what a Sunday it had been, what a weekend, like a whole lifetime. Henry slept much better that night, even though his bruises still hurt. Inside he felt content and he was looking forward to the week ahead.

Henry and Robert talked with Colin Amble before their shift began the next day and agreed that they would meet with the mine owners and managers on Wednesday evening to talk things through. Colin was grateful for Henry's part in making this happen but warned him that it would be difficult to persuade the managers and their bailiffs to give up their power.

"They treasure their authority Henry, and are suspicious of miners wanting a say in the way the mines are run. Telling the managers how to do their jobs makes them look weak in front of the owners. So, be careful Henry that this doesn't blow up in your face." Henry did not like that analogy, sounded too much like the kind of accident that could happen underground if the shot firer got things wrong. Robert and Henry agreed to get the group together on the Tuesday evening for another meeting.

Monday, the start of a new working week and what would it bring? Henry and Ritchie ate their lunch and watched Sarah, who had walked over from the Rest to paint a picture of the  pithead, the winding gear, headstock and dark, coal dust covered buildings. She lived in a coal mining community, but she was closer to nature than to man's dark and heavy industry; but she knew that both, deep down, were as violent as each other. Henry standing by the pit prop logs softened the scene and brought out Sarah's creative spirit; her man and his dangerous machine painted into history. Sarah once again felt as if she was outside herself, but this time she was not anxious, felt no fear; whatever was happening to her was nature's way and she trusted it. She smiled at the warm feeling it gave her. Sarah came back to reality to hear Henry talking to her and Ritchie about the meeting with the owners and managers planned for Wednesday, and how the working group was taking on the different aspects, safety, pay and developments. And that's all there was time for. So, before long Henry and Ritchie were back underground, hewing and carting. Sarah stayed at the pithead for a few minutes before packing up her easel and returning to the Rest.

That evening Henry had agreed to help Grampa John with some garden work at the Manor, but Grampa John really wanted to talk with Henry about coal mining and safety and suggested they sit on the garden seat.

"Henry, why do you think accidents happen." Grampa John got straight to the point.

"Well, all kinds of reasons I guess, people make mistakes,

128

aren't careful enough with what they're doing; I've seen both down the mine." Henry paused to think, but John continued.

"Yes, you're right, people do make mistakes and they can be careless, but they don't always lead to accidents, do they? There's more to it and that's what I want to talk with you about Henry. Accidents are more likely to happen when men do dangerous work, like coal mining. Or use machines to make things, but can just as easily break things. We are in a social revolution in this land of ours Henry. A revolution where machines are being made to do the work of men, and women. Powerful machines that can do the work of hundreds of men and are dangerous to use. Accidents are more likely to happen when men aren't careful using machines. Dangerous work and dangerous machines increase the risk of accidents. The men who craft and make these machines are not the landowners Henry. They are a new breed of skilled people, creative inventors, engineers who are changing the world for all of us Henry; leading the revolution. Industries for making things that the engineers create are sprouting up everywhere and men are leaving the land and working in the factories in big towns. I worry about the safety of people who work in dangerous places and use dangerous machines. I want to tell you these things Henry because I know you will see more and more of this in your life and you need to be on your guard." Grampa John placed his hand on Henry's shoulder. "Be on your guard Henry."

"I will and I am Gramps, but say more about the revolution; where will it lead?"

"That depends Henry on how men, and women because women will have a bigger part to play than they do now, shall I say behave; how they control the changes that will come with the revolution, and how they are supported by regulations, the government's laws that require changes to be made and then enforced. Did you know that this year, the Coal Mines Act will be published that requires all managers to have a certificate awarded to show they have been trained and qualified to conduct inspections? I learned this from a friend in the city who knows what's discussed in Parliament. It seems that evidence of widespread incompetence and neglect of the rules set by the 1860 Act was presented and convinced Parliament of the need for stronger rules. This neglect and the increasing number of accidents and casualties in mines is driving this. Over a thousand men and boys died in mining accidents in 1870; you probably didn't know that Henry, did you?"

"Yes, I did Gramps, a fellow from South Wales visited us on the weekend and mentioned that number. He suggested we organise ourselves into an association of mine workers to demand safer working conditions."

"I knew that this was happening Henry, and I'd heard you were involved, so that's partly why I wanted to talk with you, because it's not just about safety as you know Henry. The formation of workers' associations is growing across the country, often led by very militant men who want more than just changes to working conditions. They are trying to change the social order and will go to extreme lengths to get their way, including violent disruptions. I read that, in some parts of the country, mine workers have withdrawn their labour, trying to force the owners to increase their pay. In one case, they have got on the wrong side of some determined managers and their efforts backfired, if you understand me?"

"Yes, I think so Gramps," Henry replied, trying to make sense of what social order was and how it might change; he asked Gramps to explain.

"In the decade before you were born Henry, the nation was in a crisis. There was a general strike in 1842, people all

130

over the land withdrew their labour, with demands for a People's Charter. Leaders of a movement calling themselves The Chartists wanted to give more working people the vote to decide who represented them in Parliament, where the laws are made. I remember it as a frightening time Henry, with violence erupting all over the place and the authorities forcibly breaking up the strikes and marches. People with power didn't want to give it up; they never do Henry, that's how they are, frightened of change, frightened of losing their power, frightened that things will fall apart. But it had to come, things didn't fall apart, and Parliament did eventually pass a Reform Act just a few years ago, in 1867, that gave more men the vote, although still not people like you Henry. So, the social order is about who has the power and the authority to change things, and having a vote gives a man a voice, a stake in the power to change the social order. But now the authorities are worried about the influence of a new agitator for change, a German man, Karl Marx, who lives in London and has written about a new order, where workers have a lot more say and a bigger share in the profits, the surplus as he calls it, made from making and selling things, and digging minerals out of the ground. I worry that there will be more uprisings and more violence as the authorities clamp down on the rebels for change. I have a lot of sympathy for them Henry as they try to make things fairer for the workers. But, you need to be careful when seeking change and you need to know clearly what you want and how far you are prepared to go to get it. You need to think about the other side, what they might lose and how far they might be willing to go. Think about finding a compromise, so you go forward step by step; do you follow me Henry?"

"Yes, I do Gramps, and thanks for that, I feel educated, but also know that I have a lot to learn; can we go back to talking about safety and accidents. You see, we've formed a

131

group of mine workers who will meet the owners and managers in the district this Wednesday to talk through our proposals for change; not only about improving safety but also having a say in wages and coal mine developments."

"Henry, think about the two sides to this coin; safety at work and working safely; they are equally important. What do you think the main threats to safety in a coal mine are Henry?" Gramps looked at Henry with that enquiring gaze that always stimulated Henry to think hard.

"I'd say the threat of collapsing tunnels of course, and of gas leakage and explosions, poor ventilation and flooding; oh, and listening to you talk Gramps, I realise that the threat of injury from machines, and the consequences of faulty machines are also threats." Henry thought about this father's death and John Riddle's father's death, both caused by malfunctions.

"And what's important about working safely?" asked Gramps. Henry thought for a moment and noticed that Lady Anna was in the garden picking some flowers. He gathered his thoughts and answered John.

"Well, everyone needs to be properly trained in the job they are doing and they need to learn how to deal with problems; but not many people are good at that in my experience, so there always needs to be someone nearby who is good at that. But how do you train people to be good at problem solving, I don't know? Then, if miners are well trained they should work carefully, but I know that there are times when you need to be more careful, much more careful, than others."

"There's something else Henry, but you probably know this. Close cooperation between the men is vital to safety underground, and anywhere where men work together and depend on each other. It's about keeping an eye on your workmate's safety as well as your own, and being ready to act if there is an accident. It's good to put yourself mentally into difficult situations, what would I do if such and such happened? Or better still, talk with your workmates about it, share ideas; put your minds in the difficult situations; see who the problem solvers are, because they are among you Henry and listening to them talking about how they deal with problems can be the best training. Then you may not be taken by surprise when something does go wrong. When an accident happens, an explosion or roof collapse, the chances of survival are much greater if people don't panic, but stay calm and think about the problem. That's what good training gives you, the time to think."

"And that's good advice Gramps. You know, we do some of that talking already, but maybe a regular safety meeting would work, and we'll have to find a way of getting the messages out to all the men. I'll bring that up when we meet tomorrow." Grampa John got up to go back into the house and Henry helped him along the pathway, and thanked him again for being such an inspiration. "I always feel inspired by our chats Gramps, fills my mind with new ideas."

"You are welcome Henry; I'm getting old and frail but chatting with you makes me feel young again, so we seem to be helping each other. You know, I believe that is what is so special about us human beings, the empathy we can show to each other." Gramps had explained this idea of empathy being good for people before so Henry knew what he meant and he waved goodbye to Grampa John and headed back through the garden. Anna was standing by the gate leading out of the garden, she seemed to be waiting for Henry.

"Good day Henry, nice to see you at the Manor; I heard that we are meeting with you on Wednesday to talk about changes you would like to see happen? Can we sit together and talk for a few minutes before you return home?"

Lady Anna Fernhill owned the land and the mines in Camerton, both having been passed to her when her father died and she had decided to keep ownership of the mines rather than sell the mining rights. A single woman in her mid 40's, with strong Christian values, Anna was very sympathetic to the plight of the local working families and would help them out whenever she could. The local vicar often cautioned her against being too sympathetic. He once said that, "it helps them if they feel a little in need Lady Anna, and the men wouldn't waste so much of their earnings at the Rest." The vicar enjoyed his place in the social order and saw no need for change, saw no need for working men and their families to have a say in things. That's not the way Anna saw things. She got on particularly well with Henry and liked the way that he discussed things with her grandfather; "it keeps him going," she would say, "and he likes you Henry, likes your curiosity about things. So, you will always be welcome here at the Manor young man." She said this in a way which made Henry feel good, feel that he was wanted, and he was warmed by the attentions of this gracious woman. But now she wanted to talk about what the association was trying to do; of course she does, thought Henry, Lady Anna owns the two Camerton mines.

"Good day to you Lady Anna, and yes, I'm always happy to talk with you. You've heard about us forming an association then?"

"Yes, I have Henry and before the meeting I wanted to get some idea of your intentions, about what your association wants."

Henry explained how the association was beginning to form, made up of workers from the different mines in the district. The Camerton mines were only one of about six

134

different groups of coal mines owned by different people and companies. He went on to describe the three aspects that the mine workers had agreed needed attention and these would form the basis of the discussion they wanted with the owners and managers.

"At the meeting on Wednesday Lady Anna, we are not expecting to come to a final agreement, but rather begin the negotiations about how to improve safety, getting a fairer pay system and how the miners can influence the plans for the coalfield; we want to be involved in these things, not just leave it to the owners."

"Do you want my help with this Henry? You know that I care a lot for the miners, and particularly their families, in Camerton. But I think you will find that there are other areas where owners are less sympathetic and have employed managers and bailiffs to enforce strict rules."

"Yes, I have heard this Lady Anna." Anna interrupted Henry and motioned with a waving hand.

"Please call me Anna, Henry, or Miss Fernhill if you are more comfortable with formalities."

"No, it's not that I feel more comfortable with formalities, or maybe it is, but it will take some getting used to. I would like to call you Anna, Anna." They both laughed to defuse the awkward moment. Henry collected his thoughts and felt the urge to continue what he was saying, before his mind fogged over from the emotion rising inside. "Yes, I've heard about the strict managers and I think it's the miners from those pits who have the biggest gripes, want the changes to come quickly. I want to find a way, try to find a way, where we can all agree on what is best." Henry tried to reassure Anna about his intentions and she acknowledged this with a warm smile and gentle nod of her head.

"Thank you, Anna, I think if all the owners were like you, things would be a lot better in this world."

"In this world Henry, well that's a big thing to say and hardly true about me, but I'll take your kind words as a compliment." Anna smiled at Henry and he felt an urge to speak a thought that had been in his mind for some time.

"I hope you don't mind me saying this Anna but sometimes you look very sad and it grieves me to think you might be sad. You do so many good things and are so well liked." Anna held her hand out again and Henry stopped speaking as if by command.

"I should mind it Henry, it's a very personal observation, not one that a young man should really be saying to a middle-aged woman, but I don't mind because I know you mean well. I believe I'm right in thinking that you and your cousin Sarah are very much in love Henry; there's my personal observation in return. I've known that since you were both very small and you used to play in the garden; do you remember?" Henry nodded with a smile.

"Your father James was very helpful to my father in those days." Anna paused and collected her thoughts, wondering how much should she say? "I have been in love too Henry so I think I know how you feel now, but my love didn't work out so I put my energy, I put my whole self, into looking after the Manor, managing the coal mines, and the work I do with the church for the good of the people." Anna smiled and looked at Henry. "I'd say that's a full-time job, wouldn't you, but yes, I do have a sadness and it is under strict control and my tears are often lost in the Somerset rain Henry." Anna looked up at the sky as she said this. "Women need to find a way of controlling their sadness if they are to survive, don't you know; but men often don't know Henry, don't even know what sadness is." Anna shook her head slowly and looked back at

Henry. "Now you should return to your family and your loving Sarah, she will be missing you." Anna took Henry's hand before he had time to respond, and squeezed for longer than a formal farewell warranted; but they weren't to be formal any longer. In a few minutes of empathy, Anna and Henry had become friends and Henry squeezed Anna's hand in return, confirming what had happened.

Henry ran along the lane and up the hill to the Rest; he couldn't get her words out of his head, "*my tears are often lost in the Somerset rain*", so he ran faster and his heart pumped faster. It was late in the evening and he could see the window of Sarah's room glowing from the candle within. He gently threw a stone up and it clinked on the window pane. Seeing Sarah's face filled Henry with love. "Sorry my love, I had to see your beautiful face, and now I will sleep soundly."

"Oh, you are strange sometimes Henry Sage, but I do like that about you; please always be strange, sometimes," and Sarah blew Henry a kiss and gave him a beautiful smile; yes, he knew he would sleep soundly tonight bathed in the warmth of woman's love and kindness.

On Tuesday evening, the meeting took place in the back room at the Rest, attended by Henry and George, Robert, brothers William and James Hodge, Farnham and Archie. Archie had brought another man with him and introduced him as Arthur Riddle, who was also keen to be involved with safety. Henry shook his hand and wondered if he was related to John. Before he could ask, Robert kicked things off.

"Seems like it was only yesterday that we met up, it's good to see you all again."

"It was only the day before yesterday Robert, but it seems a lot longer to me. My Mondays are always long; feeling I have a lot to catch up with after my day of rest." Archie said this with a chuckle in his voice. Robert reminded the group that they needed to be serious and prepare for the meeting with the owners and managers the next day. Arthur described what he knew about the Royal Commission on Coal Supplies that had reported its findings the year before. It seems that, contrary to the idea of a coal famine, the Commission had estimated that coal should last about 300 years. Arthur described his ideas about how to make the local mines more efficient, using machinery to haul the coal underground, instead of the carters and ponies; making the tunnels larger so the miners could move around more easily. William and James had been looking at safety and described how improved ventilation would come from connecting the tunnels from different pits. To prevent over winding of the cages the winder would receive a signal letting him know when to stop. James had read that a new Regulation Act would be published later that year requiring managers to be certified by a board of examiners appointed by the government. Also, daily inspections would need to be carried out by trained inspectors. James looked around at his co-workers with a smile of enthusiasm.

"Things are going to get better and we need to be part of the getting better, we must have a say in all this. I wonder if the managers know about these things yet?"

"If not we can put 'em in the picture, right James," said William.

The group felt ready to take their demands, or rather their needs, to the owners; Henry had advised that they should go to the meeting with a positive frame of mind and a clear description of their needs and not make demands.

"If we say these are demands, we'll surely put their backs up from the word go, and then it will be difficult to reach an agreement. Much better that we persuade the owners that it is in their interest to improve things and let us be a part of the improving." Farnham wanted to talk about pay.

"To some, pay's the most important thing we must discuss; the thing that we must get right. The strongest anger comes from coal workers who feel they are treated like slaves and paid a pittance, while the owners and managers live in luxury. The bailiffs don't weigh the coal properly, and they do claim that we load the tubs with waste; so, we need someone there when they weigh. We must be strong on this, and some feel that we do have demands Henry that must be met, or we withdraw our labour. It's worked elsewhere, so let's see if they'll listen in Somerset." Henry thought he had done his best to dissuade Farnham and the others against being too demanding but he wasn't confident this had been enough. But they all agreed that having workers involved in the daily inspections and coal weighing was top of their list for the discussion on Wednesday. Whatever the outcome of the Wednesday meeting, they would call another gathering for all the coal workers on Clandown Hill on the weekend. The meeting ended with the miners shaking hands and agreeing a solidarity that wouldn't be broken by the artful mischief they anticipated from some of the managers; they would stand strong.

It was 7pm on Wednesday evening and men were gathering for the meeting between coal workers and owners at the church hall. The murmuring sound in the hall was of men talking, with no one conversation clear enough to be heard. As he approached the hall, Henry heard the murmurs and thought to

139

himself, this is where and how it starts. But the first sight that caught his eye as he entered the room was Anna standing and talking to a man in a tweed suit and tie. He was moving his arms and talking in an animated fashion but she looked calm and graceful, the evening sun bursting through the stain glass window and lighting up her dark hair. Henry felt an urge to protect her from the fool trying to get her attention, but he realised there was no need, she looked in complete control, but the thought persisted in his head. She looked across at Henry and smiled, moving her head slightly in a reassuring way, as if she could read his thought.

A tall bearded man walked up to the table at the front of the hall and banged a gavel to get people's attention. He introduced himself as Hamish McCartney, manager of the Radstock mines, adding that it had been agreed that he would speak for the mine managers in the district and the owners of the mines that he managed. Henry looked across to Anna who was sitting and looking at McCartney. Henry wondered what she was thinking. His wonder was interrupted by McCartney's voice.

"The mine workers have asked to meet us here today to make proposals for changes in the way we run the mines. Some of you will know that we are starting to make progress in the Radstock mines with the way the coal is weighed and how wages are determined. Not all of you agree with what we are doing but it's good that we involve all the mines in the district, so you understand what we think is realistic." A man stood up and, shaking his fist, shouted out.

"What's real to you is different than what's real to us McCartney." Henry thought he recognised the man who said this, but couldn't remember where he'd seen him, and he gave Robert a worried look.

"So, we are all here to listen and to talk; to negotiate and

140

to see if we can find common ground," replied McCartney, in an authoritative tone and with a stern expression on his face. "I understand that the mine workers have a spokesman to put their case forward. I do hope it will be a reasonable man." Robert stood up, introduced himself and described what had been discussed and agreed the day before. He spoke well, with conviction and often got a shout of support from some in the hall and even a hand of applause. One of the managers interrupted Robert with an aggressive and confrontational tone, accusing the mine workers of endangering the economic prospects of the district with their demands; in response, the fist shaker howled a curse at the manager. Hamish McCartney banged his gavel on the table, louder this time.

"Will those of you who can't contain their temper, go and cool down outside and let this meeting continue in a civilised manner. I have something important to say so I want you all to listen carefully. What the workers are asking for is not new and has been the subject of discussion and negotiation across the country for nearly a decade. Your own district's Government Inspector of Coalmines, Lionel Brough, reported in 1864, describing working conditions in the mines; let me read a line from his report. *'This account of death, contusions, fractures, amputations and surgical operations, altogether sounds like the description of military movements in the field rather than the report of industrious and peaceful pursuits.'* Does this sound familiar?" The audience responded with loud agreement. The more Henry listened to Hamish McCartney the more hopeful he felt that they would come to an agreement on the things the miners were wanting. Hamish continued.

An Act to consolidate and amend the Acts A.D. 1872.
relating to the Regulation of Coal Mines
and certain other Mines.
[10th August, 1872.]

WHEREAS it is expedient to consolidate and
amend the law relating to the regulation
and inspection of coal mines and certain other
mines :

Be it enacted by the Queen's most Excellent
Majesty, by and with the advice and consent of the
Lords Spiritual and Temporal, and Commons, in this
present Parliament assembled, and by the authority
of the same, as follows :

PRELIMINARY.

1. This Act may be cited as "The Coal Mines Short title.
Regulation Act, 1872."

2. This Act, except as hereinafter provided, (¹) shall Commence-
not come into operation in England and Scotland ment of Act.
until the first day of January, one thousand eight
hundred and seventy-three, and in Ireland until the
first day of January, one thousand eight hundred and
seventy-four, which dates are in this Act respectively
referred to as the commencement of this Act.

(¹) The exceptions are—
Payment of wages by weight of mineral after 1st
August, 1873. See sec. 17.
And—
The provisions as to double shafts for any mine not required
to have them at the passing of the Act, on and after 1st
January, 1875. See sec. 23.

"Brough's words have hit their mark at the centre of
Government and I can tell you that a new Coal Mines
Regulation Act is likely to be approved by Parliament this
summer. I have seen extracts from this and I can tell you that
many things will change and the managers will have to take
heed or find themselves out of work." He paused and looked
around the room; no response came from the other managers,
so he looked across at Robert. "Mr Barnes, you ask for better
mine inspections; well, it's coming. One of the new rules will

be, to quote from the draft, '*a competent person or competent persons who shall be appointed for the purpose shall once at least every 24 hours examine the state of the external parts of the machinery and the state of the head gear, working places, levels, planes, ropes, chains and other works of the mine.*' Another rule will require that, '*There shall be attached to every machine worked by steam, water or mechanical power and used for lowering or raising persons, an adequate break (sic), and also a proper indicator (in addition to any mark on the rope) which shows to the person who works the machine the position of the cage or load in the shaft.*' And, you'll be reassured to know that, '*the miners may from time to time appoint two of their number to inspect the mine at their own cost.*' And this will apply to the weighing as well. The new Act and its Rules will have a profound impact on how we do mining business here in Somerset, and across the Nation. We will need to get down to working together on how to implement these changes and to do it peacefully." Hamish asked the group if anybody wanted to say anything else. Anna stood up, and all heads turned in anticipation.

"Thank you, Mr McCartney and thank you Mr Barnes. I must say, an hour ago, my expectations of how this meeting would go were not high. I was worried that there would be too much animosity and that you gentlemen would be too confrontational with each other. But I feel relieved and am gratified that your spokesmen have not only used words of wisdom, but also spoken with respect for the other side, if I can put it like that. I hope that the dissent that was voiced on occasion here tonight can be ameliorated so that those with the greatest anxieties can be appeased. I will work to do this in the Camerton area and I will meet with other mine owners soon with this purpose." A roar of approval and clapping burst out from the mine workers in the hall. Managers were more reserved, and the owners that were in attendance and sitting together could be seen muttering to each other. Henry judged that the man in the tweed suit was a mine owner in the district; he looked decidedly unhappy. Henry wanted to talk with Anna, to thank her for her support, hold her hand again but she was talking with a group of men and Henry realised that she was beginning her discussions with the other mine owners in the district. A part of him was glad about this, the part with the inner voice that no-one else heard and that told him to be careful; don't let her bewitch you, it was saying.

When Henry arrived home, he found Sgt Pepper talking to his mother, stroking the handlebars of his dark moustache. It seems that John Riddle had been to the police and told them what had happened on Saturday night. But Billie Oats could not be found. When he was found, *would Henry like to press charges for assault?* Henry declined, saying that Billie had probably learned a lesson and that should be enough punishment. Sgt Pepper thanked Henry, wished him well and went on his way. Watching him walking, or rather marching, down the lane, Henry thought how well Sgt Pepper played his part in the life of the villages. His presence was re-assuring and his walk, or march, reinforced this and he would greet everyone he passed with good will. He'd been doing this for 20 years and long may we live by the rules of fair laws, enforced by honest, decent men, thought Henry.

The following evening Henry met Sarah on the canal footpath. He was bursting with enthusiasm to tell her all that had happened over the last few days, including how supportive Anna had been to the miners' cause. It all came pouring out and Henry didn't notice Sarah's puzzled expression until he paused for a breath.

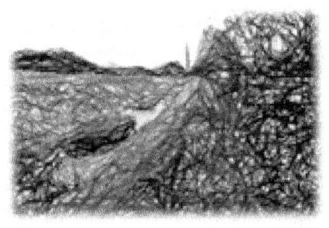 "When did Lady Anna become Anna, Henry?" Sarah asked this looking at Henry with more than a puzzled expression on her face. There was much more to the question than a simple change of name and Henry immediately realised it.

"When I visited Grampa John on Monday Sarah love, Anna, or rather Lady Anna, asked me to call her Anna or Miss Fernhill, rather than Lady Anna. I said I'd like to call her Anna, that's all there is to it, really." Henry was holding back the thoughts and feelings he had experienced that day in the garden, and those that came back to him again on the Wednesday evening. He didn't understand them himself and did not want to worry Sarah. But Sarah was a very sensual person, in touch with feelings, and could pick things up that might be hidden to others or buried inside by some. She had known Lady Anna since she was a child and was fond of her, regarded her like another auntie, but as Sarah's special awareness grew, she began to wonder if Lady Anna was holding something back. Maybe Lady Anna wanted to find intimacy with Henry, starting with asking him to call her Anna, leading to who knows where. Sarah knew that what she said now was very important. She reached out and held both of Henry's hands in hers and looked up into his eyes; she paused for a few seconds before she spoke.

"Henry, our love is strong and it will get stronger as we grow together and journey together on our adventure. Being good friends, and lovers, is where it starts and it's where we are, but the world will test our love on our journey, in all kinds of ways that we might not be able to imagine now." Sarah looked deeply into Henry's eyes to reach his heart. Henry blinked at the intensity of her gaze. He felt she was trying to read his mind but he wasn't afraid, only captivated.

"I've no reason to think Lady Anna's, Anna's, intentions are not good, but she seems a lonely woman with a sadness deep inside and I think you are drawn to protect her Henry, to ease her pain. But it may be that only love can do that and I can't share your love with another woman Henry."

"You won't have to Sarah, my love is for you alone, and I want it to grow with your love for me, day by day, week by week, year by year; but you are right, Anna has a sadness and if I can help by listening can that be wrong? I want you to trust me Sarah. Can you do that my love?"

"I trust you Henry but I'm not sure I trust Anna, or what her intentions are."

Sarah gently pulled Henry's head down until their lips met and they kissed. She led him into their loving field and they lay in the grass. Their love making was deeply intimate and satisfying. Sarah's hands explored the curves and muscles of Henry's body as he moved with a gentle rhythm above her and her body responded with a counter rhythm. He was her man and she was his woman and together they quickly reached the moment of bliss, lost to everything but their union. As the climax subsided, Henry felt a tear forming, but there was no rain to wash it away.

"This is what life is about," whispered Henry. "I disappear into a world without beginning or end Sarah,  without past or future, beside you and inside you; helpless and under your control." Sarah had also disappeared, but into her outer world, like she had experienced on the bridge the previous Sunday. She returned as Henry lowered his head to kiss her lips.

"I think we were made for each other Henry Sage, our bodies and minds, perfect fits." As Sarah wrapped her legs around Henry's back, their rhythm began again and Sarah gasped with the pleasure of love. They held each other close and warm and two ravens passed across the jealous sky above them, performing erotic aerobatics and celebrating the creation of new life, the amazing conception that would carry their genes on into the future, long into the future. Sarah wondered at the power of love and was suddenly overcome with a wave of sadness for the people who never find love or are doomed to live with unrequited love. She thought of Anna and her sadness. "What a loss," she whispered.

"What loss, where are you my love?" said Henry.

"Oh Henry, you heard my thoughts. I feel so blessed with your love and this thought came in, what a loss it is for people who never love, or never find love. It made me sad for a moment there; how can they find meaning in life?"

"Maybe we aren't all meant to find love and maybe some can get by without it; or if they never had it, they wouldn't know what they were missing. I think there are probably lots of lonesome hearted lovers with their personal tales out there in the world, but I can't imagine life without your love Sarah, without our personal tales woven together." Henry and Sarah continued to  weave their personal tales together as they sat bathed in the nature around them. As if to sanctify the moment, the ravens make another flyby heading for the woods on Clandown hill.

Friday morning at 5 o'clock and a storm is brewing over Camerton. The sun rises in the east and dark grey clouds approach from the west; which would get to the mine first is uncertain but by 5.45, as Henry and Ritchie run down the field from Tunley Houses, they see the first flash of lightning. A few seconds later the thunder clap scatters big fat rain drops into the valley and onto Henry and Ritchie's faces as they laugh and talk about Tom's visit on Saturday. Henry hears Ritchie singing a verse as they approach the mine.

"Tom's on his way, Megan's on his arm, what's he got to say, will she be a charm." But mostly the miners had serious, grim faces and were converging on the mine from all directions. Soon the industry would begin again, men hewing and hauling the black gold out from its resting place, formed from life 100 million years ago.

"Sorry Henry, I'm taking your place in the first cage." Colin spoke with Henry as he approached. "We are starting the underground safety checks this morning; you can take the second cage. There's space for Ritchie to fit in though if he wants." Colin Amble explained that, following the meeting on Wednesday, the district managers had agreed to conduct the first of the new daily underground inspections on Friday and Colin would do this for the New Pit. Henry was always in the first cage but realised that he would have to wait for the second as the cage was already full. He turned towards his brother.

"I'll see you at the bottom Ritchie, wait at the entrance to the deep vein till I come down." The cage descended as the winding gear began to turn. It would normally be about fifteen minutes before it returned to the surface and Henry could begin his shift. But this was not a normal day and as Henry watched the wheel turning, the air was punctured with a loud crack. At first Henry thought it was another thunder clap but he gasped as he realised that the cable attached to the descending cage

148

had broken and there followed a graunching sound and seconds later a dull thud from deep in the mine shaft as the cage and its occupants crashed at the bottom of the mine shaft.

The men standing around the pithead were stunned and did not move or say anything for a few seconds, frozen in their footsteps. Henry's thoughts raced around his head, his action momentarily halted by a disbelief; this cannot happen.

"Down the ventilation shaft," he shouted and raced along the canal path to the Old Pit. He was followed by other miners as the wail of the pithead siren pierced the rain-filled air in the valley. Four men descended by cage into the darkness of the old pit, looking at each other with stern, anxious faces. At the bottom, Henry was out first and made his way east through the half-mile long tunnel connecting the two mine shafts. As he approached the New Pit the dust was getting thicker and he could hear the moans of human distress. He covered his mouth with a handkerchief and made his way carefully along the tunnel, the moaning getting louder with every step. 'Thank God', he thought, 'there are survivors.' The wire-door was lying beside the buckled and broken cage. Ritchie was lying on the top of a pile of men, not moving. 'Please, please let him live,' thought Henry. Then there was a movement beneath Ritchie as one of the men gave a loud moan as he reached out an arm.

"Help me, help me," a voice cried out. "I think my legs are broken." It was Colin Amble. Henry gently lifted Ritchie out of the cage and laid him down on the ground; he put his ear to his chest and heard his heart beat.

"My brother's heart is beating; he lives." Two other men were freeing Colin Amble; "be careful with my legs men, they are hurting bad." There was no movement from the other three men in the cage. One was sitting in the corner, head slumped forward at an odd angle; it looked like his neck was broken.

The other two men lay on the cage floor and had formed a cushion offering some protection to Ritchie and Colin when the cage hit the ground. Ritchie became conscious and sat up grasping his arm.

"It's broken Henry, I'm sure of it. How are the other men?" Henry knelt beside him.

"We don't know yet Ritchie. Are you hurting anywhere else?"

"My head is sore." and he reached up to touch the wound on his forehead; a gash from where he had scraped it on something hard as he fell. "We was floating Henry, when we fell, all floating together, grasping at anything we could, each other, the sides of the cage. I'm frightened Henry." Henry picked Ritchie up and carried him back along the tunnel to the old pit shaft. More men were coming along to help. Henry would find out later who had survived but now he had to get Ritchie to safety.

The pit siren woke the whole village and everyone came running out of their homes and down to the mine to find out what was happening. Sarah rushed along the road from the Rest and met some men running the other way.

"What has happened."

"The cable broke and the mine cage has fallen with four of the first shift inside, and Colin Amble. They're bringing 'em up the Old Pit shaft." Sarah felt a pain from the sudden realisation that Henry would be in the cage. She shrieked with that pain.

"No, please God No, don't let this be." Sarah ran with the men back to the Old Pit, praying to herself. "Please God let him live, don't let him die, he mustn't die, not yet." The rain fell hard and Sarah's tears were pouring out, joining the rain, joining heaven's tears, God crying for the misery of men's folly perhaps. Sarah approached the mine shaft as the cage was reaching the surface. The cage opened and Henry walked out with Ritchie in his arms and Sarah sank to her knees. "Thank you, God, for answering my prayer, for saving my man."

"Sarah, I'm alright, I wasn't in the cage but Ritchie has a broken arm and a nasty gash on his head."

"I'll be fine, but no more hauling till my arm heals; thank you Henry. Someone should go and tell mother that we are alive Henry."

"Yes Ritchie, someone will do that." Henry sat down next to Sarah in the rain and put his arms around her and Ritchie and began to cry. Their tears became part of the rain; part of nature's sad tales that would last forever.

Later that day, the group of mineworkers at the pithead were joined by Anna Fernhill, the manager and the local vicar for a vigil. Colin Amble had survived with two broken legs but three men had died in the accident, including William Hodge, one of the workers' association responsible for safety aspects. Irony can be cruel.

The rain fell all day in the Camerton valley and the ravens were silent. The rooks flew around in their gangs, as usual, squawking their messages to each other, chained to the skyways without any idea of what lay beneath the ground; at least that's what we think.

5. A Week in the Life while the Raven Cruises

The sun's rays reflected off the spokes of the winding wheel as it rotated, sparkles of light bursting out as the cage was hauled up to the surface. The flashing reflections were powerful and the sound was distinctive, a combination of grinding and chuffing, and then it all stopped. Two men sat on a pile of logs, talking together. What were they saying? I can almost make it out; a working group for safety. Are they talking about mine safety? "Why are you talking about safety," Bran asked, but they didn't seem to hear him, let alone see him. But she could see him, she was looking at him, staring at him, holding something in her hand. Was it a stick, looked more like a wand; a fairy with a wand, but he knew it was her when she smiled and, in a moment, all was gone and reality returned.

"Here we go again," Bran whispered to himself as he woke with a start and the dream and the woman's face fading away. He quickly wrote down what he could recall. *Looked like a coal mine, sun glinting off the turning wheel; strong sounds, do we really hear in dreams? Two men talking about safety in mines, and a working group. One of the men looked familiar, the other was younger. She looked like a fairy with a wand; a beautiful fairy with a magic wand and she smiled a magic smile. She was the same one; her auburn hair shining in the sun. Who is she? And, this time I could speak in the dream; I'll try that again.* Bran had read that one theory of dreams suggests that all characters in a dream are versions, or aspects,

152

of oneself. Talking about safety he could relate to, but the woman with the wand, was that about his anima and maybe the thought that sometimes it would need magic to solve a technical problem? All stuff that he wanted to talk with Chloe about; he must call her and arrange to meet, maybe Thursday?

But it was now Saturday morning, 6am, and soon Bran and Mary were talking on the phone, sharing their stories of the day and what the weekend held for them both. Mary would be going on a retreat to Yosemite with her colleagues so they agreed that they would talk again on Monday night, Tuesday morning.

"Jos picked up a letter for you from the University, Mary. Your name and address in hand writing on the envelope but nothing else and I don't recognise the writing. Would you like me to open it and read it to you love?"

"Yes, please Bran, it sounds intriguing."

"Dear Professor Norris

I hope you don't mind me writing to you, but after reading about your work for the climate change cause, I thought you might be able to help me. I work as a researcher at the University of Slatchen, on a project funded jointly by the oil and gas industry and the Natural Environment Research Council, NERC. The project is about making sense of the environmental impact of new forms of gas production, including hydraulic fracturing and underground coal gasification. To put it bluntly, I am very concerned that my academic supervisor, Dr Clive Oats, is falsifying the data he is reporting in our published papers. I have challenged him about this but he argues that it is a matter of interpretation and if we only showed the negative side, the industry might be hampered in developing mining applications. He is accusing me of sabotaging the project and is threatening me with dismissal. It is difficult for me to prove my points because it is only a suspicion and Dr Oats won't give me access to all the data. He says that I don't need it to do my job.

So, I am looking for another research position but I wanted to alert someone to my suspicions; someone independent who might be able to explore what is going on. I would be more than willing to come and visit you with the limited evidence I have, but I wanted to check if you were prepared to listen to me. Reading about your ethical approach to your work makes me believe that I can trust you, but if you are not able to help, please say, I will understand and you won't hear from me again.

Yours sincerely

Francis Clerk PhD"

Bran finished reading the letter but continued. "It's dated 1st May, nearly three weeks ago Mary, and from the address on the front it looks like it went to the wrong Department before it got to your secretary. Dr Clerk has left his telephone number and address at his University. This sounds serious Mary. What do you think you will do about it; do you want my help?"

"Can you fax the letter to me Bran and I will think about it. Oh, and do you have time to see what his project is about and who is sponsoring it? Of course, I know you don't, but anything you can find out would be helpful. I don't want to get involved in their internal scrap but if there is an ethical issue it might be worth alerting the research council, the NERC. I won't do anything though until I know a bit more and it will have to wait till I can fit it in."

"Ok Mary, understood, I'll see if I can find anything useful next week. Hey, you know that both Julia and Dylan have got exams coming up. As usual, Dylan doesn't say a lot about his studies but we'll hopefully find out when he gets his year one results. Julia seems very relaxed about her finals, unlike me all those years ago. I remember my project was taking more of my time than it was really worth but it helped me with revision discipline; truth is I hated exams Mary, as you know."

"Yes, I know Bran, but you got through and found your way to me; I feel very lucky."

"I'm the lucky one Mary and I am so looking forward to when you get back. Please hurry up and sort them out and fly home safe to the nest. We can take that vacation we've been promising each other, pack up all our cares and woes, and head out to the hills; does that sound ok?"

"It does Bran, it sounds very good. But now I must finish packing before I go to bed; tomorrow I do head out to the hills, so I'll let you go and you must let me go, and we'll speak on Monday."

Bran always found it difficult to let Mary go. As he put the phone down he felt a pang of sadness and anxiety. He missed her so much and the only way he could deal with this anxiety was to focus on his work. This coming week would be a busy one for sure, but he had things to deal with before Monday.

After breakfast, Bran turned on his computer and checked his emails. There was one from Stuart Carter that he was expecting. He opened the attachment. Stuart made the point that the absence of any flight data or cockpit voice recorder in the Odona made things very difficult to unravel. The pilot's flight plan showed that he intended to depart from the airfield at Timly, climb to 2000ft, turn north and fly more or less direct to Bogan, a journey of about 250 miles, with 3 passengers who would be attending a meeting. The weather was generally good, with cloud at 3000ft but winds were strong, 30kts from the north east at ground-level, gusting to 45kts. Timly was in a region of low hills, with several narrow, wooded, valleys running south-west to north east. The radar profile showed the helicopter departing the airfield on a north-easterly heading, climbing to 1500ft, and levelling off before turning 180deg to the left and descending into the adjacent valley, when the radar signal was lost. The aircraft crashed onto the valley floor about one mile further down, with what appeared to be a very high descent rate. There were no eye witnesses, but some people walking in the woods further down the valley heard the crash and saw smoke rising from the valley floor. They climbed to higher ground and telephoned the emergency services. The pilot and three passengers were all killed in the crash. Stuart made the point that, from examination of the wreckage, it appeared the engine was delivering full power when the aircraft crashed, so engine failure had been ruled out. Main and tail rotors were intact. After inspecting the wreckage at the crash site, they transported it back to Farnborough for more detailed investigation. So far, they had found no evidence of any mechanical failure or malfunction.

"High rate of descent with full power." Bran was thinking aloud. "That could be vortex ring, but had the pilot lost control of the Odona, and why had he descended into the valley if the engine was working ok? Why hadn't he radioed an emergency?" Questions, questions, the answers to which we may never know for sure, thought Bran as he leaned back in his chair. Bran was one of the few engineers who had been involved in flight testing the vortex ring state, or VRS for short, in a high-risk trial undertaken in a fully instrumented Puma helicopter at high altitude. Bran was flight test engineer on board the helicopter, as the pilot decelerated to the hover at gradually increasing rates of descent. Risk was reduced, but not eliminated, by approaching the dangerous condition carefully; incrementally, as the test team described it. VRS occurs on a helicopter rotor when descending at very low speed, less than 10kts, when the flow up through the rotor due to the descent meets the downdraft from the thrusting rotor and the two flow fields coalesce  to form a re-circulating doughnut-shaped vortex above the rotor that causes the rotor thrust to reduce. The outcome is a rapid increase in rate of descent and any increase in power just makes things worse. In the Puma test, the pilot had to push the stick forward to gain speed before he could begin to climb, so several hundred feet were lost in the recovery. If a helicopter entered vortex ring at low altitude, a crash was almost inevitable.

An experienced pilot like Peter Peel would surely have known this so what was he doing flying his helicopter into this condition? If it was VRS? Who was this Peter Peel? Sandra's words came back to him, "*Peter was a very careful pilot, Dr Sage, he had a near perfect safety record.*" But was he prone to making errors, Bran wondered. Then Ron's words came back, "*Peter's mother is terribly distraught by his death and worried that he might be blamed for the crash; it's mostly pilot error these days isn't it Dr Sage?*" Well, thought Bran, it is mostly pilot error for sure, and often hard to understand, because pilots rarely admit to making a mistake, at least in public. Bran felt an urge to find out more about Peter Peel; he had promised Ron that he would help. He wondered if John Morgan's files would contain anything relevant from the previous accident and Bran decided that he would see if he could visit Suisan the next day to look through John's things. A quick phone call confirmed that would be fine so he would set off early on Sunday for a trip down to Suisan Morgan's home.

Suisan had invited Bran to join her for lunch at a local tavern that featured live jazz every Sunday lunchtime. She was still grieving over her loss so Bran was reluctant to bother her with details of the accident. They talked about old times when the two families would go hiking together in the Lake District. Both John and Bran particularly enjoyed the walk up to Dale Head and on to Robinson where the ravens would be cavorting across the sky. "Surely those birds are enjoying their flying," Bran said to John, who nodded enthusiastically and just at that moment the pair of ravens performed a 360deg roll in formation, finishing the manoeuvre by diving down to land on the rocks below Robinson. Recalling these good times lifted Suisan's spirits and she was grateful to Bran.

"How is your ancestry research going Bran, you mentioned that you wanted to find out more about, was it your great grandparents?"

"Yes, that's right Suisan, after John's funeral I visited the area in Somerset where Henry and Sarah Sage, my great grandparents, lived before they moved to South Wales. I really got a good feel for the place, and met some kind folk at the

158

mining museum down there who have agreed to try to find anything that might help me with the story."

"Oh, the story, are your writing a book about your relatives Bran?"

"No, not really; just trying to piece together all that remains of their lives in documents, newspaper articles and pictures. There isn't much and I have no idea what they look like, except…" Bran paused.

"Except what Bran?"

"I wasn't going to bother you with this Suisan but I've been having these dreams. The same woman appears in them and I'm wondering if my mind, my unconscious, is creating images of my ancestors, in particular my great-grandmother Sarah, so that I have someone I can visualise to help me. Does that make sense?

"Not really Bran; help you with what?"

"Oh, I'm not sure Suisan, maybe help me to deal with my research at a more human level, not just sorting through bits of information. Can you tell what a person is like just by looking at them? I doubt it. But I'm imagining Henry and Sarah as hard-working people with limited ambition, but strong characters; I want them to have strong characters. For some reason, that seems important to me."

"I'm also doing ancestry research Bran; you probably didn't know that. I've been building my family tree, putting a branch on the Davies tree here and there. Any piece of information I get I treat it like a leaf on the tree; adding colour and texture to the picture. I have no photographs of my Welsh relatives before about 1900, so I also am imagining what they might have looked like and wondering what they thought about. So, I think I do understand what you mean Bran. John used to say jokingly that I was bringing them back, creating memories that were not real. He thought I might start to believe these created memories; think that they really happened. We would laugh about the idea; what a shock we'd get if great-grandad Davies appeared at the door one day to say thanks for giving him another chance. He was a policeman in the town of Haverfordwest, so we would imagine that if a policeman knocked on the door, it would be Constable William Davies." Suisan lowered her head and wiped a tear from her eye; she had started to cry talking about John. "I'm sorry Bran, it's going to be a while until I get through this."

"Please don't apologise Suisan, I'm so glad you have come out with me today, I hope it's not too difficult. Please say if it is."

"No, it's good for me to get out and talk about John. I think the more I do talk about him, about our life together, the more I can reach a peaceful place, and I don't well up every time. Isn't that lovely music Bran, do you like Jazz."

"Yes, I do like Jazz, although sometimes I'm not in the mood for the more complex stuff, but this is really nice and relaxing." Suisan had changed the subject so Bran didn't try to take her back to ancestry and family. Bran looked across the room at the jazz band and found the easy sounds very soothing. The guitarist was a woman sitting alongside the bass and piano players. What a great sound he thought. They were playing the Charlie Haydon composition '*Our Spanish Love Song*'. She sounded just like Pat Metheny and the bass and guitar parts danced along together, dynamic and intimate."

"John and I used to come here as often as we could. The band creates such a beautiful relaxing atmosphere, don't you think Bran? Bran, are you still with me?" Bran was staring across at the guitarist, who had just turned her head so that Bran could see her more clearly.

"Yes, of course, I'm sorry Suisan, I was distracted there. I think I recognise the woman playing the guitar. It's a strange coincidence but I think I met her at her husband's funeral; well, it was just before John's service and I stumbled into her family group when I arrived early. The other odd coincidence was that her husband was the pilot of a helicopter that crashed. It wasn't the first time he had crashed and, in fact, John had analysed the first crash and was able to show that it was not pilot error. But the really strange thing was that I also met the pilot's grandfather at the mining museum and promised that I would let him know when the investigation report was published. The family are worried that the pilot will be blamed for the crash. I'm sorry Suisan, I didn't mean to bother you with all this, but it's one of the reasons I want to look through John's files to see what he had written about the previous accident."

"That's alright Bran, remember that I lived with John's enthusiasm for his work, and for understanding these causal factors as he called them, for decades. I think the guitar lady has recognised you and is coming over. Introduce me Bran, it will be nice to meet her." Bran rose from his seat as Sandra approached, with that same smile.

"Hullo Sandra, what a pleasant surprise and impressive guitar playing by the way, I really enjoyed it. This is Suisan Morgan. Suisan this is Sandra Peel."

"Hullo Dr Sage, or can I call you Bran since you are calling me by my first name?" Sandra had that same intensity in her eyes that he remembered as she looked at Bran but then she turned to Suisan and held out her hand. "Hullo Suisan, if I'm not mistaken I think we are both grieving widows, I'm very sorry about your husband. I find the music helps me to stop thinking about Peter and all my regrets. Those are the worst things, my regrets about what I did or didn't do; if only this and if only that. I'm glad you liked the music Bran, are you a fan of jazz?" Sandra settled into the chair beside Suisan.

"We were just talking about jazz, I do like the smooth, *kind of blue*, style but the wilder, what I describe as confused styles, usually leave me a bit cold." Bran was about to continue when Suisan spoke to Sandra.

"I really enjoyed your playing Sandra, and music does sooth my pains as well. Do you play here every week?"

"Yes, I do, our trio practice several times a week, and we play at various clubs on Fridays and Saturdays but this is our regular venue. I know the owners and we always have an appreciative audience; makes a difference to know that, to know that people are listening to you." Sandra had turned her head and was looking at Bran when she said this. Suisan picked up the chemistry and smiled at both Sandra and Bran. Sandra continued. "Jazz is about improvisation and the many styles, which in some ways are really only labels for the commercial people to arrange products on their shelves, allow different kinds of improvisation. We improvise because we want to discover, so when I perform on stage, while there might be an audience who are discovering, it's my discovery that's just as important to me. And I think that's true of most jazz musicians. I want to come away from a performance with a new discovery about myself, I want to surprise myself." Sandra gestured with her hands springing apart as she said this. "What you call confused style Bran might be the musician, the artist, on a journey of discovery. Does that make sense?" Suisan answered first.

"Yes, it does make sense Sandra and it's so refreshing to hear what you are saying. I feel a strong empathy for what you are saying. So, playing music helps you find yourself, your inner self?" Sandra responded with enthusiasm; they were on the same wavelength.

"Call it your inner self or your soul, but it's the part that isn't out there doing this and that, punching away at life every day, trying to make sense of what happens around you. It's the part of me that learns without trying, or rather can learn without trying, without reading or observing. It's all about inner processing and music switches that on for me." Sandra paused for a few moments, digesting her own words. "Playing music, improvising music, helps me discover myself, it really does. Not in a way that I could easily describe in words but more about giving me an inner peace, a self confidence that being who I am is enough. When I play I'm in the moment, as they say, but sometimes it's like I rise above myself and become part of the audience. That can feel weird and yet very real too. Sharing empathy with my audience."

Suisan and Sandra continued their dialogue for several minutes, each seeming to reinforce the other's energy and stimulate creative thoughts. Both moved their hands expressively as they spoke. Bran recognised this. He experienced something similar with Sam and Chloe, and the other band members. He excused himself and went to the bar to pay for their lunch. Looking back at the two women, he felt a comfort that their grieving was being eased by their personal sharing; at least he hoped it was. Women are so much better at this than men, thought Bran. He wondered whether he should say anything about meeting Ron Flintworth, Peter's grandfather; would it spoil the atmosphere? Maybe, but, yes of course he should. Back at the table, the two women apologised for not letting Bran get a word in edgeways. Bran laughed and explained that he enjoyed listening to them talk, exchanging views. They were reaching each other, connecting.

"It's ok really, and it sounded very creative. I'm so glad that you could meet and share your thoughts, your personal stories. What amazing serendipity, don't you think? As an engineer, and musician by the way, I can identify with the things you describe; the need for empathy, how creativity comes from just being. Sometimes if I stop struggling with a problem, it seems to solve itself and the solution turns up at my doorstep; very strange."

"Bran plays in a band called Orion, Sandra; hope you don't mind me sharing that Bran?"

"No of course not Suisan. We are very eclectic but our next concert will feature about 25 love songs by Bob Dylan. All very intense, very emotional Sandra." She smiled at him; the smile said *I know what you mean*. Bran continued, he felt that now was the moment. "Sandra, after we met last week, I visited the mining museum in Somerset, doing some ancestry research, and I met Peter's grandfather, Ron Flintworth. I told him that I would let him know when the initial accident investigation was complete, published, and what the findings were. Would you like me to share that with you as well Sandra?"

"Yes of course, I would appreciate that very much Bran, thank you. Actually, Ron did mention that to his daughter, Peter's mother Sophie, and she phoned to tell me, so I did hear that you had promised that Bran. These things can take a long time though, can't they?"

"The full report will probably take years but there might be a short summary in the public domain in a few weeks. I will let you know Sandra." It was time for Bran and Suisan to make their way to Suisan's home so they both said goodbye to Sandra, leaving her to return to making music. Bran would have liked to have stayed and listen to Sandra, talk with her about music. They now had two common interests and he thought that their roads would cross again soon, on both accounts, or at least he hoped so.

164

Back at the house, Suisan had put together two boxes of John's files for Bran to take with him.

"This is all I could find on accidents Bran and I suspect this is all that John has, or had, sorry. You are welcome to go through the filing cabinets in his office if you think there might be more.

"No, this will be good Suisan. I'll let you have them back when I have finished with them."

"I'm happy for you to keep them Bran. They won't get used here and I know that you will look after them. There is also more material on his research, old and new, so please come back and help me sort it out, will you?"

"Thanks Suisan, yes I will, in a few weeks maybe?" Bran reached out and gave Suisan a hug as he was leaving.

"It was good to meet Sandra today Bran. She seems an interesting woman and she lives nearby. I think I might ask her for some refresh piano lessons. Oh, and good luck with your ancestry research; I hope you can build that picture of Henry and Sarah you talked about. How about writing their story, bring them back to life?"

"Write their story, now there's an idea; not sure I'd be any good at that and, anyway, I'm rather too busy with engineering. Thanks for meeting me Suisan and please take care."

Bran drove back home with several things competing for attention in his mind; awoken memories of good times with John and Suisan Morgan; curiosity about what he might find in the accident files; ancestry research and the idea of writing a story; Sandra and her music. They floated around in his mind, coming to the fore, retreating to the rear but her music seemed to be there all the time. Then he forced himself to think about the week ahead – the talk with Geoff Scrag about the Holtan HoneyB on Monday, review the accident material and get back to Stuart on Tuesday; the Claston flight simulation trial including Jim's new vortex wake model on Wednesday; the safety agency wanting to meet with Tobias and him to discuss the Skycruiser2 problem on Friday. Bran would often jokingly say to himself – *thank God I'm an engineer*; although he didn't believe in a God, the sentiment was that focussing on solving technical problems had a powerful effect of releasing him from emotional entanglements and wandering thought patterns that often led nowhere; or at least that's how it seemed. After a while his mind turned to the Orion practice on Friday. He recalled that Oliver said that he would send ideas on interpreting the symbolism in Dylan's music before the meeting. He also needed to work on another of his concert songs, but wasn't sure which one. Then he remembered that he wanted to try and meet with Chloe for lunch on Thursday. *"I do hope she can make it,"* he said to himself, *"I do need to talk with her about my dreaming and I don't want to leave it till after the band meeting."* And thinking about music brought his mind back to Sandra and her guitar playing; *"she was very good,"* he thought.

Monday morning 5.28 and Bran woke from a long, deep sleep. *"What, no dream,"* he whispered to himself, *"I wonder what triggers them; must ask Chloe,"* he wrote in his dream book. Later, 8.30 and the TLeM was done and Bran called Jos in; "can you find out about a Dr Francis Clerk at the University of

Slatchen, and print off any articles that appeared in the aviation press about the helicopter accident at Timly a couple of weeks ago; thanks Jos."

The teleconference with Geoff Scrag on the issues that Holtan were having with their HoneyB helicopter was scheduled for 1400. Bran asked Roger, Colin and Felicity to join the meeting. He needed their inputs to decide whether they could take this new work on. He was also aware that the HoneyB had some of the same features as the Odona, so wanted all ears on this discussion. Holtan were developing a military version of the HoneyB, featuring a computerised control law that applied control inputs to stop the aircraft exceeding its flight envelope limits. Holtan had named this the flight envelope protection system, or FEPS for short. In most helicopters, it was the pilot's responsibility to monitor how closely the aircraft was flying to its limits, usually by scanning the cockpit instruments. In the military version of the HoneyB, Holtan had developed this system to allow pilots to fly tactical missions without having to monitor instruments; they could keep their eyes looking outside while flying close to the ground and around obstacles. If the pilot pulled too much normal acceleration, the 'g', or turned with too much sideslip, the computer would send control inputs to the rotors to prevent the limits being exceeded. 'Too much' meant if the g or sideslip exceeded the operational limits, defined in the flight manual, when the risk of structural damage or loss of control increased significantly. Fixed-wing aircraft, both military and civil had been operating with envelope-limiting control functions for decades so the rotary-wing industry had some catching up to do.

Geoff Scrag explained to Bran and his team that the FEPS had not functioned as intended on one test flight and the aircraft had entered a spiral dive. The pilot had only just

167

managed to recover control and avoided a crash. Geoff explained; "it seems that the pilot was turning hard, pulling g and pedalling sideslip to increase the turn rate, when suddenly the aircraft started to turn faster, entered a spiral dive and the pilot lost control for a few moments. He eventually managed to level the aircraft and recover control. We have the flight records, the pilot's control movements, aircraft motions and the FEPS inputs but it's a real puzzle that our engineers are struggling with. So, we wondered if you could help us to re-create this loss of control incident on your flight simulator? Our engineers could install the HoneyB flight model and help your team set up the simulator and run the trial. It could take a few days, so what do you think Bran?"

Bran wanted to know more about the fidelity of the flight model; how well did it capture the behaviour of the real aircraft, particularly in these extreme conditions.

"How good is your flight model at replicating this kind of behaviour Geoff? Have you replayed the flight data through your simulation?"

"Yes, we have done that and we've tried to replicate the incident on our flight simulator but, as you know, it is a fixed-base simulator and pilots complain that they need the body motion cues, so that they feel the changing accelerations, to react correctly. You have a motion simulator Bran. The bottom line Bran is that we aren't sure if our flight model behaves like the real aircraft outside the normal flight envelope; we haven't flown those test conditions in the aircraft yet. But, we are wondering if the pilot would react differently when he has those vestibular motion cues."

Bran turned to Roger. "What's the schedule on our simulator over the next few weeks Roger?" Roger opened his notebook.

"Phase 1 of the current project should complete early next week, then we have a few days of scheduled maintenance, followed by a couple of weeks when the University use the sim for their annual master's student projects. But often the students are not ready for the slots they've been given, so we find ourselves trying to fit them in over the summer. You may recall that we had this out with the academics a couple of years ago. Now they dock the student's mark if they fail to meet the simulator time slot. Remember, it was your idea Bran." Bran did remember; he considered it was good practice to introduce a realistic schedule pressure into the student projects. Roger continued. "Then there's the new work we discussed last week and phase 2 of the current project is due to start when phase 1 is fully reported. So, it's a busy summer but we could explore doing the maintenance over the weekend."

Bran agreed that they could support a preliminary investigation using the flight simulator but he wanted his engineers to see evidence for how well the HoneyB flight model compared with flight test data in normal flight conditions and the incident flight condition. Having an accurate flight model was critical to being able to draw conclusions from flight simulation and Bran wanted to know what Holtan might conclude from a trial on the FS2 simulator. The facility had an excellent reputation for its authenticity, its fidelity, that Bran did not want to compromise. They would help Holtan try to solve their problem but he emphasised to Geoff that an assessment of the accuracy of the HoneyB flight model needed to be undertaken before making a commitment to a trial on the flight simulator. Geoff agreed to provide the data and Roger would look at clearing space in the simulator schedule in anticipation. Before ending the teleconference, Bran wanted to mention the Odona accident.

"Geoff, just to fill you in, we've been asked by the

Investigation Branch to help them with the Odona crash; thought it worth mentioning that before we finish the call."

"Yes, Stuart Carter told me he would be speaking to you and of course we will cooperate fully with their investigation. Such a damn tragedy Bran, and the Odona has such a very good safety record; only one other fatal accident in the last 10 years and that was caused by pilot error."

After the call, Bran and his Tech leaders reviewed their actions to take this project forward. Felicity would scope out the resources needed for the preliminary investigation and send Holtan a contract proposal. Roger would receive the HoneyB simulation validation data from Holtan and check its veracity; verify that their model could be used to simulate the incident scenario. Colin would find a slot in the flight simulator timetable to host the HoneyB trial. After the Tech leaders left, Bran reflected on Geoff's comment about the Odona safety record. Although it was good compared with other helicopters it was poor compared with typical light fixed-wing aircraft. Bran estimated that the Odona fleet had accumulated about 2 million flying hours in ten years, so that's one fatal accident every million flying hours in just that one type. One in a million, is that safe enough? Bran asked himself. He knew that more than 70% of helicopter accidents involved human errors in one way or another, often pilots making the wrong decisions or taking the wrong actions.

Did Peter Peel make a mistake, Bran wondered? Sometimes, it seemed as if the pilot was not sufficiently engaged with the risks of entering dangerous flight condition. Did this make the human the weak link in the safety chain? John Morgan certainly thought so and had written several controversial articles on the subject. Perhaps a human's very best is not good enough when it comes to safety. And yet flying was, by far, the safest form of transport; that's what the

170

statistics showed. In one of his articles, John had written that, *"flight-critical systems are designed to have a flight-hour failure probability of 10^{-9}, that's one catastrophic failure every 1 billion flying hours, or the failure is extremely improbable in system-failure jargon. Pilots are clearly flight-critical, so do they meet the failure probability standard? The simple answer is no, they don't, and the accident statistics show that pilots too often fail. They may fail to notice something going wrong, or fail to diagnose the problem correctly, fail to make the right decision or fail to take the right action. The human is the weakest link in the safety chain."* John was making the case for better training and better automation aids to help pilots manage difficult situations but his campaign for improved pilot reliability drew a lot of criticism. Interestingly, it was not from pilots themselves but from operators who employed the pilots. John's obsession with safety had rubbed off on Bran, and he was developing a keen interest in safety in all aspects of life.

In his research on coal mining, Bran had discovered that, around 1872 when his great-grandfather Henry worked as a hewer in Camerton, there were about 1000 fatalities in mining accidents every year, across the country. There were about 400,000 people working in the mines in those days, so that worked out that a miner had a 1 in 400 chance of being killed at work in any year. Coal mining was the most dangerous industry to be working in during the 19th century. There was a national obsession with coal to fuel the industrial revolution and serve to expand Great Britain's global trading empire. Safety for mine workers took a turn for the better with the Coal Mines Regulation Act of 1872, applicable to coal, stratified ironstone, shale and fire clay. The Act addressed the employment of women, young persons and children; wages; the need for dual shafts; the certification of managers; mine inspections and it included a raft of general and special rules

171

that would change the mining industry forever. Accidents would continue to occur for the next 100 years and more of coal mining in the country, but the regulations set the stage for the kind of investigations that took place, inevitably leading to the discovery of human error after human error as the main causal factor. When people do dangerous things, whether its digging coal or flying aeroplanes, the margins for error can be very small, and when the margins are eroded, there are inevitable consequences. "Damn, this is depressing stuff, but also enticing," thought Bran, if one believed they could make a difference, improve safety. Just then, Jos knocked on the door and walked in.

"I can't locate Dr Clerk at Slatchen but there's plenty on Dr Oats. I printed out his biography and summaries of his research, and I've found a couple of articles on the Odona crash and printed them out for you as well; hope that's enough but let me know if you need more."

"Thanks Jos." Bran stared at the article in front of him, the words glowing like burning coal, '*the pilot and all three passengers in the Odona died in the crash*'; then came their names, '*... and Dr Francis Clerk, a researcher at the University of Slatchen. They were being transported to a meeting on greenhouse gas emissions at a country house in the Scottish Highlands.*' Bran sat up with a jolt; this cannot be a coincidence, he thought. He asked Jos to see if she could find out about the meeting and she soon came back with a programme for the joint Industry-NERC symposium on the impact of greenhouse gas emissions on climate change. Dr Clerk's talk was titled '*When is Enough, Enough?*' He was scheduled to present on the first day and then participate in a panel debate on the subject. Clearly that never happened, thought Bran. He looked through the programme and found a keynote talk by Dr Clive Oats on the second day titled '*Getting* *the Balance Right; how to reduce greenhouse gas emissions without damaging the Industry?'* I wonder if he gave that talk after what happened, thought Bran? Jos came into the room again.

"I've downloaded the presentations from the NERC website, shall I print them out?"

"Can you just print out the ones by Dr Clerk on day 1 and Dr Oats on day 2 for the moment please Jos?" Of course, there was no presentation from Dr Clerk but Bran quickly scanned the material in Oats's presentation. "Can you email me a copy of this one please Jos."

Later that day Bran sat at home, playing his guitar, waiting for Mary's call. He was working on a new song that reminded him that the way is long but the end is near. In the song, Bran was looking for the stars by which he navigated, beyond Orion, that might settle his restlessness.

Sweet shiny leather 'neath the corporate sun

Tangled metal barriers catching men on the run

Bands can't play that tune no more the pain is too intense

The audience they look quizzical, the music don't make sense

So underneath her bonnet the engine's ticking over

Flowers still grow in the field even though it's thick with clover

My songs are marching onward, are they out of control?

Perhaps they are but I'm not sure, they're coming from my soul

I'm trying to reach the starting point to tell another tale

But have this huge distraction, ideas coming in like junk mail

Please help me baby, you know that it's my fate

To be alone in the wilderness tryin to negotiate, to navigate

Searching for my stars amongst the heavens

So I can tell this tale before it's too late

This is as far as Bran had got with the song; the phone was ringing and he felt his heart jump and he reached out to speak with the most important star by which he navigated. They talked about the things they had been doing over the weekend, Mary at the retreat in Yosemite and Bran visiting Suisan. But Bran needed to tell Mary about Dr Clerk.

"The helicopter was taking them to a meeting on greenhouse gas emissions in Scotland. Dr Clerk was to give a

174

talk titled *When is Enough Enough*? You can only imagine what he might have been going to say. Meanwhile, his supervisor, Dr Oats, who he alerted you to in his letter, was due to give another talk on *Getting the Balance Right*. These guys were not on the same page Mary."

"You should hand this over to the police Bran, it sounds very suspicious. Do you know what caused the accident?"

"Not yet, the accident investigation folk have sent me some material and asked for my input, but there isn't much to go on yet. They have taken the wreckage back to their headquarters to examine it for any evidence of technical faults, or clues as to what might have happened. I'm due to talk with them tomorrow. Mary, they will be in dialogue with the police so I think I need to tell them all I know about the letter and see how they want to handle that. Would that be ok with you?"

"Yes of course, that sounds the best thing to do. Meanwhile I will send a copy of the letter to the NERC, and see what they want to do about it. They should already know about the accident of course. Maybe my imagination is getting ahead of my reasoning but I'm feeling rather suspicious of this Dr Clive Oats. Can you get a copy of his and Dr Clerk's presentation?"

"Yes, I'll send Oats's presentation as an email attachment but Clerk's was not on the NERC website. Maybe we can find it at Slatchen; shall I explore that Mary?"

"That would be very helpful Bran, thanks."

Bran and Mary talked for some time, sharing details of their lives, lived apart now for several weeks and the strange coincidence that brought their worlds together; the death of Francis Clerk in the crash of the Odona.

"Wow, that's not supposed to happen." Bran spoke out loud as he woke with his wet dream still filling his mind. Bran seeing Henry and Sarah making love in his dream, or was he making love? But it wasn't Mary, it was her but she was fading away to the call of a raven; "who are you?" Bran asked but no answer came; she belonged to an inner world where he lived on the edge of consciousness. It was Tuesday and Bran realised that he hadn't tried to arrange a meeting with Chloe to talk about dreams; he must do that today but would he talk about this dream? He would do a lot of other things today, tomorrow and the rest of the week. The intense multi-tasking of an engineer's workload appealed to Bran; the engagement with people, the problem solving, the existential pleasures of discovery, the advancement of knowledge. But these dreams were different, they seemed to be messages from within, or maybe without.

How could he connect his real world with this imaginary world? He felt the answer lay in his ancestry research and he decided to free up time the following weekend to return to this. One thing he felt sure about, that he would not be able to solve his dream 'problem' with his engineering tools. He recalled John Morgan talking once about how he saw the differences between mathematicians, physicists and engineers; a perspective guaranteed to provoke discussion and argument around the college table. They were all three familiar with the same theories but mathematicians do not concern themselves with meaning, physicists did not explore applications and it took an engineer to find meaning through application. But they all needed each other to bridge the frontiers where the three domains came together. Bran now wondered about the frontiers between these 'hard' disciplines and human life, expressed in disciplines like psychology and philosophy. He was reminded of Chloe's comment about Candice Pert's Molecules of Emotion and her dream research. Might the answer lie there?

Following the TLeM, Bran called Stuart Carter to discuss the Odona crash. He agreed to send a copy of the letter from Dr Clerk, and Stuart would brief the police investigation. There was no new information from the wreckage but Stuart had obtained radar data from two different sources and had been able to re-construct the flight trajectory of the aircraft from take-off until it disappeared below the hills to the north of Timly. Bran agreed that FS2 would apply their flight control re-construction algorithms that estimated how the pilot's controls might have been used to fly the trajectory. They would be able to derive rough estimates using their generic flight model, scaled to the Odona, but, if they could install and use Holtan's Odona flight model, the results would be more accurate and any conclusions better informed. Bran would follow this up with Geoff Scrag. The rest of the day was spent reviewing progress on three other FS2 projects including the work towards a new intensive Masters course on flight control and stability. The 4-week course would be taken in a recorded on-line problem-based format including weekly Q&A sessions for participating students. The course would start in September, and FS2 had twelve different organisations signed up with a likely audience of 60 engineers. It would be the first of its kind, a mould-breaker as Felicity Freeman liked to describe it. Felicity, as Tech Lead for CPD, had conceived this approach as she had seen the way the FS2 engineers presented their work at meetings. She was keen to develop an idea.

"We have some incredible talent here Bran, and I'd like us to share it with Industry and Academia and make some investment money for FS2 at the same time." She had assembled a plan and presented it at a TLeM the previous year. All were enthusiastic to make this happen. The course material was due to be finalised by the end of June, after which Felicity had arranged for a creative-arts company to produce the final digital package. Felicity believed that, "the engineers who take this course will be hungry to learn, and will make huge strides in their knowledge and understanding and, through the many practical exercises, be able to learn by doing; active learning is the key." With this project, Felicity was a visionary on a mission and the FS2 engineers had been falling over each other to make their contributions. She had a charisma that she would use to win over doubters. Bran felt very precious about his Tech Leads but there was something special about Felicity. She seemed to have insights that the other Tech Leads didn't; maybe because she is a woman, he wondered?

The flight simulation supporting the Claston Skycruiser3 trial was due to begin on Wednesday and a lot of time was going into preparation, and particularly Jim Waterhill's new wing vortex wake model. The FS2 office was buzzing and this was the way that Bran liked it. Sometimes, the busier it gets the more reserve energy we seem to have, he thought. But he also wanted to look at John Morgan's files, particularly on the previous helicopter crash piloted by Peter Peel. The aircraft, similar size to the Odona but different manufacturer, had suffered a tail rotor failure when flying in cruise at about 120kts. Peter brought the aircraft under control and set up a descent towards a lake at about 70kts airspeed. If he flew any slower the aircraft would begin to spin out of control because the tail rotor was no longer balancing the engine torque. At 70kts and above, Peter could sideslip the aircraft so that the aerodynamic load on the vertical fin balanced the torque. So, he would need to shut the engine off before he did slow down, and rapidly manoeuvre the aircraft into autorotation, the equivalent of a glide in a fixed-wing aeroplane, by pulling the cyclic stick back, lowering the collective and let the airflow windmill the rotor. He would need to complete this complex manoeuvre in about three seconds. If he took any longer, the rotor would slow down and lose lift, with the aircraft descending and becoming uncontrollable.

When stable in autorotation, to maintain the same airspeed, Peter would need to increase the rate of descent so that his glide slope angle would be about 15 degrees, about three times steeper than a gliding aeroplane. As he approached the water, Peter needed to slow down by pulling back on the cyclic stick and then, about three seconds before the aircraft hit the water, he would pull up on his collective lever, increasing rotor thrust and rapidly reducing the rate of descent. The problem was that this action would result in the aircraft yawing in the opposite direction to the way it turned if he applied collective when the engine was engaged. So, Peter had to approach the water yawed to the right so that pulling the lever turned the nose left to line up with the direction of flight; a very difficult manoeuvre which Peter executed perfectly. If he had got this wrong the aircraft would have hit the water with a sideways velocity and likely turned over.

"He was a very good pilot," Bran whispered to himself as he read John's report. Bran could find nothing in John's files on the vortex ring state however, a possible cause of the more recent Odona crash. Recovery from vortex ring would have been impossible at low altitude. Pilots could be taken into dangerous situations by failures of the machine but sometimes they took themselves there. Surely Peter Peel was not one of those?

179

Wednesday morning at 5.28 and another day begins for Bran Sage, but no dream to wake up to, at least not one that was still alive. What turns them on, he wondered, and what turns them off?

The test pilot pushed the thrust levers to takeoff power and the aircraft began to accelerate along the runway. After 20 seconds the aircraft passed through V_1; if one of the two engines failed after V_1, the pilot would need to continue with the takeoff run. At 30 seconds the co-pilot announced V_2; if an engine failed after V_2 the pilot would be able to control the aircraft at takeoff. At 35 seconds the co-pilot announced V_R, and the pilot pulled back on the control stick to rotate the aircraft and begin the takeoff. As the aircraft climbed through 200 feet, the port engine failed, the thrust reducing to zero within one second, causing the aircraft to yaw, then roll, sharply to the left. The pilot waited the obligatory one second before applying right pedal and stick to stop the yawing and level the wings. In another three seconds the starboard engine had automatically increased power sufficient to maintain airspeed and climb rate and the pilot had regained control of the aircraft, balancing the asymmetric thrust with a boot-full of right rudder. There were no cries of anguish or wails of fear from the passengers because there were no passengers. This was a flight simulation of the Skycruiser3 being tested with Jim Waterhill's new vortex wake model, and the test data was already being processed by the engineers in the control room.

During the de-brief, the Claston pilots discussed the differences they experienced between the normal and Waterhill wakes. They had not been told about the different wakes, a standard practice in test flying to minimise pilot expectations or to put them off trying to guess the cause of a problem. Pilots should deal with the effects and engineers will deal with the causes was the mantra that guided the FS2 simulation trials.

"The initial response is very similar but, as the aircraft reached its maximum sideslip angle, for the second case, the aircraft yawed to starboard on its own and I didn't need to apply so much pedal. But I had already applied a boot-full which turned out to be too much so I over-controlled and had to reduce my pedal input." Jim could now explain what was going on based on his new wake model.

"Because the Skycruiser3 wing has these large adjustable winglets extending vertically at the wing tips, the maximum wing lift moves inboard and the vortices that spring from the high lift flaps, that are extended at takeoff, increase in strength. As the sideslip builds up, the vortex from the starboard wing can collide with the tail and that's what you experienced. The top side of the counter-clockwise vortex applied a corrective load on the vertical tail, so your rudder input was too large to correct the yaw." Jim drew a diagram on the whiteboard to show what was going on. He started to write an equation on the board but Ralph dissuaded him.

"Ok, got it, said the pilot, this would need to go into the training manual so we learn to do it right; but only if this is correct and how do we know it is correct? And please don't try to use maths to persuade me." The pilot looked at the engineers around the table one at a time. Test pilots never missed the opportunity to challenge what the boffins had done, especially if what the boffins were saying made pilots change their learned responses. Jim looked somewhat taken aback by the pilot's forthright question and looked at Roger and Ralph with a strained expression. Ralph answered.

"We are not sure if it is correct and we'll need more time to validate the model. But we are also looking at the loads on the tail to see if they have exceeded safe levels." The Claston engineer Juergen Gmelin had joined the team for the trial and stepped in.

"I have asked our engineers back at Claston to review the wind tunnel data that we gathered to support the design. I suspect that we haven't tested this specific configuration and flight condition since there were changes during the development and we didn't go back to the tunnel. We may need to do that, go back to the tunnel."

The engineers were examining the aerodynamic loads data from the flight simulation. It seemed that the Waterhill wake had moved very close to the tail when the sideslip reached its maximum value after the engine failure, but the pilot's overcontrolling increased the tail loads beyond the safety limit. Before the trial, Jim had given a presentation to Juergen explaining how he had developed his new wake model. Bran had popped in for a few minutes to see how things were going. He witnessed the high intensity of detailed technical dialogue; engineers using aeronautical physics, computational fluid dynamics, to model complexities and create a version of reality. This was virtual engineering, practiced by amazing engineers at the top of their game, thought Bran. Innovation and creativity woven together and conceptualised by connected brains. Few people recognised the kind of creative things that go on at the high end of engineering design and analysis, and the engineers themselves are oblivious to this ignorance, immersed as they are in the existential wonders of human thought.

Bran telephoned Chloe to ask if she was free to meet for lunch on Thursday and talk dreams. No, she wasn't but, "how about Sunday Bran, I can make us a light lunch if you come around at midday?" That sounded even better to Bran as things were heating up in the Skycruiser3 trial. This also meant that he had more time to review his dreams on the weekend before meeting with Chloe. He felt it would be worth doing some homework before meeting her. He wondered if he would have any more dreams before they met up.

Quickly, I must run quickly, we must all run quickly, please God, no, don't let this be. "Sarah I'm alright, I wasn't in the cage." Thank you for saving my man, thank you. "Can I help you? Bran shouted." She looked up and put her hands to her face. "You have helped me, she cried." The three people were sitting together and there were tears, but they were safe. They didn't need Bran. They don't need me now, not just now.

Jeez, that was more than real; I could smell the fumes in the damp morning air and feel the peoples' fear. And I was with them, she could hear me and see me. She said that I had helped her. How had I helped her? Bran collected his thoughts and began to write down all that he dreamt. It was a coal mine, miners were running towards the pit head, shouting and she was with them looking desperate, but it was her, auburn hair flowing, bouncing over her shoulders as she ran along. Then he appeared carrying a younger man, a teenager, and running towards her. Other people were coming out of the pit shaft some carrying others, some stumbling along and crashing to the ground and moaning. There was a lot of moaning. They were sitting together and he was crying with his arms around them both. The young man seemed to be joking but he had hurt his arm. I had asked her if I could help and she had looked up and spoke to me; '*you have helped me.*' She held her face in her hands. Her name was Sarah. He had said he was alright, that he wasn't in the cage. What cage? Was that Henry?

Ok, that's it, thought Bran, time to get on with being Bran Sage, not some character in a dream. Thursday was a very busy day and Bran was glad to be back in the aeronautical saddle reviewing projects, developing plans, proposals for future work, and most of all solving problems. Keeping FS2 small and beautiful was a continual challenge as so many opportunities were out there. Their success rate with submitted proposals was more than 80% and the work flow had been steady for about five years; the team was stable and growing capability through taking on particularly challenging work. He would need to look carefully at the Skycruiser2 project that Claston wanted help with. The Safety Agency wanted an independent review, but sometimes it seemed as if they had already made their minds up and were looking for someone else to play the bad cop. On the other hand, it was an opportunity to get involved in the latest flight-deck technology, something that had major safety implications; right up Bran's street.

The intensity of FS2 engineering practice continued through Thursday and Friday. Staff from the Safety Agency joined the Skycruiser3 simulation on the Friday and Bran held a separate meeting with them and Tobias Hamel in the afternoon to discuss the Skycruiser2 issue. Pilots from one airline had complained about the way information was presented to them on the cockpit instruments; they became confused and had to go-around on several occasions because they weren't sure if their aircraft was on a stable approach. A stable approach was achieved when the aircraft was on the correct flight path, following a line at 3 degrees to the horizontal, at constant speed and rate of descent. If a pilot had not achieved this stable condition when descending through 1000 feet about the ground, they should execute a go-around immediately, so abort the landing and fly a circuit and be allocated the next available approach slot by air traffic control. The airline concerned had made proposals for a change but this would require re-certification and Claston's view was that the airline should improve their training procedures. They were at an impasse. Bran agreed to send Roger to the pilot training centre to get a better understanding of the pilots' concerns. He would do this in the following week and report back.

Bran stood looking out of his office window but only saw what was happening inside his head. A week full of drama and surprise. The meeting with Suisan and Sandra on Sunday seemed a lifetime ago, as did the news about Dr Clerk's death in the Odona crash. Then there was his phone call with Mary, his guiding star, and the follow-up with Stuart Carter from the Investigation Branch; the evolving work with Claston on their Skycruiser aircraft and the new project with Holtan on the military version of the HoneyB; Felicity's problem-based learning course taking shape. He was particularly pleased that Jim Waterhill's wake model had led to a re-think of the safety case for the Skycruiser3 certification. The failure situation was only a remote possibility but a safe recovery must be possible with normal pilot reactions. That was how the certification standards described it, but what was normal for what might be the weakest link in the chain? With every working week, our knowledge and understanding grow but new questions emerge that require new answers. Like John Archibald Wheeler had written, *as the island of our knowledge grows, so does the shoreline of our ignorance*. This expanding frontier of discovery was a powerful stimulus for scientists and engineers. But now attention must turn to music and the other side of Bran Sage.

As Bran drove over to the Arts Centre he reflected on Oliver's take on Dylan's use of symbolism and metaphor. Oliver had suggested this as a form of creative art, encouraging the listener or the viewer to see beyond the simple messages in black and white, of right and wrong, good and bad. We seek symbols to give expression to our own hopes, dreams and fears. They make us work at understanding which chimed nicely with Bran's pursuit of understanding as an engineer. Metaphors help people to think, Oliver had said. "So, for a start, let's talk about how our songs are helping us to think." These were his instructions for the Orion meeting on Friday night. The *Love Sick* concert was scheduled for Saturday 10th June at the Arts Centre, in aid of Medicine Sans Frontiers who were sending a speaker along to talk about their work and receipt of the Nobel Peace Prize the year before. The MSF International President, Dr James Orbinski, had said in his acceptance speech that, "*we also speak out on behalf of the people we treat and act to expose injustice.*" The speech was deeply heartfelt and drew the attention of Orion with words like, "*Let me say this very clearly: the humanitarian act is the most apolitical of all acts, but if its actions and its morality are taken seriously, it has the most profound of political implications. And the fight against impunity is one of these implications.*"

Sam had proposed raising funds for MSF and all Orion agreed. *Love-Sick* promised to be their most exciting concert yet. When all had gathered at the Arts Centre, Oliver introduced the theme of the importance of symbolism and metaphor in making sense of the world and Dylan's lyrics. He was a student of political science but also a philosopher.

"I think creative artists use both to describe what they see beyond the horizon and within the soul. You see I am already using the horizon metaphor and the soul symbol to make a point. The within and without can help us, at least try to help us, resolve the tensions between opposites like good and bad, up and down and I think Dylan uses songs as vehicles for homing in on our values, shaped by these ubiquitous tensions. All of us struggle making sense of life and love, particularly

186

love. So, with a focus on love, I'll kick us off."

Oliver: "*Blonde on Blonde* is one of my favourite albums for fantastic images, weird and wonderful characters and a feast of metaphors. There is a line in the song *Visions of Johanna* that stays with me. It goes *"the ghost of electricity howls in the bones of her face"*. I think this is Louise who held the handful of rain in the previous verse. The whole song is full of scenes that each make the leading character, maybe Dylan himself, more and more aware that he is missing Johanna dreadfully. The shadows on his face in the dimly lit room revealing an expression that howls with pain, the pain of losing Johanna, or maybe never finding her, never finding the woman in his dream. This little boy who is lost ends up with his conscious exploding, and all he's left with are the *Visions of Johanna*. I sometimes feel my conscience exploding, when I try to make sense of the world around me. This was surely a song born in the chaos of the mid-1960s. But what would I know, I wasn't born until 1972, and only really picked up the echoes from the 60's when I was in my teens. Your turn Jacob."

Jacob: "Ok, the album *Infidels* came out in 1983, when you were just eleven Oli, but I'm old enough to remember its release and the reviews claiming Dylan was on yet another new road, a secular road. It follows up the triplet of Christian albums and it seems to pulsate with anger and pain, but also wonderful images. My selection is the second song on the album, *Sweetheart Like You*. Dylan keeps asking what is he or she doing in a dump like this? We are left to wonder where or what the dump might be. He notes the sweetheart has a cute hat, a crown of thorns perhaps, and a smile that's hard to resist; it's hard for us mortals to resist a messiah; scoundrels seeking refuge in patriotism as a last refuge to make sense of their lives. We must be prepared to make our case, stand strong, not give up if it hurts, *"play your harp until your lips bleed"*. Well, that's what it means to me, maybe because it reinforces my own perspective on human behaviour and helps me stay strong when others are hissing behind my back. It's pretty emotional just talking about this you know."

Chloe: "Like Oliver, I'm going back to the heady mid-60's, to *Blonde on Blonde* and the song *I Want You*. I like Dylan's slow, Budokan-version, and I sing it even slower, sometimes getting lost in the simple words, the wanting so bad. Honestly though, I can't make sense of all the weird characters and kaleidoscope of images, like the lonesome organ grinder, or the silver saxophones, the cracked bells and washed out horns; maybe they are all sexual symbolism. But the key line for me is *"I wasn't born to lose you"*. So, he has lost her, or in my case him, and all the other stuff going on, these chaotic scenes just exacerbate the pain of his loss. Maybe the guilty undertaker had a role to play in his losing his lover and maybe he did take refuge with the chamber-maid, because she knew what he really wanted. So, that's it from me except I'll be needing you to harmonise in the chorus Bran, but you already know that, don't you?" Chloe looked at Bran with her sweet smile.

Georgia: "Me, I'm just on the road feeling lost on my journey through life cos I've experienced *Abandoned Love* and his Bobness sums it up nicely in this song. I think it was supposed to appear on the *Desire* album but eventually showed up on *Biograph* in the mid-80's. A few of the lines really resonate with my own feelings. Like when he sings, *"Everybody wearing a disguise to hide what they've got left behind their eyes"*. I've been there, hid my feelings, worn a false face, makes me cry to think about my vulnerability." Georgia paused to regain composure. "Sometimes, when I need strength to get through something, I can't find it even though I'm a strong person. My inner strength has fucked off somewhere, fighting with a ghost, leaving me to fend for myself." Georgia chuckles but she is crying and Chloe puts her arm around her; no words are needed. "One more, it's obvious I know, but I need reminding that you won't find treasure by searching. Problem is, I need to know how to find it, and old Bob is no help at all. Not sure I can do this song guys."

"This is what it's about Georgia, being real, and these songs help us find ourselves, with their lyrics and imagery. I can see its painful but I do hope you will stick with this one." Chloe was tuned in to what touched people and would always reach out to her friends.

Bran: "Thank you for that openness Georgia, I could feel your pain. I'd like to talk about a couple of things that got me thinking in the song *Journey through Dark Heat* from the *Street Legal* album, one of my favourites and I love performing it, as you guys know. First, it's in the line, *"she winds back the clock and she turns back the page of a book that no-one can write"*. Dylan seems to be singing about a lost love as he cries *'where are you tonight?'* throughout the song, but the idea of a book that no-one can write made me think about my ancestry research, me winding back the clock to the days when my great-grandad dug coal in Somerset, me trying to piece together a story. But surely no-one could write it, I couldn't write it, I only know when and where he was born, got married and died. The song is full of tension, like where he is fighting with the enemy within; just like your ghost Georgia. Now that really does mean something to me. My inner persecutor is always close by, wanting a fight, giving me constant anxiety. I hear its voice; you can do better, you can be better, you should be better, always on my tail, while I try to find my pathway to the stars. But if I got to the stars would

189

I be free of my persecutor within? I doubt it. There you are, make of it what you want."

"But you are in the stars Bran, with us lot in Orion." Georgia drew a chuckling from the group with her observation, which was spot on, as they say.

Sam: "Oooh, heavy stuff that dark heat, Bran, let's see if I can match it. Dylan used symbolism and metaphor regularly in his protest songs about social injustice, but I don't see him as a message man, or a bumper-sticker jockey, far from it. It's almost as though he is feeling the personal pain of people like Hollis Brown, Hattie Carroll and Rubin Carter or the luckless abandoned people and lonesome hearted lovers that the *chimes of freedom* are flashing for. *Abandoned Love* is a personal tale and so is my choice, and I think it's about the same person, as your song Georgia. I think it's about his wife Sara; they divorced in 1977. I think you're gonna do great with that song by the way Georgia. Any road, I've chosen that great love song, *Idiot Wind,* from *Blood on the Tracks.* I don't know a song that's as fully charged with emotion, the painful, despairing kind. It was *"gravity which pulled us down, and destiny which broke us apart".* So, Dylan blames the weakest of the four forces in nature for pulling him and Sara down and then to be broken by destiny. Does that mean he thinks it was destined to be, a *simple twist of fate* maybe? Is Dylan the lone soldier on the cross, like the soldier of mercy from that other great song, *No Time to Think*, suffering the same fate as Jesus Christ? Dylan is a great train enthusiast, not a rail buff, but rather using trains and railways to convey travelling, our journey, through life. So, we see the slow train coming and the box-car on fire, symbolising, I think, the journey ending. Perhaps the box-car that he claimed to have travelled in, as Elston Gunn from west to east, is burning; he wonders what the future holds now he realises, admits, that he's been an idiot." Sam pauses then looks around Orion with a grin on his face, "I'm planning to sing the New York version by the way."

Oliver thanked everyone for their work and they continued with their practising of those six songs, even more meaningful following their rich sharing. Later, after the pub, Chloe said goodnight to Bran and looked forward to seeing him on Sunday. "I'm particularly looking forward to hearing about your dreams Bran."

Bran arrived home late that night feeling exhausted from the week's work, but enlivened by Orion's discussions. There was a telephone message from Jenny at the Somerset Mining Museum. She had found some material that she thought would interest him. She would try to find time on Saturday to scan it and send in an email message.

"I wonder what she has found, Bran whispered to himself." He picked up his guitar and played a song he'd written.

How can I see the big picture, when I'm down a rabbit hole?

The detail can be so beautiful, but can also hurt your soul

Go right, then left, you know you've lost your way

But open your mind to see, no toll you'll have to pay

I'm not afraid of mystery, in fact it turns me on

Asking questions of real substance, your troubles will be gone

Look up, look down, both are the same, just parts of the bigger picture

And long before you've figured it out, you'll be far wiser and richer

Metaphors and symbolism can make life a richer one to live, for sure, if you can make enough sense of them. If you can allow the multitude of meanings to circulate, amazing creations can form in your mind, for use in your daily living. He wondered if coal miners could make sense of them. Another working week in the life of Bran Sage.

6. The Whistle Blows and the Ravens Cry

The air above Camerton valley was still and cool on Saturday morning. Friday's storm had receded, leaving a mist covering the lower levels. The head-frames from the Old and New Pits rose above the mist declaring human presence in the natural Somerset landscape. They also defined the place of the mining disaster on the previous day. All was quiet, even the rooks seemed to have woken up with an awareness 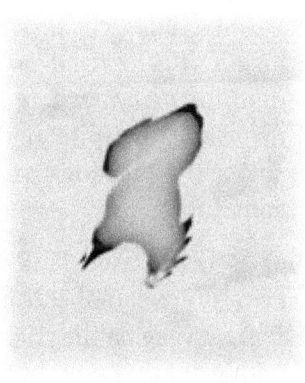 of the human tragedy below them and watched in silence. Within the mist, a group of men stood in a circle around the mine shaft. Arthur Riddle grasped the broken cable in his hands.

"Damn me, look at this cable." Arthur held the cable end out for all to see. Where it had broken, the frayed strands were hanging down; but, on half of the cable end, no fraying was visible. "Some bastard must 'ave cut this, probably last  night. Tis a vengeful act and its happened before, you remember poor Josh Parker was killed when the hemp rope broke. They suspected his bitter and jealous girlfriend, but it could not be proved. When they changed to using metal

193

cables, we thought this would never happen again. Jesus, who would do this?" The men studied the broken cable; Robert, Henry, George, Archie, Farnham, James – the working group - and Arthur who had joined them at the meetings during the week. James's brother William had died of his injuries in the cage fall. James had reached the fallen cage just as they were carrying William out, and had held his brother's hand all the way to the surface, where, sobbing he spoke quietly to him. *"Dear Will, I'll do all I can to make sure this never 'appens again; safe journey to the beyond brother and say hullo to dad for me."* Despite his grief, and perhaps because he found solace in the company of the group, James wanted to say something.

"I promised Will I would work to make things safer but how do we make things safe against vengeful criminals?" James was shaking his head and his face was deeply furrowed with grief and pain but his friends knew that he needed time to gather his thoughts. After a minute of silence, James spoke again. "Maybe we should secure the pithead area after the last shift of the day, with a fence and locked gate?" He looked at the others. Arthur spoke again.

"James, I'm so sorry about your Will, but let me be your new brother and I will work with you on making things safer. Both me and my brother John are hewers in Midsomer Norton and we know we need to push hard to get improvements in safety over there. I think you are lucky with your owner here in Camerton, she's on your side but I do believe that Jasper Crop who owns our mine doesn't give a shit about us miners. So, I'm with you brothers, and would like to be part of this working group, is that ok?". Robert didn't hesitate to support this request.

"I propose that Arthur join the working group, and if you are ok with this James, he can work with you on safety. I know

194

that no-one can replace Will, but safety is a big issue, and two can stand stronger than one. Are we all agreed that Arthur will join us?" A resounding aye burst out, men forging the camaraderie, building the courage needed to change the world, or at least a small part of it. Henry thought to himself that humans were unique in this respect, and working men particularly so. In his dreams, he knew that great things, beyond reach for one man alone, were possible when men worked together. Working men's dreams can come true, when shared. His thoughts turned to Colin Amble who had broken both legs in the cage fall; he was being treated at his home by the local doctor. He shared his thoughts with the group.

"Lady Fernhill will need to replace Colin Amble as manager of the Camerton mine and this is an opportunity to make sure the person is trained and applies the new regulations on inspections properly. Surely the mechanical integrity of the cages and cables should be checked every day before people are carried? That is another guard against anyone wanting to do mischief." Nodding his head, Robert spoke again.

"Yes, you're right Henry, we need several different safeguards to protect against the actions of wrongdoers, to guard against human failings." Henry felt strongly that this was right. Grampa John had helped him see that cooperation was vitally important when men undertake dangerous work; they backed each other up. But now he realised that machines would need to have back-ups if they were to be truly safe. So, if something broke, went wrong or stopped working, the failure would not lead to anyone being killed. How could machines be made to fail safely? The thoughts were buzzing around Henry's mind when George spoke.

"We must report our suspicions about the cut cable to Sgt Pepper today. I can run over and do that but, for God's sake, who would do a thing like that?" Arthur also wanted to say more about this.

"Pepper will want to gather evidence so we should leave all this as it is stands until he's been able to do that, agreed? And he'll want to talk with us and the men who were at the pithead yesterday morning. If someone had a gripe against one of the miners in the cage we might get a lead. Maybe someone didn't like the manager, Colin Amble, he's not everyone's friend around here, is he?" Henry spoke.

"I was supposed to be in the cage Arthur, but I arrived late and Colin took my place, to do the early inspection." Robert looked at Henry.

"Henry, do you think it's possible that one of those thugs who attacked you could have done this. Billie Oats or his friend Charlie Grange? But would they really be that stupid?"

"Oats is a nasty man." Arthur chipped in. "Doesn't seem to have an ounce of goodness in his character, like his father before him, a real neighbourhood bully. Billie seemed to be born with that same trait. Does Pepper know about your quarrel with Oats, Henry?"

"Oh yes, he was going to arrest me for assaulting Oats last Monday but John told him what happened"; Henry paused. "Arthur, is John your brother?"

"Yes, he is Henry; his judgements sometimes concern me but he told me about his chat with you and how he felt a strong kinship." Arthur paused and looked at Henry. Robert stepped in.

"I think we should now go about our business. It looks like the sun is burning the mist off and we'd better get the Sgt over here to collect any evidence before work starts on repairing the cable." The men moved off in different directions, leaving the scene of the crime behind them. Henry and George walked up the road and across the fields to their homes in Tunley.

"Noswaith dda Henry, hyfryd gweld chi eto, shw mae." Tom was laughing as he walked up the road greeting Henry. "That means, 'good evening Henry, lovely to see you again, how are you', but I don't really speak Welsh, my Megan here taught me that greeting and I bin practising it all day; that's *trwy'r dydd.* Henry, this is my Welsh beauty Megan, Megan Jones, made from the valley's love, and Megan, this is my younger brother Henry. And this is my even younger brother, Ritchie. Good Lord Ritchie, what 'ave you been doing, 'ave you bust your arm boyo?" Henry spoke to Tom, his face very serious.

"Tom, there was a dreadful accident at the New Pit yesterday. The cage cable broke and the cage plummeted down, miners were killed and Ritchie broke his arm, so it's all rather grim here in Camerton, but it is good to see you brother, and very pleased to meet you Megan. Tom wrote us about you so we had great expectations, and we aren't disappointed are we Ritchie?" Henry reached out to shake Megan's hand. Ritchie was a bit dumbstruck with Megan's good looks but managed an embarrassed greeting.

"Tom's a lucky boy, and I'm a lucky brother, even with a wonky arm. Lovely to meet you miss, can I have a kiss?" Despite the sombre mood, Ritchie couldn't resist throwing in one of his Somerset ditties, and it did have the effect of lightening the mood a little. Megan reached over to Ritchie and gave him a big kiss on the cheek, her long blonde hair covering his face for a moment.

"I've heard about you Ritchie boy, and now pleased to meet you and give you a kiss." Megan turned to Henry. "I am so sorry about the accident Henry. My brother Frank was killed last year in a colliery accident in Ebbw Vale, suffocated he did. They say there wasn't enough fresh air blowing through the tunnels. Anyway, I know how a whole community can be in pain. Thousands of crying people at the funerals stays in the memory." They all turned around to see Maria come out of the house and run to give Tom a motherly hug; she was crying.

"I am so happy to see you Thomas; Lord I think you've grown even taller, and so this is Megan from the Valleys, as beautiful as you wrote us Thomas. You are very welcome in Camerton, Megan my love, why don't we all go in and have some tea and cake?"

Later that day, Henry and Tom walked along the canal path together; they had private things to talk about.

"Megan's family in Blaina would be able to put you both up until you found a place of your own. There's plenty of work, as I said in my letter Henry, and I spoke with the manager of the Beaufort pits and the Kearsley Pit in Blaenafon before I came down. Ebbw Vale is opening up as well, with new collieries being dug further down the valley. It's an amazing place Henry. Most of the coal is used in the iron works and they are now making steel with this new Bessemer conversion process, where they blow air through the boiling pig iron to get rid of the stuff that makes iron brittle and weak. It's hot work making steel and it's the toughest metal there is." Henry was listening carefully.

"That sounds good Tom. How about the working conditions, and safety in the mines? Ivan Evans was down here last week and told us about how the Association is having to work hard to make improvements."

"That's right Henry, and Ivan is a force for good; where would we be without him? I think he's been fired up by the death of his brother last year. There was this terrible explosion in the Victoria mine when nineteen people were killed including a young lad from around here. Megan mentioned that her brother Frank choked to death before he could reach the clean air. After the explosion, what they call the after-damp gas, carbon monoxide, spread through the tunnels and the ventilation was not strong enough to get rid of it so most of the poor souls suffocated, like Frank. They've shut the mine down now. Tom paused for a moment, then continued.

"I was there Henry, waiting on the surface for the next cage to go down for the evening shift. They use a water balance to bring the cages up and down, filling a large tank with water and lowering it down the shaft so the cage with coal and colliers could be brought up. Anyway, I was waiting for the tank to fill when suddenly there was this muffled roar from deep below ground, then a blast of air and gas up the shaft. I looked at the overman Price who had already inspected the mine for gas earlier that day and he'd given the all clear. He looked distraught because his son John was underground, and he rushed to go down in the next cage. Both he and his son died that day Henry. You know, the miners would lark around, lighting up little patches of the fire-damp, the methane gas which came out of the coal workings. I learned that they call the gas damp, after the German word for vapour, dampf. It was with us all the time, but the ventilation was supposed to blow it through so it wouldn't build up in places. It wasn't good enough that day. Ivan showed us the report by Lionel Brough, the government mine inspector, where he writes that if his recommendation for better ventilation had been carried out, the explosion wouldn't have happened. Why don't people listen, then act on the recommendations from experts Henry? I'll tell you why; it's because it costs money and the owners are slow to spend money until they must. Ivan has a lot to say about this Henry. He's an intelligent man, full of good ideas; I bet you'll get on well with him." Tom paused and looked up into the sky before continuing, sharing memories with his brother.

"The funerals, or should I say funeral, it was one big funeral, took place on the Sunday, ten days after the accident and I have never seen so many people gathered together Henry; maybe twenty thousand or more along the streets, in the procession and at the cemetery. And the singing Henry, it would lift your heart even though it might be in pain from the loss of family and friends. I walked along with a friend of mine who had lost his brother and he said something like, *'Thomas boy, they say this coal is a blessing to mankind, bringing a better life to people who would otherwise be starving in the fields. But I say it's a bloody curse, taking away our dignity and humanity as we slave away in the bowels of God's Earth, to feather the nests and satisfy the greed of the rich. And look around you Tom, see how king coal and emperor iron have destroyed our beautiful land.'* I knew what he meant then Henry, we are slaves. But it's the same everywhere, and we're not going to stop the march of progress, so we must keep trying to make it better. I think you'll get involved with safety in the Valleys, like you are doing down here. Oh, and Ivan is coming down again on Sunday to meet your association and talk about the things they are doing in Ebbw Vale to stop exploitation of the workers; he'll be able to guide you. What does your Sarah think about you moving to the Valleys, Henry?"

"Sarah is a very special woman Tom, we've been bound

together for a long time, and she wants to move away, we both want this new adventure. She has difficulties with her mother who is now saying that she should move to her uncle's tavern in the Midlands. Aunt Elizabeth doesn't like me and you know she doesn't get on with our mum either, so we both want to be free of this constant anxiety. We both want a new life away and the Valleys sounds like a good place and maybe I'll be able to get some training in mine inspection and safety."

"I know what you are saying Henry. Both you and Sarah are very special, and very special to me as well brother. As we approached Somerset this morning Megan said, '*this would be a nice place to live*' and I had this thought that maybe we could move down and settle in Camerton. Megan has not been happy in the Valleys since her brother was killed, so maybe it would be a chance for her to recover. We'd get married and start a family, have lots of englwelsh children. Will you and Sarah marry Henry?"

"Yes Tom, I have asked Sarah and she said yes. You know, at that very moment, it felt like my life came together, happiest man alive I was, with a purpose that felt strong; looking after Sarah and growing in love with her every day. Can you understand that Tom?"

"I can Henry. My Megan is such a strong woman, I feel double the man when I am beside her. This is what happens when love is real and shared. Pity the poor folk who never find it Henry and they are all about us you know. This Billie Oats, he seems a mean fella, maybe starved of any kind of love, poor bloke. Do you think he was the cable cutter?"

"I wouldn't put it past him Tom, but I want to hear what he's got to say when Sgt Pepper tracks him down."

Henry and Tom carried on talking for a long while, re-kindling their deep friendship, sharing stories of their lives since Tom had left for the Valleys. They discussed the planned miners' meeting on Clandown hill on Sunday. Tom would join the meeting and get to know the new group that had formed. He knew Robert Barnes from school days and remembered playing football against Farnham Nash when Camerton played Timsbury. Tom was keen to find ways of settling back in and building a new life with Megan in the soft Somerset hills, but he knew that he would soon be underground again in the hard, dark world of coal; *I wonder if it will feel the same,* he thought to himself.

On Sunday morning Henry and Tom sat with Maria at breakfast and talked about the plan for Henry and Sarah to leave Somerset and Tom to move back down with Megan. Maria held both their hands and there were tears in her eyes.

"You will do what you must, both of you. I will miss you gravely Henry, and your Sarah too, but I understand, I really do, and Tom, you and Megan can come live with Ritchie and me till you find your own place, you know that, don't you?" Tom gave his mother a big smile and hugged her. As Tom left them, Maria spoke to Henry. "So, it will be next weekend?" It was not really as a question but more a statement of her resignation at Henry's decision. "I'd like you to have this ring to give Sarah. It was my mother's, and I think she was given it by her mother. I don't know what it's made of, but it feels like marble; I won't need it anymore Henry, so would you like to make it a symbol of your love for Sarah, just as it was for my love to your father, James?" Then it was Henry's turn to give his mother a hug, reassuring her that he would write with news regularly.

After James' death, Maria had developed a strength that

she hardly knew she possessed. Maria's eldest son, James jnr. had married and moved to Midsomer Norton. Ritchie was still a toddler, Henry a scholar, while Thomas and George were in their teens and working as haulers underground. At first, she didn't know how she would cope, but George and Thomas helped her to keep it together as her grief spilt out. The saddest thing for Maria was the strained relationship with her sister; but, perversely, not having a big sister alongside her may have helped Maria build her own independence, and strength of mind.

Maria had lost friendship with her older sister Elizabeth many years before, in their teenage years. At that time, their cousin James was kind to Maria but he seemed sad and this endeared him to her. She wanted to make him happy and soon the attachment began to grow. They would see each other after he finished his shift, walk along by the old canal, and soon they were planning a future together. Was Elizabeth jealous of Maria's relationship with James? They never talked about it, but something was keeping them apart and after James and Maria were married, the sisters hardly ever talked together. Maria loved her five sons and now Henry loved Elizabeth's daughter, and Maria's only niece. Oh, how family affairs are woven closely into the fabric of our lives, leaving pathways for stress and strain to move freely along, encouraging the ways of nature to test our nerves.

Sarah had returned home from the colliery on Friday afternoon. She had mostly recovered from the shock of the mine accident, and the fear that Henry had been killed. But it had left her with a feeling, the onset of a devastating pain from the thought of her loved one gone forever. Henry was part of her so this thought was more than she could bear. Sarah was on the point of collapse when Henry emerged from the Old Pit shaft, carrying Ritchie. It was more than a relief, it was life restoring. From that moment, Sarah knew that she had to look after her man. On Sunday, Sarah and Henry met for lunch and talked excitedly about their trip to the Valleys the following Saturday. They would only take a few things and Tom and Megan would travel with them and help them settle in. They both had enough savings to keep them going for a week or two until Henry started his new job and received his first earnings. Tom had explained that Henry would be paid monthly but he could be advanced a sub after two weeks. The pay of 30 shillings per week was more than he earned in the New Pit and he could work longer hours if he wanted to earn even more money. Sarah didn't want him to do this.

"Henry, I want us to build our lives together in our new home and we won't be able to do that if you are working all the hours that God sends. She squeezed his hand and smiled at him but with a look that said she felt strongly about this.

"That suits me Sarah love, because I'm looking forward to spending more time with you, making love and making babies." Henry paused for a moment before continuing. "The accident on Friday has sharpened my thoughts about safety Sarah, and I know I have something to give but I will need training if I am to play a role, do inspections and the like. There's more to me that a hewer, and I want to find out what it is. Can you understand that Sarah?"

"Yes, I will be with you as you find out what the more is Henry." Sarah knew that Henry had more to give, and that he was hungry to learn and hungry to grow. She knew that being alongside him was important, and she would be his support in all that he tried.

That evening, Henry and Tom raced each other up Clandown Hill to the meeting of the miners' association. Henry arrived first with Tom a close second, claiming that Henry had youth on his side. When they were younger, Tom would always give Henry a start when they raced across the countryside, but gradually Henry caught his brother up and was now faster. That's often the way with brothers, the younger with more determination in life, spurred on to do better than his brother. Robert and Arthur were already on the hill, describing the accident to Ivan, who had come down from the Valleys to talk about the report by the Truck Commission that had been published the year before, and what they were doing to make changes in Ebbw Vale. Spreading the word about how miners' associations could make things better was strengthening the metal of local groups all over the nation. Ivan turned to Henry to speak.

"Nasty business someone cutting the cable like that Henry. Any idea who did it?" Henry was reluctant to name Billie Oats as a possible culprit; there were many miners gathered around and it was often difficult to know who your friends were.

"Out local bobby, Sgt Pepper, is on the case Ivan; he thinks that if we can find the cutting tool, that might lead him to the culprit and he's interviewing all the miners who were on the shift that morning, and their families. If it was a vengeful act, he hopes to find clues from talking to folk." Henry had already met with Sgt Pepper earlier that day and the police were out looking for Billie Oats and his cronies. When a large group of miners had gathered, Ivan stood up on a box and welcomed them.

"Fellow coal miners, last year I gave evidence on behalf of the South Wales District Miners' Association to the Truck Commission, set up to investigate the excessive prices charged for goods by the Ebbw Vale Company at their shops. I want to tell you about this in case you meet it in your district. The Company had a monopoly, since they owned the land and would not allow other shops to open. The truck system, as it's called, is where the owners paid part of workers' wages with goods, like food, clothing and furniture. Well, this became illegal more than 40 years ago, but across the nation, companies are still practising a form of trucking. In Ebbw Vale, the Company owns the houses, the shops, the schools, the hospital and the damn cemetery so we go through our lives and to our death serving the Company. The Company deducts part of a man's wage to pay for all this and it damn well feels like you owe your very soul to the Company. But they were taken to task by the Commission who discovered that the Company was breaking the law by allowing 2-week subs to be paid only if the money was used to buy stuff from the Company store. I gave evidence to the Commission and we managed to force the Company to stop the practice and henceforth allow private merchants to set up shops where they could sell the same stuff at a reduced price and still make a decent profit." Ivan spoke with a lilt that the Somerset folk were not used to but found compelling. He naturally drew and kept their attention with the rise and fall of his voice, emphasising words with powerful baritone, in a way that only the Welsh can.

"But be careful brothers, because there are two sides to this affair, this clash between those that own and those that work for those that own. The Ebbw Vale Company was set up with good intentions, and by some good Christian folk. But just like mine safety, if practises aren't carefully monitored, they can drift into the bad lands. The Commission exposed a

206

paternal and profit-driven despotism that holds workers in bondage." Murmuring broke out in the crowd of miners and one shouted out, "what's depostism mean Ivan?" The man struggled with the word he'd never heard.

"Well, a despot is someone who wants absolute power over others, in control of all they do. So, despotism is what they practice." A miner shouted out, "oh, my wife Agatha is a despot," to raucous laughter from the crowd.

"I like your humour brothers, we need it to lighten things up, but you know this is very serious what I'm saying. The managing director of the Company, Abraham Darby, had built us a parish church and an amazing Literary and Scientific Institute, but he was against weekly pay and he supported this benevolent despotism that had prevailed in Ebbw Vale and the surrounding towns for decades. He claimed that making sure that the workers, but more often their wives, used their subs to buy provisions at the Company stores, served to repress drunkenness. And he was probably right, but some of us think that this kind of control deprives workers of our freedoms. What I am trying to say is that there are two sides to this, and there is good and bad on both sides." Ivan paused and looked up to the sky before continuing, like a preacher might, but Ivan was an atheist. When he continued, he spoke with even greater passion in his lilt. "I am a self-educated man and I have come to see, and to think of, these two sides as an inevitable feature of social progress. People often take sides without thinking and this can lead to conflict when they try to impose their will on people from the other side. Sometimes we, working men, need to fight for our rights and other times we need to negotiate. The Truck Commission was part of the negotiation and won a battle for working men. There is more negotiation to do and more battles to be won. Safety, pay, working conditions and mining developments; they are all on the table of negotiation and will be for a long time to come. So, we need patience and determination; we need patient, determined and educated men to lead us in these matters. Now I know that you have your own special concerns here in Somerset and Charlie Smith from the Midlands Association of Miners will now talk about what they have been doing to improve the standard of wages in their district."

As Ivan stepped down, the gathering of miners cheered him with clapping and shouts of support and gratitude. Many of the things that Ivan talked about and the words that he used were new to the Somerset miners, but they believed in him. His speech fuelled their hopes for a better future. Most of the gathering needed a leader to light the way, show them that things can get better if you want them to, and are prepared to negotiate and fight if necessary. Most were eager to follow but a handful of the men could see what all this meant in the bigger picture, and what they needed to do; understood what Ivan meant by determination and patience. They were the future leaders of the miners' association in the district. After the meeting finished, the miners walked off in all directions and Henry, Tom, Ivan and Robert walked down the hill together.

"Can it really be only last weekend that you had the fight in this very spot Henry?"

"In truth, it seems a lifetime away Ivan. So much has happened in the last week; the formation of our working group, meeting with the owners, the accident, Tom and Megan arriving and Sarah and my decision to move up to the Valleys. I have aged with these things, and out of them has emerged a new vision, something that's been forming for a while but now I see more clearly. It's about safety Ivan and my mind is set on making a difference. Can you understand that?"

"That's what I've been talking about Henry, so I do

understand. It's like a calling that religious people claim they have heard, to convert other people, to bring them to God. You and me, I think our calling is more down to Earth, more real, and so more likely to be effective. I'm looking forward to working with you on mining safety in the Valleys Henry."

As the four men walked over the road towards the Rest, the raven flew across the evening sky above them, letting out a distinctive triple kronk.

"What about me Brân?" shouted Ivan looking up at the passing raven. As he said it, the raven gave one last kronk before heading into the wood. "Well, I'll be damned," said Ivan. "I do believe he understood what I said. We have a pair on the hills above Cwm, and some folk there say they can talk. Oh, and in Welsh, Brân means raven." Henry smiled at Ivan.

"Brân, that's a good strong name. It's strange, but I do believe that Brân watches over us for some reason and tries to communicate with us?" But Tom had a different idea.

"Maybe they are waiting for us to die so they can peck our eyes out and pick our bones. Anyway, that's what folk used to think, and some still do, the superstitious ones anyway." And Robert wanted to add his pennyworth.

"I think they are magnificent birds, as mystified by us as we are by them; let's go drink a pint to the raven." And as the four men entered the Rest, Henry's face lit up with a smile as he saw his Sarah behind the bar, all thoughts of the raven vanishing like the bird itself had done just a few moments ago.

The tall man walked quickly and purposefully along the road, sometimes heading across the fields to cut off the corners. Occasionally he broke into a run over open ground and the raven flew ahead of him making the occasional kronk. He ran over the two hills that loomed above the village and continued along the farm track down into the next valley. He must have covered eight miles in the past couple of hours but he wasn't tired and he had almost reached his destination, the coaching Inn at Frome; he needed to arrive before midday. The twelve o'clock coach was waiting outside the Inn as John approached from behind and he could see people had started to board. He looked inside as he came alongside the coach; no sign of who he was looking for. He approached the Inn door, just as Billie Oats emerged carrying a suitcase and wearing a wide brimmed hat held down to partly cover his face.

"Billie, the police want to question you about the accident at Camerton New Pit last Friday. I told them I would look for you and bring you in if I found you. And I have found you so let's walk up this road to the police station."

"I had nothing to do with the accident Riddle, and I can prove it, I was with Charlie Grange all night, now let me pass."

"I spoke with Grange this morning Billie and after a little persuasion he confessed to finding a cutting tool for you last week; now why would you want a cutting tool? Then he told me you were planning to get out of the area before the police caught up with you. Come on, let's take that walk along the road Billie." Just then, the coachman called for everyone to climb on board for the trip to Bath town, and as John looked up, Billie started to run down the street. Billie had a head start but he was not very quick and soon John had caught up with him, dived at his legs and brought him down. Billie hit his head on the ground and was dazed which gave John time to tie a rope around his wrists. The local bobby had witnessed the fracas and came across the road shouting, "*all right, all right, what's all this then?*" It wasn't long before John explained what was going on and all three men tramped off to the Frome

210

police station. John had heard about the accident from his brother Arthur and had immediately suspected Billie Oats, as he knew what a vengeful man he was. "It had to be him," thought John Riddle, "he's the only one mean and stupid enough to do such a thing." John couldn't find him but caught up with Charlie Grange before he went on his shift that morning.

Monday evening and Sarah was putting her painting material together to try to capture an image in the sky she had seen the night before. Sarah liked painting the stars and had promised Ritchie that she would paint one for him before she left. He had seen a shape that looked like him hauling a coal cart, so she had a plan for what she was going to paint. Her mother came in the room as Sarah was getting ready to leave.

"I'm sorry about your sadness Sarah but you should try to put aside your feelings for Henry and think about a new life in the Midlands working in your uncle Arthur's tavern. It will be an opportunity for you to make new friends and earn some money. You might even meet a nice man who wants to marry you. Arthur is coming down next weekend and I hope you will be sensible and travel back with him. Your father and I both agree it will be good for you; new surroundings will help you grow into a woman."

"I am already a woman mother and have no intention of going to the Midlands. You have picked a terrible moment to try to persuade me about anything; now I am going out."

Sarah pushed past Elizabeth and walked out of the door into the evening air, her heart pounding with anger and fear; fear that her mother might try to stop her leaving with Henry. She hadn't told 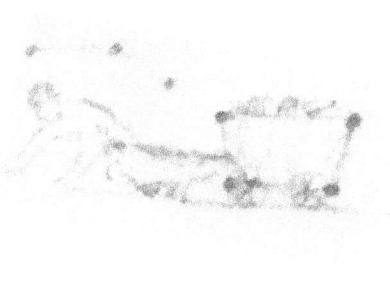 her father or mother about the plan to leave for the Valleys the following weekend. She and Henry would elope, but she would write a letter to her father; he will understand; he must understand. Sarah walked a short way along the canal and set up her easel and looked out to the north where the same pattern of stars was just appearing in the evening sky. The Great Bear was the most distinct shape in the sky, except that Sarah didn't see a bear, she saw Ritchie pulling the cart; miners in the stars above. Sarah had a wonderful imagination and could see so many different shapes amongst the stars. Earlier that year she had painted Henry in another group of stars, about to swing his coal pick into the seam, into the constellations around Orion. She knew she loved the real Henry more than the one in the stars above, more than life itself really, if that were possible. She had wondered how far away Henry's stars were and would we ever be able to visit them. Henry had told her that each star was like our own sun, a very long way away, but they were a mystery to her, a good mystery and Sarah liked mysteries, they fired her imagination. In her painting, Sarah captured her wonder and felt more settled. For a moment, she felt outside her body again, looking at herself painting the stars. She wasn't frightened by these mysterious moments anymore, she knew that they were part of her, a special gift maybe?

Tomorrow Sarah would write a letter to her father, so it wouldn't be a mystery to him why she left with Henry. As she was packing away her easel, she saw a bright star at the end of a smaller version of the bear, of Ritchie and the cart. "I wonder if that star is above the Valleys', she whispered to herself. She was looking at Polaris, the north star, and when she got to the Valleys, she and Henry would climb to the top of the hill and see that it was in the same place in the sky. She would learn that it was the only star that didn't make an arc across the sky during the night. Sarah would learn a lot of new things during her life in the Valleys.

Albert Wallace was an honest and rather sensitive man and harboured the thought that maybe Elizabeth had lured him into having intercourse and getting pregnant, so that he would marry her. He had grown to love her but, after Sarah was born, Elizabeth became distant and reluctant to share her mind or body with her husband. But she was good at keeping the books at the Miner's Rest and keeping the clients happy, so when Albert took over running the public house after his father died, they developed into a good working team. Elizabeth was very cool to her sister Maria, and when Sarah befriended Henry at a very young age, she alienated herself from her daughter. Yes, the ways of human nature are strange and test the nerves of a gentle man. When Albert read Sarah's letter he cried, although it did not come as a surprise. The only saving grace was that Tom's Megan might take Sarah's place working evenings in the Rest. Maybe Elizabeth's heart would soften when she got to know the Welsh girl; time would tell, as it sometimes does.

The Manor garden was always beautiful in spring time. The

surrounding borders full of tulips bursting into life, with colours from every part of the rainbow shining brightly. Every individual tulip seemed to be competing for Anna's attention as she walked by; did they turn their heads as she passed to keep her beauty in sight, craning to show her their beauty? But Anna's attention was focused on the person clearing a patch of ground further along the path. He stood up as she approached.

"Good morning miss Anna, the garden is so full of beauty on such a wonderful morning do you agree?" She smiled but made no reply as she moved close to him. He rose to meet her and they walked together knowingly to the glasshouse; the time had come. Inside they were both nervous with excitement. They had both known this would happen one day, but the moment had to be right and it had come on a beautiful spring morning when the tulips stood erect and envious. As he kissed her lips, he could feel her shaking and held her more firmly in his arms, moving his hands through her jet-black hair, down her back, stopping for a moment before reaching down to her thighs and around to her firm bottom. She was breathing heavily and he could feel her heart beating through their clothes. His own heart was pounding too, and he thought it would burst when he removed her blouse and began to kiss her breasts softly; Anna's nipples grew firm in his lips. He lifted her long flowing frock covered in pretty, embroidered flowers, and, still shaking, she quickly removed her underclothes while gazing into his eyes. They lay on the soft ground inside the glasshouse and when he entered her they both cried out with pain and joy; a perfect moment if ever there was one. They stayed together in silence for several minutes, prolonging the moment, their pleasure locked in time, looking deep into each other's eyes, with new-born smiles. He held his weight on his elbows and kissed her and the motion began again. When eventually he helped Anna to her feet, they both laughed at the sight of each other. Her naked from the waist up and him

214

naked from the waist down; a most erotic scene.

"Beautiful, dearest Anna, this has been the most wonderful time of my life. I never knew how good it could be; I'm in love with you Anna and I want to be with you always." Just then they heard a voice from across the garden, it was Anna's mother Florence.

"Anna, are you there, Mable needs the lettuce for making the salad, where are you girl?" They quickly dressed and came out of the glasshouse just as Florence came around the corner. "Oh, there you are Anna, and James, I wondered where you were. Have you finished sowing those seeds Grampa John gave you yesterday."

"Good day Lady Florence, yes I have been sowing this morning, I think you'll have some wonderful sweetcorn in the autumn." Anna walked quietly towards the house, picking up the lettuce on the way and turning gently to give James a smile. "Bye Anna, nice to talk with you this morning, see you again soon." As Anna disappeared into the house, Florence spoke to James.

"I can see you like each other James but it will not work you know. You are still children really; she is only sixteen and you are, what, eighteen? But, most important, Anna is destined for great things and you are a..." Florence paused, looking down before raising her head again and finishing her sentence, ".. you are a coalminer. You are from a different class in the social order; you do understand that don't you James?" Florence was looking sternly at James.

"I know what you mean Lady Florence, but I do love Anna and I think she do love me. When people are in love, what does it matter about social order? Surely what's more important is happiness?"

"Happiness and pleasure are selfish human traits James

and they don't get you very far in life. My experience is that they can get in the way of more purposeful activities, like making this Manor and the coal mines profitable. The working class can spend their time satisfying their need for pleasure, but above them are those who shape the world, create the opportunities and forge the future. Do you think you could ever understand that James?"

"What I do understand is that happiness helps me to see the world in a good light, to do things with a good intention, and to be a friend to my neighbour. These are the most important things for us humans, whatever the social order. And it seems to me that the social order you talk about is preserved by those who have a lot, to keep those who don't have much in their place. But you are my neighbour Lady Florence, and I want to be your friend, just as Anna and I are good friends and always will be." Florence did not appreciate James's attempt at reconciliation and turning around, walked swiftly back to the Manor house.

On his way home, James was filled with mixed emotions. He had experienced the best moment of his life and a new feeling, a real love, had formed in his heart; yes, it was in his heart where he felt it. But Florence's words had hurt him; would he ever be good enough for Anna, good enough for her class? Probably not. These conflicting thoughts were dancing in his brain as he walked through the woods and heard a voice.

"Hullo James, have you been to the Manor, would you like to kiss me?" Seeing Elizabeth leaning against a tree surprised James but what she said to him surprised him even more. She was several years younger than James and she had a brazen, flirtatious, manner and would often say outrageous things to James. He could mostly laugh them off but he worried that she would be vulnerable to the misbehaviour, the bad intentions, of other boys and even men.

"Elizabeth, you mustn't say those kind of things, people will take advantage of you."

"I don't mind if you take advantage of me James, I do like you a lot, so would you come here and kiss me?"

"No Elizabeth, now you come on I'll walk home with you, your mother and father will be worried about you. Why can't you be more like your younger sister. Maria is more careful about what she says, not brazen like you."

"Well I'm not Maria, am I. You like her better than me don't you, but I'm prettier and more grown up you know, look at me?" James wasn't going to look at Elizabeth showing off to him and he turned and walked off towards Tunley.

"Come on Elizabeth, race you back to Tunley." Elizabeth was spirited and innocent enough to accept the challenge and they both ran off through the woods and across the fields, James staying just far enough ahead that Elizabeth thought that she might catch him; catch him and capture his heart. But she was totally unaware that he had become a man that morning and his heart was already captured. The clouds crept across the sky above the Somerset valley and a chattering of rooks raced back towards the wood. A lone raven looked down as it crossed in the opposite direction, his mission seemingly more purposeful, but what do we know about ravens?

Thirty years later, at the end of his last working week in Camerton, Henry approached the Manor through the garden, just as Grampa John was coming out of the glasshouse. Time preserves all things, significant and trivial, and Henry had years of good memories of their talks in the Manor garden. He felt sad that they were coming to an end, and wanted to tell Grampa John how much they had meant to him. The garden held a special place in his heart and mind.

"It's so wonderfully warm in that glasshouse Henry, not surprising things grow so quickly but those delicate plants need special nurturing, just the right amount of water, the right amount of care. You know, people need nurturing too Henry, and without care we can wither away. Now, I think I know why you have come to see me this morning young man; are you leaving us Henry?"

"Yes, Gramps, I have come to say goodbye. Sarah and me, we're off to South Wales tomorrow and I wanted to say thank you for all the wisdom and knowledge you have given me. Any question I had, you would have an answer to and it was always a good answer, that made me think of another question and so I have learned so much from you Gramps. You have always been patient with me and I hope you don't mind me thinking of you as my friend." Henry felt a humility when he was with Grampa John, and always came away from their talks a better man. Gramps had a tear in his eye as he spoke.

"Ah, Henry, you are like the grandson I never had and so it has always been a pleasure to share my knowledge with you. In fact, to let you into a secret, I would often learn something new, about science, about the social evolution, about politics, just to share it with you. Your hunger for knowing has kept me going in my old age." You are like your father was when he was your age; bright and eager and a good worker, and you look just like him as well." Gramps paused for a few moments in thought before continuing. "I'd like to leave you with four pieces of advice; the four legs of the metaphorical table you might want to build on, or stand on to see further. First, keep learning Henry, never stop learning and keep your heart and

218

mind open to knowledge; remember, both need to be open to gain the full value of knowledge. Second, do your level best to find the good in others, be kind and patient, because with some people it will be difficult. Third, take care of your family; they will always be the most important and need you the most. And fourth, don't trust greedy people; you should be able to smell greed Henry and it usually stems from envy." Gramps paused to reflect and let Henry take in what he had said, then he continued.

"Maybe one more thing Henry. As I grow older, and I am very old now Henry, older than I deserve probably, I see things about myself that I couldn't see before. It's like the lake of my life is draining away and what I see are the things that were submerged, things that I buried inside earlier in my life. I remember them all Henry, as like ghosts they come back to haunt me. Meeting with you has been a big respite from these ghosts in recent years. I can't tell you how to deal with these things but when you have strong feelings about something I think it's about dealing with them when they come, in their turn. Or they'll hide away and maybe stay hidden and then come out in all sorts of ways you won't recognise or connect with. I could have been a better son to my parents, father to my children, husband to my dear wife, a better man in this world. But I think I have been a good friend to my granddaughter Anna and she a good friend to me. She has helped me grow old gracefully. She wants to talk with you before you go Henry." And as Gramps said this, Anna came into the garden holding what looked like an envelope in her hands. She spoke with a jolly tone in her voice.

"Good evening Henry, we heard about your new adventure and we'll be so sorry to see you go. I know that Gramps will miss having regular talks with you." Gramps shook Henry's hand and with a farewell gesture, walked back to the Manor. When Anna spoke again, she seemed more serious. "Henry, I have written you a letter and I make a request that you don't read it until you are on your journey to Wales tomorrow. It contains some personal information that you should know. Please don't ask me about it now but take it with you and take my affection and friendship with you Henry." Anna quickly turned and walked back to the Manor. Henry called after her.

"Anna, thank you for letting me be your friend, it's been very special for me. And thank you for caring for the miners; they will need your help even more as they develop their proposals for changes."

"I am on their side Henry, of that you can rest assured and good luck to you and Sarah in your new adventure." Anna disappeared into the Manor house, just as she had 30 years ago after making love to Henry's father.

The day had arrived. Saturday 1st June lit up with the sun rising just before 5am. Henry and Sarah had packed their bags the night before and were ready for the journey to the Valleys, or the big elopement, as Sarah liked to call it. The night before, Henry and Robert had visited Colin Amble who was at home with his legs in splints, bones set back into position. Colin agreed to give Robert some lessons in the mine inspection methods but he would need to be certified and do the proper training. It usually took a few weeks, but Robert was a fast learner and hoped to take up the role as soon as possible. Meanwhile, he would work with the inspector from one of the other mines. Henry was pleased that this had been agreed and had a final meeting with the working group that evening; Robert, Archie, James, Farnham and Arthur and Tom would be joining them as well. Six was a good number for this team; each of the three main challenges having a lead person and a backup. They wished Henry well and agreed to keep in touch, sharing news of progress in their endeavours.

It was a clear day as Henry, Sarah, Tom and Megan walked up the road to where they could take a horse and cart ride to Frome and the stagecoach to Bath. The railway network had been expanding during the previous decade so they could travel by steam train to Cardiff or Merthyr, the two biggest towns in Wales. But the journey would take most of the day so they were glad to have each other's company. As they left Tunley and Camerton, both Sarah and Henry experienced strange new feelings, mixtures of excitement and fear; fear of the unknown, excited by their adventure. They were glad to be together, and they looked up to see the early morning ravens cavorting in the sky.

"Farewell Camerton ravens, we'll miss you." Henry shouted out, and as he did, two distinctive kronks were heard. Then two more as the young ravens flew alongside their parents and they travelled together, once more to Clandown hill and beyond. "Did you hear that Sarah love, it sounded like 'goodbye Sarah.' Maybe they will miss us as well."

The journey was long and slow and at one of the railway stations, Henry and Sarah sat together on a bench at the end of the platform.

"I'd like to read Anna's letter out loud if you are ok with that Sarah." Sarah gently squeezed Henry's hand and nodded her head slowly. Henry opened the letter and began.

Friday 31st May 1872

My Dear Henry,

I heard yesterday that you and Sarah will be leaving Camerton to make a new life for yourselves in South Wales. I have held a secret for thirty years but have decided to share it with you in this letter. I am hoping that doing this will free me in a good way, so I don't want you to be concerned for me. What I said about women learning to control their sadness was true, and it works for me, most of the time.

Your father James and I had a small affair, before he was married of course. I say small because it didn't last long but it was very intense and I'm sure we were in love; maybe like you and Sarah are now. My family were strongly opposed to me seeing James but we used to meet in the garden and talk about life, like young innocents do. After a very passionate encounter, I became pregnant and when my mother found out she sent me to live in Bath for about three years with my auntie and uncle.

I never told your father about his daughter and when I returned to Camerton he had married your mother Maria and your brother George was a baby. He had stopped coming to the Manor garden by then and worked as a miner, so we hardly saw each other.

Your sister's name is Wendy Arton and she was born in Bath on February 20th, 1843. When she was six months old, she was taken from me and adopted by John and Mary Arton, a couple who lived in a village just outside Bath. That broke my heart at the time and I pined for my daughter but my uncle sent me to a finishing school, where I was taught how to control my emotions, behave like a lady and look down on the working class. I wasn't a good student but I endured it as a kind of punishment for my getting pregnant.

That is my secret Henry and that is all I know about my child, your sister.

I will miss our talks and our growing friendship which have meant a lot to me; I will preserve the memories. We need to preserve the good things in life Henry, to get us through the difficult times.

Please give my love to Sarah and be sure to look after her.

Affectionately Yours,

Anna Fernhill

Camerton Manor

Henry turned to Sarah with a stunned look on his face.

"I have a sister. Her name is Wendy and she is, she's 29 years old. My father knew nothing about his daughter. Can you imagine that Sarah? I wonder where she is now and does she know who her real mother and father are?" Sarah reached over and embraced Henry in her arms. She held him tighter when she heard him sobbing.

"I don't think so Henry. Wendy probably grew up thinking that John and Mary Arton were her real parents, otherwise Anna would have heard from her, but we don't know; maybe we'll never know Henry." Henry read Anna's letter again before putting it back in the envelope and into his pocket.

"No wonder she looked so sad, carrying the memory of her daughter that she never knew. She was a remarkable woman Sarah. I think I will write to her after we settle in the Valleys."

Later in the day of their travels, Henry and Sarah stood on the top of the hill that separated the Ebbw Vale and Blaina valleys. They looked down on their future homeland, more than a thousand feet below. The pit heads of the coal mines scattered along the valley at Waun-Lwyd, Victoria and Ebbw Vale were recognisable to their Somerset eyes but what was different, and much more dramatic, were the landmarks of the iron and steel works, particularly the four towering blast furnaces belching out fearsome fire and clouds of smoke, lighting up the sky with man's industry. But it wasn't only their eyes that were stimulated.

The sooty smells and crunching sounds joined with the fiery sight to pervade their senses. Coal and iron ore seams outcropped at the head of the valleys and these deposits were the first to be accessed but now, the deeper seams underground the valley floor were being mined. Without speaking, Henry and Sarah held each other close, both wondering what the future would bring in this sensual valley. Henry would become very familiar with these mines and their network of underground tunnels, deep shafts and seams of alternating iron ore, coal and limestone. They would be the focus of his attention and source of his learning for decades to come. As he looked down on humankind's dark footprint, Henry wondered if his descendants would follow in his footsteps in the mining industry. He turned to Sarah.

"What a sight Sarah, I was wondering if our children will

work in the mines."

"Who knows Henry, maybe one day our descendants will stride out in a different direction but first we will see how it works out for Brân." As Sarah said this, in a wood below them a pair of ravens rose out of the trees heading their way.

"Who is Brân...," but as he said this, Henry suddenly realised what Sarah meant.

"Sarah, are you pregnant, please be pregnant?" Henry held Sarah close and looked into her eyes.

"Yes, Henry and I think I am carrying our son and I would like to call him Brân, after the Welsh for raven; what do you think my love?"

"Brân, yes that's a good name, a strong name. Sarah, I have already asked you this but I will again. Will you marry me, and marry me this week? In that little Chapel that Megan's family go to? Then our life together can really begin." The two ravens passed by calling out with gurgling croaks. Sarah smiled and held both of Henry's hands.

"Yes Henry, I want to build our new life together with what we are, and with what we have brought from Camerton. I am excited and yes, we will get married in the little Chapel, if they'll have us." Sarah knew that they would face many challenges living in the valleys. But it would be their new home, their children's home. And they were not alone. Most of the population were immigrants from all over the nation, come to work underground, bringing the habits and dialects from their home towns with them. Henry would have his work cut out. Many of the mines were very gassy, and the district was notoriously dangerous with a history of accidents due to explosions. Henry would soon be a very busy man but, for now, the couple on the hill were rejoicing in their union.

There was an eerie silence in the Camerton valley that Sunday. The mine had closed for a week and would start working again on Monday morning, but it was as if time had stood still and the villagers were waiting for the daily routine to begin again. Some folk would miss Henry and Sarah badly, but this branch of the story will not return to Somerset to hear what they say. Of course, the lives of the Camertonians will pick up from where we first began the story just over two weeks ago, on May 16th. Whether this will be, or was, for better or worse, time or maybe the ravens, will tell.

7. Playing Hide and Seek as the Raven Turns

Early Saturday morning, with no dream to wake him up, Bran rose later than usual, made a coffee and telephoned Mary. She had returned from Yosemite on the Friday evening, but it was close to midnight on the West Coast and she was too tired to answer all Bran's questions – who did you meet? what did you discuss? did you climb Half Dome? have you solved any of the World's problems? Are you missing me? Mary was missing Bran and would be glad when her sabbatical was over and she could return to the nest, as Bran liked to describe their home. Bran brought Mary up to date with the helicopter crash saga and had sent her Oats's presentation. Oats was clearly in bed with the oil and gas companies and did not mention his colleague Clerk's data and concerns in his presentation; it was as if Dr Frances Clerk didn't exist. Bran agreed to see if he could obtain a copy of Clerk's presentation, *'When is enough enough?'*, from the University. Bran and Mary agreed to talk again in the week and they let each other go.

By mid-morning, Jenny's email had arrived and Bran felt excited as he downloaded the attachments. Jenny summarised what she had found in the email; there were three files. *"I'm sure you will be able to make sense of these Bran but please let me know if I can be of further help; meanwhile I will continue to explore on your behalf. There may be more where I found these."* The first was a newspaper report on an accident at the Camerton New Pit on the morning of Friday 24th May 1872. The cable that lowered and raised the cage to and from the coal seams had broken and the cage had fallen about 50 feet. Three miners were killed, the mine inspector had broken legs and a teenager had broken his arm, saved from serious injury by falling on the other miners. Bran read the names and whispered one of them to himself; *"Ritchie Sage, the young man who broke his arm"*. Bran was struggling to make sense of his thoughts but he couldn't escape the idea that this was the accident in his dream from the previous Thursday. *"Almost 128 years to the day; what is this about?"*

Bran stared out of the window into his garden trying to control, and to organise, his thinking. *"Come on, you are an engineer Bran. There are physical laws that govern things in space and time. Cause and effect can be explained, and only explained, by these laws. But something is connecting the present with the past; crossing over from one century to another."* He remembered his grandfather George used to tell stories about his life as a miner; did he also share stories about his own father and mother and these were buried in Bran's memories? *That's possible he thought, but is it possible that we carry the memories of our ancestors in our body-mind system, embodied in our genes, in the molecules of our emotions?* "If so, it is beyond my understanding," he whispered. The article went on to report that there were suspicions that the cable had been cut by someone and the police were questioning several people. *"I wonder why someone would do that."* Bran thought to himself, *"and did they ever find the man, or woman?"* Bran looked at his dream notes. … miners running towards the pit head; she was with them looking desperate; he appeared carrying a younger man, staggering towards her; people moaning; he was crying with his arms around them both; I had asked her if I could help and she had looked up and spoke to me; *'you have helped me.'* *"Yes, that was Sarah,"* whispered Bran, *"and Henry carrying who? It must have been Ritchie. I was back there with them*

229

and she spoke to me. It really happened, but how had I helped her?" There were many things that Bran did not understand but he felt sure they were all explicable, or would be one day, through rational scientific exploration. This idea was exciting to Bran and he believed that the revelations of science served to free people from being mystified by false prophets proclaiming weird and wonderful pasts and futures. But this was starting to shake his foundations; and yet, it was exciting as well. *What will Chloe have to say, he wondered?*

The second file was a set of minutes of the Somerset Miner's Association which formed in 1872; the names of the attendees of the inaugural meeting were recorded. Three names drew Bran's attention; James and Thomas Sage and Archie Flintworth. *"James and Thomas, those will be Henry's brothers."* Bran knew this from the various records he had obtained, including census documents from 1851, 1861 and 1871 and so on, showing who lived at the Sage household on those dates. The censuses showed that Henry had lived in his mother's home in Tunley in 1871, but lived in Ebbw Vale, with wife Sarah, and four children, in 1881. Their eldest child, Brân, spelt with the Welsh accent, was eight years old on the census date in 1881 so would have been born, probably, in 1873. Looking back at the list of people, Bran wondered if Archie was an ancestor of Ron's from the mining museum; could be his grandfather or grand uncle. Bran made a note to check this with Ron. The Association was made up of miners from the various collieries in the district and the members were allocated roles relating to Safety, Pay, Working Conditions and Mine Developments. *"They seem well organised, focussing on important things"* thought Bran, *"I wonder who their leader was, and did his great grandfather, Henry, play a role? Maybe Henry was as obsessed with safety as his great grandson."* The minutes noted that the Camerton mine owner, Lady Anna Fernhill, was very sympathetic to the miners'

230

cause and she supported their aims for improvements across all fronts.

There was another newspaper cutting from the Bath Chronicle, reporting meetings of hundreds of miners on Clandown hill in 1872, just before the Association formed. Visiting miners from South Wales and the Midlands gave rousing speeches that spurred the Somerset miners into action and so began the process of implementing the requirements of the Coal Mines Regulation Act of 1872. Their motto was 'for union and for right'. Bran felt he was getting closer to understanding what it must have been like for Henry as a coal miner in Somerset. *"Thank you, thank you Jenny"*, Bran whispered to himself, *"you've given me a big piece of a very big jigsaw.*" If Henry did rescue his younger brother in the accident, then Bran knew that he and Sarah were still in Somerset in May 1872, but Brân Snr was born in Ebbw Vale in 1873. So, they must have moved to South Wales after the accident and, from their marriage certificate, Bran knew they were married in the Old Blaina Baptist Chapel in June 1872. Things were fitting together.

Bran decided it was time to turn his attention to his great grandparent's life in the Valleys and he would try to locate the Chapel where they were married. A quick online search showed that such a chapel was no longer functioning, but there was a link to a website featuring the work of a builder who renovated old churches and chapels. The chap was currently working on a Chapel in Blaina which just might be the one. Bran sent an email to the builder asking if the Chapel he was renovating was the Old Blaina Chapel that was operating in the 1870's. He would have to wait for a reply which suited Bran since he felt unsettled by the discoveries he'd made that morning and wanted to take a break from ancestry and think about aeronautics and then music, two of the other passions in his life. He would return to his dreams tomorrow with Chloe's help.

It was a beautifully clear sky and the stars in the Plough shone abnormally bright. Bran imagined he saw the outline of a man in the pattern of stars. "So well defined, like a young man hauling a coal tub. I wonder how far away they are," thought Bran; "Henry had said that each star was like our own sun, and a very long way away. So, you knew something about the stars Henry, and Sarah says she loved you more than the stars above; now that's what I call love." The stars began to fade away but in a rhythmic manner and there was a tune accompanying the fading image, getting stronger as the image grew weaker. Bran reached out and switched his alarm off. Sunday morning, 5.28, and Bran opened his eyes to reality, again. He quickly made a note of this short but vivid dream. He had been thinking of his band, Orion, before he went to sleep so that might explain why stars would feature in his dream, but what were Henry and Sarah doing there? The star pattern had become a coal tub in Bran's dream; who had Henry said these things to, about the stars? "*Sarah; he had said them to Sarah.*"

Later that morning, Bran packed his dream journal into a small rucksack and cycled into the city to Chloe's place. He wasn't sure what to expect and he thought that he might come home even more confused and unsettled, but he enjoyed Chloe's company, so what the heck! Chloe welcomed Bran into her house. They walked passed a side room and Bran peeped in.

232

"We won't go in that room if you don't mind, that's where I meet my private clients for psychotherapy, and I charge for my time in there." Chloe always spoke in a calm, easy way that made Bran feel comfortable in her company, and very trusting of her. Bran had heard from others that she was very good at what she did, helping people whose lives had collapsed into dysfunctionality to find a way to recovery. If ever he needed that kind of help he would be only too happy to enter the therapy room where Chloe charged for her time. "I've laid out some lunch on the table Bran. Would you like to tuck in or start by telling me about your dreams?"

"Thanks for agreeing to meet and help me with this Chloe; I think I'd like to tell you about my dreams first if you don't mind, I've been thinking about what I might say to you for most of this morning, so would like to get it out."

"Really Bran, sounds serious. Many people have recurring dreams that bother them. But I recall that your dreams aren't so much recurring ones, but did you say the same person appears in your dreams, a woman, but you don't recognise her; have I got that right?"

"Yes, that's it, but there's far more going on and I'll start from the beginning if you don't mind." Chloe sat in an armchair and invited Bran to sit opposite, signalling that she was 'all ears'. Bran opened his dream journal and read it word for word, adding some context, the dates and times, how he felt. So, Chloe heard about the woman on the bridge over the canal, the woman with the wand at the coal mine talking with the two men, the accident and the woman, now with the name Sarah, speaking to him, the intimate love scene in the field and last night's star-gazing, the Plough as a coal tub. Bran could now describe Sarah clearly, her auburn hair, her strong facial features and gaze, and her smile, the sound of her voice, all very captivating.

"You said she spoke to you Bran; she said that you had helped her. What do you think that was about?"

"I've no idea Chloe, really, this is all a mystery to me. I'm someone who normally gets stuck into mysteries, aeronautical problems are bread, butter and jam to me, but this, I hardly know where to start."

"Ok Bran fair enough, I'll try to be more scientific; but I'm not a scientist, right? Some people think that dreams are a way our subconscious communicates with our conscious, tries to alert the part of our brain that works at making sense of things to what's going on within. When I say, going on within, I mean the stuff that hasn't been properly processed. I'm sure you've heard or read about this." Bran nodded in agreement and Chloe continued. "I'm talking about the things that happen to us that we don't fully deal with at the time. We have an emotional response to pretty well everything that happens to us and sometimes if we don't, or if we can't, deal with it, we just park it somewhere. It doesn't go away and it can creep back and bite us, or bring us down, when we are not expecting it. This is going on throughout our lives so I often find with my clients that we need to work together to mine for the stuff that's hidden deep within; stuff that might be the source of a problem. It often goes back to childhood, where trauma can be very destructive because children don't understand what's going on and really can't deal with things unless they have someone who they can trust to share it with, to help them deal with it. A common ailment is when children have been repeatedly told they weren't good enough, so they then carry that thought, or that belief through their lives. Some people are then motivated to strive to do better but others are dragged down by it. I've met both in my work. But to come back to you Bran, I asked you what you think Sarah meant because that might be a key to unravelling your dreams. You said that she said you had helped her and ..." Bran interrupted Chloe.

"I asked her if I could help her because she was crying, but Henry was safe and she didn't need me or maybe she thought I had helped Henry, I don't know Chloe, it was a dream."

"Ok Bran, lets imagine that you are the characters in your dream. Remember I said that this is one way of trying to make sense of dreams. Some aspect of you is embodied in everything in your dream, people and things. What would Sarah be?" Chloe paused but Bran's face told her he was perplexed by the question. She continued. "Jung called the feminine side of men that reside in the subconscious, the anima. Your anima might be struggling if you have suppressed your sensitivities, your gentle side, over the years. So maybe your anima is talking to you, trying to make itself heard through your dreams, in the form of people you are creating in your imagination, like Sarah. You said you thought she had a wand in her hand in another dream, so your anima might be able to conjure up magic spells or maybe it was a paintbrush and she was painting a picture, painting your dreams."

"All sounds plausible Chloe; you're good at this, aren't you? I do know about the anima, but I thought that I was quite a sensitive chap, you know the way I put emotion into my music in Orion. Why would I suppress my sensitivities?"

"You've worked in a man's world, been an engineer, for 30 years Bran, and my guess is you have had to hold back your emotions to manage conflict, to be able to focus on the problems and their solutions. I imagine your rational thinking skills are very well developed and you don't do much fantasising, but rather stay close to the edge of reality; am I right?"

"Maybe Chloe, but how do you explain my seeing something in my dreams that happened 128 years ago. Jenny from the mining museum in Somerset sent me a newspaper cutting on the mine accident in 1872; I didn't know about that."

"Who knows what you heard as a child Bran. As a two or three-year-old, you probably listened to your grandparents talking to your parents and other family members, and things stay in the memory, even though you can't remember them. If you had any traumatic experiences around this time, then there might be a lid shut tight on all this stuff." Chloe paused for a moment and she could see that Bran was deep in thought. Then she continued with something she thought would interest Bran. "Some folk think there may be a genetic memory that connects us to our ancestors. Darwin understood that humans must have survival properties, problem solving skills, passed on from generation to generation. Individual humans shouldn't have to re-invent these things or we wouldn't last long as a species. He called it pangenesis but this was way before we understood genetics. I don't know of any scientific work relating to the kind of genetic memory that might bubble up in dreams though. Well, not in the real world but remember in Alien Resurrection, Ellen Ripley is re-constructed and has memories from her previous incarnations, but I don't think fictional stuff is going to shed light on your dreams Bran." Chloe continued before Bran could comment on the genetic memory concept. "The love making sounded fun Bran, what were your feelings around that?"

"Oh, embarrassment Chloe, I felt embarrassed and surprised. And, as I reflected on what had happened I realised how exciting it had been, which made me feel guilty; it was as if I had been unfaithful to Mary." Bran and Chloe sat quietly for a while, both in their own worlds. Bran started to wonder

236

if he was asking too much of Chloe, straying into personal things that perhaps should be off limits in their friendship. Was he being unfaithful to Mary again, for sharing this with Chloe? But they had paused so maybe Chloe was thinking something similar. Then she spoke, taking them out of their musings.

"Enjoying sex in a dream is quite normal Bran, and it's not really under your control, is it? But, on that note, shall we have some lunch?" Bran felt relieved that Chloe had pulled them out of what might have been a difficult moment.

"Yes, that sounds good and I'm sorry I mentioned that dream Chloe; probably crossed a boundary that was better not crossed, if you know what I mean."

"Maybe, my professional instincts were becoming aroused and I'd prefer to be your friend than your therapist." Bran and Chloe changed the subject to the upcoming 'Love Sick' concert, now less than two weeks away. They had a practice session planned for the coming Friday and then the big rehearsal the following Friday before the concert on Saturday 10th June. Chloe had worked out a slow version of the song *Has Anybody Seen My Love* and sang it with oozing emotion. Bran would accompany her on guitar and harmonise in the middle eight. She wanted to practice this after lunch. "Now you know my selfish reason for inviting you around Bran, can we run through it please?"

"Of course, Chloe, ready when you are." Chloe began playing the piano, a moving introduction, so unlike Dylan's *Empire Burlesque* version. During the choruses, Bran tried a variety of different harmonies until he found the right one; he knew that because of Chloe's warm smile, she was happy with it. "We do that well together Chloe, and that is a great variation on the original; pretty well a new tune, did you compose it?"

"Yes, I felt the original was too jaunty. Too jaunty for the lyrics and the meanings I attach to them. Goodness knows what Dylan was thinking of, but don't we always say that?" Bran was looking across the room.

"Chloe, that pattern of stones you have in that case, is it Orion?"

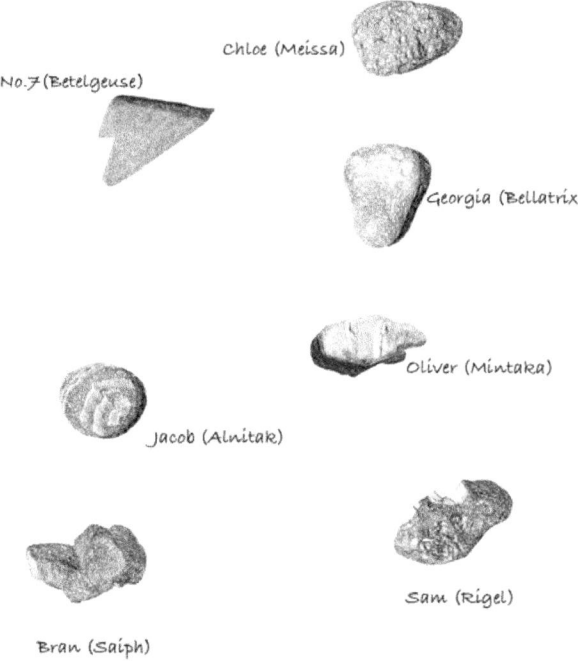

"Ha, ha, well spotted Bran, come and have a look. You may remember I'm a stone collector; stones are like history's bones to me and a big tension calmer. See, I've given them names, what do you think, do they fit?"

"I look very misshapen Chloe, is that how you see me?"

"No, not at all, but you are the most complex, multi-

238

faceted member of the band. You do this amazing engineering and then sing a sad song like Most of the Time; that seems to hold a memory for you Bran, anything in that?"

"Yes, I think so; I think it catches a lot of my memories of past love, unrequited love, confused, immature love from long ago. I'll take that 'complex' thing as a complement if you don't mind Chloe. But what about Meissa, up at the opposite end, you look like you've been bombarded by meteorites, what does that mean or is that too personal a question?"

"Its personal, but not too personal. I think I'm good at therapy because in many cases I've been there myself, and that particular stone speaks to me of survival and resilience."

"I see, yes that's you Chloe, and I can see Sam, Georgia and the others in their stones too. I think they would love to see how you see them. You are a good artist Chloe and I guess that goes with the sensitivity?"

"Not sure about that, but I do know that I have to be in the right mood for art and that usually means at peace; at least for the kind of art I do." Chloe and Bran sat down again to finish their lunch and continued talking about this and that, staying clear from personal stuff. When they had finished, Bran thanked Chloe for listening to him and for sharing her interesting ideas on dreams.

"Thanks, Chloe, you've given me much food for thought about all kinds of things actually, and a great lunch. But I forgot to mention the Ravens, in my dreams, I could hear them."

"You should speak with Georgia about that, she's into ravens, but remember to write your first thoughts about your dream down; they could be important to understanding."

They were standing next to Chloe's therapy room and

Bran noticed a painting hanging on the wall inside. "I see Orion keeps you company in the therapy room as well Chloe."

"Yes, he does and since you've seen him, come in and have a closer look, come meet my Orion. But no more than a minute or I'll charge you. The original might have been a hunter, but what do you think my Orion does?"

"I can see, he's playing a guitar and, is that Jim? How is Jim by the way Chloe, and the kids, are they away for the day?" Chloe's head sank but she looked at Bran again when she spoke.

"Jim and I have separated and he's looking after the children this weekend. I wasn't going to mention it Bran, would have rather spoilt our chat, and, no, that isn't Jim. He told me he was having an affair with someone from his work, at the University, said that she excited him in a way that I didn't anymore, and I told him to leave. That was a month ago." Chloe put her hands to her face as she began to cry.

"I'm so sorry Chloe; what a fool he is." Bran felt Chloe's pain and sadness and he felt his own tears rising. When Chloe saw this, she put her arms around him and their tears merged together in empathy.

"Just hold me tight for a minute please Bran." They held each other for several minutes until the empathy started to dry the tears and Chloe relaxed her hold on Bran. He didn't want to let go but she managed to loosen his strong hold and, with a light laugh, reached for the paper hankies and handed one to Bran. She folded her arms across her breasts and smiled.

"Thank you Bran, that was very helpful, if a little crushing, but that's ok. Where did your tears come from?"

"I felt for you Chloe, the pain you must have, can't help thinking what a fool Jim is. Anyway, I don't know what turns the tap on but it doesn't happen very often; can I blame you?"

"No, you can't, I didn't touch your tap; go figure for yourself and I'll see you on Friday." They walked quietly out of Chloe's house together. They were now more than good friends. They had shared personal things and deep empathy, the best kind, and knew they could trust each other. "Cheerio Bran, cycle carefully and keep your eyes open for stupid motorists coming home from the pub."

Cycling home, full of thoughts, images of the things that had happened; Chloe's tears, the special value of their friendship, unbroken because they hadn't crossed the line, his dreams were even more alive now that he has shared them, Chloe's beautiful song now even more poignant. The thoughts danced around his mind as he kept his eye open for stupid motorists and fools like Jim on the road; he would knock him down if he saw him. As the thoughts settled, one came back and demanded his attention; children who were told they weren't good enough. Had that happened to him? His father Alwyn had been a strict man who would get angry at Bran's misdemeanours, but Bran had always seen this as a normal, and justifiable, reaction to his wayward behaviour. Even as a child, especially as a child, Bran would push the boundary every day. "It's just the way he is," his mother Aoife would say to his father, "give him some slack". Yes, it was just the way he was, but where it came from in the foggy ruins of time he didn't know, and hadn't wondered much about it, until now. Maybe he should talk to his mother about this, something he'd always found difficult, for some reason.

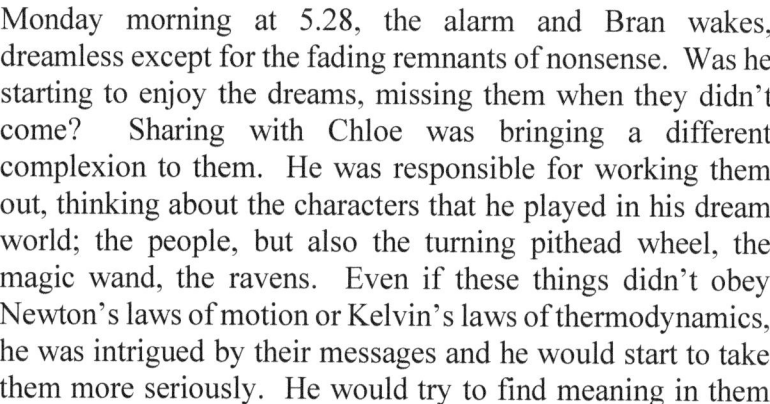

Monday morning at 5.28, the alarm and Bran wakes, dreamless except for the fading remnants of nonsense. Was he starting to enjoy the dreams, missing them when they didn't come? Sharing with Chloe was bringing a different complexion to them. He was responsible for working them out, thinking about the characters that he played in his dream world; the people, but also the turning pithead wheel, the magic wand, the ravens. Even if these things didn't obey Newton's laws of motion or Kelvin's laws of thermodynamics, he was intrigued by their messages and he would start to take them more seriously. He would try to find meaning in them that could improve his life, his mental state. Yes, he would try.

Bran liked Monday mornings because the FS2 staff often came in restored, fresh and eager to return to their tasks, had even solved problems over the weekend and wanted to share their discoveries. There were rarely *Monday-Monday* blues or hangovers at FS2, like you might expect from organisations involved in more routine activity.

This week was particularly important because they would be exploring the HoneyB-M flight envelope protection system to see if they could explain the malfunction; that was pencilled in for Wednesday. The Safety Agency would be coming in later in the week to discuss the Skycruiser2 cockpit problem, if that was what it was. The Skycruiser3 work would now pause until Claston had carried out a new wind tunnel test. Perhaps the most important activity was a simulation of the Odona crash scenario. Bran picked up from Roger at the TLeM that Holtan had provided FS2 with a simulation model of the Odona over the weekend, and they could look at that on Tuesday.

The Accident Investigation Branch would send a pilot and engineer to support this preliminary simulation trial. Friday, and the next Orion get-together, seemed an age away, both in time and space, but part of Bran was looking forward to that, especially seeing Chloe again.

Robert lowered the collective lever as he turned onto a south-westerly heading, descending into the valley north of Timly. "Airspeed 60kts, descending at 500 feet/minute, and pulling back to slow down; descending below the hill line."

"I need to descend into this valley to check the airspeed folks, but it shouldn't take more than a few minutes." Peter lowered the collective and set up a descent at 500 feet/minute. The hill top was at about 1000 feet so Peter thought it should only take a couple of minutes to get down and check the airspeed indicator and pitot-static tube; maybe it was blocked. He reached forward and tapped the glass; "sometimes the needle gets stuck on these early Odonas," but the airspeed still read 60kts.

"Airspeed holding at 60kts but I've had about six degrees nose up pitch for the last ten seconds so speed should be less than 40kts by now. Doesn't look like that when I see the valley sides racing by though; you guys must have added a strong tail wind."

"Damn it, airspeed sensor isn't reading correct, I need to land and find out what's wrong. Sorry folks, we are going to have to put down in the field up ahead; hopefully it won't take long to sort it out." Francis Clerk was sitting nervously next to Peter and spoke with a chuckle; "well maybe I won't need to give my talk after all; save me a lot of stress."

243

Robert maintained his deceleration for another 10 seconds and was sure the airspeed should now be below 20kts, even though the ground speed looked about 60kts; the tailwind was creating a powerful illusion that the aircraft was moving faster through the air than it really was. "Rate of descent building up and I now have nearly full power but still going down; I think we've hit vortex ring Bran, is that what is happening? Ok, rate of descent over 2000feet/minute and increasing, we are going to hit hard here, you have control."

"I have control." Colin took control of the simulation from the control desk, recorded the run details in the log book and downloaded the flight data onto the analyst's computer; the engineers in the room next door were already preparing to put the data through the flight path analysis routines.

Peter could not call out 'you have control' and as he pulled in maximum power, his aircraft only increased its rate of descent. "Damn it, vortex ring; brace, brace, tighten belts and brace, we are going to crash." Seconds later, the Odona hit the ground hard, at more than 2500 feet/minute descent rate and with a forward ground speed of about 30kts. The aircraft bounced but stayed level on its skids for a few seconds, then entered a shallow ditch and pitched down, the rotor blades ploughing into the ground ahead. The broken skids punctured the rear fuselage and fuel tank, and the aircraft was ablaze within seconds. All four occupants were incapacitated in one way or another by the hard landing, were unable to open the doors and became asphyxiated as the fire enveloped the broken fuselage.

Another tragic air accident with four fatalities that would add to already poor safety statistics for small helicopters. The lives of dozens, if not hundreds, of people would be affected, some shattered. Sandra Peel would receive a telephone call

244

later that day with the news and would be distraught, and wishing she had some time over again, so that she and Peter could make up. But now there was no making up. The investigation would take time but would be thorough and lessons would be learned. The primary causal factors would become part of the database that informed the industry, recommendations would be made to reduce the chance of such an accident happening again. Some people, like John Morgan and Bran Sage, knew that was a forlorn hope; accidents were waiting to happen when humans do dangerous things.

"Can we try that once more Bran and I will begin my corrective action a little earlier? I'd like to find the edge, the critical condition in terms of airspeed and height, beyond which recovery will be impossible, ok?" Robert was a test pilot working for the Air Accidents Investigation Branch. He had a great deal of experience exploring accident scenarios and always wanted to find out how much margin was available before a crash was inevitable; this often said a lot about the pilot and their ability to analyse situations, take corrective actions and so on. After the sortie, the pilot and engineers sat around the de-brief table drinking coffee. Robert had crashed nine times, laughingly saying that he'd used up his nine lives, but he had managed to recover the aircraft on the tenth run; he had found the edge. The formal de-brief was complete, each run gone through with a fine toothcomb, using the data already analysed and plotted out for scrutiny. The team were now more relaxed and Robert was interested in the maths of the simulation model. "How realistic is your vortex ring model Bran?" It was a Holtan model, so Bran looked across at the Geoff Scrag, the Holtan Chief Engineer, who was shaking his head.

"We are not sure Robert. We don't have the flight data to validate the model in vortex ring state, but we are using the best model we could develop to run in real-time and one that has been checked out on a different aircraft. Then we tailored it to the Odona rotor system which, as you know, has a high rotorspeed."

"Well, it was a powerful effect, like flying into a hole in the sky. If that's realistic then a pilot wouldn't have much chance of recovering below about 200 feet. The vertical motion cues on your simulator are good at cueing that by the way Bran; I probably wouldn't have realised it had happened just by looking out of the cockpit. Visual cues aren't enough and I'd say that sinking feeling gave me a couple of seconds' advanced warning; it might be worth checking that out, run the simulation again with motion switched off. As an aside here, the training schools are trying to persuade the safety agency to allow the use of flight simulators without motion systems. I think that's risky if they want to train recovery from vortex ring entry or tail rotor failure and other large acceleration manoeuvres." Bran asked Colin to plan for another sortie where they could check out the impact of the motion system, the so-called vestibular motion cueing, as opposed to the visual motion cueing.

As the afternoon ended, the trial team starting packing things up. Bran looked at Stuart.

"Do you think you've got what you need from us Stuart."

"Yes, thanks Bran, that's enough for the moment. As I mentioned earlier, we need to verify our suspicion that the airspeed sensor was blocked, but it looks that way. The pitot-static tube was damaged in the crash and subsequent fire so we can't be sure, but one of our engineers speculated that this could be a causal factor. In some ways, it would be better to take than pilot error. Maybe Peter Peel could have found another way out of the difficult situation but he was not to know that the winds had increased to such high levels in that

246

valley. Treat this as confidential for now Bran, we must keep our speculations out of the public eye until we know more. I anticipate getting a preliminary report out next week but we may not include this; let's see what else we find. Because of the Clerk-Oats issues, the letter to Mary etc., we need to keep the Police in the loop with our investigations as well. They may want to initiate a fatal accident investigation in the short term, before we have concluded our full assessment. That would be unusual, so we do need to get a move on. We'll let you see our analysis of the sim tests, probably by the end of the week, ok?"

"That's fine Stuart, can you send to Colin and he will get you our analysis of the flight path reconstruction you requested." Stuart and his Investigation Branch team left as the afternoon came to an end and Bran also bid farewell to Geoff Scrag who had sat in on the Odona simulation trial. Geoff had come to participate in the HoneyB-M simulation trial the following day. Bran had been concerned that anything they did to re-create the incident with the flight envelope protection system on the HoneyB-M, used a simulation model validated for the application. The Holtan and FS2 engineers had been going through the validation evidence throughout the day and Roger came into Bran's office to report that he was confident that they would be able to re-create the problem with acceptable accuracy.

Bran decided to sit in on the HoneyB-M simulation on Wednesday morning, including the briefing for the test pilot who had joined them from Holtan. FS2 had developed a protocol for conducting flight simulation trials that mirrored real-world flight testing. Communication between the control desk and the cockpit, the engineers and the flight crew, was always formal, tight and to the point, using normal communications parlance; "trial 206, sortie 1, run 1, recorders on, aircraft trimmed at 120kts, 3000 feet above ground level," "simulation ready," "pilot ready", "motion system engaged," "you have control", "I have control." And so began the first run of the sortie. The pilot would try to recreate the scenario he experienced in flight two weeks ago. He would set up a turn at 60-degree bank angle, pulling 2g, and then apply pedal to increase the turn rate. As the sideslip built up and turn rate increased the pilot could feel 'lateral g', absent from the Holtan fixed-base flight simulator.

"That feels right, like I'm leaning to the left even though I'm turning to the right. Increasing turn rate with pedal and I can feel the FEPS fighting me, stopping me from turning faster. I guess that's the sideslip limiter working?" Geoff Scrag was at the control desk with the Holtan engineer and he answered the pilot.

"Yes, that's right Bob, do you otherwise have full control, any suggestion of departure?"

"No, not yet, and I seem to have full control; I'll try to turn a little harder." Bob applied more pedal but the turn rate stayed at 16 degrees/second. The aircraft was on the sideslip limit and the FEPS was preventing the pilot from applying more tail rotor thrust. "No suggestion of incipient spiral dive. Levelling out. You have control."

"Pilot close eyes. I have control." Colin took control from the pilot and paused the flight simulator. "Re-initialising. Ok to open eyes now." The pilots were always told to close their eyes before the simulator was paused and during the transition to a new flight condition to minimise the risk of bursting the 'bubble of illusion' created in ground-based flight simulation. Ensuring that pilots behaved, used their controls, in a similar way to the real-world flight testing made the read-across to reality possible. If the bubble burst, then the simulation became more like a video game and pilots could quickly resort to unrealistic patterns of behaviour. Getting this right was something that Bran took very seriously.

During the de-brief, the engineers and pilot discussed the results of the sortie, comparing the data from the simulation with that from flight test. There was a strong correlation for the flight trajectory before departure, so why did the real aircraft then depart and the simulation not? Colin suggested that a more detailed examination of the tail rotor control actuation system should be undertaken. He had a suspicion that the simulation might not be the same as the real aircraft in this area; and were the computer commands from the FEPS being relayed to the control actuators correctly? Also, Roger had asked what kind of math model of the rotor wake interaction with the tail rotor was included in the Holtan simulation. Seems like it was not very detailed, but might the wake have interfered with the flow through the tail rotor, enough to stall the blades perhaps? Colin suggested that Jim Waterhill might be able to create a higher-fidelity rotor wake model if they thought it would be helpful. The Holtan engineers would take these ideas away for further exploration. A new project tasking would be prepared for FS2 to undertake more simulations, since the pilot was convinced that motion cueing was critical to preserving the bubble of illusion for this problem.

"Tobias Hamel from Claston called while you were in the sim Bran; said it was urgent, shall I call him back?" Jos was waiting for Bran as he returned to his office. Bran agreed to take the call and waited for Jos to put him through to Tobias.

"Bran, if you haven't heard already, one of our Skycruiser2's crashed this morning. It was one from the same airline that have complained their pilots have difficulty with information on the cockpit displays on approach. Seems like the aircraft was on finals but way outside limits and they tried a go-around, but were too late. They hit the runway hard, the undercarriage collapsed and the aircraft skidded off and came to a stop on the grass. No fatalities thank God, but a lot of injuries and hull damage. We'll pause the assessment this week as the Safety Agency and the national accident investigation bureau need to turn their attention to the accident investigation. I'd like to keep you involved when the dust settles if you don't mind."

After the phone call, Bran's thoughts were on safety, on how precarious things can sometimes tip over when man and machine interact, and how simulation can explore these in relative safety. There were human factors, and art, as well as science, involved in flight simulation. Bran had spent his career learning about reality from examining creations in the virtual world and reflecting on comparisons with the real world. He would usually learn more when comparisons revealed disagreements. He reflected on his ancestry project; was he creating a virtual world of his ancestors that were re-living in his subconscious and dreams? Just as he wondered what had really happened in the Odona crash, the HoneyB-M FEPS malfunction and the Skycruiser2 crash landing, so he wondered what really happened to Henry and Sarah, at the mine, on the footpath, in the field? Would he ever really know?

That evening Bran phoned Mary. She was in one of her meetings but stepped out for a 'brief chat'. She had reviewed some of Dr Clerk's research and had discussed it with her colleagues. They thought he might be onto something and were keen to see his conference presentation if Bran could find it.

Mary had agreed to talk with the funding agency about the

work. Their chat was indeed brief but long enough to remind Bran of the special sanctuary inside his heart where he and Mary dwelled.

The train was smoking down the track, hauling carriages around the bend as it left the station. The sounds of the big machine on the move, the smell of soot and steam, fumes from burning coal and hot oil filled the air. The platform was empty, apart from a group of four people, two sitting down talking to each other, luggage stacked up. I'm close to them now.

Friday morning and Bran woke with a start. "I've got to write this down. Steam train disappearing around the bend. She was sitting, looking at me, listening to him talking; about Sarah leaving Camerton, and a secret held for thirty years. It's a letter, someone was reading a letter to Sarah. Your father James and I had an affair; I became pregnant; my mother sent me to live in Bath, three years with auntie. Damn, careful to remember as much detail as you can Bran, stay with it, don't let it fade. Never told him about his daughter and when she returned to Camerton, he had married Maria. Maria and James, I know who they are. Henry is reading a letter to Sarah, and whoever wrote the letter to Henry is talking about my great great-grandfather, James Sage. Henry's sister is Wendy Arton, born in Bath on February 20th, 1843, adopted by John and Mary Arton. It broke her heart, sent to finishing school; taught how to control emotions, behave like a lady, look down on the working class; punishment for her getting pregnant. Wow, that is some punishment. Look after Sarah. Its signed *Anna, Anna Fernhill from Camerton Manor*. Anna Fernhill, the woman in the newspaper cutting who owned the mines in Camerton valley. That's more than a dream. How can I be hearing someone reading a letter in the 19th century? What are my first thoughts; Chloe told me to write my first thoughts? I missed the train, did Sarah miss the train? Who were the other two people on the platform? I could hear Henry's voice, soft with a Somerset accent. Were Henry and Sarah on a journey, leaving Camerton? Yes, they must have been travelling to South Wales. This was when they moved. I've been wondering when they moved, so that's been in my head at all levels for a while. Wendy Arton, James's and Anna's daughter, Henry's sister; was Wendy Arton real? I am going to find out. If Wendy was real and born in Bath on the 20th February 1843, I should be able to track her down from the census records. Now this is exciting and warrants another trip to Camerton and the Somerset Mining Museum." Bran made a note to call Jenny at the museum that morning to see if he could visit on Saturday. He also wanted to find out more about Anna Fernhill, the woman with the broken heart, who'd had the affair with James and had been punished for getting pregnant; she was a real mystery. Bran reached for the document he'd downloaded from Jenny's email; the minutes of the Somerset Miner's Association. *Lady Anna Fernhill was very sympathetic to the miners' cause and supported their aims for improvements across all fronts.* "Maybe Anna's broken heart had healed", Bran whispered to himself.

Orion would be having a longer practice session that evening. They needed to work through twelve more songs to complete the set, so would need at least four hours. It would be a shorter Friday than normal at the office for Bran. And the TLeM ran for longer than normal, because they needed to discuss the fallout from the simulation trials and the consequences of the Skycruiser2 crash; how might FS2 prepare for involvement? Friday was turning out to be anything but normal. After the TLeM, Bran saw that Jos had sent him a copy of the presentation that Francis Clerk was due to give at the Bogan conference. He forwarded it to Mary,

252

with a message that he would be heading out early on Saturday on his ancestry research journey and would phone late on Sunday. Bran also received an email from Jim Owen, the carpenter who was renovating the Old Blaina Chapel; he would welcome the chance to meet Bran. Bran arranged to visit on Sunday, on his way back from Somerset; time to visit the Valleys. It was going to be a busy weekend, but first something that Bran had been looking forward to all week.

He was the last to join the band and he found them peering over a picture Chloe had brought to show them; it was a photograph of her stones. She said it was time to reveal all. Sam was the first to comment.

"I'm more than a stone Chloe love, especially one with a chunk bitten out; is that supposed to be my chip?"

"Well, I thought that was very you Sam, and don't you underestimate stones, or chips, they carry a huge history and you can make of it what you want, like Dylan's songs. Rigel is a blue supergiant, blue cos its used up all its hydrogen gas. Doesn't that fit Sammy?"

"No, you know I'd prefer to be Betelgeuse, can I swap with No.7? Now he's a red giant, more fitting, considering my football team, and, besides I've always fancied Betelgeuse's girls *'who'll do anything you like, real fast and then real slow.'* And, I've always wanted a *'point of view gun'*, then I could fire it at Bran and he would agree with everything I say. Come on Chloe, let me swap with No.7, please?" Sam was laughing as he made his plea, but there was also something serious in the tone of his voice. Georgia had always been very happy with Bellatrix, saw herself as a female warrior and said she would have been ok with a chip in her stone; "gives you character". She had told Sam she was more comfortable with him beneath her, as Rigel, than alongside, as Betelgeuse. Sam looked puzzled at this. And Oliver was uncertain about Mintaka's stone, like some weird creature, and said he needed a few light years to think about it, while Jacob was very comfortable with Alnitak. He knew the star was one of the most complex in the night sky and his stone's surface patterns reflected this complexity, reflected his percussion. He joked with Oliver about their role in the star system.

"Come on Oli, us on the belt need to keep the band's trousers on, keep 'em up, which reminds me, shouldn't we be practising our songs?" The stones seemed to charge up Orion's emotions, unsettle them actually, and Georgia tried to bring them back with the usual five minutes of meditation before anyone played a note. But it was not enough to break the spell, the disquiet. They knew this was the last practice. Next week would be the rehearsal and then the concert and everyone seemed slightly on edge. Dylan had said something about hiding things in songs, if you wanted to, bad enough. And so, Orion began their practising, each member hiding their personal stuff in the lyrics or the way they played their instruments. They all knew this was going on, and deeply respected others for it, even helped each other with the hiding, all in the subconscious of course. Oliver reminded them that they were running through two songs each.

"You all know the parts that need polishing so let's be efficient and work through them. I suggest Bran gets us going with *Baby Stop Crying* and then *Something There is About You*, followed by Chloe with *Has Anybody Seen My Love* and *It's All Over Now, Baby Blue*. Georgia, can you come after that with *All I Really Want to Do* and *Boots of Spanish Leather*, with Sam playing the guy part, ok? Then, while you're up Sam, you can follow with *Simple Twist of Fate* and *Don't*

Think Twice. Now to the Belt Boys, first Jacob with *True Love Tends to Forget* and *I'll Remember You*. I'll finish up with *It Ain't Me Babe* and *Where Teardrops Fall*. That should cheer us all up, but we did all agree the Love-Sick theme, didn't we? Maybe we should have a break after Georgia's set."

And so, Orion began their final practice session. They stuck religiously to the agenda, 20 minutes for each song, kept working them until the clock struck. To the observant, hidden things peeped out for brief moments, and were revealing. Both Georgia and Sam had tears in their eyes as they shared a dying romance, the stars forsaken for a sweet kiss and all she wanted were the boots, made from Spanish leather, of course. As Sam went walking down the long and lonely road, whereto he hadn't a clue, or at least he couldn't, wouldn't maybe, tell, he closed his eyes and paused before admitting that goodbye was too good a word; where did that come from, wondered Oliver? Bran seemed obsessed with her crying, but wasn't that the way Dylan wrote it, and he knew the sun would always shine, but Bran seemed unsure from the expression on his face. Perhaps he was captivated by something crossed over from another century; now there was definitely something in that. Chloe shared her pain and Bran helped her with the harmonies they had practised the previous Sunday; has anybody seen her love? Bran had seen her love and hoped that Chloe would be able to share it again soon, with someone. When she sang, strike another match, Bran knew that the words held her truth, and the tears flowed again; what was he hiding there? And, who was the tearjerker that Jacob sang about? He'd clearly been under her spell at some time in his life, breaking free after his weekend in hell, perhaps. We don't know because Jacob had it well hidden, but perhaps it would be revealed in the expressions on his *FACES* exhibition they would all see next weekend. Now it was Oliver's turn. Oliver the political scientist, who delved into the meaning of life from a whole other level, denied to most because of their ignorance. Where do the tear drops fall Oliver, come on tell us? But were we all thinking of her, or him, when the sun comes up, that's where teardrops fall. Bran thought of Mary, oh Mary, can we sharpen the senses that linger in the fireball heat? Yes, we can, we can, just come home safe to me.

Dylan's lyrics brought out the boys and the anima in the men, and the girls and the animus in the women, brought out the hidden things that needed to be cared for. The whole band, all of Orion, were aware of this in their own ways and that's what brought them together; a remarkable symbiosis. Although things were hidden, they knew that bringing them out using the symbolism and metaphors in the lyrics was sufficiently revealing, and helped them manage the confusion arising from emotions being brought back to life through their memories. The past brought into the present, never really gone no matter what Dylan said. Mind you, Bob was good at that kind of thing, whether he wanted to be or not.

"Sam if you really want to be Betelgeuse, you can, the space is free, but you don't get a point-of-view gun, or get to see starships on fire, unless you close your eyes and let your imagination do the rest." It wasn't just Chloe who had picked up Sam's angst that evening, but she was the first to try to coax him into talking when they were in the pub. The practice session had lasted the best part of five hours so they were all weary but needed the chill-out time in the pub. Sam looked around at his friends and his tears suddenly flowed.

"My dad had a heart attack yesterday, when we were watching the match; he got a bit too excited. He nearly died but I laid him down and gave him CPR, cardiopulmonary resuscitation, for those who don't know. I had my father's life in my hands, beating at his heart, that big heart, and was scared that I would lose him, that he was slipping away. I was shouting at him, don't die dad, don't die and I kept it up for about 20 minutes until the medics arrived and took over." Georgia quickly moved over and sat next to Sam, putting her arm around him.

"Oh Sam, we're with you and you saved your dad, right? How is he now?"

"He survived and when he woke up he looked at me and asked if we'd won, then he gave me a big smile. Most dramatic moment of my life, I tell you; can't recall my birth mind you. My dad shaped my thinking big time; in fact, he taught me how to think, how to think like a socialist and behave like a socialist. You know he walked with Bertrand Russell on the *Action for Life* march in London. I have a photograph; 18th February 1961, and there he is, I can see him in the photo. He is very proud of this and I am very proud of him." Oliver leaned forward and held Sam's arm.

"I'm so sorry about your dad Sam, sounds like a good man and thanks to you he has a new lease of life." Oliver paused for a moment before changing the subject. "Talking about thinking, you know Russell once said something like, '*most people would rather die than think, and most people do.*' He was very aware of the fragility of democracy, the tension between freedom and democracy. Governments in power, with a majority, claim to speak for the people while they plough their furrows of ideology."

"That's it Oli, my father taught me to see the twisted ideology of the Tories. They say they want people to be independent but all the time they want to chain us up, play the ruling class and deny us our freedom. We'll only be free when we have control." Georgia wanted to ease Sam's pain, but something inside of her had been woken.

"I wish I could say the same about my father Sam; he was too busy trying to stay still to give my mum and me attention. I was glad to see him go; he didn't die, just left us to fend for ourselves." Bran wanted to say something about democracy.

"I think it's more about governments, the modern elite that drift into power, frankly being unable to manage the complexities of democracies. For some time, I have thought that we need a second chamber, made up of professionals, appointed for their knowledge and skills, particularly relating to technologies; a proper balance of the two cultures that C P Snow wrote about. That way, more informed decisions could be made, enabling private enterprise to support public enterprise fairly." Sam didn't agree.

"No Bran, you're another idealist hoping for socially responsible capitalism. I'm afraid it will always serve the selfish instincts of the greedy; there's no design for life there. And if you want to make a difference you need to stop playing with planes and digging up the past and get stuck into what really matters." Sam had drunk a few pints so he was letting off steam, not thinking clearly, despite what his father had taught him and fortunately Bran could see this. Chloe rose in Bran's defence.

"Ease up Sam, that's unfair and unfriendly, you know Bran does a lot of good work investigating accidents, making aviation safer. Come on, let's get off politics, we know it always divides us." Jacob wanted to bring them back to thinking and Dylan.

"Ok, what about this; do we think about Dylan's lyrics when we sing them? I do because that's the only way I connect with them but I remember you saying that you didn't, Sam. Please explain?" Sam was quiet with his head hanging down.

258

He put his pint down on the table and looked up at Bran.

"I feel them but don't think about them. Hey, I'm sorry Bran. You're like my big brother and I lost it for a minute there. Truth is, I'm a little bit envious of your passion for what you do. Forgive me?"

"Of course, Sam, felt a slight pang for a moment but its passed now and maybe it's because I'm like your big brother that you did it; you know what they say about sibling rivalry. And by the way, I'm a bit envious of your ability to interpret Dylan, maybe it's because you feel the lyrics. When you sang, *"they walked along by the old canal, a little confused"*, well I was there, I really was, I mean that. You have a real skill projecting the scenes into my imagination." Oliver raised his glass.

"Before we break tonight can we drink to that thought, Orion projecting into each other's imaginations; such a lovely thought."

Bran dropped Chloe off at her house on his way home.

"Thanks again for the other day Chloe, it was very helpful and got me thinking about all kinds of things. Sorry about you and Jim as well, I hope you find a way...." Bran had not finished his sentence but Chloe interrupted.

"I don't want to find a way with him Bran; I need someone better than Jim, someone who can love me. See you next week." Chloe was gone in a moment and Bran thought what he said was stupid, and insensitive. Did he really want Chloe to find a way with Jim? No, he wanted Chloe to be happy, that's what he wanted.

Bran poured himself a glass of Burgundy and sat looking through an old family album; there were his father and mother, father long gone and mother living in peaceful retirement in the village of Crickhowell, only 10 miles, but so very far, from the scarred landscape of the coal mining Valleys. He would call in and see her on his visit to Ebbw Vale, maybe even stay

 with her. And there was an old photo of him flying a Harvard. He liked to look down on the countryside from 2000 feet up. On a clear day, you could just make out the hills in mid Wales; that was far enough he'd say to himself. But his mind turned to what Sam had said, and he felt the pain, the shame, again. "Do I play with planes, dig up the past, don't I do things that matter?" Bran knew that, deep down, he did these things because he enjoyed them. Sam said that he was envious but maybe his inner persecutor was less demanding than Bran's because Sam did things that matter, wrote articles that shook foundations, made people feel uneasy, changed the way they thought and proudly followed in his father's footsteps. Bran wondered if Sam ever sang Dylan's song '*Gonna change my way of thinking*'. Sam was not a religious man but reckoned that Jesus was one of his heroes, so perhaps he'd be ok with the lyrics. Perhaps we all need to put our best foot forward, stop being influenced by fools. How would Bran's ancestry research help him with that he wondered and why was he digging up the past? He'd said on page seven that it was to do with his mortality but he wasn't sure now; there must be more, if there ever could be more.

Bran closed the photo album and remembered the chat about hidden stuff in the songs and thought that photo albums

were like that too. He pulled out one of his poems and worked out a couple of tunes; one real fast, the other real slow, like the pretty girls from Betelgeuse.

The pictures tell it all, I think it's plain to see

Some hanging on a wall, some hanging up a tree

You've got to have an eye for seeing through the stare

Into the deep beyond, into the pain and joy

Meet the little girl, meet the little boy

They're beckoning you to come

Play hide and seek in the family album

As he drifted off to sleep, Bran remembered the canal path in Camerton. Sam's singing had taken him back there. "I must visit it again, maybe she'll be waiting. No, don't be daft, she's moved to Wales. Get a grip Bran, Sarah has long gone, right?"

8. Yn rhydd o Unigedd, mae'r Gigfran yn dathlu

Free from Solitude, the Raven Celebrates

"So, we'd like to get married this week in your chapel, do you think Mr. Lewis will do that for us?" Sarah was speaking with Megan's mother, Gwen, but looking at Henry as she asked this.

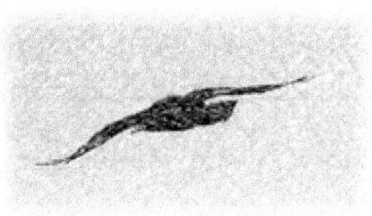

They had finished breakfast after their first night staying with Megan's family, and were sitting around the table with her mother, her father Rhys and younger sister Siân. The kitchen was small and cosy, the rich smells of freshly baked bread and roast ham warming the room. Gwen kept her house spotless, especially her kitchen which she cleaned every morning after Rhys had left for work. She was proud of her home, proud to make it a special place for her husband to come home to after his hard day hewing coal at the Rising Sun pit. Gwen replied to Sarah, looking at Henry first then back to Sarah.

"Well now Sarah love, you can ask him yourself when you come to service with us; put on your best, we'll be leaving in about 30 minutes. But yes, it would be good if you could marry, that way you wouldn't have to sleep on the floor Henry, would you? I hope it wasn't too uncomfortable?"

"Not at all Gwen, I'm only to grateful to you both for putting us up. I was exhausted after our day's travel and then the walk up the hill last night, so slept like a log. Beautiful view from up there by the way. Looking down on the valley below and across the hilltops. I've never seen so deep or so far in my life; looked like there was valley after valley stretching out as far as we could see."

"They say you can see England from up there on a clear day, across the river; never seen it myself mind you. Some people, outside the valleys of course, like to think that this is England, but everybody hereabouts is Welsh, even the English immigrants, if you get me. Rhys and me would go up there a lot in our courting days, didn't we love? There were some nice little hollows we could hide in, get to know each other better. Now we have our own bed so don't need no mountain top hollows, do we Rhys?"

"Henry and Sarah are not interested in our love life Gwen dear, now I got to get ready for Chapel and I think you have to as well." Rhys was a kind man who worked hard for his wife and three children but was easily embarrassed by Gwen's explicit language, although this had drawn him to her when they were young. The wonder of her sexuality rather overpowered him so he'd offered little resistance. She was direct and forthright in a Welsh way, just like her mother before her and two daughters, Siân and Megan, after her. Her son Dafydd was more like his father, reserved and careful with his words, careful with his actions and faithful to his non-conformist code. He lived in Ebbw Vale and Henry and Sarah would be meeting him at lunchtime on their first visit to the town of iron and steel. Tom and Megan were staying with Dafydd for a few days before returning to Camerton to build their new life together. Henry was eager to find out what the job prospects were in Ebbw Vale. Megan had said that Dafydd would be able to help. So, after Chapel, they headed over to Ebbw Vale and found Tom and Dafydd talking with two other men in the street outside the terraced house in Waterfall Row. They were dressed smartly, in Sunday best, so Henry guessed they had also been to Chapel.

"Tom brother, we've just come from the Blaina Baptist Chapel and Minister Mr. John Lewis has agreed to marry us on Wednesday, but we need you and Megan to be our witnesses, is that alright?"

"Well now I'm sure that can be arranged brother Henry, and good morning to you sister Sarah. Can I introduce you to Megan's brother Dafydd and his friends Gethyn and Wyn. They work at the Victoria mines, although Gethin here can't do any mining or labouring since his accident." The men greeted each other with strong handshakes, like men do when they make a new friend, relaxing their grip when greeting Sarah, not wanting to spoil the new friendship. She acknowledged their sensitivity with one of her Somerset smiles.

"It's good to see you again Thomas and very pleased to meet you Dafydd and you too Gethyn and Wyn. Do you live here in Ebbw Vale?" Sarah was anxious to find a home for Henry and her, and she wanted to know more about the town. Gethyn answered Sarah.

"Yeh we do love, Wyn and I lodge with Mrs Morgan in number eight." Gethyn pointed with his one good arm down the narrow street and he continued with a chuckle in his voice; "next door to Dafydd and his noisy family. I'm not saying it's a bad noise mind you, just a noisy noise." Dafydd was laughing as well and explained to Sarah who looked a little concerned.

"We had two lots of twins, or rather Rhian did, within about eighteen months, so they are a handful and an earful at times. But we love them, don't we uncle Gethyn?"

"Yeh, too right we do. I'm looking forward to when I can take em up to the stute and show them books, with stories and pictures that will make their eyes water and their minds wonder. I work most of the time in the library at the Literary and Scientific Institute, or stute for short, Sarah. I lost my arm in a roof fall a few years ago so I'm pretty useless at anything that needs two arms. But reading and sorting books, I can do that till the sun goes down, and that can be quite early in these deep valleys. Sometimes I think my accident was a blessing cos it brought me to books. Do you like reading Sarah?"

"Yes, I do like reading Gethyn but I don't do much of it; I do paint though, pictures and sketches of anything that takes my fancy."

"You'll have to come up to the stute Sarah, there is a painting class showing off their work this Friday. Let me take you and introduce you to some of the artists, you'd be amazed at what people round here can do, what they see in their mind's eyes."

"I'd love to come over Gethyn, thank you." Dafydd brought them back to the question of where to live.

"Listen Sarah, I know you're looking for a home here in Ebbw and I do know that there is a family moving out of number 15 this week. They have eight kids so need more space and we can find out if that house will be free. It's one of the EVC's houses, that's the Ebbw Vale Company's, and I know that Tom has been speaking to the manager at number 6 colliery about you working there Henry, sort of taking his place. How's that been going Tom boy?" Tom spoke to Henry and Sarah.

"I think that's going to work out fine. I've arranged for you to meet Arthur Rogers tomorrow to talk about it; he wants to find out what you can do. Arthur is a hard man but fair, lost his father in one of Bailey's pits in Beaufort and is obsessed about safety; he also lost his sense of humour so be wary. But let's go and have some lunch. Dafydd's Rhian has done a

Sunday roast for us and Rhian's roast is a real treat."

The small group walked down the narrow street towards no.10. People stood outside doorways of the small terraced houses that made up Waterfall Row; women with folded arms and speaking with an intensity that was unfamiliar to Sarah. They seemed to be mostly talking about other people in a way that was not always complementary; Jones did this and Evans did that, well I never; where will it lead, how will they do, did you ever? The flow of gossip that coloured people's opinions and outlooks, reinforcing already fragile and limited understandings about the  world around them, but providing some tribal comfort and security. She heard the Welsh language spoken several times but everyone exchanged friendly greetings, bora da, shwmae, hylô and warm smiles as they passed by. Sarah was aware of the strong smells, some obviously from the kitchens, but others more unpleasant pervading the air. She wondered where they came from. The sound of babies crying filled the air; a new generation wanting to be heard or just crying for food, or maybe both. As they passed number 15, Henry squeezed Sarah's hand and gave her a warm smile. This might be their home soon and Brân may be crying too.

Rhian's and Dafydd's home was spotlessly clean inside, just like Gwen and Rhys's. Henry and Sarah were made to feel welcome and soon all seven were sitting around the small kitchen table eating Rhian's fabulous lamb roast. This was the only time they eat proper meat in the week, but Rhian would always have a broth cooking on the stove. The men talked about the changes that were taking place since the EVC had been damned for its continued use of trucking, whereby the weekly subs could only be used to buy goods from their shops. New shops were opening, selling groceries, furniture and hardware, run by local businessmen. The strikes by sale-coal miners against reductions in pay was starting to involve the miners at the EVC mines but Ivan Evans was working on an agreement to limit the pay reductions to 5% and avert a strike in Ebbw Vale. Sarah looked around the room, taking in the details of how Rhian had arranged her kitchen, noticing the things she liked and didn't like. Sarah was designing her own kitchen and felt excited by her thoughts, when there was a loud knock on the door. Dafydd squeezed by the others and made his way to open the door. Standing there was Bryn Williams, a friend who worked at the local iron and steel works.

"Shwmae Bryn, what's up on Sunday boy?"

"Sorry to disturb your day of rest Dai but there's a gang of miners down at the works, come over from Aber I think. They are threatening our men down there, saying they should come out on strike with them. Just like when the scotch cattle used to come over in their bloody herds."

"Damn it, not them again, I thought they had packed up more than 20 years ago. Hang on Bryn, I'll come back down with you." Dafydd explained to Henry what was going on and he and Wyn quickly changed into their working clothes. They tried to persuade Henry to stay at the house but he was determined to join them. He felt his adrenalin starting to flow and his instinct was to stand alongside his new friends. As the three men approached the works, they saw a group of about ten men surrounding a few of the iron workers. They were speaking loudly with crude language. The loudest turned as he heard Dafydd approach.

"Hey, we don't want no trouble boys, just come over to

ask for your support with our strike this week. The owners are cutting our wages by 10% and we need you Ebbw boys with us. Come on now, don't be blacklegs, stand with us against the bastard slave drivers." A tall burly, mean-looking man stepped forward, looking at Henry and spoke in a growl.

"You with us or against us, that's what I'd like to know?" As the man was talking, another group of men was coming down from Ebbw Vale. One of them, Mervyn Jones, strode up and he didn't mince words with the intruders.

"Bugger off from where you come from or we'll help you on your way." Whatever happened next, it happened very quickly; they'd done talking and wanted to sort things out with fists rather than brains. It was like someone had stepped on the proverbial cat's tail. One of the intruders threw a stone he'd been holding and it hit Merv on the head, at the same time as the man who had, moments ago, claimed that he didn't want no trouble, in that double negative way, lashed out at Merv knocking him down. Dafydd punched the double negative in the face, breaking his nose, while Henry punched mean-looking man in the gut, doubling him up, followed by a left to his head. Henry made it quite clear that he was against him with a final punch that put the man down. Stone thrower was wrestling with Wyn, and there were about six other one-to-ones going on. By now Merv was back on his feet and wanting to repay the intruders with interest for his bloodied head. The fight was fast and furious without quarter given. In slow motion, if it could be imagined, it was quite theatrical, almost a dance, accompanied by grunts and groans, squelches and cracks of flesh and bones. The natural life on the mountainsides paused their Sunday business, and looked down in silence as if the audience in the play. Men at war, whose instinct is to fight, the reason for fighting long forgotten, every movement charged by the urge to win, to defeat the enemy; it would only end in a win and a defeat. Henry had laid three of the intruders out of the fight and wrestled stone thrower off Wyn, hurling him to the ground, where he stayed. As another group of Ebbw miners came running down the road, the intruders began running off, back from whence they had come. Merv ran after them, but Dafydd called to him.

"Come back Merv, let 'em go, they've got the message." Merv shouted a curse after the intruders and Dafydd turned to Henry. "Damn it Henry, you are one good fighter, that guy won't look the same again, they won't recognise him back in Aber, if that's where they came from." Dafydd sat down on a pile of railway sleepers before continuing. "Ivan said that we might expect this from the miners at the sale-coal pits; told us that the owners claim they weren't getting a good price for the coal that goes off to England. Here in the Victoria mines it nearly all goes to feeding the coke ovens for iron and steel making and we just can't make enough of that stuff. So, us miners feel a stronger kindred with our friends and family who make iron and steel than miners from other valleys." Henry was wiping the blood from his face as he listened to Dafydd.

"I thought Ivan said there was a National Union of Mineworkers so we would all work together, for union and for right; aren't they the watchwords now?"

"Yes, that's the way it's supposed to be but we haven't got there yet in the Valleys; too many separated communities. There's the Rhondda and Aberdare way off to the west, six valleys away, Blaenavon and Abersychan to the east and even close by we have Blaina, Abertillery and Sirhowy; we hardly ever talk to each other, let alone build an association. Ivan is trying to bring us together but when these thugs come over and try to force things on us, it sets things back. I think they just want to stir up trouble, got their own personal axes to grind, just like the scotch cattle used to. Those no-goods would smash people's homes and beat them silly just because they disagreed with them; empty headed wasters. In the end the army had to come in to sort them out. Let's hope to God that's not starting up again." The group of miners sat quietly attending to their wounds. One of Merv's friends was wiping the blood from the cut on Merv's head under continuous instruction from Merv; "not there damn it, over a bit, not so bloody rough will you, you'll make it worse." Henry's knuckles were bleeding, as was his left ear and he could feel bruises on his cheekbone in the same place that one of Billie Oats's cronies had hit him with a club just over two weeks ago. Scars and bruises, there to remind us of our humanity. And so, it went on, the victors joking and congratulating each other for their strength and prowess while their bodies and minds settled down, heart beats and adrenalin rush slowing.

Back at Rhian's home, after Daffyd and Henry had left, Gethyn offered to take Sarah and Rhian up to the stute. Sarah was anxious about Henry. She knew he was very decisive and would always do what he thought was right, but she hoped he would not take foolish risks. Her memory of his fight with Billie Oats and his gang was still fresh. But she was also very curious to know what went on in the Literary and Scientific Institute and Gethyn was only too pleased to share his knowledge. Rhian wanted to finish cleaning up after lunch so told them to go without her. When they arrived at the Institute, Gethyn welcomed Sarah in and began to describe what was inside.

"You can see we've this large lecture hall with a stage, a reading room and library over that side and three classrooms over there. We started a course in technical drawing and basic mechanics principles for adults last year and hoped that the younger scholars would sign up as well but they just haven't had enough basic education, reading and arithmetic and the like. We are hoping that will change since the education act of 1870."

Sarah hadn't realised what this meant so Gethyn explained. "Our Bedwellty school board was set up last year and has been trying to get the Ebbw Vale Company to improve the schooling for the young kids. Thankfully some of those in charge up in London can see the  benefit in government taking over education, rather than leave it to the land owners and the church, neither of who really care to educate the people properly; suits 'em better to keep us under their thumb if you ask me. Give a man a hunger and a thirst for knowledge and there's no stopping him, he'll do the rest. This is where it starts Sarah, when a man learns a skill he wants to use it and when he learns something new he's ready for the next thing. Well, that's the theory; and is that how it was, or is, for you Sarah?" Sarah was wondering if Gethyn thought that education applied to women as well.

"Oh, now there's a question Gethyn. I went to school in my village of Camerton, learned to read and write and, yes, I enjoyed it. I learned practical things quickly and Henry would help me with reading and my homework. He's a very good, and a very patient, teacher. But we both left school when we were young. I worked for my father at his Inn and Henry started in the mine when he was only 10 years old. He also worked in the garden of the local Manor and learned a lot from the owner's grandfather who had travelled the world. Henry would come back from his day at the Manor and tell me all the things he'd found out from Grampa John, about the stars in the sky, the seasons and weather, places and people around the world and their different cultures, the politics of England and what went on in our parliament. Almost too much sometimes, but Henry took it all in. Me, I would make clothes and paint or sketch pictures of things I see, in the way I see them." Sarah was aware that she was starting to share her personal story with a stranger, a man she didn't know, something she hadn't done before, but Gethyn seemed trustworthy, and it felt safe. Perhaps it was because she was in a new place, with new people who didn't know her as Sarah Jane Wallace, daughter of Elizabeth and Albert Wallace, barmaid at the Colliers Rest and secret lover of her cousin Henry Sage. Sarah felt like she was learning something new about herself, a change, and like Gethyn had said when a woman learns something new, she's ready for the next thing, except that Gethyn had referred to men; maybe he was ready to learn something new as well.

"Sounds wonderful Sarah, so you paint and, look, you can see the easels we have along the side over there. They are for the painting classes every Friday, so you must join us." Sarah wasn't ready to commit but thought she would like to find out what happened at the painting class. Gethyn was excited by Sarah's interest and invited her over to the library, talking as they walked.

"When I got involved in this library, and we bought a pile of books, my dad said that miners would never read Dickens. So, I decided to prove him wrong. I'm reading this one now, Barnaby Rudge, a story set during the Gordon riots, the anti-Catholic protestations, about 100 years ago. I do like Dickens because his detailed descriptions let me see what it was like in the past, brings it to life; just close my eyes and I can see it, feel it even. But, it's a complicated story with lots of characters, sometimes I think too many, but I can see he uses

273

them to make lots of different points, that just a few people wouldn't; see what I mean there Sarah?"

"I think so Gethyn, but I haven't read much. My mother would try to force me to read but I resisted so I think that's dampened my enthusiasm; I didn't get on with my mother." There I go again, sharing personal stuff, Sarah thought as she said this.

"I'm sorry to hear that Sarah; but you know, this story is about a young man, Joe, who leaves his father's Inn because he's always quarrelling with him, and he leaves his girl Molly behind, but they come back together later. But Joe has lost his arm in the American war of independence so I feel a bit like him, with my one arm and all."

"Sounds a good story Gethyn, but who is Barnaby Rudge?"

"He's a fascinating character Sarah, I do like him. Dickens portrays him as a rather simple person, travelling around with his mother trying to escape a stranger, who turns out to be…, I won't say Sarah in case you want to read it. I reckon Dickens uses Barnaby Rudge to help the reader along, connecting the different things going on; quite clever really. But the amazing thing in the story is Barnaby's raven, his pet raven Grip, who can talk. Dickens himself had a raven he named Grip and he wrote about the bird's preternatural sagacity. I love words that sound good, but I had to look those words up." Gethyn could see that Sarah looked confused so he thought he should tell her what the words meant. "Preternatural is like 'out of the ordinary', or 'special' and sagacity is like 'a wisdom' or 'thinking carefully before deciding on something'. Grip had a preternatural sagacity, doesn't that sound good? Grip would entertain people with his talking, saying things like "*halloa, halloa,* or, *never say die, or, what's the matter 'ere.*" Some people say that ravens watch

274

and learn from humans, learn how to talk and even learn how to think like humans. You know, there are a pair that live in the wood up on the hill above Tynyfid farm at Waunlwyd. Farmer Evans would have shot them but he thinks they are mystical and any harm to them would come back on the culprit tenfold; well, that's what he says and everyone believes him so they leave them alone. One day a buzzard came over the top and seemed like he was going to attack a new born lamb, when suddenly the giant raven, pulled in its wings and swooped down to attack the buzzard, who then took off with a squeal. Farmer Evans do love his ravens for sure."

"We saw the ravens last night from up on top of the hill Gethyn; it's like they were saying hullo to us, welcoming us to our new home." Just then, Henry and Dafydd came into the hall, Sarah immediately noticing  Henry's bruises, and her expression revealed her mixed emotions.

"I'm alright Sarah, just a bruise, some thugs from the next valley came over trying to persuade the miners here to join their strike, but we chased 'em off." Dafydd explained more about what had happened and then spoke to Gethyn.

"Are you trying to recruit Sarah to work in the library Geth?"

"Never crossed my mind Dai, we were talking about Evans's ravens, seems like they welcomed Sarah and Henry to the Valleys last night." Dafydd had something to say about ravens.

"Ah yes, ravens, let me say our Lord has told us many things about Ravens. In Genesis, the raven is the first bird that

Noah sends out to search for land, before he sends the dove. I think that's because the raven could talk to Noah, tell him where the land was; the dove then brought back the olive branch. I was talking with Robert Evans after Chapel last week; he'd read from Luke 12.24, where Jesus asks us to *"consider the ravens, that they sow not, neither reap; which have no store-chamber nor barn; and God feedeth them: of how much more value are ye than the birds."* Robert thinks they are spiritual and who am I to argue with him, a man of God?" Henry wanted to say something and he took Sarah's hand and looked at Dafydd.

"Sarah and I would go to the church in Camerton, but I don't really think of myself as a strong Christian Dafydd. I do, we do, follow the Christian way but our local vicar down in Camerton, well he thought that workers should respect their place in the social order, as he called it, which he made clear was on the bottom. So, he put me off the church, not Jesus Christ mind you, but the religions organised in his name." Dafydd felt a chance to recruit.

"I'd like you both to try our Chapel here in Ebbw Vale, when you move over. I think you'll find it quite different to what the Church of England say and do, which is mostly very different if you get my meaning. But first you are going to try the Blaina Baptist, right? Henry and Sarah are getting married over there on Wednesday Geth." Before Gethyn could say anything, Sarah felt an urge to speak her mind.

"I would like to try your Chapel Dafydd. Henry is right that we've both been put off by the church, where the vicar preached more about what you shouldn't do, and members of the congregation were more concerned about how they looked, than being more caring to each other, or learning about Jesus's love, his way of life. So, if your Chapel is about learning how to love your neighbour, then maybe I'll, maybe we'll, come along and see if it suits us." Sarah looked at Henry for approval and welcomed his smile.

"Yes, Sarah love, let's do that, maybe next Sunday Dafydd."

"That would be wonderful, and before that you should come here to the stute on Saturday night to see some theatre. A touring troupe are putting on a short play, *Efa and Dylan*. It's a coal miner's version of Shakespeare's Romeo and Juliet. Seems that Efa's dad works in the sale-pits in Aber and Dylan's dad works in the iron and steel pits here in Ebbw and they hate each other. Just like those thugs who we met today Henry. So, when Efa's father finds out that she is seeing Dylan, he goes crazy, threatens to disown her. The guy who wrote it, William Parnell, says that he tries to help communities see the different sides of local issues, using theatre as education. Six o'clock on Saturday, ok?

The afternoon was wearing on and Henry and Sarah decided to catch the train back to Brynmawr and then walk down to Blaina. On their way back, they shared all that had happened to them in the way that lovers and close friends do.

"Are you keen on the Chapel Sarah, you seemed forthright about it back there, in a way I hadn't seen before."

"Ah, you noticed that Henry. It was something Gethyn said earlier. He was telling me about the Institute and he asked me how I learned and if I read books. Simple enough questions but they got me thinking about myself and what I want, who I want to be here in Ebbw Vale." Henry looked confused.

"I want you to be Sarah, my lover and wife to be in a few days. Who else do you want to be Sarah?" Henry asked this in a rhetorical kind of way, almost as if he wasn't asking Sarah at all.

"Henry, I am 18 years old and maybe I have another 50, 60 or even 70 years to live. I will be your lover and wife and mother to our children, but that will only be a part of me, not the whole me. Nobody asked me how I learned before and Gethyn was really interested and wanted to share his learning with me. I didn't know how to answer him Henry but I know that I must find out, so that I can talk with people, share ideas, explore new things. You must know what I mean Henry, you have been doing that with Grampa John for years, and more recently with Lady Anna or should I say, Anna." Henry felt a deep confusion and anxiety. He didn't want to share Sarah with anyone. Yet, he knew that their life journey together would involve them becoming not only closer, but also more independent; himself with his passion for safety and what that would bring? and Sarah? The uncertainty made him anxious.

"Your words give me anxiety Sarah but they also excite me, so I ask that you be patient. I am jealous of any attention that you get from other men, you must know that from down in Camerton; why do you think I never came to the Rest? I am jealous of anything that takes you away for me Sarah. I know that's daft, silly, but I can't help it, can't help feeling the way I do. We'll be together more than ever here in Ebbw Vale, but that'll make me want you even more."

"It's not only daft but also unnecessary Henry my love. I am your woman, bonded from birth don't you know. You mustn't let your jealousy get the upper hand. But, how did what I said excite you Henry?"

"I'm not exactly sure Sarah, but something about how we can grow in new ways, become new people almost; in ways that we might never have been able to as Henry Sage and Sarah Wallace in Camerton. Yes, that excites me but also scares me; can the two go together Sarah?" The couple from Somerset walked and talked all the way back to Gwen's and Rhys's

278

home in Blaina. Emerging new pieces of the growing young couple, new surroundings, new ways of living and getting close to being wed. New hopes and dreams growing out of their sharing.

On Monday morning Henry met up with Daffyd at the Victoria number 1 pit. They were joined by the manager of the Victoria mines, Arthur Rogers, originally from the Midlands, who was doing his rounds, and Ivan Evans who wanted to meet Henry again. The miners' inspector Hugh Griffiths, who used to be a puddler in the Beaufort ironworks before they had closed the previous year, also joined the group. Ivan spoke first and welcomed Henry to Ebbw Vale.

"Very glad that you could make it here Henry; Camerton's loss will surely be Ebbw Vale's gain. This is Arthur Rogers who manages the Victoria mines and this is our own inspector, Hugh Griffiths. I told them you were more than a hewer Henry, and had good ideas for improving safety in the coal mines." Henry thought that Ivan was exaggerating rather but maybe he had a good reason for this, so he decided not to contradict him.

"That's right gentlemen, I do have a passion for safety and hope I can be helpful here in the Valleys, but first I need a job to support my wife to be. Sarah and I are to be married this coming Wednesday." Arthur Rogers had an answer for Henry.

"You can start on

Friday Henry. I want you to get familiar with all the active Upper Ebbw pits so you can join a hewer team, starting in number 6 and working your way through them, ok? This one here is number 1 and we shut it down last year after a nasty accident, nineteen men died. There was an explosion and Inspector Brough's report cited poor ventilation as a likely cause so we're putting that right. It was a fiery pit mind, and the men knew that, so God knows what set it off; maybe someone with a naked flame. Only one shaft and furnace ventilated so we got to put some blowers in to improve the ventilation. We can walk down to the other mines this morning but first let me show you where most of our coal goes." Henry was taking it all in, with eyes, ears and nose; man's industry pervaded all the senses; even taste as the chemical dust settled on Henry's tongue. As they walked along, Ivan spoke with Henry.

"Good to have you with us Henry. I was impressed with your pulling together that working group down there in Somerset, and the men there seemed to have a respect for you and trusted that you were on their side. That is so important and we've had problems in other districts with managers using dirty tricks to divide the Union. Last year's strike in the Rhondda was because the coal owners and iron masters reduced the wages by 10% in one shot, but the strike failed because the workers were not together. Only this year has the Ironworkers Union come to the Valleys, but now we have a tension between miners who work in the mines that sell their coal on the open market, and those in the collieries owned by the ironmasters, like here with the Ebbw Vale Company. I hear you got a taste of that conflict yesterday. This is the third time I've met you Henry Sage and on two of those occasions you've been fighting; you'll get a reputation boyo." Ivan was laughing as he said this but Henry thought about what he and Sarah had talked about the day before; he could be a new person in Ebbw Vale but he didn't want people to think he was a fighter. As they continued talking, Henry was aware they were approaching the tall towers that he and Sarah had looked down on from the hill when they arrived on Saturday.

"Talking of iron Henry, I know that Arthur wants to show you how the coal is used." Arthur caught up with them.

"We just passed the coke ovens Henry where we heat up our coal to get rid of organic substances, leaving almost pure carbon. Then we bring the coke to these four blast furnaces, where we turn iron ore into wrought iron.  As I said, the main fuel is coke, but we sometimes use anthracite coal from the western valleys; our own bituminous has too many impurities for iron making, so we must coke it. The hot air is driven in by the blast engine in that building on the left, then the iron ore, coke and limestone tipped in through the top and molten pig iron pours out on the other side. The Darby blast engine is the largest in the world, named after our managing director, Abraham Darby, and each of these furnaces produces about 800 tons of iron every week. That's a lot of iron Henry, I can tell you, but it doesn't end there. We then turn it into steel using the Bessemer convertors further up the valley, getting rid of impurities and leaving just the right amount of carbon. I've given a chemistry lecture at the stute to educate people about how we make good steel, though not many understand it. I'm afraid they haven't had enough basic education if you ask me. Anyway, Darby decided that Ebbw Vale would change to steel making a few years ago and we haven't looked back; it's so much stronger and durable than pig or wrought iron. Hugh here used to puddle the molten pig iron up in Beaufort and they didn't change to steel so all the Beaufort iron works have closed now. Seems like the owner didn't have a vision for what was coming, and he wasn't very kind to his workers either, flouted the safety regulations. Anyway, that's history now thankfully." Henry made a mental note to find out more about the flouting, and he wanted to hear the chemistry lecture as well. The small group walked around the various sites in the Ebbw valley, coal mines, ore mines, furnaces and ovens and the steel convertor, Ebbw Vale's pride and joy. Hugh spoke to Henry as they were gazing at the machine.

"Steel Henry, stronger than anything man has ever made, and here we are in Ebbw Vale leading the world, doesn't that make you feel good, feel you are in the right place?" Henry did feel he was in the right place but something Sarah had said to him the previous evening kept coming back; "*being your lover and wife will only be part of me.*" Isn't that the same as me saying being your lover and husband will only be part of me? But Sarah knows that I am the bread winner and that will need to be a big part of who I am, that's the way it is, always has been, surely? Henry was clearly not convinced by his own argument, which unsettled him. Lost in his thoughts, Henry had paused on the pathway and heard Dafydd calling him.

"Come on Henry, I know those furnaces are fascinating to look at but there's more to see down here." Henry caught the others up as Ivan was discussing the wage reductions with Arthur. He and other Union leaders had got the managers to agree to a 5% wage reduction but was making the point that the owners should be suffering, and seen to be suffering, as much as the workers during lean times. Arthur was shaking his head and began his forceful argument.

"No, Ivan, it comes down to the price the owners can sell our coal for and that's about supply and demand. If someone else offers cheaper coal, of the same quality, then why should the railway companies buy ours, which is more expensive because we pay our miners more? The biggest part of the cost in coal mining is the labour, so that's where the owners look to make reductions when they need to."

"But the owners don't go without their Sunday roast or eat less every day Arthur, do they?"

"Ivan, you heard the argument that Darby made during the Ebbw truck shop dispute. If the miners drank less, didn't get so drunk, they would have more money for their families, and be able to work harder, so earning more. It's a vicious circle with some of the workers Ivan and you know it. Present company excepted of course and I know that Daffyd and Hugh are Methodists so I think you must agree with me." Daffyd spoke next.

"I agree about some of the miners spending far too much money on drink, but even those who live very frugally and have big families suffer from these pay cuts Arthur. Don't forget that some of their earnings is taken out to pay for house rent, schooling, the church and the Institute, so a 5% cut can be more than what a day's food costs. And remember that Darby lost the case Arthur, and the Company had to stop the practice of only giving subs through purchases in their shops. The wives and mothers can now buy the same goods cheaper in the new shops."

As the discussion, verging on argument, continued, Henry thought that he could see both sides and, just like in Camerton, careful and respectful negotiation was going to be crucial to progress, when such strong opinions were involved. He also knew that the Union would need to be strong to stand up against the greedy bully, the worst combination of character traits to find in a fellow human being, especially when they have power over you, as the owners did. There would always be tensions between those that have more than enough and those that don't have enough. Henry believed that he and Sarah would have enough to live on, maybe even be able to save a little, but soon Brân would arrive and before long his brothers and sisters, more mouths to feed. Henry smiled to himself as his dreams started to excite him and financial worries faded away; he and Sarah would find a way. As he bid farewell to the group of new friends, thanking them for all they had showed him, Henry's main thought was, it's time for me and Sarah to get married.

The Old Blaina Baptist Chapel looked resplendent in the sunshine on Wednesday morning, as the small group of people walked up the pathway and entered the front door. They were welcomed in by the Minister, Mr John Lewis, who asked to have a private word with Henry and Sarah first.

"The normal process for getting married is to read the bans in your place of residence for three weeks, in case there are any fundamental objections. However, Henry and Sarah, here we are very much nonconformists and Rhys and Gwen Jones have explained the situation, you just arriving from Somerset and wanting to set up home in Ebbw Vale. So, I am very pleased to lead this Christian service to unite you together in marriage. I see you have your brother here Henry; but

Sarah, do you have any relatives joining us?" Sarah was suddenly struck with a sadness. Henry saw this and put his arm around her.

"No Mr Lewis, the truth is that we eloped because my mother did not look kindly on Henry and my love. I think she was envious of our feelings for each other. I don't have any brothers or sisters."

"And what about your father Sarah, did he object as well?"

"I don't think so; no, he didn't object, he wants me to be happy; but I think he was afraid to go against my mother's wishes. They were planning on sending me away to my uncle's place in the Midlands, where I would 'grow up', as my mother put it. But I am already grown up Mr Lewis, and Henry and I want to build a new life together here in the Valleys." Sarah looked at Henry, tears in her eyes. "And we want to be married to begin the building."

"Yes Sarah, you are grown up; she is the most grown up person I know Mr Lewis; she can see and feel things that other people don't or can't."

"Sarah, I like to hear your conviction and I've no doubt that you are grown up, but marriage will bring trials and challenges as well as joy and happiness. I sense you are both ready for all these things and you will need each other on your journey, building your new life. Henry, I've heard that you fight for good and safety and I pray your endeavours are fruitful here in the Valleys. Lord knows the poor people here need a champion for that noble cause. I look forward to hearing about your new life together, but first, shall we go back into the Chapel and begin the marriage ceremony?" As they walked back into the Chapel, they were welcomed by the smiling faces of their family and friends; Henry's brother Tom and his wife-to-be Megan, Gwen and Rhys, Dafydd and Rhian, Megan's and Dafydd's sister Siân, Ivan Evans, Gethyn and Wyn and Mervyn Jones with a bandage around his head covering the wound from stone thrower. As Sarah arrived at the centre of the aisle, she stood directly in the path of the sunbeam bursting through the stained-glass window at the side of the Chapel, lighting up her hair so that her natural auburn blended with the colours in the sun's rays, burning bright. The gathered were transfixed with her beauty.

Henry hardly heard the words that minister Lewis spoke. He gazed into Sarah's bright eyes now that their special moment had come; *do you take this woman, in sickness and health, richer or poorer, for ever, until death do us part.* Henry found those last words chilling. He didn't want Sarah to die, ever. He didn't want to part with her, he wanted to cherish Sarah for ever, she was the missing piece in his life, without her he might fall apart, they were born to be together. Then he saw Sarah's lips moving as she was gazing into his eyes; she whispered *yes, I do.* He heard minister Lewis speaking to get his attention.

"Henry, are you still with us? Do you have a ring for Sarah? It's not essential, but if you do."

"Yes minister, sorry, yes of course I do." Tom took the ring from his pocket and handed it to Henry. "Sarah, this ring is a symbol of my love for you, binding us together forever. Will you wear it to know that I love you?" Henry softly eased the marble ring onto Sarah's finger, until it was part of her hand.

"Yes, I will wear it to know that you love me, and it will show that I love thee."

"Then I pronounce you man and wife." Minister Lewis's words had hardly left his lips when the assembled gathering, led by brother Thomas, let out a cheer, like breath released after being taken away. Another generation of Sages were hinged together in matrimony. Their destinies would be shaped by their love for each other and their personal dreams of what might be would merge in ways that none could predict; such was the force and wonder of human love. Their child Brân, and his siblings, would grow up as Valley children. Some would welcome the security of the surrounding hills and be at home with the camaraderie of the tightly knit mining community, others would

want to escape the shadows and the claustrophobia, become people of the world. As the group walked out of the Chapel a raven turned in the sky overhead, seeming to greet the married couple with three gentle croaks. Sarah gazed at the dark shadow above and, for a few moments, was lost in an inner world; she came back when she heard Daffyd talking to his father.

"Well, well, I never seen 'em over here before, 'ave you dad?" Rhys was shaking his head.

"I think it's that big fella from Ebbw; all the ones over here were shot down by farmer Rees long ago. Go back home boyo before they get you too." The raven turned once more and headed back west; he would be back in Ebbw for lunch.

Henry and Sarah also travelled back to Ebbw Vale and, arriving at their new home in Waterfall Row, Henry carried Sarah through the small Welsh door, lowering his head as he did so to avoid bumping on the doorframe.

"Here we are Sarah, my love, our new home, our first home, at last we are together. Looks like our friends have been furnishing the place over the last few days; a table and four chairs, a dresser with plates and bowls. We'll have to put some pictures up on the walls, make it our own."

"Oh, it feels so good to be here Henry, can it be real? And where did this lovely ring come from, that was a surprise?" Henry explained the history of the ring, hoping Sarah would be alright about wearing his family heirloom.

"I love it Henry and it fits perfectly, and I wear it to show that I love you." Sarah wanted to repeat what she had said in the Chapel, because it meant so much to her. "Oh, and I would like to put some of my paintings and sketches on the walls Henry if you are alright with that?" Of course, Henry was alright with that. "It will help to make this our home. Shall we go upstairs and see if we have a bed?"

Sarah led Henry up the stairs and peeped into the back bedroom; it was empty, except for a small chest of drawers. In the front bedroom, there was a double bed, made up with sheets and a blanket. Whoever had made the room up had pulled back the sheets inviting the newlyweds in. Henry held Sarah in his arms and kissed her with a passion that almost overwhelmed her. He kicked the door shut from the readers' view, so the rest is left to your imagination, which is unlikely to come close to reality.

A   A   A

On Thursday, their first full day as a married couple, Henry and Sarah worked on their home: windows open wide beckoning the wind to blow away the cobwebs, sweeping and scrubbing, painting and plastering, old and new friends appearing, bearing gifts of function and ornament to adorn their home; fuel for the fires, pots, pans and other kitchen utensils, flowers and flower pots, beautiful reds and yellows, and food for the larder, enough to last a few days. A week ago, Sarah had been working as a domestic in her family home so she knew what was involved, but now this was her own home and everything she did, she did with care and with a feeling of deep pride that was new to her. She was indeed grown up and just needed the space and opportunity for her maturity to shine. Henry saw what was happening and would regularly pause with his chores to embrace Sarah, reminding her of his love. He wondered if anybody could be so lucky as him. A week ago, it seemed just a dream but now that dream had come true. He also knew that tomorrow would need a different aspect of his manhood, of his maturity. He would be starting work and going deeper underground than he had ever been; the thought was faintly erotic.

A heavy crunching thud sounded as the cage reached the bottom of the shaft, seven hundred feet below the surface. Arthur and Henry climbed out of the cage and, carrying their Davy lamps, and lowering their heads, proceeded along the main tunnel to the coal face, a half mile away. Without man's presence, there would be silence at this depth but the sounds of heavy industry and men at work filled the air, echoing along the dark passageways. A roaring sound from the cage being lifted to the surface by the water balance system, a different roaring from the blowers that formed part of the ventilation system, a graunching from the coal tubs scraping the tunnel walls and wheels screeching on their rails. The occasional crashing sound as tubs hit each other on their journey back and fore. Then Henry heard a more natural sound coming from a side tunnel. A man was hitting a pony from behind with a whip to try and encourage it to haul his tub faster, but it only resulted in the animal lifting its head and letting out a loud groan.

"Bloody animal is not worth the grain I feed it on; come on get a move on." Crack and neigh, crack and neigh, and then the horse stopped, looking at Henry as they joined the main tunnel.

"Stop hitting the animal, can't you see it's distressed and in pain?"

"I want it to be in pain don't I, that's the only way it will bloody work for me." As the man raised his whip to strike the animal again, Henry reached out and grasped the man's arm.

"I told you to stop hitting the poor creature." Henry snatched the whip out of the man's hand and threw it to the ground. Arthur Rogers looked perplexed.

"Come on boys don't fight over a damn horse. Henry, some of these animals get lazy down here and need encouragement."

"I've never known any animal to be encouraged by a beating, more likely fearful and discouraged." Henry stroked the pony's main and, taking the halter, gently pulled, whereupon the horse began moving forward slowly. "Mr Rogers, we need to show respect for each other working underground and that includes the ponies. This animal looks sick and should be taken above ground to recover." The miner who beat the pony was cursing under his breath as Henry spoke to him. "Why are you not carrying a safety lamp? Don't you know that the candles are unsafe in these gassy tunnels?" The miner spoke to Arthur Rogers.

"Who is this bloke Mr Rogers, I don't want nobody telling me how to do my job."

"This is Henry Sage, Gwyn, he's going to be joining the

hewer team here in the Victoria's and he'll be working with Ivan Evans on improving safety. And you shouldn't be wearing the candle no more, you know what the report on number 1 accident said."

"Well I can't afford a damn safety lamp Mr Rogers and the candles are much brighter anyway and there's only a danger if the gas builds up between shifts and the new ventilation is supposed to clear that." The disgruntled miner took the halter from Henry and pulled the horse on up the tunnel, cursing as he went. Henry had kept his foot on the whip so Gwyn wouldn't pick it up again but he suspected that beating was probably common practice. He spoke to Arthur Rogers.

"It would be better if the miners weren't cruel to the animals down here Mr Rogers." As he said this, Arthur Rogers shouted after the man pulling the horse.

"Take the horse up to the surface with you Gwyn, let the vet look at him." Henry and Arthur walked on, crouching more as the tunnel roof got lower in places. "You're right Henry, but the mining regulation act didn't say anything about the treatment of ponies and mules underground, so we rely on miners taking care of the animals."

"It was the same in Somerset Mr Rogers, a horse working underground might only live for three years compared with twenty working in the fields. Beating the poor beasts doesn't make them work any harder." The pair continued walking and talking, sometimes having to lower their heads to avoid the rock roof. The air was warm and damp, pungent with odours not found in the fresh air on the surface. The wooden pit props seemed to creak and groan from the weight of the world on their shoulders.

"We've been using the pillar and stall at the face for years but we are trying the long-wall method down 'ere. There can be a build-up of the firedamp in the old stalls so we need good ventilation to clear it out; with the long-wall method, we don't get the stalls. Some of the miners don't like it though, they all got to work at the same pace; so, the fast miners must slow down and don't earn as much. You'll have to meet the folk from the Institute of Mining Engineers Henry, who are trying to get us to introduce such things to make it safer working underground."

"I'd like to meet them Arthur. Sometimes you must pay a price for improved safety but I've heard that with the long-wall system, there's less waste, so the mines should be more profitable. This is where the owners need to be sharing the risks and benefits of change with the workers."

"You're right Henry and I do believe that our director, Abraham Darby, is open to hearing these arguments. Anyway, you'll see the long-wall up ahead." As they approached the coal face, they heard sounds of hewers at work, so familiar to Henry. They stood aside as a hub was hauled through by another pony, led by a boy. "Men, this is Henry Sage, an experienced hewer from Somerset, he'll be working with you from Monday and Henry's going to train to be an inspector so look after him." One of the hewers sat up from his contorted position and reached out his hand.

"S'mae bachgen Henry, dwi'n Griff, croeso I uffern." Arthur helped Henry out with the translation.

"Come on Griff, I know you speak good English; he just welcomed you to hell, Henry." The men introduced themselves to Henry and they sat and talked hewing methods, ventilation and haulage for some time. The miners had heard from Mervyn about the fight on the weekend so they were pleased to meet the man everyone had been talking about. Soon they wanted to get on with hewing so Arthur bid farewell to Henry and headed back up the tunnel to the shaft, the cage and up-cast to the surface, to what was left of heaven in the Ebbw valley.

Henry spent the rest of the day at the coal face, the six hewers gradually cutting their way further into the seam, fitting the props behind them as they went. Walking home, he was tired but in a healthy way, mind bubbling with ideas. Grampa John was right, he thought, close cooperation between men is vital to safety underground; keeping eyes on your work-mates' safety as well as yours. But more than that, Griff had pointed out that when they were working as a team, the normally slower workers would speed up trying to match the faster ones. They would settle at a pace that allowed them to be more productive than was possible in the individual stalls; and they could better look after each other's safety. Henry noted that this was happening because Griff was a good leader; a team needs a good leader, then productivity and safety can improve together. The mineral landlords and colliery owners need to understand this, especially those who saw the working miner as primitive and slovenly.

In the stute, the painting class had started in the early afternoon and Sarah sat at her easel, deep in thought. She was remembering what Gethyn had said about the raven; it had a preternatural sagacity, she liked the sound of the words. Earlier, Gethyn had showed her Edgar Allen Poe's poem, The Raven, and while she was reading it, a man whispered in her ear.

"Are you frightened by the raven my pretty girl?" He was a strange looking man, dressed in black overhauls and his eyes were wide open and staring. He looked a little like a raven, but Sarah was more at ease with the real raven than this strange man. "His soul is trapped in the raven's shadow dancing on the floor; do his fiery eyes burn into your bosom? Has his beak gone deep into your heart? Why does the raven keep speaking, Nevermore?"

"I'm not frightened, just trying to make sense of the poem, I'll have to read it again to get the meaning, it's not obvious."

"Nothing is obvious my love, at least nothing worthwhile and words are inadequate. We can only really see the truth through metaphors and the images that words create in our minds. Black and white, good and bad, no doubt they exist but I've never found them; it's the in-between that makes life worthwhile, makes life possible." The man's gaze was making Sarah uneasy and she stood up and took a few steps away and noticed Gethyn running towards them across the library floor.

"Come on John, leave Sarah be. I'm sorry Sarah, this here is John and he is in the painting class but nobody understands what he paints, do they John."

"I do understand my paintings Geth, they speak to me of the wonders of life and the phantoms within, like this poem, lights a fire in the mind and I can't put it out until I paint. Real artists all have fires in their minds. Do you have a fire miss Sarah?" While Sarah felt uncomfortable, she was also intrigued by the things John was saying. She thought that she mustn't let her apprehension close her mind to new things, even though they might be weird.

"Sometimes my mind is full of thoughts, too jumbled to make sense. I've never thought of this as a fire but, yes, painting does calm them down." Gethyn had come to gather the painting class together, back in the main hall.

Sarah had decided to paint a picture of a raven. She had many images in her mind; the pair that flew around in the Camerton valley, often intruding on her love making with Henry; she had seen one after coming out of the Chapel after the wedding. But the one that was strongest was the image she had of the raven she and Henry had seen when they walked up the hill on their first evening in the Valleys. She had thought then that the bird was welcoming them. *Ravens are black, but tinged with blue. Ravens can talk and see right through you.* As Sarah painted, so the words of a poem started to form in her mind. *The raven is smart, her shape is a mystery. The raven is smart, knows all her own history.* "Where did that idea come from," Sarah whispered to herself as she sketched her memory onto the sheet in front of her.

Henry walked along the back lanes of the street of mining cottages, still processing what had happened in the day. Earlier, he had met Ivan who had asked him to give a talk on mining safety at the stute before the play on Saturday; "you'll have a good audience Henry but don't talk for more than ten minutes or you'll get booed." What he might say was burning like a fire in his mind. As he walked along he could smell the odours of human habitation, some pleasant from the cooking, others unpleasant from decaying garbage and sewage. He heard a man shouting, cursing his wife about something; he sounded drunk and his wife let out a shriek as she hit him with a pot and the man went staggering off down the lane, back to

295

the pub, where he would share his troubles with other victims of the darkness.

Henry arrived in Waterfall Row and was warmed by greetings from neighbours as he approached his new home. Sarah had made a fulsome vegetable soup which smelt wonderful as he entered the house and they held each other for a long slow time. As they sat and ate their supper, they shared stories from their day apart. This was new to both, and powerfully enabling for their growth as individuals as well as a married couple. Of course, in 19th century Ebbw Vale, they may not have seen or thought of it that way but future generations would be grateful for the foundations that Henry and Sarah were building.

"I like being married to you Henry Sage, I feel very fortunate; can we stay friends forever?"

"Of course, we will Sarah. Hey, I've just noticed our first pictures on the wall. Did you paint that raven Sarah love? And is that me digging for coal in the stars?"

"Yes, I painted that picture last March, from a quiet place on the old canal path. I could see you in the stars, so there you are, and always will be for me. And I've learned a few things about ravens from Gethyn at the stute today Henry; seems there is a pair who live on the hill that the local farmer protects because he thinks they are spiritual and they can talk?"

"I've heard that too Sarah. I find it hard to believe, but I do think all animals have feelings and can be happy or sad, depending on what happens to them. And they watch what we do and remember, yes, I do think they remember. Talking of remembering Sarah; today, in the mine, for some reason I thought of Wendy Arton, my father's daughter, my sister. Where is she? What is she doing? What does she look like? Maybe we'll never know." Henry looked at Sarah with his perplexed expression; she knew it well.

"Let her go Henry, if she's made of the same stuff as you, she'll be alright. Someday, who knows, we might find the answers to those questions, but now we need to build our lives here in the Valleys, right? Tomorrow's another day and who knows what it will bring, and you need to think about what you are going to say about safety."

They held each other again, nourishing their friendship with love. Sarah knew it would not always be so good and filling the reservoir for times of drought seemed very important to her.

9. The Raven is Smart as She Begins her Descent

Bran wanted to draw a line under his ancestry research, get to a place where he felt he knew enough that he could write the story, so that his children and future generations could know a little about Henry and Sarah. As far as Bran knew, they were the first Sages to re-locate, in modern jargon; Somerset folk bringing their family up in the culture of the Valleys. Despite his strong kinship with his mother Aoife's Irish lineage, Bran had grown up a Valley boy and had some of those cultural traits welded into his personality; like grit and determination and a weird sense of humour. He was forming a picture of Henry and Sarah but felt that most of the detail in the picture that was visible through his microscope was now filled in; time to draw that line. To prepare for his trip to Somerset and Ebbw Vale, Bran had sat down and wrote a summary of what he knew of his great grandparents, from census material, genealogy organisations that he had subscribed to, and anecdotes from his memory of chats with his parents. He was particularly interested in the period when they moved from Somerset to the South Wales Valleys, in the early 1870s.

He'd written this down in the form of a list.

1. Henry Sage was born in Tunley, near Camerton, Somerset in 1851. Henry's parents were James and Maria Sage (neé Mears). He had four brothers, James Jr, George, Thomas, and Ritchie. Henry's father was killed in a mining accident in Camerton, Somerset, in 1862. Henry's mother Maria died in 1903. In the 1871 census, Henry was a coal miner, living with his mother in Tunley Houses. In the 1881 census he was a coal mines inspector, living in Waterfall Row in Ebbw Vale, married to Sarah Wallace. They had four children, Bran (8), Alice (6), Henry Jr (3) and George (10months). Henry died in 1920, aged 69, then living in Brynheulog Street in Ebbw Vale.

2. Sarah Jane Wallace was born in Midsomer Norton, Somerset in 1854. Sarah's parents were Albert and

Elizabeth Wallace (neé Mears). Elizabeth was Maria's sister, so Sarah and Henry were first cousins. Sarah was an only child. Her mother and father both died in the 1890s. In the 1871 census, Sarah was a domestic in her parent's public house, The Miner's Rest, in Camerton, Somerset. In the 1881 census she was living in Ebbw Vale with Henry and their four children. She and Henry continued to grow their family with at least twelve children born alive according to the 1901 census. Sarah died in 1946, aged 92; she still lived in Brynheulog Street.

3. Henry and Sarah were married on Wednesday 5th June 1872 in the Old Blaina (Baptist) Chapel, in the Aberystruth Parish of Monmouthshire. The marriage certificate states that the minister was Mr John Lewis and witnesses were Thomas Sage and Daffyd Jones. They moved to Ebbw Vale sometime after that.

4. Henry's and Sarah's first child, Brân, was born in Ebbw Vale in 1873 and was killed in Belgium during WW1. There were no records of his death and, like many of the casualties of that desperate conflict, his body was never found and Bran Snr was declared missing, presumed dead, referred to in the documents as MPD.

5. George Sage, Henry's and Sarah's fourth child, a coal miner in Ebbw Vale from the age of 12, was my grandfather. I was born in George's home in Ebbw Vale in 1950, before my parents, Alwyn and Aoife, moved to the next valley to set up home.

Then there were the few snippets learned from chats with his parents and grandfather, although the latter were few and far between.

1. During his time as a mines inspector, Henry developed a reputation for having uncompromising principles, and a determination to improve safety in the face of complacency and deviousness from coal owners and colliery managers, as well as slovenliness from some of his fellow colliers.

2. He also had a reputation as someone not to pick a fight with; if you did and Henry hit you, you would stay down for a while, and you wouldn't look the same when you eventually got up. It was as if he had fists of iron, or maybe steel.

3. When Henry died, his coffin was the largest ever

made in Ebbw Vale. He had just returned from visiting family in Somerset, where he had picked up a virus that led to pleurisy from which Henry did not recover.

4. Sarah had some, undefined, involvement with the Ebbw Vale Literary and Scientific Institute and she attended the Mt Zion Primitive Methodist Chapel on Briery Hill.

5. She would paint and sketch pictures of her family and the natural world.

6. Sarah Sage's obituary in the Merthyr Express was brief but noted that she *"displayed a profound compassion for the vulnerable"*. This line had always intrigued Bran and lingered in his mind.

His ancestry research drew him closer to his great grandparents but Bran was sufficiently rational to realise that he could never truly know them. But, while these images from the real world made a strong impression, there were no photographs of either Henry or Sarah.

And what about Bran's six dreams, what did they add to the picture? Bran was careful to remind himself that these were the fictional parts of his knowledge.

Henry and Sarah walking along the canal path; did she look at me? I must go back there during next visit.

Sarah painting picture of two men standing in front of coal mine; yes, Chloe was right, it was a paint brush, not a wand. Was one of the men Henry?

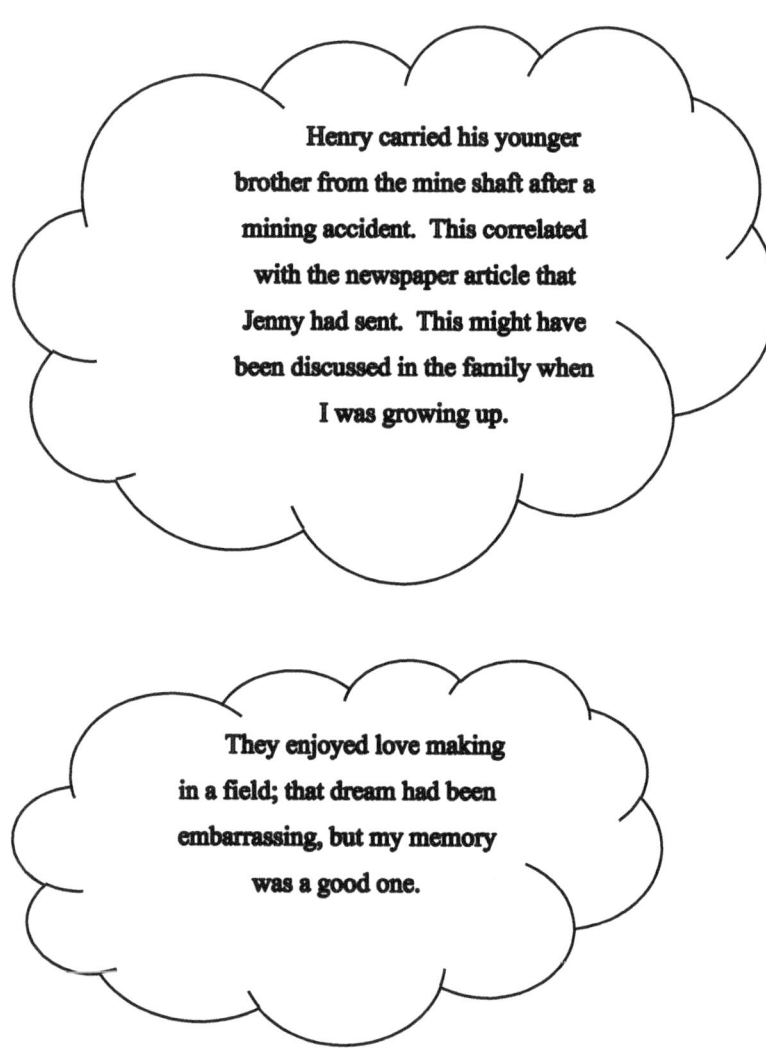

Henry carried his younger brother from the mine shaft after a mining accident. This correlated with the newspaper article that Jenny had sent. This might have been discussed in the family when I was growing up.

They enjoyed love making in a field; that dream had been embarrassing, but my memory was a good one.

Sarah painted a picture of the Plough, not the Great Bear version but rather a collier hauling a coal tub. This might have been a consequence of seeing Chloe's Orion painting, with the guitarist instead of the hunter.

A woman named Anna wrote to Henry about having his father James's child, named Wendy Arton. This must be pure fiction but I will send a request to the ancestry research organisation to find out if such a person was born on the date in the dream and, if so, request they send her family tree. I will be very surprised if she existed but I need to know for sure.

Bran remembered that in some of the dreams he could hear a raven croaking. Chloe had suggested that he talk to Georgia about ravens and he intended to do that. But what was it that Chloe had said about dreams? Think of all the characters and artefacts as aspects of yourself. That was easy with the ravens; his name, Bran, meant raven in the old Celtic language. She'd also said something about Freud believing that our unconscious creates our dreams to solve problems; dreams lead us down the '*royal road to the unconscious*'. Bran liked that notion, being a problem-solver himself, although he'd come to consider aircraft flight problems as a lot simpler than human psychological problems. Aircraft were deterministic, with predictable behaviour; with people, anything can happen and usually does. That was ok with Bran. He had known some people who seemed more like robots; very clever but rarely had a creative thought, at least that's the way it seemed. He generally preferred people who wanted to explore, to examine their lives and find deeper meanings. Socrates had said that the unexamined life was not worth living. Bran thought that was a bit harsh, but then Socrates was on trial for his stand on the critical importance of wisdom and self-knowledge to living one's full life and to relieving the fear of death. Bran's ancestry research was shining a light on his mortality, but was he trying to relieve his fear of death?

He was recalling these things as he drove into the car park at the Somerset Mining Museum on Saturday morning; "*I wonder what else Jenny has found?*"

"Good morning Bran, very nice to see you again. Ron is up in the office so let's go up and chat; would you like a cup of tea?"

"Good morning to you Jenny, is it really only two weeks

since I was here; feels longer than that, don't you think? I'd prefer coffee, black please, no sugar, and thanks for the material you sent by the way, very helpful, I'm really grateful."

"Well, I've found a few more things, maybe small pieces of the jigsaw you are trying to assemble. I like this detective work, so much more interesting than just cataloguing stuff." They walked into the office to find Ron Flintworth sitting at the desk reading what looked like a newspaper cutting.

"Hullo Bran, very good to see you again. Since Jenny turned up all this material on the Somerset miners' union I've been finding out a lot more about Grampa Archie and I've got you to thank for that. He was in what they called the miners' task force, responsible for mining developments. Things that the coal owners wanted to do to develop the mines in the area had to be discussed with the union first and my Grampa was at the centre of this. I never knew this Bran and it looks like a couple of Sages were in the task force too, George and Thomas."

"Yes, I read the article that Jenny sent but there was no mention of their brother, my great grandfather Henry Sage." Jenny placed another file on the table.

"But I've found a mention of Henry Sage. This is another article about the mining accident. Seems like the local bobby, Sgt Pepper, what a great name, arrested a local, Mr William Oats, and he was charged with cutting the cable. Seems like he'd had a quarrel and a fight with a Henry Sage; now who could that be I wonder?" Jenny loved playing the detective, revealing the clues like in an Agatha Christie novel. "Turns out that Henry had given this Oats chap a good beating for some reason and Oats wanted to get revenge and cut the cable because he thought Henry would be in the cage for the first shift of the day. Luckily your great grandad, can I call him the

307

fighting Henry, missed the first drop for some reason, but his younger brother Ritchie was in the cage and broke his arm; lucky not to be killed I'd say Bran. Anyway, it doesn't end there. Seems like a John Riddle, friend of Henry's, tracked Oats down and took him to Sgt Pepper. It doesn't say if the bobby had a band by the way." Jenny was full of spirit telling the story. Bran was wondering where he had heard the name Oats before. "Oats was convicted of manslaughter. Seems like he persuaded the judge that he didn't mean to kill anyone. He'd been in prison for a few weeks and escaped when he was being transferred to another prison. The article suggests he had an accomplice, a Miss Rita Jenkins, maybe his girlfriend, who disappeared after the escape. They were never found. That's all it says about Henry, Bran, but it's another piece of the puzzle."

"Yes, indeed Jenny, I really appreciate all your efforts. I think Henry and Sarah eloped soon after the accident to live in Ebbw Vale, and I'm planning to visit there tomorrow, try to find a few more pieces. Do you know anything about the Camerton Manor, by the way, and a lady by the name of Anna Fernhill?" Ron was quick to answer.

"Jenny's the one for the Manor, Bran, wrote a little booklet on it a few years ago, didn't you Jen?"

"I certainly did, what did you want to know Bran?"

"Well, it said in the article you sent me that Anna Fernhill was very supportive of the miners' cause hereabouts. What was that about, and did she have a family, are there any ancestors still around?"

"No, she stayed single, surprising really because by all accounts she was a very attractive woman, and probably had lots of admirers. The family donated her diaries to the museum when they cleared the house. They were more notebooks than diaries, her impressions of the way the mining practices evolved into the 20th century. She owned the land and the mines and from what I've read she was very influenced by her grandfather, more so than her father it seems. Grampa John, as he was called locally, had travelled a lot and was the wise man of the village of Camerton in the mid to late 19th century. He had radical ideas about politics and democracy, was a philosopher and kept a beautiful garden. Anna followed in his footsteps and looked after his ravens when he died." That got Bran's attention.

"He had ravens; what you mean he kept pet ravens?"

"Yes, that's right. There was a massive extermination of wildlife in our country in the 19th century, all enabled by the vermin act which declared certain animals as a threat to the crops. Many farmers did not discriminate and shot everything that moved. Some took a particular dislike to ravens and Grampa John took in the last two ravens in Camerton valley, around the same time we are talking about, in 1872; just a coincidence I'm sure. He would feed them and I've read that he used to talk with them, but that might just be the old wives' tale of the story." Bran interrupted Jenny.

"I've heard that ravens can learn to talk Jenny; don't forget Dicken's Grip in Barnaby Rudge. You said that Anna kept the ravens after her grandfather died."

"Yes, she did but, one day, about a year later I think, one of the ravens was shot by a farmer from over Clandown Hill. It's said that the other raven died soon after of a broken heart, another old husband's tale. The ravens have only recently settled back in Somerset and we do see the occasional one cross over the valley."

"I don't suppose there was anything in Anna's diaries about my family Jenny?"

"No Bran, I'm afraid not; as I said they were mostly about mining and very few people get a mention."

The three carried on chatting about the past until Ron suggested they went down to the café and have a sandwich lunch. Bran and Jenny both agreed and Bran insisted on paying.

"Good idea and please let it be on me."

After lunch, Bran said that he wanted to have another walk along the canal path, and he wanted to find out if he could visit the Manor. Jenny answered him.

"You'll have to be quick. The owners are moving and clearing out the house; actually, I think there's a car-boot sale on today."

Walking along the old canal path, Bran was deep in thought about his great grandparents. Thinking that they had probably walked along this very path, talking about their future, maybe planning their elopement, comforted him. He wondered what their dreams were, what their expectations were, were they both as committed to the adventure? Did they see the move as an adventure? He tried to stop the thinking and allow his mind to absorb the peace of the place. The birdsong helped, the robin and the blackbird competing for attention; is that the way it is? Bran entered the gate into the Manor grounds and could see a lot of activity in the courtyard outside the house. He walked through the garden which looked like it needed a lot of attention. Ivy was growing over the greenhouse. Someone will have to cut through years of growth to get in there, Bran thought as he tried to look through the glass, but the growth of fungi had made it opaque. I'll just have to imagine what's in there he thought, but he was good at that. His muse was interrupted by a woman's voice.

"Good morning, I know what you're thinking, they don't look after their garden. You'd be right. I'm Vanessa Caldecott, my husband and I are selling the property, downsizing you'd say. We aren't really gardeners so have given this area very little attention over the years. The greenhouse is just full of old plant pots and boxes; I'm sure its had better days. Are you here to see what's on sale?"

"Well, yes, kind of. I'm Bran Sage. I visited the mining museum this morning as part of my research into my ancestors who lived in Camerton in the 19th century, before they moved to Wales. The owner of the Camerton mines, Anna Fernhill, owned this Manor at the time my great grandfather was a collier here. Seems like she was very supportive of the community."

"Oh yes, indeed she was; our Anna was a strong feminist as well, born before her time I'd say. You probably met Jenny at the museum. She has Anna's notebooks and they give a good picture of a strong woman in a man's age; a forerunner of the suffragettes, so it can't have been easy. But she did own the land and the mineral rights so she was in a fortunate position. She didn't need a vote to have power. How is your research going?" Bran wondered where he should start, how much he wanted to say. He gave Vanessa a summary of where he was at. "You said your great grandfather's name was Henry, is that right?"

"Yes, Henry Sage and he lived in Tunley, married his cousin Sarah Wallace whose family owned the Collier's Rest." They had arrived at the car boot sale and people were strolling through the courtyard, cluttered with furniture, crockery, paintings and sculptures, old machines and strange objects; like an outdoor antique store. Vanessa had walked away, rather abruptly Bran thought, and gone into the house. Bran mingled with the other visitors, hearing conversations about whether someone did or didn't need that; and where would we put it, it's never worth that much, that's a bargain, etc. Bran had no intention of buying anything, but he'd often say that and come home with a boot full of junk. "I'm just like any other guy Mary; something takes my fancy and I have to have it." "You're not like any other guy Bran Sage, that's what I love about you, that's why I married you." He smiled as he recollected great times with Mary and he wanted them again, more than anything he wanted them back again.

"Bran, hullo Bran, Bran Sage, over here." Bran heard his name being called through the clutter of multiple conversations; thought it was in his daydream, but it was Vanessa, calling him from the front door. "Bran can you come inside for a minute please?" Bran looked up and waved in acknowledgement, following Vanessa into the foyer of the Manor.

"You looked lost in thought there, Bran; I have something inside you may be interested in."

"I've promised them to a taxidermist in Bath Van, he can't have them."

"This is Robbie my husband, let's go into the library." Bran was more than curious.

"Can't have what?" As they entered the library, Bran saw what they were talking about and he was taken aback. "Wow, I knew they were big but I hadn't imagined this huge." On the table in the middle of the library was a large glass dome with two ravens inside, one looking up at the other and the other looking out at the onlookers, large curved beak slightly open. Vanessa handed Bran a card.

"This was attached to the underside of the dome Bran; you

312

may be interested in what it says." Bran took the card and read it to himself.

After we took these ravens in and cared for them, they began to talk to us, copying our voices, saying 'good morning', 'how are you' and 'where's my dinner'. But they would talk to each other as well, very quietly. After the male was shot, the female would cronk at me, 'where's Henry'; she became very melancholy, stopped eating and died soon after. They were wonderful birds, with preternatural sagacity, and I miss them terribly; we all miss them. The note was signed Anna Fernhill, and there was a date, 2nd March 1876.

Bran was stunned and stared at the ravens. The large male bird stared back and, to relieve the intensity, Bran walked across the room to sit down but the bird's eyes followed him. His feelings were a complex mix of fear and wonder, the fear he thought he'd shaken from years of rational science and engineering, the wonder was like electric charge.

"I thought you might be surprised. Why do you think the raven would say that, 'where's Henry'? If we believe Anna Fernhill that is." Bran was still staring into the fierce eyes.

"I don't know, surely it's a coincidence."

"There's something else Bran, come over and look in the jar." Bran hesitated but walked over to see what Vanessa was pointing at. The ravens were standing on a branch, their feet wrapped tightly around its bark. Below the large bird was a small brass plaque with the name *Henry* inscribed. Bran's eyes moved lower down the branch to the second plaque, and why should he be surprised at what he saw? The name *Sarah* was slightly hidden by some blades of grass, dry and dead for more than a hundred years, like the birds above. "Why would Anna Fernhill give her ravens the same names as your great grandparents Bran; any ideas?" Bran was shaking his head slowly, in a combination of wonder and an 'I don't know', in answer to Vanessa's question.

"Are these for sale Vanessa?"

"I promised them to a taxidermist in Bath, so sorry they've already gone." Robbie was repeating what he had already said, this time with more fervour.

"What price is he offering, I'll match it, give you another ten percent?" Vanessa interrupted the conversation.

"Robbie, I want Bran to have these ravens. Somehow, they are connected with his ancestry and I know he will look after them, and probably they will stay in his family; is that right Bran?"

"Yes, they will and I will look after them. It's strange but I sometimes dream about my great grandparents and I hear ravens calling, although I've never seen them." Bran sat down again, that same emotion taking over. "I would be happy to pay you what they are worth Robbie." Before Robbie could begin his bargaining, Vanessa spoke again.

"We found these inside a small cupboard in the corner of the attic; looked like it hadn't been opened since the dome was put inside, goodness knows when. They are not our property Robbie and I want to give them to Bran. It's like they'll be going back home, a place where they will be valued and cared for, not just as ornaments but for what they were, for what they are."

"Well, I'll be darned, that's quite amazing Bran." Ron and Jenny were gazing into the dome as Bran shared the story of how he had stumbled upon them at the Manor car boot sale. "So, these are the ravens that Grampa John looked after; the last two in the Camerton valley in the 19th century, and named after your great grandparents. Look at the size of 'em, especially Henry. Did you say he had the biggest coffin in Ebbw Vale Bran?" Ron looked at Bran with a smile as he said this. Jenny was curious what sense Bran was making of the find.

"Not sure how you will fit this in Bran but it's a big piece for your ancestry jigsaw. What do you make of it?"

"I really don't know Jenny but I'm not one to anthropomorphize. Also, my scientific training and knowledge, and my experience as an engineer, both make me very cautious about jumping to irrational conclusions. Maybe the human Henry and Sarah befriended them when they visited the Manor, so the birds learned their names. From what I've read, Barnaby Rudge comes to mind, I am persuaded that ravens can learn to speak like humans, but I find it difficult to believe that they think like humans."

As Bran prepared for his departure from the mining museum, he thanked Ron and Jenny for their help. "I'm extremely grateful to you both. I sense that I'm drawing a line under my great grandparents' lives in Somerset. If I think any more about them I might start making things up."

Bran also wanted to say something to Ron about his grandson's accident. "We did some tests on our flight simulator last week that gave us clues as to what might have happened. I can't say too much but I think there will be a police investigation Ron. Something suspicious about the circumstances of the crash; it'll be in the papers soon. From what I've seen so far, Peter did everything he could to avert the crash, but his options may have been very limited. I'll keep you, and Sandra of course, informed if anything tangible comes through that I can share."

"Thank you, Bran, what you've said has already eased my anxiety. I'm so sorry that Sandra is left with such grief about the unresolved difficulties she and Peter had. She's a fine woman Bran, and I get on well with her. Such a pity that she and Peter couldn't make a better go of it. She was, she is, a free spirit, while Peter was quite a strict, disciplined man, comes from serving in the forces. Or maybe he joined the Royal Air Force because that need for discipline was already in his nature. In which case, it's probably my fault; usually comes from the male lineage, doesn't it Bran, the sins of the father and all that?"

"You shouldn't be hard on yourself Ron, every new generation has to figure out a lot of things for themselves, and I think that's the way it should be, always will be actually." They walked through the foyer as Ron opened the door for Bran carrying his glass dome with the ravens staring at him, but he stopped as he saw the pictures hanging on the walls. "I thought you were going to pass these pictures on to the artist's son Jenny." Bran put the glass dome on the floor.

"Turns out that Sonia Johnson wasn't an artist after all, so the S.J. must be someone else's initials. I thought we would just keep them there." Bran was overcome with emotion, his voice trembling as he spoke.

"My great grandmother painted these Jenny. S.J. is Sarah Jane, Sarah Jane Wallace, Sarah Jane Sage. She must have left them at the Collier's Rest when she and Henry eloped to the Valleys. I know because they have come into my dreams, Sarah painting. My research is stirring up a lot that I probably heard from my grandad when I was very young. The stirring is fuelling my dreams and in one I saw a woman painting at the colliery, just like this one." Bran pointed at the painting of the man standing next to the winding gear at the Camerton New Pit. "And, could this one be Henry and Sarah walking along the canal path I wonder? Can I please buy these paintings from you Jenny?"

"No, but you can have them Bran, although would you mind if we kept the kingfisher, it's the most beautiful picture I've ever seen?"

"Thank you, Jenny, yes, please keep the kingfisher. It will be good to know that its looked after here in the mining museum. Perhaps you could add a little piece below the picture saying who painted it."

As Bran drove over the Second Crossing to Wales, he was still thinking about all that had happened during his few hours in the Camerton valley. He occasionally looked through his rear-view mirror to check the dome was still safe on the rear seat. Henry and Sarah on their journey up to the Valleys, once again.

Bran arrived at his mother's house in Abergavenny late in the evening, weary from his early start and busy day in Somerset, but looking forward to seeing his mother. Aoife had prepared dinner, a sausage and bacon casserole, Bran's favourite when he was growing up and he could smell the rich aromas as he entered the house, bringing back good memories. His parents had moved from the Valleys to the greener grass of Abergavenny after Alwyn had retired. They enjoyed a few good years together but Alwyn had developed emphysema from smoking and working underground, his health deteriorated and he was diagnosed with cancer. He had passed away nearly twenty years before. To begin with, Bran worried that Aoife did not seem to have the will to overcome her grief and wouldn't be able to cope on her own. Thankfully, she was part of a local church community who rallied around and helped get her life back on track. Since then, she had developed in new ways, painting with water colours and sculpting with clay, but Aoife's passion was social care, rooted in her experience as a district nurse for many decades, particularly treating miners and their families. She would say that all people really wanted was a good friend who would listen to their woes and comfort them. Their inner healing resources would then be found and put to work.

Aoife greeted Bran warmly with a mother-bear hug and wanted to care for his every need.

"Please don't fuss mum, I can do that myself; it is very good to see you again." Bran would speak with his mother every week on the phone but the conversations were not very deep. He wasn't sure why.

"Tell me what you've found out about them Bran, our Sarah and Henry." So, Bran proceeded to tell his mum all he had found out in Somerset; the mining accident, when they travelled to the Valleys, the ravens and paintings. He didn't mention his dreams, and he wasn't sure why. Aoife had only met Sarah on one occasion during a visit to Ebbw Vale. Sarah was old and frail but welcoming and something about her had stayed with Aoife, the way she looked at you, questions in her eyes. "She was quite a woman by all accounts Bran, worked hard to get the Cooperative Society established in Ebbw Vale and she was involved with the Literary Institute; quite an artist as well, apparently. Your grampa George told me that when his dad, Henry, died, Sarah became a recluse for a long time, lost all her energy for life. Then one day, it was like she woke up out of a dream and began living again. I think I was inspired by that when your dad passed away Bran; if she could do it then so could I. Of course, you know that she'd said to us, quite firmly, that she hoped we would call our first son Bran, after her own first son. She never believed that he had died in the trenches in Belgium; always hung onto the thought that he would come home. Maybe that kept her alive for so long? When our first child turned out to be a daughter, it kind of upset her plan, but we named your sister Sarah and your great grandma seemed content with that."

"Mum, I must have forgotten Sarah had asked that I be named after her son. I had it in my mind that was dad's idea." Bran's relationship with his father was complex. They were good friends as adults but didn't talk much about the years when he was growing up. Alwyn was strict and uncompromising and Bran was sure he'd developed his strong work ethic from his dad, and his softer, more artistic side from his mum, and maybe Sarah as well. That's the way he liked to think about it anyway. But his father never seemed to be satisfied with Bran's progress, always wanting more; Bran should always be trying harder, doing better, being better. *You'll thank me when you're grown up*, he'd say, even when Bran thought he was already grown up. Maybe Alwyn had caught this from his father George, who'd caught it from Henry and before that James? Or perhaps he was living vicariously through his son; getting Bran to do what he didn't, or couldn't. Such a lot goes unspoken, unexamined, but it was too late now. Too late for the talking, but not too late for ancestry research, not too late for re-creating their history.

And, it wasn't too late to talk with his mum. Bran and Aoife chatted until well after midnight and Bran told himself that he must make sure he finds out all he can about his mother's family for when he turns to her side of his ancestry research. But not just that, talking with his mum was awakening his past, his own journey through adolescence that he'd closed the door on. And he valued his friendship with Aoife, and decided he wanted to re-build it anew. He wondered if Sarah and Brân had talked much, were they good friends, before her first son became MPD?

"You should visit aunt Alice, Bran, she lived with Sarah during her last few years and she still lives in Brynheulog Street. She's never been very communicative, and she would complain about your behaviour when you were growing up, so she may not welcome you, but you never know. Do you remember her Bran?"

"I think so but my memory of visits to Ebbw Vale are faded; what relation is she?"

"One of your Grampa George's brothers, Farnham, married Florence and Alice is their daughter. So, she's your dad's first cousin, so once removed to you, I think. She must be about ninety and I haven't seen her in years. Amazing how valleys can be cut off from each other, but the truth is more that we didn't get on, or rather your dad and Alice didn't get on. Let sleeping dogs lie Bran, but if you're brave enough, you could visit her and ask about Sarah. I can try to call her if you want?" Bran agreed that he would do that.

The next day, Sunday 4th June, Bran arrived at the site of the Old Blaina Chapel at the agreed time, 1030, and saw a man standing outside the old building. He guessed this was Jim Owen, the builder who was renovating the property, turning it into a home. Jim welcomed Bran, introduced him to his wife Joyce, and they walked through the entrance and around the building together.  It was hard to imagine that it was once a Chapel. Did Henry and Sarah come through that door, stand here and say, yes, I do, to each other? Yes, they do, I mean did, and Bran had that same déjà vu that he'd felt walking along the canal path in Camerton. But the past leads through the present into the future and one day this would be someone's home, which gave Bran a warm feeling; that same stone wall would enclose this special space for many years to come. Jim shared his plans for the building and Bran thought they were very fitting. They agreed to keep in touch and Bran thanked Jim and his lovely wife Joyce for hosting him and he headed over to Ebbw Vale. Would there be any trace of Sarah in the Literary and Scientific Institute, he wondered? Would he feel the presence of Henry in 21st century Ebbw Vale? Like so many places that were trying to recover from the industrial revolution, that had left scars and bruises in the landscape and the communities, Ebbw would probably be unrecognisable to the people who lived there in the 1870s. The mines and ironworks were gone, unemployment was over 30% among young people, many of who had insufficient skills to be socially mobile. Something had gone badly wrong.

"We were expecting you Dr Sage, I hope you had a good journey; I'm Janet Jones, we emailed each other. Would you like to come over and sit in the library, it's the most comfortable room and they'll be starting the dancing course here in the hall soon. Of course, we don't refer to it as the Literary and Scientific Institute any more but we are proud of, and we do value, our history. We are just the EVI now, the Ebbw Vale Institute. In the old days, they called it the stute, but I think EVI sounds better, don't you?"

"Well, it's certainly more modern and acronyms are used so much these days; but I think they sometimes take the character out of a place."

"Yes, I can see that, but you said that you were interested in finding out about your family connections with the EVI; sorry I mean the stute, and in the latter part of the 19th century, right? As I said in my email, we don't keep records here and you'll have to go down to Cwmbran to the Gwent County Archives. Same for all the documents about the mines and mining. One day we might bring them back to Ebbw Vale, where they were born, so to speak, but right now I'm afraid there's nothing here."

"I do realise that Janet but just visiting the places my relatives would have known, and I think Sarah Sage had some involvement with this place, is enough for me."

"Feel free to look at the books Dr Sage but I hear the dance music starting so could you leave by the side door when you are finished please?" Janet said her goodbye and left Bran on his own. But there was no trace, no sense of a presence, the modern acronym and the vacuum of the post-industrial revolution obliterating the past, like it didn't happen, leaving the present unanchored. Bran had to get out of there, fast. He made his way to Brynheulog Street, passing his birth place without stopping, trying not to remember. A very old lady answered the door.

"Yes, can I help you?" The Welsh Valleys accent was almost like song, one word connected to another without space.

"I'm sorry to intrude, I hope my mother was able to let you know I would come today. I'm Bran, Bran Sage, Alwyn's and Aoife's son."

"No, she didn't but I don't answer my phone anymore. Bran Sage eh, dear God I remember you making fun of me when you were young, I hated you, still do."

"I'm so sorry aunt Alice, I really am, can you forgive the

322

stupid boy inside the grown man who would really like to be your friend." These words flowed out as if rehearsed but they weren't and they were meant, as heartfelt as anything Bran had ever said. Alice was rather taken aback by the plea from the visitor.

"Come in, you might as well, where have you come from? I heard you and your sister and brother had moved away from the valleys years ago, deserted us for greener pastures in England."

"Yes, we both moved away a long time ago aunt Alice, but I'm staying with my mum for a couple of nights while I do some ancestry research here in Ebbw Vale. I want to find out as much as I can about my great-grandparents, Henry and Sarah." Bran slowly walked into the house behind the frail and delicate old lady who invited him into the sitting room. It looked like nobody had sat there for years and the aroma was of age, nothing else could describe it.

"Can I make you a cup of tea Bran, but I don't have no milk, nor no sugar neither." Bran held back a smile at the quintuple negative of valley dialect.

"No thanks Aunt Alice, can we just talk do you think?"

"What about Bran, I don't like talking these days, done enough in my life, mun. Did you know that we only have a certain amount of talking in us before the landlord calls us in. I think I've done most of mine. Ancestry research, what's that now? You trying to dig up the past? And call me Alice, Bran, auntie makes me feel older than I am, and I am old."

"Not dig it up, Alice, more try to understand how my ancestors lived."

"Now why'd you wanna do that? What good will it do? Will it make the sun shine brighter, or the grass grow greener, heal the sick, feed the poor, make anyone happier?" Alice's questions floored Bran. He was not expecting an inquisition, such profundity.

"No Alice, none of those things, but it may help me know myself better, be able to lead a better life; knowing how my family endured might help me be more caring to, to anyone I am with. Does that make sense?" Alice did not answer immediately but just looked at Bran with an expression that both confused and re-assured him. She did understand, but where was it taking her thoughts? Bran decided to get to the point. "Mum told me that you looked after Sarah in her late years, did you know Sarah well Alice?" Again, a silence and Bran felt he knew what Dylan meant when he sang about silence being like thunder.

"This was 54 years ago Bran, when Sarah died. I was working every day to keep us both going, but we would talk in the evenings and go for walks on the weekends. Sarah loved to walk on the hills but couldn't do that no more in her last few years so we'd just go up round the ponds. You been up there too, used to laugh at me, remember? She was a very special woman Bran, very serene, is that the word, serene?" Bran couldn't, or wouldn't, remember but he knew what serene meant.

"Like calm and peaceful?"

"Yes, that's it, well most of the time anyway, but one day she became very unsettled, not at all serene, and shared something with me that I've kept to myself for all this time. Can I trust you Bran Sage?"

"Yes, you can Alice, you can trust me to be sensitive regarding personal information, but are you asking me to keep a secret?" Bran wondered whether he was about to hear something that he should not include in his ancestry book; he'd wait for the thunder. In any case, Alice didn't answer but continued talking, looking down into her open hands as she spoke.

"Sarah always believed that her first son, your namesake, Brân, didn't die in Belgium during the war. She could not accept the MPD notice on the letter she received. Brân was a medic with the South Wales Brigade on the Western Front and was supposedly killed when shells hit the hospital tent. After the war, Sarah attempted to find out more about how Brân died and contacted one of his army mates, a Derek Painter from Blackwood. Derek told Sarah that Brân was in love with one of the nurses, Caragh Lynch, and talked about escaping with her, making their way back to her home in Ireland. Brân was not a fighter like his father, would never hurt a fly. On the night of the shelling, Derek was sure that Brân and Caragh had gone off into the woods to 'perform some tests'. Derek said that's what they used to say when they made love, 'perform some tests.' He never saw them again; the hospital was obliterated, no-one could be identified and Derek assumed that both Brân and Caragh had been killed. Sarah was determined to try to find out if they had escaped the Front. She eventually managed to find out from the war records where Caragh Lynch came from and she tried to contact the family. Caragh's father wrote back to Sarah with condolences for her loss and invited her and Henry to visit them in Ireland so they could share memories of their loved ones. Sarah thought the father was trying to tell her something that he couldn't write. They decided that Henry would take a few days off to visit the Lynch's. They told friends that he was visiting family in Somerset. When Henry came back it seems that he had been injured, and it took a while to realise that he had broken ribs but by then he was suffering from pleurisy. He died a week later. Sarah was desperate of course but she never told me what Henry had found in Ireland, if she ever knew. So, there you have it Bran Jnr, and it's good to get it off my shoulders."

Bran was trying to take this story in, a huge missing piece of the jigsaw, and one that made the picture more confusing than ever. What had happened to Brân? What had happened to Henry in Ireland? Ancestry research throws up unexpected questions; very much like accident investigations, Bran thought but he pushed that idea back downstairs.

"Thank you, Alice, I'm rather lost for words. I wasn't expecting to hear this, and you've no idea what Henry found in Ireland, how he got injured?"

"Sarah didn't want to tell me and I respected that. After Henry died she became a very private person and burned all her letters and notebooks before she died, left just a couple of her paintings behind."

"Could I see those Alice, please, I really would like to? This will sound weird I know, but I've had a couple of dreams where someone, I think its Sarah, paints pictures." Alice asked Bran to follow him upstairs and they walked into one of the bedrooms. The two paintings hung on the wall above the bed. In one, the raven's wings were open wide as the bird glided above the landscape. The second showed the miner woven into Orion; Bran had seen something like this before, in his dream. "That's like one I saw in my dream Alice, except it was the Plough, Ursa Major, not Orion. I think she saw Henry in the stars above Camerton, where they lived in Somerset. You probably think I'm crazy Alice but I've been having dreams about my ancestors; not surprising as they've been on my mind quite a lot. And I hear ravens too."

"Not crazy Bran, just very imaginative, why don't you take these paintings with you; I won't need them anymore." Bran thanked Alice for her generosity and they continued talking for a long time. Alice wanted to know what else he'd found out about Henry and Sarah, and she asked him about his profession; she was interested in his work as an aeronautical engineer. So, it was Bran's turn to talk and describe his life and, as he did so, he felt closer and  closer to Alice. "Sounds like you've had quite an exciting career Bran, something you wouldn't have found in the Valleys for sure." She was right there but Bran was curious about Alice's life.

"Did you never want to get married and have a family Alice?" As soon as he'd said it he realised it was too personal a question. Alice looked at him and smiled.

"It's alright, I don' mind you asking, and I don' hate you any more Bran Jnr. Men aren't really my cup of tea Bran, with or without sugar. But I grew up in an age where I couldn't reveal my true self; different now isn't it and good that it is. But now you must be on your way, and I'm feeling tired." As Bran was leaving and thanking Alice once more, she took his hand. "I do welcome Sarah into my dreams like you Bran, listen to her soft voice; I've got a good imagination as well.

Farewell for now, give my best wishes to Aoife."

Although Alice hadn't asked him to keep the secret, Bran decided it would be better not to mention the story to his mum; it didn't feel right yet, anyway. The next day Bran drove Aoife to Alwyn's grave in Ebbw Vale and they stood in silence with their own thoughts, remembering the good times, and the not so good times, that teach us how to do things differently next time, and how to manage the shame. But there wouldn't be a next time with Alwyn. Bran would be leaving the Valleys that morning to head back up north, back to his real world, but he carried treasures, some material, some deep inside his psyche. Ancestry research was not just about digging up the past. More importantly, it was about navigating a better path into the future.

When he'd woken up that morning Bran had another dream to record. He knew immediately where it was, the Old Blaina Chapel, except it wasn't an old, broken building being refurbished, it was a splendid Chapel, stained glass windows and a group of people were walking out. Did Sarah look up at him and did he hear the raven cronk three times? Yes, she did and yes, he did, and he wasn't surprised anymore, it was all part of his rich imagination, like Alice had said.

Bran arrived back at the FS2 office at lunchtime and the

TLeM had been delayed until his return. He looked around the table at his staff, wondering for a moment what lay behind their eyes, in their thoughts. Felicity always looked directly at him when she spoke. She was looking for approval, but her eyes also shone with confidence; she always knew the approval would come. Roger was deeply reflective, held so much knowledge behind his eyes and could draw it out in a wonderfully logical way so that Bran always knew what he meant. Colin was more circumspect, shaped by many years involved in flight testing. Colin would say that when you've been exposed to the real world of flight test like he had, and survived, you question everything that moves. Colin would often avoid direct eye contact when speaking; said it put him off his thinking. What a great team, Bran thought, so different from the characters on the road and along the roadside of his ancestry journey. They took Bran through the progress over the weekend and Monday, often the busiest day at FS2. The results from the simulation of the Holtan Odona accident had been sent to the Investigation team who were now required to liaise with the police enquiry since there was compelling evidence of foul play. The flight path reconstruction analysis was continuing and Roger expected this would be complete by the end of the week. The investigation into the Claston Skycruiser2 cockpit displays and related human factors on unstable approaches, had been put on hold since the crash, and it was now in the hands of the country's national investigation bureau. Then there was the exploration into the Skycruiser3 wake interaction with the tail, following engine failure on take-off. Roger reported that Claston were scheduling a new wind-tunnel test this week and they would endeavour to get the data processed and available to FS2 for their model and simulation the following week. They would be able to fit this into evening slots on the simulator after the student project work was complete. The HoneyB-M work was more complex. It seems that Colin had been having further discussion with Holtan regarding the actuator system and said that he had an idea what might be going wrong; their system might be demanding too much from the actuators, but in an unusual manner. They would try that out in simulation before improving the rotor wake interaction model using Jim's theory. Bran considered this a very important piece of work.

"All we do is important guys but if we help them solve this problem, it really does ramp up our credibility and brings us a new opportunity; you know I'd like Holtan to try out some of our envelope protection solutions. I think they've resisted because they didn't invent it, and we've patented our design concept so they'd have to pay us to use it, but let's take the opportunity to explore if our approach could solve their problems without the increased actuator authority. It's a potential win-win solution and we can make some money to fund the simulator visual improvements we want." There were nods of agreement around the table.

As the TLeM ended, Bran wondered at the depth of engineering analysis and skills required to do the work that FS2 did. He also reflected on the differences between the Chief Engineer role that Geoff Scrag played at Holtan and the Chief Designer role that Tobias Hamel played at Claston. Two powerful positions of authority, of influence, in the aerospace world. Tobias's focus was the aircraft, its form, fit and function and all the trade-offs involved in the optimisation process that involved dozens of highly specialised engineers. Geoff's focus was ensuring that the design met all the engineering standards for safety, strength and performance. And the way to do this was to use engineering tools through the product life-cycle that were fit for purpose; simulation modelling, virtual prototypes and the manufacturing jigs and processes. Geoff was responsible for these tools and their accreditation by regulatory authorities. The roles were distinct but complementary. Bran would enjoy discussing how these roles played out in practice with student groups, helping them grasp key aspects of the career routes to these senior positions. Jos disturbed his musing with a message from Geoff Scrag confirming the delay in the Odona work. The Police were following up on the Oats-Clerk issues with the University and research council; seems like the letter Mary had received had really got people's attention.

"Oats, that's where I remembered the name! The guy who cut the cage cable at the Camerton mine. Good grief, can it be that another amazing coincidence has stretched over 128 years, or could it be that...?" Jos interrupted Bran again to remind him that he had agreed to give a talk on aviation safety to students at the University on Friday morning; she handed him a folder with papers from the last one he had given.

That evening Bran phoned Mary and they talked for a long time. Bran was excited, and relieved, to talk about all the things that had happened during his visit to Camerton and Ebbw Vale. It was almost like it wasn't real until he shared it with Mary, just a dream or at least his memories were swilling around inside his head, only loosely hinged with reality. He hadn't had time to write it all up in his notebook but that would be his first task after the phone call. Mary had been writing a paper for presentation at the United Nations Conference for the Parties, COP 6, to be held in The Hague in November. It would be co-authored by colleagues from Berkley, but Mary would give the presentation. Bran could feel her excitement about her research findings as she described it. What discovery does to people? It can make you hide or crave for the light. Mary and Bran were both light cravers, wanting to light up the darkness, build new understandings. Mary did this in fundamental science, Bran in applied science, engineering.

Bran explained to Mary that the police were now following up on the Clerk-Oats situation, so better that they let them get on with it; and Mary and Bran would let each other get on with their own lives. Wednesday and Thursday would be busy days in the office for Bran but he was looking forward to getting out and breaking free on Friday.

"Now, for the most important thing friends. Close cooperation between us miners is vital to safety underground, mark my words. It's about keeping an eye on your butty's safety as well as your own, and being ready to act if there is an accident. I've seen with the long-wall method that close cooperation is better for production as well as safety, so don't think it's one or tother. And, it's good to think about difficult situations, what would I do if such and such happened? Talk with your butties about it, share ideas, listen to the ones who have solved problems underground before. Listening to the problem solvers talking about their experience can be the best preparation. When an accident happens, an explosion or a roof collapse, the chances of survival are much greater if people don't panic, but stay calm, think about the problem and work together. That's what good training gives you, the time to think. My father James might still be alive, if the people around him had better training and thought about what was going on. Finally, I would like to recommend that we undertake a review of all safety issues relating to working practices in the EVC mines; I'll need help with this and we'll need to get the managers on our side." Bran could hear clapping and cheering and the uproar broke the spell, waking him up.

Friday morning 5.28 and Bran sat up with the dream still playing out in his mind. Someone, was it Henry, talking to a group of people in a hall. Bran thought he knew that place, the shape of the stage, the rooms off to the side. He had been talking about safety underground, the importance of working together, wanting a review. Bran wrote it down in his dreambook and realised that he had to modify his safety talk to emphasise the criticality of cooperation between engineers. The specialists in the new technologies, that would continue to roll in relentlessly, needed to be part of the failure analysis teams; only the specialists would know how the new devil works with the new details, and improve the safety above ground.

"Thank you, Henry," he whispered, "I wonder if they listened to you."

Later in the morning Bran sat down with one more cup of coffee. He was pleased with his talk, which took the form of him presenting a series of case studies on safety, followed by discussion with the student group about the failure assessment process, causal factors, human behaviour and ethics. In every case, he tried to bring in Henry's point about cooperation between team members and the need for constant vigilance on safety matters. He would also draw on John Morgan's work on accident and risk analysis. What a huge influence John had been, what a good friend; a close colleague and good friend are hard to find as Bran recalled the eulogy he had given, all those weeks ago.

Generally, Bran was only pleased with a presentation if he had a receptive audience and this student group were receptive, responsive to his calls for engagement. It only took one or two to get the flow going and stimulate the courage in others to ask what they might think a stupid question. Pilot error drew the most questions. Bran had described accidents where the aircrew had not fully monitored the changing flight condition presented on their cockpit instruments, leading to the pilot-in-control misjudging the safety margin and the aircraft entering a dangerous flight regime from which recovery was impossible. One student asked why were these occurrences so frequent? That led to a heated discussion. There was not a simple answer but training shortcomings, workload and fatigue, complex automation systems and poor communication all got onto the list of culprits. One student declared that aircrew needed a computer assistant, a pilot's associate, that monitored everything going on and would warn the aircrew well ahead of entry into dangerous conditions. If they ignored the warnings, the computer would take over. Another student challenged this by asking could we always trust the computer? Young minds grappling with almost existential issues that orbited the hard core of engineering. They would need to consider both as they developed into professionals. Bran would emphasise that, whatever practices they had picked up in school or at home, to be a good engineer you shouldn't be afraid to ask the question that you can't answer with your own resources. Showing your vulnerability is a strength; isn't it ironic? Bob Dylan would often do it, but in rather hidden ways, so you needed to be tuned in to pick it up. Staying tuned in is a full-time job.

Talking of Dylan, and tuning in, Friday night was dress rehearsal time for the *Love-Sick* concert and Orion met early to ensure they could work through the concert, narratives and all. As Bran walked into the Arts Centre, he couldn't fail to notice the pictures hanging around the hall and he remembered Jacob's exhibition on facial expressions would be running for a few days.

"Some amazing expressions on these faces Jacob and I see that your artists have made some interpretations. Are the pictures in this group all done by the same artist?"

"Evening Bran, good to see you, yes they are. The chap has this huge collection of pictures and photograhs of his family and ancestors and thought he'd put a few in, have a go at describing what the people are thinking, what's going on behind the eyes. There seems to be depth in every one; its what makes us human. But you can't really tell what people are hiding can you, only guess?"

Bran looked at the faces, some looked happy, others sad, some serious, another quite funny. Just like his own ancestors, the pictures only captured a moment in these people's lives; but a moment when they looked at you, well most of them; he noticed that one seemed to be asleep. He was reminded of Henry the raven who always looked at him and had been asleep for a long, long time. I wonder when that little fellow woke up?

"Time to get going fellow Orions." Oliver's words echoed around the hall, getting the band member attention. They were all gazing at pictures, reading the descriptions, deep in thought, but at the call, they all came forward to the stage. Twenty-four songs plus an acapella version of *Girl from the North Country* to finish off interspersed with colourful narrative descriptions from the band members on their song selections. Two seventy-five minute sets and a break of 30 minutes; all very organised by Oli. "This is the framework guys, you know the running order and it's our job to be creative and entertain within this; give the audience something to remember." And so, Orion began their rehearsal. Jacob's father Toni had agreed to make notes, pick up any flaws and share with the band after they had finished. But as Sam said, "tonight's flaw could be tomorrow's loveable imperfection."

Later, in the pub, the band were quiet, talking about other things, not wanting to burst the wonderful balloon full of love and the compressed feelings they had created; they could prick it tomorrow night after the concert and listen to the big bang and sighs of relief, help each other manage the post-concert blues. Chloe and Georgia were good at that and those who held their weakness strongly, like Sam and Bran, would surely need help. Before the night was out, Bran asked Georgia about ravens. "Do you think they are mystical Georgia?"

"Oh Bran, you interested in Corvus Corax, my favourite bird. My sister Elsie keeps a pet raven she found with a broken wing; she took it in and it wasn't long before they had bonded, really bonded. She's jealous of me though, kronks her head off, or her heart out, when Elsie gives me attention. But are they mystical? What a question from a scientist like you Bran, what's it all about?"

"I know, silly really, but I've had a few dreams where I hear ravens; not sure what that means."

"You should talk to Chloe about dreams Bran; but anyway, I do know that ravens have been revered, feared and even hated by humans throughout history. They've been symbols for all kinds of things. Poe's raven is scary, kronking '*nevermore*' over and over, leaves the poor love-sick bloke in a state, with his soul trapped in the raven's shadow on the floor; a symbol of love never to be recovered, or something like that. So, what might they represent in your dreams Bran?" Bran was shaking his head thinking of nevermore; the very thought of nevermore seeing Mary again made him shiver. "And then there was Odin, the Viking God of wisdom and knowledge, a wanderer by trade. He had two ravens, Huginn, or thought, and Muninn, or memory. Legend has it that Odin used to send the ravens off every day to find out what was going on in the world; they'd fly back and tell him, keep him up with the news. Just like Noah, who sent the raven off to search for land. I know it doesn't say so in Genesis, but some think that when the raven told Noah where the land was, he then sent out the Dove to bring back the olive branch, yet another symbol. And if that isn't enough Bran, they can learn to speak our language. Jennie's raven has learned a few words, thankfully not nevermore or curses, but *good morning* and *can I have a pizza*. There's this book that Jennie has, *Mind of the Raven*, by an American biologist, Bernd Heinrich; he writes about the raven's intelligence and consciousness. Now you should look at that if you really want to find out about them. Sorry Bran, you asked if they are mystical; no idea love." Georgia smiled at Bran, hoping she hadn't overwhelmed him with her out pouring. "Well, you did ask!"

"Yes, I did and thanks Georgia, you've given me food for thought."

Bran sat at home looking at the ravens he'd placed on the table in the lounge and Sarah's four pictures which he'd hung

337

on the wall, so he could see them and the ravens at the same time. Spoils from another century, authentic relics from his history; Bran felt the past was beginning to settle down, if that were possible. Henry stared back at Bran from his perch and Sarah still looked up at Henry. Anna's preternatural sagacity, Odin's memory and thought, Camerton's Henry and Sarah; symbols of mortality perhaps. He picked up his guitar and sang a ditty he had penned earlier.

The Raven is black, the Raven is blue

The Raven can talk, can see right through you

The Raven can fly, oh boy can she fly

Up down, right or left, the oyster's her sky

The Raven is smart, her shape is a mystery

The Raven is smart, knows all her own history

She turns upside down, folds one wing in tight

The Raven flies on right into the night

The Raven is black, the Raven is blue

And so are you.......

"Time to draw a line under this ancestry research, its driving me crazy; but what do ravens have to do with mortality?"

Bran noticed a message and attachment from the ancestry research company. *Thanks for your request, details of Wendy Arton attached.* A task for tomorrow, he thought.

10. Listening to their Hearts as the Raven Passes by

Henry and Sarah missed walking along by the old canal, listening to the birds of Camerton singing their songs. But here, in Ebbw Vale, there were different walks, ones that  stretched their legs more as they climbed to the top of Mynydd Carn-y-Cefn, the spinal cord hill that separated the Ebbw Vale and Blaina valleys. They reached the same point that they had climbed to one week ago, the day they first arrived in Blaina. They looked down and saw the Baptist Chapel where they wed just 4 days ago; they could see Gwen and Glyn's house.

"Is that Gwen on the doorstep arms folded, chatting to another woman."

"You've got good eyes my love, can you see down the valley to the next town, where is that?"

"Yes, I see it, that's Abertillery. The mines down there are mostly sale-mines, so the owners sell their coal on the open market. They try to get the best price they can but Ivan says there is such fierce competition and some of the owners are mean people; won't pay their miners a decent wage. That sparks discontent and an envy of the miners in Ebbw where most of the coal gets turned into coke for steel making. That was the reason for the fracas on Monday, remember, although I think those blokes were just trouble makers?" Henry pointed to the bruise still healing on his head. "When the sale-coal miners call for strike action, the Ebbw miners ignore them. Ivan is trying to get all the miners in the different valleys to work together for action so that the coal owners listen to them. He's finding it hard work, but he's a good negotiator Sarah, already persuaded the owners to reduce the wage cuts they were planning."

"But what are you going to say tonight Henry, your ideas about safety; how are you going to get them to listen if they are all knotted up about pay?"

"Ah Sarah, I got to get this right or the men won't listen to me, I know that. I wish I had a bit more time to prepare, but not sure that would make a difference. I remember Grampa John talking about safety; he had a wonderful way of explaining ideas Sarah, made so much sense. The idea that safety and productivity should be the twin goals, equal in value, in the industrial revolution that's been going on for more than a century. The importance of cooperation between workers to make things safe; watching out for your mates, or butties as they're called here in the Valleys."

"Sounds to me like my man has got it all there in his head, just needs to let it out with that passion I know about, then they'll listen to him."

 "Talking about passion Sarah, look at those ravens up there, don't you think they fly with passion. Oh, did you see that, one of them rolled over; now why do they do that if not for the fun and the passion? Showing off to his mate I reckon. Can you keep reminding me about fun Sarah; a man could go crazy working underground without fun." Sarah held Henry's hand tightly, reassuring him that she was there as his best friend and, to reinforce the point, she suggested it might have been the female raven that rolled over. As they walked along quietly, they noticed two men walking up the hill from Blaina. One of them was waving.

"Henry, good morning, nice day for a long walk." As the two pairs closed in on each other, Henry recognised Ivan, but not the other man. "This is William Parnell, and these are my friends Henry and Sarah Sage, moved up from Somerset last week. William has written the play that will be performed in the stute tonight. Can we walk along with you Henry; I wanted to have a chat with you about your safety talk, if you don't mind." Sarah and Henry shook hands with William, who wanted to say more about his play. Sarah was enthusiastic.

"Please Mr Parnell, tell us more about it."

"Ok, briefly, if I may, but please call me William. We are a travelling theatre, based in London and our aim is to bring what we call social-conscious messages to communities around the country. We want to help people understand some

342

of the changes that our Liberal politicians are working towards. Our troupe has been performing *Dylan and Efa* across the Valleys for the last few weeks and our final performance will be in Ebbw Vale tonight. Although it's roughly based on Shakespeare's Romeo and Juliet, we tailor it to the local audience, try to weave in local issues. So, Dylan Rees's family are from Abertillery and Efa Jones is from Ebbw Vale. Dylan is infatuated with Efa and she is, well, she's simply in love. If you don't mind me saying, you two look like you might understand that. But, their fathers hate each other because of the disputes about pay. And, just like the servants of the Capulet's and Montague's in Shakespeare's play were fighting on the streets of Verona, so the miners fight on the hills and the streets in the towns in the Valleys. Ivan tells me you've had a taste of that already Henry. We try to mix humour and tragedy, to keep the audience entertained, but the message in the end is that fighting is futile and leaves most people unhappy, and some people, well sadly, dead." Henry wasn't sure about the futile bit.

"Sometimes you need to fight to make a big change, like in the American civil war. Men fought for freedom, for the abolition of slavery, just a few years ago. That wasn't futile." Henry was remembering what Grampa John had told him.

"Yes, you're right Henry, very right, but I think if we, as a troupe, went around the country encouraging people to fight, they would soon shut us down, so we try to be subtler, build the messages into the drama; it usually works and leaves people wondering. Often metaphors help people see the truth more clearly you know. On the other hand, my wife Erica is more direct. She belongs to the Society for Women's Suffrage, who want to get women the vote and more equality in society. I think she would agree with you Henry, but you can ask her yourself, she's going to give a short talk just before the play starts this evening. We try to take advantage of any gathering of people to get messages across."

As they walked on, Henry and Ivan broke off to talk about mining safety, while Sarah and William talked about the play and Sarah wanted to know more about women's suffrage. It seems that Erica had been drawn into this movement by William's sister who was a friend of Helen Taylor, the step daughter of John Stuart Mill. Helen had helped her step father produce his 1869 essay *The Subjection of Women*. Erica felt she'd been awoken by reading this, realising that those with power over women, generally men, would only give this up with a struggle. Some so ignorant or blind that they believed that domestic slavery, and sexual inequality in all matters, were the natural way of things. The church generally supported this viewpoint so a battle had to be fought. The battle had several fronts; the first and foremost with the men of power who had the most to lose, or thought they had; second with the women who colluded with the men in power, and third with all the institutions like the church who preached and practiced the dogma. Some men were so bloated with entitlement that their superiority over women was woven into the fabric of the social order, but the fabric was wearing thin, the writing appearing on the walls.

"The time will come Sarah when women will put their lives on the line for this cause. And with women like my Erica and Helen Taylor, and those to come, laws will change and right will prevail, I am sure." Sarah was stirred by this cause and looked forward to meeting Erica later in the day. What bravery, what courage to take on these battles knowing that there will be casualties, knowing that you might be one of them. Where does it come from? Deep inside, from the parts that have always been there and always will, yes always will.

Henry was angry with himself that he had missed Erica's talk, but he needed the time to think about how he was going to give his own talk. He was nervous, like he'd never been before. Twenty-one, a stranger in a new land, trying to persuade seasoned miners to adopt a new code of working, where safety was number one and he only had about 10 minutes. Ivan introduced Henry, explaining that he was training as a mines inspector, helping the Ebbw miners to implement the rulings of the Coal Mines Regulation Act, likely to be passed by Parliament in August. "Henry is our friend brothers, help him make things better."

Henry began by telling his audience, a mix of miners, iron and steel makers, managers and their families, who he was and why safety was important to him. He'd lost his father, James, in a mining accident when a roof collapsed, he'd witnessed the aftermath of the Camerton cage-fall accident, an act of vengeance by a discontent miner. He knew the cost of poor ventilation underground, felt for the families who had lost loved ones the previous year. The changes would make mining accidents much less likely; one day hopefully eliminating them. Henry talked about safety lamps; no other light than a locked safety lamp would be allowed in the arcas known to be gassy. There would be rules on the use of explosives, on places of refuge along the underground roadways; on securing the roof and sides of all travelling roadways; training for enginemen and all who used machinery that could maim or even kill if it failed; rules on communication from top to bottom; no single linked chains would be allowed, and all miners must have access to two shafts."

"To repeat brothers, when these changes, these rules, are

fully implemented the accidents will reduce and one day, we hope, they will cease." Henry paused and looked around at his audience. Sarah smiled at him and the woman next to her looked familiar; something about her face, what was it? But it was time to finish off. "Now, the most important thing. Close cooperation between us miners is vital to safety underground, mark my words. It's about keeping an eye on your butty's safety as well as your own, and being ready to act if there is an accident. I've seen with the long-wall method being tried in number 6, that close cooperation is better for production as well as safety, so don't think it's one or 'tother. And, it's good to think about difficult situations, what would I do if such and such happened? Talk with your butties about it, share ideas, listen to the ones who have solved problems underground. Listening to the problem-solvers talking about their experience can be the best preparation. If an accident does happen, God forbid, an explosion or a roof collapse, the chances of survival are much greater if people don't panic, but stay calm, think about the problem and work together. That's what good training gives you, the time to think. My father James might be still alive today, if the people around him had better training and thought more about what was going on. Finally, I would like to recommend that we undertake a review of all safety issues relating to working practices in the EVC mines; you can all help with this and we'll need to get the managers on our side. Thank you for listening."

Henry's talk was well received and Ivan congratulated him. "It begins now Henry, well done." Sarah beckoned to Henry to come sit beside him to watch the play.

"Well done Henry, they're on your side, and that's a good start. This is Erica Parnell. You missed her good talk."

"I'm so sorry Mrs Parnell, it's my loss I know but I needed time to gather my thoughts together."

"Erica please, and glad to make your acquaintance Henry. I enjoyed listening to what you said; you'll have your hands full making all the changes you talked about. Sarah can tell you about my cause, women's suffrage, its starts with us getting a vote." Henry was staring at Erica but his thoughts were interrupted as William appeared on stage to introduce the play.

Dylan and Eva started with a mock fight, played out to music from a harpsichord, lute and symbol. The audience became involved with hoots and jeers, cries of support for the Rees's, then for the Jones's, bursts of laughter at the moments carefully planned by William. The play lasted about 90 minutes, the story gradually unfolding, the love quickly blooming, the tragedy finally overcoming everything and everyone, leading the families to reconciliation. But, just as in the Verona original, William didn't want to paste over the cracks in the underlying fault that led to animosity, and the audience saw the villains rising once more to continue the affray. But, by then, the audience had been persuaded, the villains were out of favour, and maybe, just maybe, miners would value friendship more than enmity. Henry thought how important that was underground; good lessons to be learned from the play.

Outside the stute, the actors and musicians were climbing aboard the charabanc that would take them back to their hotel in Abergavenny before their long haul back to London the next day. William was talking to Henry and Sarah.

"Good luck with your efforts Henry, you have a good cause to fight for and I hope our little play helped." Erica joined them and they said their farewells, hoping to meet again but knowing it would be unlikely.

"Come on William, let's get on board before they take off without us."

"Alright Wendy, I'm with you." Henry's mind was spinning.

"Are you Wendy?"

"I'm Wendy to my friends and family, but Erica is my fighting name, well my middle name actually. What is it Henry, are you alright?"

"You are Wendy, I recognised you." Sarah put her arm in Henry's and whispered, *"she doesn't know Henry, let it be."* It was dark and only Sarah could see and feel Henry's tears, share his dilemma.

"And I'll recognise you next time Henry, go make the world a safer place." The charabanc clattered off with the troupe singing a song from the play, Wendy looking back at Henry.

The following evening, Henry and Sarah walked up the track through the Silent Valley, to the accompaniment of the ravens. Henry was so grateful to farmer Evans for protecting the birds. Something about them made him feel secure and he needed that to balance his other feelings that day. "I know it was her Sarah, she had Anna's eyes and the shape of her face, the cheek bones and dimpled chin. And she is my sister Sarah, do you think she might be pleased to know that."

"You took more notice of Anna than I did Henry, I know that. But I think it was right that you didn't say anything last night; maybe you could write to her? You both have causes to fight for so, yes, I think she would be very pleased to know you as a brother."

"I could send her Anna's letter. She seemed a strong

woman, did you get that impression from her talk Sarah?"

"Yes, I did. But she thinks that Mr and Mrs Arton are her parents and they will have helped her be strong. If she knew about Anna and James what would she do, how would she feel? She may want to visit Anna and that would stir things up in Camerton if the truth were out. What would that do for Anna?"

"Sarah, you think of things that I don't and it's good that you do. But it's a big secret to keep to myself. Maybe I could write to Anna; she wanted to tell me, to share her secret and maybe because it was getting too heavy to carry. She might like to know what has happened to her daughter."

"You don't keep it to yourself Henry, you share it with me." Henry and Sarah continued to talk and share ideas as they reached the top of the hill and the sun was sinking in the north-western sky. They sat on a rock and looked out across the landscape, stretching out westwards, with the dark shadows of each valley separating the hill tops. Deep within the shadows, the communities went about their business; like life in a city, mining communities never stop, the urgency of need is too great.

"I had one of my moments today Henry, when you were talking about safety. I'm used to them now, but they still take me by surprise and make me wonder. It's like I am the ears and eyes of the world for you Henry Sage, and that makes me feel good, know what I mean."

"Henry, Sarah." Two men were approaching, waving and shouting the names of the main actors. "Over here, jeez that hill was steep, what a place, and what a view. Look at the red glow from them furnaces." Henry and Sarah were pulled out of their musing by the presence of two familiar faces.

"Ritchie, and John, John Riddle, well I'll be. What are

349

you doing here?" Ritchie came running up and laughing as he spoke. Henry gave him a big hug.

"Couldn't let you escape on your own, all alone in this strange land, thought you might need a helping hand." Ritchie could always find a rhyme for the moment. "So, after we met with Tom last week and he said there would be plenty of work in the Valleys, John and I decided to come and look after you. What do you think to that sister Sarah?"

"I am very pleased to see you brother Ritchie and you too John, but this is a lot rougher and tougher than Camerton; how is your arm, and where are you staying?"

"Its healing well, should be able to work with it in a week. Megan's mum is putting us up until we can find work and a place to stay." Henry was still looking bemused.

"It is so good to see you both. Come over to Ebbw Vale tomorrow and I can introduce you to the manager of the Victoria mines. I'm sure there'll be a place for you John; are you still able to shift twelve tons."

"I am Henry. I tracked Billie Oats down by the way, and they've locked him up before his trial." Henry was shaking his head.

"There will always be an Oats; people devoid of good heart, who gain pleasure from other's misfortune and do anything to make their way in life. Thank you for that John, you're a good man. But tell us about life in Camerton, are people missing us? Ritchie, how is mum and what have Sarah's mum and dad said?" The four friends sat on the rock together, Ritchie and John regaling with stories from Camerton, Henry and Sarah recalling what they had been doing all week. Just one week and there would be many more to come in the valley of fire, coal and steel.

Towards the end of the 18th century, the population of the Ebbw Vale and Beaufort farming communities was about 150. The valleys were green and the living was subsistent, and hardly easy. By the beginning of the 19th century, the Beaufort iron works had been established, and coal mining began, increasing the population to about 1200. In 1802, the Rev Walter Davies was touring Wales to report on the state of agriculture, and following his trip from Crickhowell through Beaufort and Sirhowy, he wrote in his notebook, "*Farewell beautiful Cwm Clydach, welcome dreariness, filth and wealth.*" One man's view of progress. By the early 1870s, at the time that Henry and Sarah Sage moved to Ebbw Vale, the population had increased tenfold to 12,500 and would double again by the end of the 19th century, Sarah and Henry making a healthy contribution to this growth. The provision of social support, in the form of housing, clean water and sewage facilities, health and welfare, education and leisure facilities was slow and did not match the population growth. One consequence was infant mortality from diseases like measles and diphtheria. If you were lucky enough to be born, you had a fifteen percent chance of dying as a baby. At least four of Sarah's and Henry's children would die as infants.

While the Ebbw mines were relatively free from accidents for the remainder of the century, and early 20th century, other districts in the Valleys were not so fortunate. An explosion underground at the Prince of Wales colliery in Abercarn in September 1878 killed 268 workers, and the single worst industrial accident in Britain's history occurred at the Universal colliery in Senghenydd in October 1913, when 439 workers were killed. In the Ebbw valley, an underground explosion in the Marine colliery killed 52 miners in 1927; the number of casualties would have been much higher if the manager, Edward Gay, had not ordered the ventilation fan to  be slowed, reducing the fanning of the flames. A good example of what a good problem-solver can achieve. The explosion occurred during the night shift so Henry's son George, Bran's grampa, was not underground at the time. George continued to work at the Marine until he was 70 years old, in 1950, the year of Bran's birth. The Marine was the last colliery in the Ebbw valley when it closed in 1989.

Industrial disputes continued in the depression that lasted through the 1870s and 1880s, but the efforts of the coal miners' unions, that were in any case fragmented across the Valleys, were weakened by lockouts and collusions between mine owners. Coal mining seems to be an industry that brings out the worst in the greedy capitalist and the best in hard-working men and women. How such forces managed to survive is a wonder of nature; but we are talking of human nature.

Whatever way we look at it, life in the Valleys must have been grim for most working families in the 19th century. Yet, incredibly, people endured and could laugh at their troubles, be thrilled by moments of gladness, joining together in song with power and passion about the social injustices they endured; forging a character found in only a few other places.

But, returning to fiction, what's in store for Henry and Sarah I wonder; lots of children for sure because they enjoyed love making; well that's the way I like to imagine it, as you should know by now. They would have hardship, but I hope that their union from such an early age, fortunate to be attracted by the other's strengths and weaknesses, and to be stimulated by the wonder of the opposite sex, would help sustain them for the little time they had together, in the grand scheme of things.

"She seems a nice young woman Alice, do you think that Alwyn will be happy with her; how do you say her name again?"

"Its spelt *Aoife* and pronounced eefa. It's an Irish name and means beauty; so, very fitting don't you think nan. Yes, I think she will make Alwyn happy. He's been depressed since coming back from the war and it seems that Aoife is breathing new life into your grandson. He's getting under George's feet as well and, if he gets that job in Abertillery, they can move there and hopefully start a new Sage family. Uncle George likes Aoife a lot nan, so I think she will help the family stay connected."

"I'm sure you're right Alice dear and it will be good if they have children. I hope they will call their first child Bran, after my first son, your uncle Brân. If I forget, could you ask them to do that please Alice? Now, I want to write a letter so could you bring me a pen and some paper and then leave me alone please." Sarah looked up at her raven painting and smiled. Writing her letter brought back memories, some as fresh and sweet as the aroma of pineapple mayweed along the Camerton canal path in spring. She was familiar with melancholy, strangely comforting in the night time of her life. As she finished writing her letter, her tears were flowing and splashing

on the paper below. That same old feeling came over her and she wanted to send the letter before it disappeared. She opened the back of the painting frame and placed the letter inside, replacing and securing the wooden panel and holding the painting to her bosom. *The raven is smart, a natural mystery, she is so smart, knows her own history, the raven is black, the raven is blue, and so are you.*

11. Heading for the Light as the Raven Touches Down

"What a week, it really was such a week, it was." Bran talks to himself as he wakes, his brain searching around for a remnant, but no, nothing there, all undreamt. "Who needs dreams when reality is awaiting to fill the space with wonder." Reflecting on his journey in the footsteps of Henry and Sarah reminded

him of Sam's challenge about wasting time on the dead and gone; but he knew it was much

more than that. And thinking of Sam reminded Bran that he would be meeting up with Orion at 4pm to set up on the stage and run through a few songs, smoothing out some edges. Sam would say, *"why smooth 'em out, the audience won't know, and anyway, I like the sharp edges, more real, more risqué and more fun."* Bran felt like that as well but Oli was a bit of a perfectionist and nobody wanted to argue with Oliver. Georgia would change things every time, saying, *"right, that's how I'm doing it on the night."* All her versions sounded great; a different twist, a new colour, another facet, brought out at every turn. Orion did not perform concerts often enough for them to become either easy or taken for granted. For Bran, each one was a hill to climb, but he liked the view from the top, and he liked the ovation, which usually came. But part of him felt a fake, a fraud, using Dylan's lyrics to convey his feelings, or Dylan's metaphors to untangle his twisted thoughts. But he reassured himself that it was all very genuine, and a kind of positive transference; that's what Chloe had said to him. And surely Dylan knew this when he wrote lyrics like *"someone had to reach for the rising star, I guess it was up to me."* Thinking that Dylan was speaking to him always helped Bran overcome these thoughts of being phoney. He liked to imagine that Dylan would feel affection for those who travelled alongside him. And Bran had travelled with Bob Dylan since his age of enlightenment, since he passed through "the smoke rings" of his mind. Did Henry have an equivalent source of inspiration, Bran wondered as he was on his Saturday morning cycle ride. Sounds like Grampa John may have opened his eyes to a thing or two; *"Grampa John, Anna Fernhill, Wendy Arton, ah"*; he'd forgotten that he'd received a message from the ancestry research company. Bran turned his bike around and raced home.

"Well, well so she was real." Bran opened the attached file showing a family tree stretching back to the early 19th century. The Artons of Bath had five children, Wendy Erica is number four, born in February 1843. "That's right, that's the date in the letter, didn't know about the Erica part though and no mention of adoption." Bran was not surprised and he didn't expect to be. She had married William Parnell in 1872; they'd also had five children. "Ok this is where it gets complicated with branches growing off in all directions." The side note said that Erica Parnell was an active member of the Society for Women's Suffrage. "Good for her, must have been tough though, social forces against her, but what happened to Wendy I wonder; where now, which direction? They had a daughter Olivia, born 1880, let's head up that branch. Olivia married John Watchtower in 1906. "Now, that's a great name., and what a coincidence, same name as Mary's mother's." They had lots of children, Julia was born in 1919; an ocean child with seashell eyes, I imagine." Sometimes, Bran's

356

thoughts wandered off at the slightest cue. But then he paused, staring at the screen. "That can't be," he whispered, "surely, it can't be?" Julia Watchtower married Ralph Norris in 1946. Their daughter, Mary Anne Norris, was born in 1951. Bran read it again, and again, and again, shaking his head but smiling with wonder. Mining for gold and finding a diamond. "Mary, my Mary. Married Bran Raymond Sage in 1975, and here we are. I have to phone her."

Bran could hear the ring tone ending and Mary's voicemail begin; "*I'm not available to take your call right now, please leave your message and I'll get back as soon as I can.*" "Mary its Bran, about 10am Saturday and I've just realised you'll be fast asleep, sorry my love; can you give me a call later please, but I'll be wrapped up in the Orion concert from four-ish. Hope all is well over there, bye for now." Bran thought it might have been better to wait until after the concert so he could focus on how he was going to break the news to Mary. Go back far enough and we are all related to the common ancestor of course, but to discover that they had the same great, great grandfather, and the whole Wendy Arton story, was quite amazing. And for all of this to come to light from a dream was hardly believable. Bran recalled that Mary knew that her great-grandmother had been involved with the Suffragettes. "*Wait a minute,*" thought Bran, "*you just said it, this all came to light from a dream; this doesn't say anything about Wendy Erica Arton being James's and Anna's daughter. That could be a figment of my imagination.*" He realised that he needed to be careful what he said to Mary. He hadn't shared anything about the dreams he'd been having over the last month. "*Slow down Bran boy, hold on tight, anchor yourself to the facts and let the other stuff orbit around, but don't go believing it. Best not to worry Mary with this, wait till she gets home in the summer. I'm so glad she didn't answer the phone; she'd have thought I'm going nuts; which maybe I am.*"

The doorbell rang. Georgia jumped inside as Bran opened the door, waving a book in her hand and giving him a big kiss. She was pure drama and Bran loved her for it.

"Hi Bran, can't wait till tonight but my nerves are starting to flutter, how about yours?" How good it was to see Georgia, pulling him out of his mixed-up confusion. "I thought you might like to look at this book; I mentioned it last Friday, remember Corvus Corax?" Georgia lifted the book up for Bran to see the cover.

"*Mind of the Raven*, by Bernd Heinrich; yes, I remember you mentioned it Georgia, can I offer you a coffee?"

"Got any herbal tea, anything will do, but no coffee thanks. I didn't want to leave you frightened by all that mystical stuff I put on you about ravens. This guy is a scientist so should appeal to you; you prefer facts to myths, right?"

"Well, most of the time I do, but I like the myths as well, provided I can keep them out there, beyond the horizon, the frontier of what I know; beyond harm's way, separated from the facts if you like. It's when they merge together, and I can't tell them apart, I start to get confused. It is good to see you Georgia, I've got dandelion or honey and ginger?"

"Dandelion please, so do they merge for you Bran, and what do you mean by that anyway, sounds a little scary?"

"Does it really? I'm not scared by it Georgia, I guess I'm saying that I don't always know which side of the frontier I'm on. It happens in my profession. I think I understand some aspect of flight behaviour and then up pops something new from a flight test that challenges my thinking. Suddenly, I'm beyond the frontier and I need to, kind of, re-calibrate my understanding, my baseline, build again from what I know for sure."

"That makes good sense Bran. For me that's how I learn, having my mind open when new experiences come along. But we were talking about myths and truths weren't we. There are lots of myths about ravens but I don't think this author is caught up with those. He portrays ravens as problem solvers, drawing on experience and memory to anticipate what might happen; all in all, quite clever birds. It's my sister's book but she's happy if you want to borrow it."

"Thanks Georgia, yes I would. It might help me make sense of why they appear in my dreams. I was thinking that Dylan's lyrics can take me over the frontier as well, where things don't look familiar. But like you, I know that's where I can learn. That *long-distance train rolling through the rain,* that I'll sing about tonight, those tears falling on the letter he's writing. I feel it, you know, right here." Bran holds his hand to his heart. "Sometimes I'm on that train, on that long journey through life, and my tears are flowing as melancholy grips me; why I don't know, but I do miss Mary. I'm stuck in this ancestry research, getting caught up trying to make sense of who my great grandparents were. But I'm bringing it to a close, any day now." Bran wanted to say more but Georgia interrupted him.

"Bran, where did those ravens come from? They look, well, big and very serious. You really do have a thing about ravens don't you."

"Ah those, I brought them back from Somerset. Apparently, they are very old, flew around the area where my great grandparents lived before they moved to the Valleys." Bran held back from mentioning their names and Georgia didn't seem to notice them.

"I get it, the ravens are connecting you with your ancestors. Maybe those eyes actually saw your great-gramps and great-grannie, maybe even felt sad after they left. Blimey Bran, you've got me making up the story." They both laughed at the idea. "So, is that what you are doing, anthropomorphising them? You wouldn't be the first you know. Remember Aesop with the fox and the raven, and the morals? Don't trust flattery, watch out for the deceiver and don't let your ego get the better of you; but you wouldn't do that would you Bran?"

"Well, I try not to Georgia, but I'm not going to deny that my ego plays a big role, just needs controlling. And, I am on my guard against deceivers. I think I have a built-in deceiver-detector, comes from my holding dear the ethical principles of my profession. Oh, that sounds very serious Georgia, and it is."

"That's alright Bran, it's one of the things I like about you, and your harp playing of course; still good for joining me on *Big Girl Now*?"

"Yes definitely, I've been practising it. Your idea of harmony between harp and fiddle is very creative Georgia, can we try it out again this afternoon?

"Yes, we must, but now I'm on my way. Enjoy the book and let me know what you learn from it, ok?"

"I will, thanks Georgia, see you later."

After Georgia left, Bran sat down gazing at the two ravens, holding Heinrich's book in his hands, thinking aloud. "They draw on their experiences and memories; memories, that's it. We all do it. It's what make consciousness, the ability to draw on our memories. I draw on my knowledge from my training and experience to do my job, to solve problems; residing in my brain, my body, as memories. Pilots fly aeroplanes relying on memory, including muscle memory for moving the controls in response to the motion of the plane. They need to see the impending dangers soon enough, and react quickly enough, in the right way, to avoid a crash. My guitar playing draws on my memories; I know the chord sequence, the process; I know where my fingers go, but I don't need to think it through every time, it's all from memory. What changes is how my emotions shape the way I play and sing. But even then, I'm drawing on my emotional memory. And they don't go away; the process memories, the muscle memories, the emotional memories are all there, ready for action, some deeper down than others. Yes, that's it. Whatever memories I have from way back, when my parents and grandparents talked about Henry and Sarah, they are still there, even though I may not be able to remember them; isn't that a contradiction? No, some are so deep they need to be carefully mined for, like some of the rich coal seams that Henry would have found underground in Camerton and EbbwVale. And the analogy doesn't end there. Some seams would be fiery, unleashing the firedamp as the miners hewed with their pics; a slight spark causing ignition and devastation, more lives lost, taking their unique and precious memories with them. So too, some memories are trapped within a fiery trauma, could blow you to bits if recalled. What was it that Chloe had said to him?" *Who knows what you heard as a child Bran. As a two or three-year-old, you probably listened to your grandparents talking to your parents and other family members, and things stay in the memory, even though you can't remember them. If you had any traumatic experiences around this time, then there might be a lid shut tight on all this stuff.* "The lid shut tight; shut tight on what?" This was getting rather too introverted for Bran's liking and he felt he'd gone far enough for one day. "But I'm so glad Georgia came along, its helping me move on."

Bran phoned Mary again before he entered the concert hall; still no answer. "Probably out jogging in Wildcat Canyon, but why didn't she call me back earlier? I hope she's ok." Sam arrived just behind Bran.

"Into the breach Bran, seems like Jacob's brother Luke has new sound kit in the hall and has designed a new set-up system."

"Hi Sam, good to see you; new system eh, will it make us sound better do you think?" As they entered the hall, they could see the other members of Orion were gathered around and Luke was explaining about his new sound system. Bran and Sam were greeted by a cheer from the other stars and then followed the ceremonial hugging, the first step in the bonding which would need to be strong to fully work its magic. Luke was eager to continue with his instructions.

"Ok, I'll begin again. This is important guys, my

reputation as a sound engineer depends on Orion performing well; they'll blame me if it sounds bad." Sam wasn't going to let him get away with that.

"Do you have a reputation then Luke, I thought you were a teacher?"

"I am a teacher but have other ambitions, and my reputation starts here so be patient with me. Anyway, please listen to my plan and you'll see it could make us all great." Fortunately, the band could see he was half joking, but only half; here was a man building his ego, but they would listen to his plan. Georgia wanted to set a condition.

"If it doesn't constrain our creativity Luke, we're with you. But performance is where we need max flex, get it?"

"Yeh, yeh, I'm with you. See look, this is the template." Luke held out a sheet which he had removed from the sound desk. "It overlays the channels on my mixing desk, like this. Twenty-four altogether, each of you having four, two for your mic, on the left, and two for your instrument, on the right. Each has a volume and a tone; just showing the volume here. I have made one of these for each of your songs; blame Oli if I've got this wrong. This one is for Bran's *Journey Through Dark Heat*, written on the top see; final song, so, second set, song twelve, just an example. There are a lot of you on this one, plain to see, and the height of the bars on the sheet tells me how much volume and tone texture to add with the slides. Got it?"

2/12 Journey Through Dark Heat (where are you tonight)											
Chloe keys		Bran acoustic guitar		Georgia violin		Sam bass		Jacob percussion		Oliver electric guitar	
Mic	Inst.	Mic	Inst.	Mic	Inst.	Mic	Inst.	Mic	Inst.	Mic	Inst.

Luke was, indeed, a teacher, sharing his knowledge and looking around for affirmation, confirmation that his students were impressed.

"So how do you know how high the bars need to be Luke, you haven't heard us?"

"That's where you're wrong Sammy boy, I've listened to Jacob's recording from last week. That was mostly acoustic of course but I think it's a good start; I'd like you to do the first few bars of each song and I can refine the bar heights. You'll need to stand in the same place for the whole concert of course, use the same mics and instrument leads, ok?" Sam had another question.

"I see some bars get darker as they go up, what does that mean?"

"Well spotted Sam, this is where I can be creative as well." Luke pointed at the chart. "These are Chloe's and Georgia's voices between verses, and this is Oli's solo in the break. Or, it tells me to increase Chloe's piano during her solo in *Sweetheart Like You*. I've thought it all through you know."

It took over an hour for Orion to set-up 'Luke-style'. They all agreed that the process discipline was likely to make for a smoother performance; less worrying about whether they were all 'coming through' ok. What was 'coming through' of course, was down to them. Luke was pleased with himself.

"There, that didn't hurt, did it Georgia love?"

"Not yet Luke love, but sometimes pain takes time to work its way through." Georgia was smiling, half joking, but only half. After they had finished the set-up and final polishing, Orion retired to the 'green room' where they could rest in peace for 30 minutes before the audience started to arrive. This was an important time of meditation so no more chatting, and especially no more practising; what will be will be. Bran had been impressed by Luke's methodological approach; building a process memory to guide him through the concert, leaving enough for him as the sound engineer to be creative. Human beings were good at building up and using their process memory; no other species came close. In the concert, Bran would be relying on his muscle memory and emotional memory; a huge reservoir and so important to draw on the right stuff, from the right place. He was also struck by Luke saying, *"Bran's Journey Through Dark Heat."* Dark heat, like underground in a coal mine, like his journey tracing Henry's and Sarah's footsteps. But let that go now; let the dust kicked up by the footsteps settle, time for music.

Orion were behind the curtain, like their stars behind clouds, as Toni welcomed the audience to the Centre and talked about Médecins Sans Frontières, the charity that the Orion *Love Sick* concert was supporting. A speaker from MSF would give a talk in the break, referring to material from James Orbinski's Nobel Peace Prize acceptance speech the previous December on humanitarian law and values. Bran wondered whether Orion's first set could in any way prepare the audience for this; there would be stark contrast. Maybe they should have chosen a theme featuring Dylan's protest songs; too late now. In any case, surely if humans could only get the love thing right, there would be no more crimes against humanity. Very wishful thinking Bran, don't you know that getting the love thing right, even if you are lucky enough to find it, might be the hardest thing humans try to do.

But, back to Toni's introduction; he liked to raise the curtain on the performance and he was good at building up a sense of drama; our very own house-band, the shining stars of Orion showing us what it's like to be *Love-Sick*. The lights beamed onto the stage as the curtain was lifted and Orion began performing their first number, *Has Anybody Seen My Love*, Chloe-style. Bran harmonised during the refrain and this was real for him; had anybody seen my Mary, he almost sang those words, but surely was thinking them. As the song ended, some lights were rotated so that the band could begin to see the audience giving their appreciation; loud clapping, whistles, hoots and cheers from the locals. Bran could see a table full of staff from FS2, waving at him. He wasn't expecting them; he was the other Bran tonight, but he nodded his head in respectful acknowledgement. Then, on another table, he saw Suisan Morgan and was that Sandra Peel sitting next to her? Yes, it was, wonder what she'll think of Orion.

A moment in space and time, an event like none other, lasting an instant and forever, and Bran's senses captured in time because they were made of dreams and he remembered what her lips felt like, as soon as the coloured lights surrounded her, lifted her up as she smiled at him and blew her kiss his way. The smile he knew so well, but was he dreaming? He stood up and shouted out loud – "Mary!" Bran was about to undo his guitar strap and run across to her, but Mary was gesturing to him to stay there; we'll meet when you've done. Chloe was also waving to Mary and deliberately took a little time introducing the members of Orion to the audience, letting Bran settle before she started her next song, *I Want You*. Bran harmonised during the chorus and smiled at Mary, wanting her so bad. As if the set sequence was made for the moment, Bran was next on with *Something There is About You*. All those years before, when they'd first met, Mary had struck a match in Bran and the fire was still burning. The words rang even truer now, and perhaps something had crossed over from the last century. Bran harmonised during the chorus with more intensity and passion than ever before. How deeply the lyrics touched him and awakened his soul, but while Dylan might not be able to put his finger on why, Bran

Sage was very clear; Mary had filled the missing piece in his character.

At the break, Bran rushed through the audience and held Mary in his arms. She felt just like he remembered, all the curves, soft and firm spots and indentations.

"Hope you don't mind the surprise Bran. Forgive me, I thought you'd probably need to keep your mind on the concert, are you ok?" Bran was unusually lost for words but she could see from his face that all was indeed ok. Bran waved to his work colleagues as he went back to the green room.

The second set was launched with Jacob singing the title song, *Love Sick*, Dylan's painful song from the *Time Out of Mind* album, still fresh with the Dylanites. Did she destroy him with the smile in his dream? Dreams could be very powerful, Bran knew that and, once more, Dylan was there with him. The final song in the set was Bran's *Journey Through Dark Heat*. In *Street Legal*, Dylan had thrown a window open wide, reminded us that Eden was burning. One could search forever within the lyrics for meanings that made some kind of sense for you. This was Bran's strongest song, and the passion turned up full like the slides on Luke's control desk. He'd arrived at the new day, and he had survived the journey through his ancestry; but without Mary, it just didn't seem right, but there she was, with him, tonight. Georgia and Chloe boosted the drama joining in with rich, sexy voices, at the end of the lines. Jacob played the congas like his life depended on it, creating a beat that seemed to fill the hall with anticipation, duelling with Sam on bass between the lines. Oliver's lead guitar solos punctured the air in the hall. Chloe turned her keys to emulate a saxophone and caressed the punctured space, denying Oli domination in the dark heat. The sounds of the tubs being pushed along the underground rails by young boys, the guss and crook biting into their skin; the echoes of the hammerings and clashes from the hewers at the face; men cursing and crying out in pain and joy. The silent memories of colliers working deep underground were indeed like thunder.

For an encore, Orion sang *Girl from the North Country*, a cappella, with three-part harmony. Each of the band had their own girl or boy in their minds as they sang. The Orion star pattern was projected onto the ceiling above their heads, the star names alongside a picture of the band member who played that part. In the real world, these stars were hundreds of light years apart. For example, the light from Chloe (Meissa) would take more than 100 years to reach Sam (Rigel) and then another 700 hundred years, or thereabouts, to reach the real Chloe and Sam here on Earth. Maybe they had the same great, great etc., from when those photons were launched from Rigel? Bran stopped his brain there, let someone else go down that long and lonesome road if they dare. Anyway, his mind had turned to an old poem he'd scribbled down many years ago when he and his brother were in a band together. He smiled as he recalled the words.

Long before the curtain came down they should have left the stage

If it wasn't for the sweet taste of fame they'd have gone back into their cage

But all in all, 'twas best that they left, for who knows how they'd have coped

With the struggle and fuddle, the all-consuming muddle in the dark bright world of the doped

Indeed, who knows how they would have coped, but musical fame was not to be for the young Sages, even though they were good, at times very good. Back in the Hall, the audience were very appreciative and the talk by Margaret from MSF had stirred their consciences, and their generosity; she took home more than £1500 for the charity. And, apart from the fun, the adulation and the opportunity to dig deep into their emotional memories, that's why Orion did what they did. Bran and Mary agreed to meet Suisan and Sandra for lunch the next day, and then went with the band to the pub, but they wanted to be alone with each other, so excused themselves early and headed home. Orion would meet the following Friday for the usual review of the concert and to pick up recordings from Luke. Their lives would continue to unfold in numerous ways, but there we say farewell to this band of fellow, starry-eyed, travellers, until the next time.

Bran and Mary arrived home late but they had a lot of catching up to do and, to begin with, all Bran wanted to do was to look at Mary, gaze into her eyes, let his emotional memories come back, hold her body and kiss her lips, take her clothes off and then? Well, that's none of your beeswax and, anyway, extraordinarily private and likely to lead to national arousal and devastating envy; and, also, quite unlike what you might be used to in run-of-the-mill love stories and sexual encounters.

After making love, Mary and Bran were hungry and sat on their terrace with a light supper and bottle of Saint-Aubin. And there was the Plough in the northern sky, the light from hundreds of years ago twinkling at them, and pointing to Polaris. They were catching up with each other's news; how Mary's report on Climate Change was coming along. She

369

would present results at the COP 6 in November. Hearing Mary describe her work reminded Bran of just how transfixed he could be by her. She had given a written statement to the police about the letter she had received from the late Dr Francis Clerk, and sent a copy of Clerk's presentation to the research council, with her comments on its veracity.

"He was onto something important Bran and they'll need to locate this Dr Oats to find out why he was blocking it." Mary would have to fly back to San Francisco on Monday to finish off her paper to meet the submission deadline and complete her sabbatical project, so they only had a few hours of precious time, and she wanted to hear about Bran's ancestry research. She knew he had been digging deep and she had stood looking at Sarah's paintings for some time.

"These are amazing Bran, so much going on in them, your Sarah really did have an eye for detail. See the sun bursting off the winding wheel and, here, she's caught the spread of the raven's wing tips; helps to reduce the drag someone once told me."

"That would have been me, love. Are you sure you're up for this Mary, it's after 1am?"

"But only 5pm in San Francisco and I'm still on Pacific time. Yes Bran, I'm ready when you are Senor." And that brought a smile from Bran.

"Thanks Mary, I'll start with the dreams. They started about a month ago but I haven't been keeping you up to date with them, didn't want to worry you, and have you thinking I was going nuts. I've kept a record in this little notebook; I call it my dream book. First one was on 17th May, the day I went down to John's funeral. At the time, I didn't pay much attention; the woman was talking but I couldn't hear the words. Then after I arrived home, after visiting the mining museum,

370

she appeared again on a canal path with a man. Mary, she was staring at me and I couldn't move until the raven flew by and gave a loud kronk, which woke me up. It was the same old canal path in Camerton that I had walked along Mary, but the canal had long gone when I visited."

"Are you sure she was the same woman Bran, and who do you think the man was, what did they look like?"

"Well, I've seen them both a few times now. He's Henry, and tall, well built, distinct facial features, wavy hair, a bit like Burt Lancaster. She is, or rather was, good looking, kind of handsome with auburn hair; her eyes seem to be asking questions. Then, the next day, we're on Saturday now, three weeks ago, there were three of them, a younger man with Henry and Sarah. I think she was painting the picture with the coal mine. At first I thought she was waving a wand but Chloe suggested that she might have been painting." As soon as he'd said this he realised that he hadn't told Mary that he'd shared his dreaming with Chloe, and felt embarrassed. "I'm sorry Mary, I should have said, I asked Chloe if she could help me make sense of the dreams." Mary was too strong to be upset by this; or if she was, she didn't show it.

"That's fine Bran, was Chloe helpful?"

"Yes, she was, very helpful. She talked about unresolved stuff in the unconscious bubbling up; and then how all the actors, everything that featured in a dream, can be interpreted as aspects of one's own character. The very aspects that one needs to get stuck into, to work on the unresolved stuff. I've given these things a lot of thought Mary. I can't put equations to them, so don't have any predictions, and I'm not kidding myself that I understand any underlying science, but looking at them this way, things do begin to make a kind of sense."

"Do you know what the unresolved things are Bran? Is

this to do with your father? You've mentioned that he would always be telling you to do better."

"Yes, I think it may be Mary, but that's as far as I've got; thinking it may be my response to being told I wasn't good enough. In the dream, I heard the men talking about a working group for safety. I've written here that I asked them why they were talking about safety, but the two men paid no attention. But she smiled at me Mary. So, I think to myself that my great-grandmother approved of my commitment to aviation safety. My inner self is using my dreams to pat me on the back, tell me I'm good enough. See how badly I'm missing you Mary?" They could chuckle at Bran's interpretations, but Mary was listening carefully, becoming more and more intrigued, and not a little concerned, by Bran's story. What would she think of his next dream I wonder?

"Then, on Tuesday, I dreamt that I was with Henry and Sarah making love in a field and the raven kronked again. See how badly I'm missing you Mary? I thought it was you to begin with but then I could see it wasn't. When I woke, I felt embarrassed, and shamed that I had betrayed you Mary."

"Really Bran, did you enjoy it?" Mary reached out and held Bran's hand.

"Well, in my dream, yes, I think I did, but not after I woke, left me rather unsettled that day."

"Did you have any more dreams like that Bran?"

"No, thank goodness, that was the only one but there are four more, shall I continue?" Mary nodded and settled back in her chair.

"This next one is important because it relates to something that really did happen, 128 years ago. She was running towards a mine, very upset, crying, and then he appeared,

Henry appeared, carrying the younger man in his arms. Sarah said *thank God* and I asked her if I could help and she looked at me and said *you have helped me.* Jenny from the mining museum sent me a newspaper cutting about a mining accident at the Camerton New Pit. One of the injured was Henry's younger brother Ritchie Sage. Chloe suggested that I might have heard my father and grandad talking about this when I was very young; and yes, when I thought about, it I faintly recall grampa talking about his uncle Ritchie. If I had experienced a trauma around that time, the lid might be shut tight on the memories, until the unconscious prizes it open."

"When it thinks you are ready to handle it, or need to deal with it."

"That's it Mary, but I'm not sure the unconscious can think. Chloe talked about the integrated mind-body and I did get that. So many of the latest flight automation systems need careful integration with the physical aircraft or things can go terribly wrong. The plane gets into some unique condition that the designers haven't thought about, the automation behaves in an unintended way, the pilot gets confused and can exacerbate things by taking some learned action based on memory; but it turns out to be the wrong reaction, the memory was unreliable. What good training does for pilots is help them to problem solve, rather than rely on outdated memory. Does that make sense?"

"Just about, but don't change the subject. She said that you had helped her, how?"

"I don't know Mary, but Chloe suggested that Sarah could be my anima being released, and she was thanking me for releasing it. A bit of a long shot but plausible."

"Do you think it's time your anima was released Bran? Perhaps your unconscious is warning you that too much science and technology can harden a man's heart; that you should do something about it before it's too late."

"Gasp, not another mid-life crisis." And they could chuckle again. "The next dream was short; I think Sarah was painting the stars in Ursa Major, creating the image of a young man hauling a tub, the bowl of the Plough." Mary walked over to look at the painting of the miner forged into Orion.

"So, it wasn't this picture Bran. Of course, Orion is not visible in the night sky in June. Sarah must have painted this picture in the winter months. There's no date on it so might have been after they moved to Ebbw Vale. I wonder what happened to the painting in your dream."

"I don't know Mary; there is so much I don't know, but maybe it just doesn't exist? The next one is probably the most important, and just eight days ago. They were sitting on the platform at a train station and Henry was reading a letter to Sarah. The letter was to Henry, from *Anna Fernhill*, the woman who owned the Camerton manor and the coal mines in that area. She told him that she'd had an affair with his father James, my great great-grandad, before James was married, and she'd had their child. But she had been sent away so James never knew about it. I wrote this all down Mary, let me look; her name was Wendy Arton, born in February 1843 and adopted by the Arton's of Bath."

"How strange. I wonder if that actually happened Bran, or is it another bubbling up from your unconscious? But how would you interpret it?"

"I got the ancestry research company to find out all they could Mary; this is the tree they sent me." Bran handed Mary the sheet of paper. Mary studied it carefully and her expression changed to one of perplexion as she reached the conclusion.

374

"This says that Wendy Erica Arton was my great-grandmother, but it doesn't say anything about her being adopted by the Arton's, just that they were her parents. Could your dream be trying to connect you with me Bran? Reminds me of the Roy Orbison song, *In Dreams*; could be my favourite song of all time. And that would link with you missing me Bran; glad to hear that by the way. I think I told you that my great-grandma was a suffragette, although I never knew her as Wendy, only Erica Parnell. I've often thought that I'd like to find out more about her; it could make a good story."

"You should Mary, but I warn you that fact and fiction start to merge together when you try to piece things together, at least that's what I'm finding."

"Yes, I can see that Bran; what's next."

"Two to go. Last Tuesday I woke up with a dream about their wedding in the Old Blaina Baptist Chapel going around in my head. They were walking out of the door with a group of people and she looked up at me. She always seems to look up to see me Mary, and then the raven kronked and I woke. I know it was the chapel because I have a copy of their marriage certificate and I'd been in touch with the guy who is renovating the place."

"Maybe she looks up to you Bran, or maybe you would like her to look up to you."

"That's plausible Mary, connects with my seeming to need more than my fair share of praise."

"Ravens seem to play a role in all this and you've brought these back, Henry and Sarah. And, she's looking up at him. What do you think this means?"

"I've talked to Georgia about ravens and she loaned me a book her sister had, about the mind of the raven, written by a zoologist; some good scientific discussion in the book. Seems like they are very intelligent birds. But I don't understand what they mean in my story, except that they do show up in most of the dreams, usually at the end, waking me up. Although not in the last one. This was last Thursday and Henry was giving a talk on safety in coal mining. I knew from my father that he was a mines inspector and, in this dream, he was really spelling out the importance of safety initiatives. This all rang true for me, chiming with the work that John Morgan and I had been doing on the underlying aeronautical science that underpins accident analysis."

"That makes sense Bran; so, with a good imagination, all your dreams are explicable in terms of the bubbling unconscious and possibly traumas from when you were very young, your father getting angry with you, telling you that you weren't good enough. And you do have a very good imagination, I know that. Have you completed your ancestry research Bran? Are you done with this investigation?" Mary put her arm around Bran and kissed him.

"Yeh, I think I am. One of the things I did last week was visit my mother and her cousin Alice, one of Sarah's and Henry's many grandchildren. I think I said that's where I got the paintings of the raven and the miner in Orion. My mother and I had a really good talk by the way, and I am intending to stay in closer touch with her. I've neglected her Mary. But Alice told me that Sarah didn't believe that their first son, Brân, was killed in the war. She said that Henry had gone over to Ireland to meet the family of a nurse who had been killed at the same time as Brân. Well, that's what the war report stated; both missing presumed dead. Apparently, Henry died soon after he returned and Alice never found out what her grandfather had discovered and Sarah wouldn't talk about it. That's another avenue of exploration I suppose, but definitely for another day, or another year."

Both Bran and Mary were exhausted by their dialogue but Bran felt relieved to have been able to share it all with his closest friend, his soul-mate, his wife. He felt that the lurking demons had been, like the kronking ravens, freed from his inner self; or at least exposed for what they were, and he could begin to connect with them without fear of failure. They both thought they would sleep well that night, or rather morning; it was 3am before they went to bed and they were hoping to have a long Sunday lie-in. But, that wasn't to be.

"What is it Bran? Bran, wake up my love, it's just a dream." Mary took Bran's hand that seemed to be grasping at the air and he was shaking his head back and fore. She put her other hand to his cheek, stroking his hair and trying to gently bring him back to reality. "Come on Bran, it's alright, you are here in bed with me; I'm with you my love." Bran woke with a start.

"It's time to go." Then he looked at Mary and his expression changed from one of deep anxiety to relief. "Oh Mary, I'm so glad you are with me. I was with her. It felt like I was her."

"Who Bran, is this Sarah again? Come on, I'll make some coffee and you write it down in your dream book while you remember it. Are you ok with that Bran?"

"Yes, that's a good idea Mary; this wasn't like my usual dreams, something happened, I'll write it down and, yes please, coffee would be good." Mary brought the coffee into the study and found Bran sitting at the table still writing. But he stopped as she put the coffee pot on the table and looked

377

up. "I was writing a letter. No, I mean she was writing a letter. She was holding the picture tightly in her arms, and she was crying Mary. And I felt this powerful urge to go to sleep, go to sleep in my dream, but no ordinary sleep. I wanted to resist and I started struggling to wake up, grasping at the arms of the chair to push myself up but I couldn't get a grip. Then I felt your hand on my cheek and heard your voice. You brought me back Mary."

"Good job I am here Bran, is this how it is every time you wake up from a dream?"

"No, this was the first time it was a struggle. I was scared Mary, felt I was trapped in the dream; trapped as Sarah. I think she was dying Mary. Part of my unconscious was dying; what does that mean? But she didn't die until 1946; why has the story jumped more than 70 years?"

"What story Bran? You said that as if your dreams are episodes in a story. And to dream of dying might be your unconscious letting go of something. You said she was holding a picture; could you see it?"

"It does feel like a story, or at least a jigsaw and I am searching for the pieces. I can't see the painting, but wait, another part of the dream is coming back. The letter she was writing, she put it behind the picture, why would she do that?"

"For someone to find Bran, try to remember what the picture was." Bran held his head in his hands. He had felt all kinds of emotions springing from these dreams over the previous month, but never the distress that he was feeling now. He wondered if Mary being with him somehow allowed his inner self more freedom, more courage even; courage to be vulnerable.

"It's the raven Mary, that painting of the raven, I know it. Ravens have journeyed with me through these dreams and somehow, I know." Bran paused and looked at Henry and Sarah, Henry imperious at the top of the branch and Sarah looking serene and confident. She once flew with style and grace, and it was as if she knew she'd had a good life and would survive for as long as someone cared for her. Bran got up from his chair and reached up for the painting hanging on the wall. The backing board was held firm with tabs and Bran removed these one at a time.

"How would you know about this Bran, and If you didn't know until your dream, what does this mean? Are you sure your aunt Alice didn't mention this?"

"Well, I'm sure she didn't mention it when I met her last week, but who knows what's lost in my memory, right?" Bran lifted the backing board and the attached mount card, revealing the glass and back of the picture beneath. That was all there was, apart from the sweet aroma of age gone by. Just then, the mount card fell away from the backing board to reveal an envelope. He reached down and carefully, very carefully, picked up the envelope. He looked at Mary who was staring back at him, shaking her head with incredulity.

"You must open it Bran, read what she says." Bran opened the envelope and lifted out two sheets of paper, with neat handwriting.

"It starts '*Dear Brân*', so it's a letter to her first son, who was killed in the war. I can't make out the date. There are smudges here, there and everywhere."

"I think those are from Sarah's tears, and read the first couple of lines Bran; she isn't writing to her son, she's writing to you. Can you read it out loud?"

Dear Brân

I am so glad you have found this letter and I hope it will comfort you and not disturb you too much, although I realise that it might. I met your mother-to-be, Aoife, last week and I liked her very much. I'm sad that I won't have time to get to know her, but there we are. Now, I have just asked my granddaughter Alice to request of Aoife and Alwyn to name their first child after my first son, Brân. I am hoping that this will draw you to finding out about him and how he carried the torch from his father. I will explain more later in this letter.

I have so many good memories from my life and I have learned to hold these dear, to protect them, because the darkness is always close by. My first darkness was the absence of love from my mother. I can only think that she did not experience real love, and so didn't know how to give it. My second darkness was the loss of two of my sons in the war and that almost broke my spirit. But when I lost Henry, I broke down because we were one. He was half of me and I was half of him. I hope you never experience losing half of yourself Brân. But if you love, truly love, that is the risk you take, and the consequence is inevitable when the moment comes. But your life will be richer from giving and receiving love; I now believe that's all we really need to make us whole.

But to the good memories. I remember the early summer flowers along the Camerton canal path, walking along with my Henry; the aromas are still fresh in my memory. Before we were married, we would talk about our plans for a life together. We were so excited about it and some wonderful things happened on those walks. Your great grandad was a good man of purpose Brân, full of ideas about how things could be better. It was exciting talking to him and others found this too; looked to him for leadership. Henry would think things through and, when he decided, that was it. It was as if he knew where the truth was, and then he knew when he'd found it. He was also a loving man, and I had heaps of love to give, so we were incredibly lucky.

My memory of our elopement to Ebbw Vale (yes Brân, we did elope) brings back the excitement I felt that whole day and the days leading up to it. When we set up our new home and we knew that Brân was coming, we would walk on the hills and Henry would say that he could see forever, that if he looked carefully he could see the Somerset hills, which sometimes made us sad. But I knew that we could not have both the old and the new and I drew on some of Henry's purposefulness to build a big nest for a big family. And as you probably know, we did have a big family!

My energy is almost gone dear and I need to ask something of you. When our first son was born, we knew he was special. Brân took after his father in many ways, and this worked because Henry would always give him the approval he sought. So, Brân picked up Henry's values, his code of safety, his instinct to face problems, not let them pass by unsolved. Brân turned this to caring for the injured and he became a medical officer for the mines in the Ebbw Vale district. When the first world war broke out, he volunteered to join the Welsh regiment as a medic. Most of his brothers worked underground as hewers, so they escaped the call, but Brân's young brother William could not endure the mines. He cried the first time he went underground and couldn't work because he was so distressed. He worked on the surface so got the call and Brân made sure he was with him at the front. William was killed when his trench was shelled, on the same night that the hospital tent that Brân worked in was blown apart. Where Brân was strong and purposeful like his father, William was delicate and confused by life, and he should never have been sent to fight. I'm sure that Brân tried to look after him but he couldn't be at his side every moment. They found William's body in pieces, blown apart. The people in the hospital were burned beyond recognition and Brân was declared missing, presumed dead. War is unforgiving and indiscriminate but behind all this are people making decisions and giving instructions. I've come to think these people are the men who have not known love.

I do not believe that Brân was killed that night. After the war, we found out from one of his friends that he was having an affair with a nurse in the regiment, who was also missing presumed dead. Her name was Caragh Lynch, from a place called Fermoy in Ireland. After we found this out, Henry visited the family. Something happened to him there that he would not tell me about. I think that was the only time he held a secret from me and I worried that shame might have held him back. But, I never found out because he became ill and died a few days later of pleurisy. The doctor told me that his ribs were broken and this had damaged his pleura. I have only ever told your aunt Alice about this Brân and asked her to keep the secret. Something happened to my Henry in Ireland. He said that the Lynch's were still grieving from the loss of their

382

daughter and didn't know anything about Brân. But I think he did find something and he would have told me if he had recovered.

You must know some of our story from what George and Alwyn have told you, but you won't know this part. If you ever journey down this path of discovery, find the truth and make it part of our history.

So that is my request of you dear Brân and I know you will receive it when you are ready. If you have followed the ravens, you will find my letter. Brân means raven in Welsh and old English, but of course you will know that by now.

Protect your memories, dear Brân, they can get lost in the fog as time passes, but one day they will be all you have left.

With all my love, your great-grandma,

Sarah

Bran touched the writing on the paper, touched the dry tears and felt the warmth of Sarah's message deep inside. Mary held his other hand and put her head on his shoulder, that wonderful loving gesture that brought a gust of comfort through his body. So, this was Sarah and he had found her, or rather she had found him. The couple sat quietly together looking at the letter for long enough that thoughts settled and their realities came flowing back.

"Will you try to find out about your namesake Bran, or rather Brân; do as she requests?"

"Maybe, maybe one day I will. But now I feel like I want to get back to being Bran Sage, the aeronautical engineer, draw a line under this episode of my ancestry; pick up the torch, the one passed on by Henry to Brân. Feels even more urgent to me now Sarah."

"Bran, you just called me Sarah."

"Did I, I'm so sorry Mary. I want to continue the journey through our life, with you by my side, sometimes more than half of what I am. I realise we don't know what our journey holds but I do know that we will be able to see by the light of our own wisdom and love." The two lovers sat together quietly reflecting on Bran's words.

They met with Suisan and Sandra for lunch as planned. They talked about the concert. Sandra had lots to say about the music, showing that she had a good memory for details and a good sense of humour as she drew attention to some of Bran's 'deliberate' mistakes. But Bran pointed out that one of the 'mistakes', when he sang "*she's so close behind*", rather than "*she's so far behind*" in the song *Most of the Time*, his Bobness himself had been known to sing it this way in concert and Bran preferred these words, most of the time. So, was it a mistake or not? They briefly discussed the police investigation into Peter's crash and scorned the Oats's of this world; the unlucky fools unable to love. Suisan passed a folder to Bran. It was titled '*Tau Theory of Flight Control; early ideas.*'

"I found it in a draw in his desk, underneath a newspaper, almost like it was hidden. I thought if you could make sense of John's 'early ideas' Bran, you might be able to continue his work."

"Thank you, Suisan, I will try. John had told me he was working on a new theory of control in collaboration with a Professor from Edinburgh. This might be it."

After Bran and Mary had said goodbye to Suisan and Sandra, they walked up one of the local hills so they could look out over the city and beyond to the distant mountains. The view never ceased to inspire them both and they sat quietly taking it in. Soon they would be apart again and focussed on their own worlds but now they shared the same world. In the few hours they had spent together, Bran and Mary had renewed their closeness, rekindled their love and remembered how important their friendship was. Mary had been with Bran for the drama of *Love Sick*, and for the epiphany of Sarah's letter. We don't deserve all we have but it's what we make of it all that counts, surely?

On Monday morning Bran drove Mary to the airport for her flight to the West Coast. They held each other close for long enough and then let each other go.

"I'll be back in July Bran, be ready for me."

Back in the office, the TLeM started with Roger, Colin and Felicity sharing their thoughts on the '*Love Sick*' concert and it felt strange for Bran to be mixing his two worlds together. And yet, as the compliments and the critique flowed, it felt more real to him bringing them together; integrating the left and right sides of his character. His staff were seeing a different side to their boss, his vulnerability expressed through singing Bob Dylan's lyrics.

After the TLeM, Bran looked out the window of his office. It felt good to be back in the saddle again, good to have been with Mary, good to have the Orion concert done and good to bring his ancestry research to a place of relative rest. He felt that he had discovered there was magic involved in all these things, connecting the different strands in his personality that went back through the generations. He imagined himself carrying that torch and it felt good, lighting up the road ahead for him to be creative while drawing on his memories; memories of the process, emotional and muscle varieties.

There was a knock on the door that brought Bran back to the moment, and Jos appeared.

"You have a call from a Mr O'Reilly from Kinsale in Ireland, can you take it?"

"Yes Jos, please put him through." Bran picked up the phone. "Hullo, Bran Sage here."

"Hullo Dr Sage, Dermot O'Reilly, curator of Kinsale Museum here so, we met a few years ago when you visited with your brother. Now, I've some news. I've been informed that your grandfather's letters to your grandmother, from when he was in prison in 1920, are being auctioned in Dublin this coming Friday. I thought you might be interested, so. You did say you were planning to do some ancestry research, did I recall that right?"

Meet the Characters

May | June 2000

Bran Raymond Sage	The modern-day protagonist, an aeronautical engineer
Mary Anne Sage (née Norris)	Bran's wife; an environmental scientist
Dylan Sage Jnr	Bran's and Mary's son
Julia Sage	Bran's and Mary's daughter
Sarah Sage	Bran's sister
Dylan Sage Snr	Bran's brother
Alwyn Sage	Bran's father
Aoife Sage (née Ryan)	Bran's mother
George Sage	Bran's grandfather
Elizabeth Sage (née Rees)	Bran's grandmother
Farnham Sage	George's brother
Florence Sage (née Jones)	Farnham's wife
Alice Sage	Farnham's and Florence's daughter
Brân Sage	Henry's and Sarah's first child: George's uncle
Derek Painter	wartime friend of Brân Sage
Caragh Lynch	nurse and wartime lover of Brân Sage

John Morgan	Bran's professional mentor and friend
Suisan Morgan	John's wife
Kenneth Morgan	John's brother
Peter Peel	pilot of helicopter that crashed
Sandra Peel	Peter's wife and jazz musician
Frank	Sandra's brother
Sophie and Philip Peel	Peter's mother and father
Ron Flintworth	curator at mining museum and Peter Peel's grandfather
Jenny Partridge	curator at mining museum and retired teacher
Tony and Sonia Johnson	owners of the Collier's Rest Inn in Camerton
Ollie Johnson	Tony's and Sonia's son
Jim and Joyce Owen	owners of the Old Blaina Chapel
Vanessa and Robbie	owners of the Camerton Manor
Janet Jones	staff member of the Ebbw Vale Institute

FS2 Office and activities

Joselyn Amble	Bran's secretary
Roger Thomas	technical lead for modelling and simulation
Colin Blunt	technical lead for flight science
Felicity Freeman	technical lead for continuing professional development
Jim Waterhill	specialist in aerodynamics
Ralph Jones	simulation engineer
Rosie Lynch	therapist at the University
Frances Rogers	member of the Royal Aeronautical Society
Geoff Scrag	chief engineer at Holtan Aircraft
Stuart Carter	engineer with Air Accident Investigation Branch
Tobias Hamel	chief designer at Claston Aircraft
Juergen Gmelin	engineer with Claston
Robert	AAIB test pilot
Francis Clerk	environmental scientist at University of Slatchen
Clive Oats	environmental scientist (Clerk's supervisor)

Orion

Sam Hunter (Rigel)	bass
Georgia (Bellatrix)	fiddle
Chloe (Meissa)	keys
Oliver (Mintaka)	guitar
Jacob (Alnitak)	percussion
Bran (Saif)	guitar and harp
Jim	Chloe's husband
Toni Bow	Owner of the Arts Centre and Jacob's father
Luke Bow	Jacob's brother and sound engineer
Dermot O'Reilly	curator at Kinsale Museum

May – June 1872

Camerton

Henry Sage	a coal miner, Bran's great grandfather
Sarah Jane Sage (née Wallace)	Henry's wife, Bran's great grandmother
Maria Sage (née Mears)	Henry's mother
James Sage	Henry's father
George, James, Thomas, Ritchie	Henry's brothers
Elizabeth Wallace (née Mears)	Sarah's mother and Maria's sister
Albert Wallace	Sarah's father
Arthur Wallace	Albert's brother, Sarah's uncle in the Midlands
Brân Sage	Henry's and Sarah's first child
Anna Fernhill	owner of Camerton Manor
Florence and Charles Fernhill	Anna's parents
Grampa John	Anna's grandfather
Mable	maid at Camerton Manor
Wendy Arton	adopted daughter of John and Mary Arton

Archie Flintworth	member of miner's task force and grandfather of Ron Flintworth
John Riddle	friend of Henry's
Arthur Riddle	member of miner's task force and John's brother
Robert Barnes	member of miner's task force
James Hodge	member of miner's task force
William Hodge	member of miner's task force
Farnham Nash	member of miner's task force
Charlie Smith	miner who visits Somerset from the Midlands
Martin Ferris	miner in Somerset
Colin Amble	manager at the Camerton pits
Billie Oats	farm labourer from Somerset
Sgt Pepper	local policeman in Camerton area
John Cooke	miner from Somerset who died in Ebbw Vale
Hamish McCartney	manager at Radstock mines
Rita Jenkins	friend of Billie Oats

The Valleys

Ivan Evans	miner who leads the association
Idris Owen	manager at No 6 Victoria colliery

Megan Jones	Tom Sage's fiancé
Daffyd Jones	Megan's brother
Frank Jones	Megan's deceased brother
Siân	Megan's sister
Gwen and Rhys Jones	Megan's parents
John Lewis	minister at the Old Blaina Baptist Chapel
Abraham Darby	Director of the Ebbw Vale Company
Griff	collier in No. 6 colliery
Mrs Morgan	householder in No. 8 Waterfall Row
Gethyn and Wyn	friends of Daffyd and lodgers with Mrs Morgan
Mervyn Jones	Ebbw Vale miner
Arthur Rogers	manager of Victoria collieries
John	man at the stute
Dylan Rees and Efa Jones	Romeo and Juliet in the Valleys
William and Erica Parnell	leaders of the travelling theatre company

Acronyms

AAIB   Air Accident Investigation Branch

COP   Conference Of the Parties (United Nations Climate Change)

CPD   Continuing Professional Development

CPR   Cardio-Pulmonary Resuscitation

EEC   European Economic Community

EVC   Ebbw Vale Company

EVI   Ebbw Vale Institute

FEPS   Flight Envelope Protection System

FriBri   Friday Briefing

FS2   Flight Science for Safety; Bran Sage's consultancy company

IEE   The Institution of Electrical Engineers

kts   nautical miles per hour

MPD   Missing Presumed Dead

MSF   Médecins Sans Frontières

NERC   Natural Environment Research Council

PhD   Doctor of Philosophy

RFC   Royal Flying Corps

TLeM   Technical Leaders Meeting

V1, V2, VR   Critical velocities during aircraft take-off run

VRS   Vortex Ring State; a dangerous flight condition for helicopters flying at low speed

Acknowledgements

This book is a product of the author's imagination, but what lies within has been shaped by a lifetime of observing, wondering, striving to understand; thankfully, it doesn't let up. But there are huge positive influences I want to acknowledge, and first and foremost I would like to express gratitude to my family and close friends for helping me feel safe and secure being myself.

And then there is Bob Dylan. I have travelled with and been influenced by Bob's music since the early 1960s and it has always felt fresh and uplifting; at moments, quite awakening. So, thank you Bob. The reader may have picked up this influence on occasion throughout my novel, from the message on the front cover to the song choices of the members of the band Orion as they prepare for the Love Sick concert. I would like to acknowledge the 30 songs and occasional brief quotes from the lyrics as listed below.

Most of the Time, *Oh Mercy (1989, Columbia Records), Tell Tale Signs (2008, Columbia Records)*

Love Sick, *Time Out of Mind (1997, Columbia Records)*

Wedding Song, *Planet Waves (1974, Asylum Records)*

Make You Feel My Love, *Time Out of Mind (1997, Columbia Records)*

You're a Big Girl Now, *Blood on the Tracks (1975, Columbia Records)*

Born in Time, *Under the Red Sky (1990, Columbia Records)*

Series of Dreams, *The Bootleg Series, Volume 1–3, (1991, Columbia Records)*

Death is Not the End, *Down in the Groove (1998, Columbia Records)*

Visions of Johanna, *Blonde on Blonde (1966, Columbia Records)*

Sweetheart Like You, *Infidels (1983, Columbia Records)*

I Want You, *Blonde on Blonde (1966, Columbia Records)*

Abandoned Love, *Biograph (1985, Columbia Records)*

Where are You Tonight (Journey Through Dark Heat), *Street Legal (1978, Columbia Records)*

Idiot Wind, *Blood on the Tracks (1975, Columbia Records)*

Simple Twist of Fate, *Blood on the Tracks (1975, Columbia Records)*

No Time to Think, *Street Legal (1978, Columbia Records)*

Tight Connection to My Heart (Has Anybody Seen My Love), *Empire Burlesque (1985, Columbia Records)*

Baby Stop Crying, *Street Legal (1978, Columbia Records)*

Something There is About You, *Planet Waves (1974, Asylum Records)*

It's All Over Now Baby Blue, *Bringing It All Back Home (1965, Columbia Records)*

All I Really Want to Do, *Another Side of Bob Dylan, (1964, Columbia Records)*

Boots of Spanish Leather, *The Times They are A-Changin' (1964, Columbia Records)*

Don't Think Twice, it's All Right, *The Freewheelin' Bob Dylan (1962, Columbia Records)*

True Love Tends to Forget, *Street Legal (1978, Columbia Records)*

I'll Remember You, *Empire Burlesque (1985, Columbia Records)*

It Ain't Me Babe, *Another Side of Bob Dylan, (1964, Columbia Records)*

Where Teardrops Fall, *Oh Mercy (1989, Columbia Records)*

Gonna Change My Way of Thinking, *Slow Train Coming (1979, Columbia Records)*

Up to Me, *Biograph (1985, Columbia Records)*

Girl from the North Country, *The Freewheelin' Bob Dylan (1962, Columbia Records)*

Some excellent choices by the Orion band members, even if I say so myself.

*

I wanted my story to be as authentic as possible regarding the coal mining experiences of my great-grandfather Henry and the aeronautical experiences of modern-day Bran. The latter was relatively straightforward, because I have deep personal experience, but being a coal miner in the 19th century stretched my imagination, to say the least. And yet, I felt an affinity with the kind of safety issues experienced by miners. I recall the stoicism in my grandfather, a coal miner for 60 years, and I had tasted the true grit of steelworkers in vacation jobs during the late 1960s. But I reached out for what others had written and found the following two books particularly helpful.

Macmillen, Neil, Chapmen, Mike, Coal from Camerton, Lightmoor Press, 1990/2000/2014

Gray-Jones, Arthur, A History of Ebbw Vale, Starling Press Ltd., 1970/1971

*

Some other books that I have drawn on to weave my story are listed below.

Peace, Maskell, W., Coal Mines Regulation Act, 1872, W.M. Hutchings, "Colliery Guardian" Office, London

Morris, J.H., Williams, L.J., The South Wales Coal Industry 1841–1875, University of Wales Press, Cardiff, 1958

Francis, Hywel, Williams, Sîan, Do Miners Read Dickens? Origins and Progress of the South Wales Miners' Library, 1873–2013, Parthian, Cardigan, 2013

Coombes, B.L., These Poor Hands, University of Wales Press, Cardiff, 2002

Bellamy, David, Images of the South Wales Mines, Sutton Publishing Ltd., 1993

*

For the reader interested in ravens, there are three excellent books I have sought knowledge from about these wonderful birds.

Heinrich, Bernd, Mind of the Raven, Ecco Press, 2007

Ratcliffe, Derek, The Raven, A Natural History in Britain and Ireland, Princeton University Press, 1997

Shute, Joe, A Shadow Above, Bloomsbury Natural History, 2018

I want to acknowledge that I have quoted, in Chapter 5, from the 1999 Nobel Peace Prize acceptance speech by MSF International President Dr James Orbinski.

The owners and restorers of The Old Blaina Chapel, Vic and Sue Owen, were very hospitable and welcomed me during a brief visit to the place where my great-grandparents were married; thank you both.

Thanks to staff at the Somerset Mining (Radstock) Museum who were very helpful during my visit to the Camerton area as part of my ancestry research.

Thanks to NASA for the images of the Moon and the Earth from the Moon, in Chapter 1.

All the photographs of the ravens were taken at various times on my travels through the Lake District and North Wales; these real and wonderful birds provided me, unknowingly I think, a source of inspiration, as well as preternatural sagacity, of course.

Most of the illustrations have been created by the author, sketched or based on old photographs. But a few were created by Mark Straker, for which I am grateful; notably the characters in the stars in Chapters 7 and 9, the 'restored image of the Old Blaina Chapel in Chapters 8 and 9, the faces and aircraft concept in Chapter 3 and the vortex ring in Chapter 5.

While some of the characters in my novel, particularly my relatives, are based on real people, their names have been changed and their stories are mostly fictional. However, I consider that my imagination has been well-informed and I like to think that they might enjoy aspects of their fictional existence. Outside family members, there are a few real people mentioned in my novel, but generally my characters are truly fictional and any resemblance with real people is accidental.

Davies Lynch, November 2020